THE WORLD MADE RIGHT

Kate's hands were unsteady as she unlaced her gown. Suddenly, she felt herself spun around. Jack stood before her naked, and she saw that his breath was as uneven as her own.

The sun was hot on her bare skin, but it was a poor rival to the burning she felt. His kiss seared her. His hands cupped her breasts, fingers teasing her nipples into taut aching peaks, as her own hands explored the hard muscles of his chest and arms and back. And when he pressed her still closer, she willed her muscles to relax against his demanding masculine onslaught.

As her senses exploded in ecstasy, Jack's shuddering cry joined her own. And Kate knew that her world had come right again. . . .

THE HEART REMEMBERS

by

Barbara Hazard

AN ONYX BOOK

*To all those who love Bermuda
and know it well, my apologies
for rearranging some of it,
and its history, to fit my story.
Still, I hope I have written an apt
description of God's Own Garden
and captured, at least in part,
the spirit of its early settlers.*
—BH

ONYX
Published by the Penguin Group
Penguin Books USA Inc., 375 Hudson Street, New York,
New York 10014, U.S.A.
Penguin Books Ltd, 27 Wrights Lane, London W8 5TZ, England
Penguin Books Australia Ltd, Ringwood, Victoria, Australia
Penguin Books Canada Ltd, 2801 John Street, Markham,
Ontario, Canada L3R 1B4
Penguin Books (N.Z.) Ltd, 182-190 Wairau Road, Auckland 10, New Zealand

Penguin Books Ltd, Registered Offices: Harmondsworth, Middlesex, England

First Printing, July, 1990
10 9 8 7 6 5 4 3 2 1

Copyright © by B. W. Hazard Ltd., 1990
All rights reserved

 REGISTERED TRADEMARK—MARCA REGISTRADA

1

London, 1772

"PRITHEE don't slouch, Katherine!"

Kate Hathaway stifled an impatient sigh as she moved her already straight spine another quarter of an inch away from the back of the little gilt chair she was seated on. Beside her, her Aunt Mary nodded slightly before she continued in her soft, complaining voice, "How many times must I tell you, niece, that with all your handicaps, it is essential you at least *try* to appear the epitome of well-bred young womanhood?"

Kate refused to answer. She was beginning to dislike her aunt, a most grievous fault, no doubt, but one she felt was perfectly justified. The woman seemed determined to make her life miserable!

She looked around the large drawing room, trying to forget why she was here—not only here in the Duke of Dartmouth's formal house in Grosvenor Square, but in England at all. On her other side, her mother raised her fan to whisper, "Do be patient, dearest! Remember Mary knows best what is required of a young girl appearing in society for the first time."

"I know, Mama," Kate whispered back. "I . . . I shall try."

Olivia Hathaway nodded a little before her eyes sought the richly dressed throng parading before them again. Her daughter thought she looked just like a child with her nose pressed to the window of a sweetmeat shop, so eager, so interested, so hungry! She herself tried to look at the guests with the same attention, but she knew hers was a feeble effort in comparison.

Around her, the buzz of many conversations swirled, and she caught a phrase or two. "M'lady, how charming you look this evening!" . . . "Sirrah, I say the man's an abomination, and furthermore—" . . . "La, my love, do

5

look at Miss Harford's gown! So *English,* is it not?" . . .
"Fled the country, ye say? Ecod!" . . . " 'Tis called Oil
of Lilies, and—" . . . "And I say we have mob rule in the
countryside now—" . . . "Yes, just off Bond Street, the
most taking little shop!" . . . "And so I replied, 'Sir,
much as it desolates me to contradict you, I must—' "
. . . "He's gone to Methodism, you say? Damme!"

Ah, the *beau monde*! How often her mother had spoken of it at home in Bermuda. How often she had ex-
tolled its members' wit and wealth, and elegance! Kate
had soon wearied of the oft-told tales, but she had listened even so, knowing that remembering the land of her
birth was one of the things that made her mother truly
happy. She had never returned to England after her
marriage to Roger Hathaway some thirty years before,
but Kate was sure that not a day of that time had gone by
that she did not think of it with longing. And now that
she was here at last, was it any wonder she looked so
entranced?

For herself, Kate knew she would never feel that way,
even as she lowered her eyes to her clasped hands when
an older gentleman in a gray periwig and a puce coat
heavy with silver lace peered intently in her direction.
She did not consider the *beau monde* either witty or wise,
although she was willing to admit they were very elegant,
and most assuredly wealthy.

No, to her, England—London, especially—was a trial
to be endured. It was so large and crowded and filthy,
and it smelled—of manure and coal smoke, decaying
garbage, dead animals, and the offal from butcher shops
that was thrown into the kennels that ran down the
center of the streets. And the clamor, the omnipresent
noise! All those iron-shod wheels and clattering hooves,
the watchmen's and the venders' cries, the wandering
musicians and beggars—why, even the newsboys had horns!
And there were the hand bells on the carts, the apple
women and Billingsgate wenches, the roars of the crowds
that gathered to mock those in the pillory or some poor
soul at a hanging. Sometimes Kate imagined that no one
in London was ever still, the babble was so widespread.
She was still not sleeping well even after almost a month
here, for London itself never seemed to sleep. And when
she remembered Bermuda—the fresh soft air, the sound

of birds and the low thick flow of the slaves' voices, even the lapping of the waves against the shore—she wanted to weep.

She shivered a little then as a cold draft from the nearby doorway touched her shoulders and eddied about her thin-clad ankles. It was cold here, too, even though it was April now. Yet she was not allowed to wear a heavy shawl or thicker stockings. Such things were for peasants, not young ladies with noble relations, or so her Aunt Mary had claimed. Eyeing the other women at the reception, Kate had to admit she would have cut a most unusual figure of fun, so dressed. All the women here tonight wore silks and satins and muslins, cut low to the bosom and laced tightly below over unforgiving stays. Feeling the ones she wore, too, digging into her rib cage, Kate grimaced. She hated stays!

As she watched the ladies, she saw how the full skirts they wore looped up to show elaborate petticoats adorned with all manner of lace and ribbons and embroidery, swung gently over their hoops as they moved. They reminded her of gorgeous yet improbably upended flowers.

And only some of the most elderly ones had a light stole to shield them from the drafts. Although she searched hard, Kate could not discover a single goosebump on any of the younger women's bare shoulders and bosoms, gleaming as they were in the candlelight.

"I fear that wash I prepared for Katherine has not been as efficacious as I had hoped," Mary Townsend remarked to her sister-in-law. "Her face is still most sallow. Tch, tch! I wonder if perhaps a stronger solution might not be of benefit, since you will not permit the use of some discreet cosmetics?"

"Now, Mary, you know Kate's . . . er, Katherine's father is adamant about a young girl using paint. But I am sure her complexion will soon be all you could wish. Her tan is almost faded, after all."

"Yes, leaving her looking yellow," their kinswoman declared. "And she has freckles as well! Why you ever permitted the gel to acquire such an affliction, Olivia, I shall never know! Gently bred ladies are supposed to shield their faces at all times from the injurious effects of sunlight. Yet when you first arrived, 'twas all I could do not to swoon, she was such a blackamoor!"

Kate was furious at being discussed as if she were not even there, and she interrupted to say, "The sun is very strong in Bermuda, and it shines almost all the time. It is quite unlike the fog and incessant rain you have here."

Ignoring the smug satisfaction she heard in her niece's voice, Lady Pelton retorted, "All the more reason to avoid it, then! Prithee, did you never wear a bonnet?"

Kate had a sudden vision of herself stretched out on a patch of grass overlooking the ocean, her face raised to the warm sun with her discarded riding hat thrown down beside her. Or how she used to remove her bonnet when she was sailing with her brothers, because it always got in the way when the sloop was close-hauled in a steady breeze. How she had loved the feel of the salt spray on her face, the tang of it when she licked her lips. And dear Gregory and George! She wondered if they missed her as much as she missed them.

She had to close her eyes for a moment then, and swallow hard, she was so homesick. So very homesick! Yet she knew her stay in England might be a prolonged affair. Although her mother had never said so in so many words, Kate was well aware why they were here. She had been sitting at her open window one night last September, admiring the sparkle of the moonlight on the waves, when she heard her mother and father enter the garden below her.

She had not intended to eavesdrop, but her mother's first sentence made her gasp and lean closer to the window. "You must see there is no one here for Kate, my dear, no one suitable at all. Unless, that is, you are willing to have your daughter marry Aaron Evans, or perhaps William Younge?"

Roger Hathaway gave a lazy chuckle. "Neither a shopkeeper nor a sailor, madam, and well you know it. But Kate has just turned nineteen. Surely there is time yet before she must consider matrimony."

Unseen in the darkness above them, Kate had nodded eagerly in agreement, even as her mother went on, relentless, "Nineteen is quite old enough, husband. As you should remember, I was but eighteen when I married you."

There was a long pause, and Kate almost withdrew. Then a slightly breathless Olivia Hathaway continued,

"Prithee now, be serious, Roger! It is of the utmost importance that Kate have a Season in London, for it is only there that she can meet suitable young men of standing and wealth. Perhaps even a titled gentleman. Remember, her uncle is Viscount Pelton. I know she is not an outstanding beauty, but she is a well-enough girl, with much to commend her, and her dowry is adequate."

"I think her beautiful," Mr. Hathaway protested. "But, Olivia, have *you* thought? If Kate marries abroad, there, in all probability, is where she will stay. I cannot see any English lord giving up his estates to reside in Bermuda permanently. And just think how we will miss her, so far away!"

"As to that, we cannot be sure, of course. It may not come to that. Besides, I am sure Bermuda would be a charming home for any number of adventuresome young men, those with the money to maintain themselves here, of course. You may trust me to watch over her and guide her choice most carefully, Roger."

"Ecod, I know that," he replied quickly. "But tell me, my dear, can it be you are pretending that this visit you propose is only to secure an advantageous match for Kate? Aren't you looking forward to it as well? Come, wife, be open with me!"

"I will not try to dissemble," Olivia Hathaway said with dignity. "Yes, I have missed England sorely. I quite long to see my old girlhood home again, my dear brother, and his family. Why, just think, I have never even set eyes on my niece and nephew, and they are grown now and married themselves. Now, now, husband! Prithee do not look so grim! I have been happy here with you, you know I have! Still, I admit I have missed the dear hills and dales of home, the bite of a winter wind, the first snowdrop, the changing seasons. And I have missed my kin. So much—so very much."

Above them, Kate could not hear it, but she could imagine her mother's gentle sigh of regret and longing. For a moment she forgot the topic of conversation and tried to imagine what it would be like to be carried away and exiled from the only home you had ever known, and brought to live far across the ocean. And then her gray eyes widened. If what her mother planned came true, that is what she would have to do herself, in reverse migration.

"Niece, attend me, if you please," Lady Pelton said sharply, emphasizing her remark with a rap of her fan on Kate's arm. Unwillingly Kate focused again on the drawing room, the brilliant jewels of the guests sparkling under the light of many candles. A hum of gay conversation and muted laughter filled her ears again.

"I do beg your pardon most humbly, ma'am," she said. "I was thinking about something else."

Her aunt did not appear to be mollified by this handsome apology. "You should only be thinking of the reception, the people here. A vacant, bemused expression will not add to your consequence, you know. Try to cultivate a look of interest, expectation—vivacity!"

Thus chastised, Kate was resolute in pushing Bermuda from her mind. She inspected the guests once again. Her eyes wandered from one group to the next without pause until she saw several young men standing together on the opposite side of the room. She would not have lingered there, except her attention was caught by something that made her smile to herself. "Do you know who that young man is near the window, Aunt Mary?" she asked. "The one in the dark blue coat with the bob wig? And the very dark tan?"

Lady Pelton ignored the provocative words, spoken in such a demure voice, as her eyes inspected the group Kate had indicated. Then she nodded. "That is the baronet Sir John Reade. He has but recently returned from a voyage around the world."

"He sailed around the world?" Kate asked, her eyes beginning to shine. "I quite long to ask him about it!"

Her aunt turned to see her leaning forward, with the most interested expression she had ever beheld on her fine-featured face. Her brows rose slightly as she said, "I have no acquaintance with the baronet, however, so I shall not be able to present you. Indeed, even if I had, I would be most reluctant. His background is not . . . not quite nice."

"Not nice? How so?" Kate persisted, her eyes never leaving that tall, well-built frame. As she watched, he said something, and the men surrounding him began to laugh. In only a moment he joined in, throwing back his head in complete enjoyment.

Kate was sure she had never seen anyone so gay, so much at his ease, since she had arrived in London. And m'lord did not appear to care that his complexion was vastly different from that of the men around him. Kate thought his tanned face under the neat white wig he wore the handsomest she had ever seen. And he had sailed around the world!

"What do you mean, Mary?" her mother asked, her eyes as wide as her daughter's. "He appears a most popular young man. La, see the crowd he has attracted!"

Lady Pelton pursed her thin lips. "No doubt he is regaling them with tales of his adventures," she said. "I did not mean that he is not well-regarded, although there are some who look at him askance. His late father was also Sir John Reade. He was the well-known historian and author, but he was not in general favor for he expounded the most ridiculous theories about the welfare of the poor. And then there was his mother. Fah!"

"What did she do?" Kate asked, dragging her eyes from the gentleman in question to stare at her aunt. She could see that Aunt Mary looked quite indignant. Why, she was ruffling up just like one of Keza's bantam hens did when it was annoyed.

"Would you believe that Lady Reade had the audacity to marry only *two months* after her husband's demise?" Lady Pelton asked, her voice outraged. "To not even maintain a decent mourning period—ecod! There are those who refuse to acknowledge her to this very day for that lapse. And then there was the man she married—well!"

"Who was it, Mary?" her sister-in-law begged. She was so starved for gossip of the *ton* after her long years abroad, she could never hear enough.

"Alexander Maxwell, the mad Earl of Granbourne, that's who," Lady Pelton said with distaste, quite forgetting how ardently she had pursued that same earl for her daughter Eleanor only a few years ago.

"But why would she marry a madman?" Kate persisted.

Olivia Hathaway looked apprehensive. For a young girl, Kate was very inquisitive and tenacious, traits of which her aunt did not always approve. But for this evening at least, Mary did not reprimand her, and Kate's mother could relax. She was glad of the reprieve, for she wanted to hear the story too.

"Of course, he is not mad all the time," Lady Pelton told them. "But what else can you call a man who turns his servants and tenants off and then proceeds to burn his most noble hall to the ground? And when it was destroyed, they say he locked the gates behind him and left it to return to its former wild state. And he has never since gone near it, not even once!"

"My word," Olivia Hathaway said faintly. She noticed that Kate did not appear in the least discomposed by this intelligence, and she was not surprised. She knew it took a great deal to shock her irrepressible daughter.

Tilting her head to one side, Kate mused, "I wonder why he did it. He must have had a good reason, although it seems very singular!"

"No one knows," her Aunt Mary admitted, sniffing a little. "The earl is seen very little in society these days. Indeed, I believe he and his second countess live in the west country somewhere, at another estate he owns. A small place—nowhere near as imposing as Granbourne Hall was in its heyday. They have a hopeful family now, for Lady Granbourne was many years younger than Sir John. Ha! Much good that family will do them!"

She sounded so smug and satisfied that both Hathaway ladies stared. "There are only two little girls, I believe," she explained. "La, it serves him right, after defying convention the way he did. Now he will never have an heir, since his union has produced nothing but females!"

Kate longed to remark on the loathing she heard in her aunt's voice, saying that surely such antipathy for her own sex was most perplexing, but she stifled the impulse. She had learned that Lady Pelton had very little sense of humor. Instead, she said brightly, "But if he has burned down his noble hall, there would be nothing for an heir to inherit anyway, now, would there?"

Mary Townsend turned to face her niece. That merry face, the girl's dancing gray eyes and little smile, made her forget the earl's indecent wealth and other landed properties. "Mind your manners, saucebox!" she said, rapping Kate's hands with her fan again. "La, such pertness to your elders! I never!"

Kate raised a hand to her lips and coughed a little to

stifle a chuckle. At her mother's urgent nudge, she subsided.

A short time later, an elderly lady came over to be introduced to the newcomers, and only moments after that she was beckoning her grandson to her side. Kate was forced to converse with the thin young man while the older ladies looked on in satisfaction. Which one of them disliked it more, Kate could not tell. The gentleman was polite, of course, but so indifferent to her she longed to slap him. And she, who had never had any trouble talking about any subject under the sun, was strangely tongue-tied with this supercilious London fop. Surely it was most inexplicable!

When she was free to glance around the room again, she saw that Sir John Reade and his cronies had disappeared, and she was not surprised. Why would he want to waste his time doing the pretty here in this chilly yet stuffy drawing room? Not he, a man who had sailed the seas, seen the world, struggled through storms off a dangerous lee shore, and known the tropical sun on his face while the fresh breeze ruffled his hair. She sighed.

But as she curtsied to other guests and made halting conversation with more superior young men, Kate Hathaway told herself that the intriguing stranger was sure to be at other affairs this spring. She might have a very good chance of meeting him and talking to him then. She did so long to ask him about his voyage!

But Miss Hathaway did not see the baronet again for some time. Unbeknownst to her, he had ridden down to his estate near the southern coast of Kent the morning following the reception.

Although his stepfather, Alexander Maxwell, had found him an excellent agent before he sailed, Jack Reade knew this was a duty he could neglect no longer. His own presence was necessary for the continuing prosperity of Hythe. It was, after all, that prosperity that brought him a great deal of his wealth and allowed him the freedom to travel and do as he wished. Besides, when all was said and done, he had a great affection for the place. He had been born at Hythe, and it was there he had spent his boyhood years with his dear father and lovely young mother. But in spite of loving the place and knowing full well how much he owed to it and its care, Jack Reade

Barbara Hazard

knew, deep in his heart, that he would never make a farmer. Not for him to find contentment just sitting quietly in the country totting up the revenue from the harvest, or spending the long winter planning next year's crops and improvements. No, he was still too much of an adventurer for that.

He grinned to himself as he rode along, his teeth very white in his tanned face. His stepfather knew this as well as he did, and shook his head over it, although he never tried to stop the wandering. Just as well, Jack thought to himself, spurring his horse to a canter as he came closer to home. For as much as I admire and revere the earl, I go my own way. And I have to answer only to myself, now that my father is dead. I am Sir John Reade now, and what I want is all that matters.

The bright spring morning lifted his spirits, and he imagined he could catch a whiff of salt air now. He inhaled deeply and then laughed at his fancies. Even if there had been any tang to the air, it would have been impossible to isolate it from the pungent smell of the newly manured fields around him.

Looking about, he was reminded how lovely the land that comprised Kent was. The county had been named England's garden, and with its fertile fruit trees, its hops and rich grain harvests, Jack thought the title most apt. Maybe someday, he mused. Maybe someday there will come a time when Hythe will be a welcome respite from my travels, and I will settle down here with a pretty little wife to raise children as well as crops. Hythe deserved an heir.

Jack laughed again at the domestic picture he was painting, and at the merry sound, some birds took flight from the hedgerow he was passing.

He knew he would find Hythe just as he had left it, although it would be nowhere near as warm and welcoming now that his mother had remarried and lived in Devon. Of course, she and Alex also owned Willows, the estate that adjoined his. His godmother had left it to them at her death some years before. He knew they were not there at present, however. He had had a message from the earl's estate in Devon only last week, telling him the family intended to come to London soon, to open Granbourne House in Berkeley Square. Jack was

looking forward to seeing them all—his beloved mother,
his good friend and mentor, the earl, and his two little
half-sisters. He smiled to himself then, wondering what
changes he would see in the girls. Constance had been
five when he left two years ago, and Grace only a baby of
two. He hoped they would remember him. He had brought
them some wonderful presents.

And then he forgot them as a picture of Lady Arbel
Stanton invaded his mind. He shook his head a little. He
did not consider himself an impressionable fool, but surely
it would take a man made of stone to forget or ignore
that young lady. Only eighteen, and in London for her
first Season, Lady Arbel was nothing short of breathtaking. She was not especially tall, but to his eyes she was
perfectly proportioned. That slender waist, that deliciously
lavish bosom, those tantalizing hips! Even her neat ankles would cause remark. And her lovely face had perfect
features, and skin like cream. It was such a contrast to
her dark blue eyes and arching brows. Her hair was as
black as his own. She had an endearing little dimple, too,
right by the corner of her tempting, rosy mouth. Damme,
he thought, she was a desirable little baggage!

He had met her at Lady Cowdin's one afternoon when
he had been invited there for tea. M'lady's son, Sir
Dudley Cowdin, was one of Jack's best friends. He and
Tony Emerson, Lord Weil, had accompanied him on his
voyage. And to think that Dudley was related to such a
piece of perfection, and he had never even known it!

Lady Arbel had smiled at him kindly, and her eyes had
been wide with interest as the three of them took turns
regaling the company with stories of their adventures.
Jack could not be sure, of course, but he fancied her
smile for him at parting had been a little warmer than the
one she had given her cousin or Tony.

As he reached the gates of Hythe, he promised himself
he would return to town as quickly as he could. He had
to see her again; had to make sure she was indeed the
paragon he remembered, one who now invaded his dreams
both sleeping and waking with such regularity.

Reluctantly he put Lady Arbel aside to greet his gate-
keeper's wife and children and ask how they did. As he
trotted up the drive, Hythe came into sight. It stood
before him as it had for so many years, an old stone

building with narrow mullioned windows surrounded by its terraces and gardens. It looked like an ancient fortress, but his heart lifted at the sight, for Hythe was his home.

He had sent the coach ahead with his clothes, so he knew he would be expected, and everything would be in order for him. Even as he prepared to dismount, a boy came running to take his horse, and at the front door Greyson, his butler, was bowing and smiling. Jack stretched and looked around. The gardens were just beginning to show tender green new shoots, but by June they would be a riot of color. And from what he could see of the distant orchards and newly tilled fields, all was well there. He grinned at the stableboy and called him by name before he climbed the shallow steps to the terrace that fronted the house, well content to be home, at least for now.

His people were not best pleased when he left Hythe again little more than a week later. Many of the older ones pulled down their mouths and bemoaned the young master's restlessness.

"But he's always been this way, as I myself can tell you," Mrs. Nearing informed the butler after the baronet rode away again. Greyson had been butler for only four years, and the housekeeper never failed to remind him of it. "La, when he was a boy he was never still! And since all is going so well here, why should he stay? It's lonesome for him here alone, poor dear man. No, he's off to London to see his friends and amuse himself. It was ever thus."

"Mayhap if he had a wife it would make a difference," Mr. Greyson remarked. "I quite long to see the day when the master settles down at last and takes up his permanent residence here."

Mrs. Nearing's eyes brightened at the thought of the coming family; the nurseries full and the laughter of young children echoing through the halls. "Aye, that'd be prime, that would," she agreed. Then she chuckled a little, and her round face under the white mobcap creased in a smile. "But m'lord is only twenty-four. Plenty of wild oats to be sowed before that happy time, I'm afraid.

"He's such a handsome young man, isn't he?" she went on. "I'm sure there's many a young lady would love to snare him and tame him. We shall just have to be patient, Mr. Greyson. The time will come—just you mark my words!"

She was chuckling again as she left the hall, the keys of her office clinking together at her ample waist.

Sir John Reade arrived in London a day later. He had taken temporary rooms in Jermyn Street, until such time as his mother and the earl arrived in Berkeley Square. After he had changed to town clothes, he decided to stroll over there to see if the shutters were off Granbourne House as yet.

To his delight, as he entered the square, he saw the earl's traveling coaches in the act of drawing up before the door, and he hurried his steps. He was just in time to motion the footman aside so he could hold out his hand to help his mother alight.

"Jack! Oh, my dearest son, how I have missed you!" she cried as she threw herself into his arms and pulled his head down so she could kiss him soundly. Behind her, the earl raised a hand in salute, his hazel eyes alight with pleasure at the homecoming.

Jack felt an answering lump in his throat when he saw his mother's tears.

Hugging him tight, the countess said, "It has been so long, Jack . . . so long! Oh, darling, I am so glad you are safe home at last!"

A very young voice interrupted the reunion. "Who's dat man kissing Mama, Boodle?"

Jack turned, his mother still held tight to his side, to see a small girl staring at him from the shelter of her nanny's arms. There was doubt in her eyes, and as he watched, she put her thumb in her mouth.

Smiling at her, he said, "But you must be Grace. I see you have not outgrown that bad habit yet, now, have you? Do you remember me? I'm your half-brother, Jack."

The little girl's face reddened, and she snatched her thumb out of her mouth and put her hand behind her, as if to avoid further temptation.

"Jack, Jack! Is it really you? Is it? Is it?" another high young voice called, and when he looked, he saw Constance Maxwell climbing out of the coach behind them.

She ran toward him, her arms outstretched. Jack re-

leased his mother to catch her up and spin her around.
The little girl's skirts flew out and she chortled in delight.

"But how much you have grown, m'lady," Jack teased.
"Why, I can hardly lift you, you are so heavy!"

"That's 'cause I'm seven now, Jack," she confided.
"Grace is still only a baby, you know, but I'm grown up.
Well, almost grown up," she added, as if to be perfectly
truthful. She grinned at him and Jack laughed aloud at
her gap-toothed smile. Lady Constance was in the
process of losing her baby teeth, and she looked like a
miniature clown.

"Did you bring us some presents, Jack, did you?" the
little girl asked next. Behind her, the nanny made a
clucking sound of disapproval, but she continued, as persistent as he remembered her, "You promised you would!
You did! Where are they?"

"That will be quite enough, Constance," the earl reprimanded her. As he held out his hand, Jack lowered the
little girl to the pavement to grasp it between both of his.
A moment later, the earl threw his arms around him in a
rough hug. "You're looking well, my boy, but that dark
face of yours is not at all the thing here in town, you
know," he said, his voice rough with emotion.

"I'll admit it has been much remarked," Jack told him.
"You're looking well too, sir. It is so good to see you
again—all of you."

As Constance grinned and Grace hid her face in her
nanny's shoulder, Jack studied his mother and the earl.
Camille Maxwell was as beautiful as he remembered, and
besides the serene happiness on her face, she had an
animation, a glow, that she had not worn all those
years he had been growing up. Not for the first time,
he wondered at it. It was obvious how much she loved
the Earl of Granbourne, and he was glad for her. He
could not have wished a better man for her after his
own father died. And although he had been upset at the
short time she had mourned Sir John, he had come to
accept it in the face of the couple's devotion to each
other.

He saw that his mother looked a little older, and there
were a few strands of white in her black hair, but she was
still lovely.

As for Alexander Maxwell, he was as upright and strong-looking as he had ever been, in spite of the lines in his lean face.

"Do come inside, Jack," the earl was saying as the nursemaid shooed Constance before her up the steps. The countess had turned to speak to her maid and the earl's valet, and footmen were scurrying from the mansion to unload the coaches. "All will be confusion for some time, I fear, but I'm sure we three can find a quiet nook somewhere so we might hear how you have fared these past two years."

He hugged Jack briefly again before he offered his arm to his wife. "Come, my love! Let us adjourn to the library and stop providing the vulgar with a raree-show. I am sure you would welcome a cup of tea after the journey. And, Jack, some sherry?"

The three entered the house to find the butler bowing and awaiting his orders. After he had greeted his master and mistress, he turned to Jack to say, "M'lord! I am delighted to see you safe home at last. Welcome, sir, welcome!"

"Thank you, Kemble," Jack said as he clapped him on the shoulder in friendly fashion. "And I am delighted to be here. But you'll be seeing too much of me, I fear, in the weeks ahead. That is, you will if I am still permitted to use Granbourne House as my base here in London."

"As if you would ever be refused," his mother scolded as she handed the light pelisse and the bonnet she wore to her maid. "I wish you might move in today, for I want you near me as soon as possible."

Taking Jack's arm, and then her husband's, she led them to the library. "How happy I am to have my two best-loved men beside me," she said softly.

Jack smiled down at her, and then he shook his finger at the sparkling tears that threatened to wet her cheeks again. "No watering pots, now, Mama, if you please!" he ordered. "I say, Alex, can't you stop her?"

"Those are tears of joy, my boy, and you must allow her the moment. It's not every day the prodigal son returns, you know."

The earl left them to order refreshments, and Jack took his mother to her favorite chair. Before she sat down, she kissed him again, and then she took his face

between her hands to study it intently. She did not smile
as she did so, and Jack returned her gaze just as seriously.

"Well, Mama, are you satisfied?" he asked as the earl
returned. "You may believe it is truly me."

She patted his face and smiled. "I know, dearest. I was
only enjoying my first real look at you. You have changed,
Jack," she went on as she took her seat. "You are a man
grown now."

"And what was I when I went away, madam?" he
teased. "After all, I was no child then, but all of
twenty-two."

His mother nodded. "That is of course true, but you
were still young. Young at heart, I suppose, is what I
mean, and your features still showed their boyhood cast.
Now you are mature. You have seen much these past two
years, have you not? You have grown, and not only in
the breadth of your shoulder."

"Aye, that I have," Jack admitted as he took his own
seat.

The earl leaned against his desk, watching the two of
them with a little smile on his lean, stern-featured face.

"I would not have missed it for the world, Mama, sir,"
Jack went on. "Sometimes, it was not always pleasant,
and on occasion it was dangerous. There were many
things I wish had not occurred, things I wish I had never
seen. But overall, it was everything I had dreamed it
would be. A once-in-a-lifetime experience."

For well over an hour the three sat in perfect harmony
over the tea tray, the earl and countess asking question
after question, and Jack catching up on all the family
news. And when he rose at last, he promised to return
for dinner and have his belongings fetched from Jermyn
Street first thing in the morning.

At the door of the library he turned and bowed, a
twinkle in his unusual turquoise eyes. "Be sure and reassure my lady Constance that I will bring her presents this
evening," he said. "I know how eagerly she is awaiting
them! And I pray the baby will come down as well. I
don't think Grace quite accepts me as yet, but maybe the
doll I brought her from China will help!"

2

LITTLE over a week later, Lady Grace had not only accepted her strange new brother, she had begun to demand him with great regularity. "Want Jack," she could be heard to say several times a day, and she would pout if he were not immediately available. Lady Granbourne told her son that he was spoiling the child, but Jack would only laugh and shake his head before he took the little girls to roll hoops in the park at the center of the square. He always put Grace up on his shoulders, where she would clutch his collar and giggle, while Lady Constance swung his other hand, chattering away as if he had never been gone at all.

He thought them both pretty children, with their mother's dark hair and regular features. Constance had her father's hazel eyes, and Grace the blue eyes of her mother. They had the engaging manners of the well-brought-up young, and they often made him laugh. Jack knew he could not have loved them better if they had been Reades rather than Maxwells.

Of course he did not spend an excessive amount of time with them, for he was busy with his friends, busy pursuing the number of activities that the London Season offered gentlemen.

Kate Hathaway saw him often, but as yet she had had no opportunity to make his acquaintance. She watched him as closely as she dared, at every party they both attended, and she was one of the first to notice with what fervor he always greeted the lovely Lady Arbel Stanton, how long he lingered by her side, and how warm and attentive he was to her. Kate found herself suffering pangs of regret, and she was surprised that it was so, for she had never fancied herself in love before.

As of course I am not now, she told herself stoutly as she sat between her mother and her aunt one evening at a ball given by Lord and Lady Hanover. Why, it is ridiculous to even think such a thing, when I have never even spoken to the man! He might well be impossible—a bore or a conceited idiot.

But somehow Kate knew he was none of those things. If he had been, he would not have attracted such a crowd of friends, nor would every female from the age of sixteen to sixty brighten whenever he smiled at her.

Now Kate smoothed her new gown with thoughtful fingers. She knew she looked nice tonight. Her chestnut hair was arranged very high on her head in the current mode, and powdered as well. It was crowned with a wisp of lace and flowers, a modest headpiece worthy of a young woman making her come-out. In a way she was glad she did not have to wear the plumes, tassels, and caps her mother and her aunt sported. Her gown was modest too. A soft aqua silk with elbow-length sleeves, it had a low square neckline both front and back. Completed by creamy lace at the cuffs and bodice, it was opened over a quilted white satin petticoat, and her hoops were as fashionably large as anyone could wish. But even though she knew how attractive she looked, there was no way she could compare with the Lady Arbel, who was a vision, dressed in a deep blue gown that matched her eyes.

Kate sighed at the warm way the baronet was clasping the lady's hand, how he bent closer to whisper something in her little ear. Lady Arbel laughed up at him and pursed her lips for a moment in a little moue of warning. To Kate it appeared Sir John was having the greatest difficulty in refraining from kissing her right then and there.

"My love, with whom are you to dance next?" Olivia Hathaway asked, interrupting her musings.

"A Mr. Franklin Farnsworth, Mama," Kate said as she turned away from the handsome couple across the way.

"Excellent, excellent!" Lady Pelton exclaimed. Then she lowered her voice to whisper, "Brother of Viscount Farnsworth, a good, neat estate in Oxfordshire, five hundred pounds a year, no bad habits, family everything they ought to be."

Kate stifled a giggle. Aunt Mary certainly had the *ton* at her fingertips, she thought, even as she wished she would refrain from detailing the assets of every gentleman who came near her niece. It was so hard for Kate to concentrate on any conversation with them, when all their good points were dancing in her head. Sometimes, just for a change, she imagined her aunt saying, "Bad, very bad! Mortgaged estate falling down around his ears, no income to speak of, a drunkard, a womanizer, and a bounder. Mother insane, father simple, both brothers in Newgate for bad debts."

But that would never happen, of course, for she would never be allowed to meet such a man. Her mother watched over her carefully, but although she too was quick to approve any suitable man, Kate was not concerned. She had her father's promise, extracted just before they sailed, that if she found no one to her liking, she was not to be coerced into a loveless marriage. And she had every intention of returning to Bermuda at the end of this Season, to take up her life there again. Some of the men she had met had been superior and lordly, treating her like a rude provincial, but some of them had been both amusing and pleasant. Even so, she wanted none of them. She wondered if the day would come when she would know what she wanted. She certainly did not know now.

The next dance was a minuet, and Kate was delighted to find that she and her partner were to be next to Sir John Reade. He had led Lady Arbel into the set, and although they were not acquainted, the two girls had exchanged small smiles.

Mr. Farnsworth was treated to a very quiet Miss Hathaway, who, if he had but known it, was barely attending to him. Instead, she listened hard to catch a word or two of Sir John's teasing conversation. At the end of the dance, as he raised his lady from her curtsy, Lady Arbel said, "La, sir, I fear you have been among the savages too long! You know I cannot do that, it would cut up everyone's peace. And how my father would frown! No, no, prithee do not ask it of me!"

Kate could not hear what the baronet replied, for he was whispering now. As she smiled at Mr. Farnsworth and thanked him, the young man preened a little and patted her hand. Kate could have told him it was no use. Mr. Farnsworth thought so well of himself, he was a bore. And he was of short stature, with a round face and close-set little eyes, surely no match for the handsome gentleman she had been admiring. Not that Kate realized she should not be taking his physical attributes into account. Close-set eyes made no never-mind to five hundred clear per annum, as she was sure her Aunt Mary would be only too quick to point out.

Jack Reade left Lady Arbel's side reluctantly. She had told him he must not be too attentive, or there would be gossip. For himself, he did not care how much gossip there was, but he would not distress her. Since his return to town, he had fallen in love with the lady, and he would do anything she wished. Or not do, he told himself a little grimly. The slow, gentle courtship she expected would be hers, no matter how he longed to take her in his arms and kiss her until she was all breathless acquiescence. No, he would go slowly, so as not to startle her. Arbel was very young and innocent, and well worth waiting for, he told himself as he joined Sir Dudley and Tony Emerson in the salon set aside for refreshments.

He was surprised later to see his mother and the earl enter the room. He had not known they were to be guests here this evening too, for they rarely attended social functions. Then he remembered that Lord Hanover was a close friend of the earl's.

He bowed to them, and they all exchanged smiles. The young lady he was standing next to turned to him and said brightly, "That must be your father, is it not, Sir John? I would have known him anywhere, you are so much alike! Your facial structure, your smile . . ."

As her companions tittered, she looked confused. "Have I . . . have I said anything wrong?" she asked, one hand going to her lips in confusion.

Jack smiled down at her. Nancy Goodwin had only recently come up to town, and she was not awake on every suit as yet. It was not her fault, that little blunder.

"No, no, mistress, 'pon my honor," he reassured her. "But that is my stepfather, the Earl of Granbourne. My own father died some years ago."

Mistress Goodwin looked puzzled, and her eyes sought the tall, lean figure of the earl again. As a frown creased her brow, she said, "Oh, I am so very sorry, sir! I did not know. But surely . . . I mean, la, those cheekbones . . ."

Her voice died away in confusion, and Lord Weil took

pity on her and changed the subject. Jack studied the earl, his own forehead creased now. Alex wore a powdered wig, as he did himself. Perhaps that was the reason she had made the mistake, for his own black hair was vastly different from the earl's chestnut, he told himself. Then, too, we are much of a height, and our general build is the same. As for our cheekbones, I see no resemblance there.

He saw his mother lean closer to whisper to her husband, and the way the earl's stern face softened for a moment before he put his head back and laughed. Jack felt a tiny tremor of unease—at what, he did not know.

He had forgotten the episode completely the next morning when he joined the family at breakfast. His mother held Lady Grace in her lap, although there was no sign of her sister, Constance.

"Want Jack!" the child demanded, holding out her arms with an enchanting smile.

Obediently he lifted her and gave her a kiss before he set her down on the floor. She pouted up at him, looking quite fierce until he said, "Just a moment, poppet! I must select my breakfast, you know."

The little girl's smile returned, and from the sideboard he said over his shoulder to his mother, "She'll break some hearts one of these days, mark my words, Mama!"

Lady Granbourne nodded, her face serene as she watched Lady Grace tag after her tall son as he took some eggs and a chop from the silver dishes spread before him. At the other end of the breakfast table, the earl was deep in his post, a little frown on his face. He looked up only when his younger daughter climbed onto Jack's lap.

"What a good thing it is that I am not a jealous man," the earl remarked to his wife. "I fear I have been quite cast in the shade by this handsome gentleman so newly returned to civilization."

Camille Maxwell smiled at him over her coffee cup. "As if you would ever permit Grace to climb into your lap before your second cup of coffee, Alexander. Coming it much too strong!"

They laughed together, and Jack looked from one to the other. His mother's eyes reminded him of Arbel's, such a deep, glowing blue. The earl's eyes, he noticed afresh, were hazel, with golden glints in them. And mine are blue-green, he could not help remembering.

As Grace demanded a piece of his muffin, he shook his head at himself. What madness was this? he wondered as he gave it to her. Alex was his good friend as well as his stepfather, his mother's husband, and his half-sisters' father. Nothing more. If it had not been for that flighty girl's remark . . .

Still, later, when Grace had been removed by her nanny for a walk in the square, he could not help asking when the two had first met. "I don't believe I was ever told," he added.

"We knew each other briefly when we were young," the earl told him. Jack wondered if he were imagining that the earl's eyes had grown watchful and cold.

"Yes, we grew up quite close to each other in Kent," his mother contributed. Jack looked at her carefully, but there were no shadows in her clear, honest eyes. "But then, I met your father while on a visit to Bath, and I married him almost immediately. I have never been back to Saxford village since."

"But eventually you and Alex did meet again, of course," Jack persisted. "When was that?"

He saw the two exchange a little glance, but he could read nothing in it.

"Yes, in London, when your father was in the Americas," the earl told him. "But why do you ask, Jack? It seems strange that any of this would interest you."

Jack threw down his napkin and rose. "Oh, it was just something someone said last night, sir. It is not important. And now I must beg to be excused. Tony has planned a tilbury race to Richmond this morning, and I must not be late to the starting post."

He blew his mother a kiss and waved to the earl, and a moment later he was gone.

"Alexander?" Camille asked, her voice only a thread.

The earl did not answer, for he was staring at the door Jack had just closed behind him. The countess waited for a moment and then she rose to come and put her arms around his neck. "We must not borrow trouble, my dear," she said, sounding as if she was trying to convince herself as much as him. "Surely it was just a careless remark, and Jack will forget it in no time."

The earl turned in his chair so he could gather her into his arms and draw her down on his lap. "No doubt you are right. But I think that as soon as Sir Joshua Reynolds finishes the portrait of you and our daughters that I commissioned, we will remove to Willows. The countryside will be better for the girls. And Jack's path here in town will be easier if he is not constantly connected with the mad Earl of Granbourne. In any way."

"Mad earl, indeed!" Camille said sharply. "You are no such thing!"

Alexander kissed her cheek. "Thank you, my dear. But you and I are the only ones who know what happened at Granbourne—and why. And we both care for Jack too much to see any, er, trouble come to him. No, better we abandon this mad social scene. I shall not miss it, nor, do I suspect, shall you."

Camille assured him he was right as she nestled closer to him. As she rose a little later to take her own seat again, she asked, "What do you think of Lady Arbel Stanton, Alexander? After watching them together last evening, I suspect Jack is more than a little attracted to her."

The earl looked puzzled. "Duke Stanton's daughter? Which young thing was she? Ah, yes, I recollect now! The little beauty with the luscious figure!"

As his wife's brows rose at the enthusiasm in his voice, he smiled and added, "I only noticed her because of her blue eyes, sweeting. I thought them much like yours, but when I had the chance to observe them more closely, I could see they were nowhere near as fine."

Camille chuckled. "Why, Alexander, how adroit you are!"

She reached for the salt trencher and he eyed her empty breakfast plate.

"What on earth do you want salt for now, my dear?" he asked.

She held up a pinch. "Why, to take with your words, Alexander, what else?"

After their shared laughter died away, the countess excused herself. She had a sitting with Sir Joshua this morning, and she had to dress and see that her daughters were ready to accompany her to the artist's studio. Camille was very pleased with the family portrait. Sir Joshua had

caught Grace's expression so well. Even Constance, forced
by her missing baby teeth to appear uncommonly solemn, had a certain dignified charm in her simple frock
with her black curls arranged in artless ringlets.

As she crossed the hall, the countess wondered if she
could possibly persuade Jack to have his portrait done too.
She quite longed to have even a miniature of him now
that he had reached full manhood. For, after all, there
was no telling when he might not take it in his head to be
off on his adventuring again. It would comfort her to
have his likeness to look at in his absence. Of course, the
Lady Arbel might have something to say about any lengthy
journey. How nice if it should be so!

In the days that followed, Jack Reade continued to
press his suit with the Lady Arbel Stanton. He discovered she was more than willing to be in his company,
indeed, she appeared to find him as intriguing as he
found her. And if her cousin, Sir Dudley, made one of
the party, her father allowed her to dispense with the
escort of a servant or her chaperone.

It was on one such occasion that Jack finally kissed
her. He and his friend had called at the Stanton home
that afternoon, and when Sir Dudley left them alone for
a moment to deliver a message from his mother to the
duke, Jack was quick to seize the advantage. He reminded himself to go slowly, carefully, but her lips were
so soft and sweet, he forgot himself. When he raised his
head at last, Lady Arbel was blushing.

"Oh, sir, you must not! You know you must not!" she
whispered, walking away from him to pace the drawing
room, while she waved her fan frantically before her
heated cheeks.

Jack wanted to go to her and take her in his arms
again, but he made himself stand where she had left him.
"Forgive me, my love," he pleaded, feeling every inch
the lovesick fool he knew he appeared to be. "I could not
help myself, not when I have wanted to kiss you for such
an age!"

Lady Arbel smiled a little, now that she was at a safe
distance. "To be sure," she said demurely, "we have
known each other for almost four weeks now. Such a
length of time, is it not?"

"Four weeks, two days, and, er, fourteen hours!" Jack invented, hoping she knew as little of mathematics as most girls. "I have been counting them!"

He saw she looked pleased at the compliment, and he went and took her hand in his. "M'lady—Arbel—say I may call on your father and ask for your hand. I do so long to make you my wife!"

She pulled away from him, looking startled. "Oh, no, it is too soon for that!" she exclaimed. "Why, I have only been out for such a short time!"

As Jack stared down into her rosy face, those turquoise eyes of his ablaze, Lady Arbel felt her heart move in a very strange way.

"But I knew of my love almost at once," he told her. "What can it matter how long we have known each other? Can you not give me some hope, my dear, that my suit will prosper? I want you so!"

The lady lowered her blue eyes to her fan. Her heart was pounding in earnest now, for who could not be pleased when such a handsome, sought-after beau claimed devotion? Even so, she had no intention of succumbing to him, or to the demands of her thudding heart. She had waited too many years for the time when she would take her place in society, to contemplate forfeiting it to become only a wife. Then, too, she had dreamed of marrying someone of higher rank than a mere baronet. She was Duke Stanton's daughter, was she not? There was no one who would not have been honored to claim *her* hand. Still, Jack Reade was a handsome young man, and she had enjoyed his kiss, his embrace. She must go carefully, for it was pleasant to have him dancing attendance on her.

"Arbel?" Jack said slowly, as if he were tasting her name in his mouth. "Your name is like music, the sweetest music I have ever heard. I long to say it every day for the rest of my life."

"But . . . but I don't know, Jack," she whispered. "You must allow me time to think. It is such a serious move, marriage, and, well . . ."

"I promise I will make you happy, love," he pleaded, taking her hands again and squeezing them in his earnestness. "I will do everything in my power to see to that!"

As the lady took her seat and spread her skirts, she

motioned to a chair nearby. "And of course you will stop your wanderings then, won't you, sir?" she asked. "You do intend to remain in England henceforth, don't you? See to your estates, enjoy the London Season?"

"With you beside me, how could I help but enjoy it?" came his swift rejoinder. "And Hythe can only be graced by your beauty."

"Well, you are mighty persuasive, sir," she said. "Still, I cannot answer you today. But perhaps by the end of the Season?"

Jack wanted to demand that she give him her answer now—right now!—but he restrained himself. Slowly, slowly, he told himself. Arbel is young, and it is only fair to allow her her girlhood before she must put it behind her. For himself, however, now that he knew how much he loved and wanted her, he could have cursed her coyness. But he reminded himself Arbel was worth any delay. He would woo her every chance he got, and maybe, just maybe, she would relent and agree to an earlier betrothal.

Held up by a press of traffic, he was late to the soiree they were both attending that evening. He saw her sitting with Tony Emerson, deep in a *tête-à-tête,* and he hurried to her side. Lady Arbel's voice was cool as she told him she had already accepted his friend's invitation to the supper dance. As Tony grinned at him, Jack forced himself to bow and leave them.

Looking around the room, he saw Nancy Goodwin smiling at him hopefully, and he was quick to turn away. Not that he escaped feminine eyes even then, for a young lady sitting against the wall with a pair of older women was regarding him with steady gray eyes.

Jack noticed that everyone was preparing to dance the supper set, and he knew he would only call attention to himself if he delayed finding a partner any longer. He looked around, but every one of the girls he had met this Season was already taking her place. Even Nancy Goodwin had been claimed.

Desperately he went and made his bow to the gray-eyed young lady sitting so properly with her chaperones. He remembered he had been introduced to her a few days ago, and to her relatives as well.

"M'lady, ma'am," he said to them as he bowed. "I

hope you remember me. I am Sir John Reade. Mistress? If I might have the honor?"

He noted with a little amusement that this young lady showed no girlish reluctance, for she accepted at once with a warm, delighted smile. As he took her hand and bowed to the ladies she was deserting, he wondered why one of them looked so bemused and the other so indignant.

"Forgive me, but I have forgotten your name, mistress," he said in an undertone before they joined the others waiting for the music to begin.

"I am Kate . . . oh, I mean Katherine Hathaway," she said, and then she chuckled. He looked down at her, and was surprised to see a sprinkling of golden freckles on the bridge of her nose. It was such an honest display, as artless and endearing as a daisy dancing in a little summer breeze, that he smiled at her.

"My Aunt Mary, Lady Pelton, you know, has decreed I am to be called Katherine, you see. It is hard for me to remember when I have been 'Kate' all my life," she said.

"I shall remember your name now, Mistress Hathaway," he told her. "Was it your aunt who looked at me in such disapproval? I wonder why."

Kate joined hands with him, feeling as light as air in her anticipation. She knew she could not tell him the real reason for Aunt Mary's chagrin, so she said, "I fear my aunt wanted me to wait for another gentleman to take me in to supper. But I cannot like her choice, so I am delighted to escape him."

She paused, but noticing the baronet's eyes looking over her head to where Lady Arbel and Lord Weil were standing, she added quickly, "But I will be going home to Bermuda soon, so what care I for her frowns?"

His attention caught, Jack forgot Lady Arbel. "Bermuda, did you say? Why, I have always wanted to see Bermuda."

"You have not done so?" Kate asked, her gray eyes wide. "But I have heard you sailed around the world. Surely your ship must have called in Bermuda."

He chuckled. "We did not go quite around the world, mistress, and somehow those islands were not on our itinerary. Instead, after we left England we sailed down the coast of Africa to Dakar before we crossed the Atlantic

to Brazil. But tell me, is Bermuda as lovely as I have
been told?"

Kate nodded. "It is the most beautiful place in the
world."

She sounded so convinced of her statement, so preju-
diced, that Jack could not help teasing her. "But I have
heard it was once called the Isles of the Devil. Is that
so?"

His partner nodded reluctantly. "Yes, that is true,"
she admitted. "But that was only because there have
been so many shipwrecks there. Bermuda is guarded by
reefs on every side but the east. Some of those reefs
extend for eight, even ten miles offshore. For a long
time, sailors avoided the place for that reason. But now it
is known as God's Own Garden. And that is a prettier
name, don't you think, as well as being more accurate?"

Before Jack could answer, she went on in a rush, "But
never mind Bermuda now! I have been longing to speak
to you ever since I heard of your voyage. Where did you
go? How long were you at sea? Oh, how I envy you the
adventure!"

Remembering some of the more unattractive aspects of
his trip, Jack wondered what the lady would think of the
howling winter gale they had faced rounding Cape Horn,
the long days drifting aimlessly in the doldrums, under a
hot tropic sun, the monotonous food and cramped quarters. Or how much she would envy him the adventure if
she were to know of the two sailors they lost—one overboard on a stormy night, the other who fell from the
rigging. He knew he would never forget that sailor's
scream, the sound of his body hitting the deck, but he
decided to say nothing of any of this. Instead, he would
give her the highly expurgated, romanticized version he
had given other ladies so many times since his return.

The dance ended long before his story was told, and to
his surprise, he found himself looking forward to continuing it at supper. Miss Hathaway had shown him, by her
comments and questions, that she knew more about sailing than any girl he had ever met. And when he taxed
her with it after they were seated at a table for two,
enjoying their repast, she admitted she had sailed since
she was a child.

"My three older brothers, you see, are avid sailors. So

of course I tagged after them as soon as I was old enough. I have my own little sloop now. Oh, she is not much— only twenty feet long, but I can handle her by myself. I am ashamed to admit I called her *Sea Sprite*, she is so yare. How my brothers teased me for that!"

She sighed then, and her eyes grew sad. "I do miss home so!" she confided.

Looking around the crowded room, hearing the stilted conversations, and seeing the social smiles of the other guests, Jack could well believe it. "I am sure London and society must be rather stifling in comparison, are they not?" he commiserated.

He was delighted to see her smile again, and nod in complete agreement. She was a taking little thing, this Katherine—no, Kate!—Hathaway. In fact, she was yare herself! Of course, she had not a tenth of Arbel's beauty, but she was still attractive with her intelligent gray eyes, those fine, aristocratic features. Even her golden freckles, her generous mouth, were appealing, and she was so quick, so vital. He glanced down at the hand toying with her wineglass. It was feminine, yet it looked competent as well. He could imagine her steering her sloop, adjusting a sail, or dropping the anchor. How refreshing she was, how different!

They were still talking when he noticed that the supper room was almost empty. Of Lady Arbel there was no sign, and he rose at once. Still, when he took Katherine Hathaway back to her relatives, his bow and thanks for her company were genuine. "I shall look forward to seeing you again, mistress," he told her. "I have yet to tell you of China and the South Seas, after all. M'lady. Ma'am."

Kate was still smiling as she took her seat again, and Lady Pelton looked at her askance. The girl was showing an animation she had never seen before, and the hint of roses in her cheeks made her almost lovely, she thought. But Mary Townsend had already made up her mind that her niece was to marry Mr. Farnsworth. He had been the most attentive of all the girl's small circle of acquaintance, and she had no reason to suspect he would not be successful if he should ask for her niece's hand. And since she herself desired the match, she had convinced herself that both Olivia and Katherine would agree to it

at once. Such a good family, so much wealth! It was most
satisfying after all her work and effort in bringing out an
unsophisticated provincial. Katherine, she was sure, must
be grateful.

Sir John Reade did not approach Miss Hathaway again
that evening, much to her regret. She noticed how he
hovered near Lady Arbel for a time, and when he finally
took his leave a little later, Kate saw that he looked
angry. She wondered why. She could not know that Lady
Arbel had decided to tease him, setting up a light flirta-
tion with some other young sprigs of the *ton*. It was her
way of testing Jack's devotion, and a pleasant game as
well. The men who clustered around her were only too
anxious to fall in with her plans, and she felt a surge of
real power at the way she was able to manipulate them.
She was, after all, very young, not that Jack appreciated
her behavior. Instead, he went home with a black frown
on his face, and when he found the earl sitting alone in
his library, could not even be persuaded to join him for a
nightcap.

The earl wondered at it when he went up to bed at
last, but since he knew it could be any number of things,
not the least of which might be a little lady with blue
eyes, he was not troubled. Jack had always been emotional
—volatile, and given to moods. But he would come to
Alexander Maxwell in time, as he always had since they
had met, shortly before Sir John's death. Until then the
earl would not pry. Not only because it was not his way
but also because he had too much respect for any young
man's sensibilities. And as he remembered all too well
from his own experience, the throes of first love could be
devastating.

As he claimed the stairs while Kemble and the footmen locked the house and snuffed the candles, Alexander smiled to himself. He was remembering a time when
it had been the most important thing in the world to keep
his love a secret hidden from the world. Perhaps that was
what Jack was feeling now.

3

"DAMN!" Jack exclaimed at breakfast the next morning.

He threw the note he had been reading down and looked up to see two intent pair of eyes regarding him from either end of the table. He flushed a little at their scrutiny.

"I do beg your pardon, Mama, sir. That was not well done of me, was it? But you will understand my reaction when you learn that this note is from Martha Reade. She says she and Cousin Robert have recently arrived in town, and she invites me to tea in two days' time. Of course she also bemoans the location of the rooms they have taken for reasons of economy, their lack of standing in society, and . . . and . . . *and!*"

The countess smiled at his look of frustration. She knew the Reades well, and she did not like them any more than her son did. Cousins of her late husband, they had long had hopes of inheriting Hythe and all Sir John's wealth. Well she remembered their barely suppressed chagrin when she had come to Hythe as a young bride, and their anger when Jack had been born. She had known even then it was not because they were poor, for they were not. They were only greedy. And greedy people were so very unattractive!

"Of course you must see them, Jack," she said as she passed him the toast rack. "But since they do not move in your circles, you will not have to be more than passing polite. And one tea party is not such a terrible ordeal, now, is it?"

Her son stared at her, his turquoise eyes dark with dissatisfaction, and her brows lifted. Suddenly the earl remembered he had yet to tell Camille of Jack's behavior the evening before, so she could have no idea of the reason for her son's bad temper this morning. He was sure Martha Reade's invitation had simply been the last straw for the young man.

Suddenly Jack smiled. "How easy for you to say, Mama! I notice she has not honored you with an invitation!"

Lady Granbourne shook her head, her face serene. "No, nor is she likely to do so. You know she has not spoken to me since I wed Alexander. But I must admit, I have not found that any . . . shall we say, hardship?"

Jack laughed, his good humor restored. "No, she cut up very stiff about your marriage, as I recall. How fortunate for you!"

"Well, she is your father's cousin's wife. You must be polite. And no doubt Robert is wanting to see you after your long absence. I wonder why they came to town at all. It is most unlike them."

"But, Mama, it is as plain as the nose on your face. Can you have forgotten that the youngest Reade, Clorinda, is still unwed? And she must be twenty-seven now. No doubt their arrival is all in aid of procuring her a husband at last. I wish them good fortune!"

"I don't believe I have ever met Clorinda Reade," the earl remarked as his wife handed him a cup of coffee.

"You are to be felicitated, sir," Jack told him. "Short, fat, plain, and to add to her charms, she has a most disagreeable voice. It is so loud and rasping, it reminds me of a fingernail drawn down a slate."

"A most delightful girl, I see. I wonder you are not all breathless anticipation," Alexander remarked, and the two burst out laughing.

Camille Maxwell looked from one to the other, her heart full of her love for them both. She reached out to touch Jack's hand, and when he turned to her, his eyes were alight now with good humor.

"Nevertheless, you will go to tea, won't you, my dear?" she asked. "It would be rude to refuse."

He sighed as he threw down his napkin. "Oh, yes, I shall do the pretty, never fear. For half an hour, no more. But I shall not be cozened into taking Clorinda about, nor introducing her to my friends, which is no doubt what Cousin Martha is scheming. I value my friends too much to inflict her on them."

"Poor girl," Camille murmured. "It must be hard for her."

"I assure you she does not think so," Jack retorted. "She considers herself a diamond of the first water—a real catch. I have never seen anyone so blind to so many staggering faults. And now they will be hailing me in the park, inviting me to dinners, perhaps even a small evening party, and begging me to bring such of my friends as are worthy of dear Clorinda's attention. I know them!"

"Possibly you could escape to Hythe," his stepfather remarked. "A timely retreat is not always cowardly, but good strategy at times."

Jack had risen to take his leave; but he paused to say, "No, I cannot leave London, not at this time, sir. It . . . it is impossible."

He bowed and left them, his color heightened. To his mother he appeared very young and self-conscious, and she looked to her husband for an explanation.

"I suspect Jack has fallen deep in love, my dear, and it is not going well for him. His face when he came in last night! Was I ever that young? My, my, I cannot remember."

"Indeed you were, Alexander," Camille told him, her eyes dancing. "I wonder if it can be Lady Arbel he loves?"

"We shall have to wait until Jack tells us, my dear. But since I trust your woman's intuition explicitly, I am sure you are right. And it would be an excellent match for Jack. Duke Stanton has no other children, and he dotes on his daughter, or so I have been told."

His wife made a deprecating gesture. "As if I cared about titles or standings or money!" she scolded him. "I just want Jack to be happy, to have the kind of marriage we do."

The earl rose then and came to draw back her chair. "If he succeeds, he will be blessed indeed, my love," he murmured into her hair as his arms came around her waist. "But love such as ours is rare. We are the lucky ones."

"I shall pray Lady Arbel is worthy of him, then. And that she truly loves him."

"As you love me?" the earl persisted, his hands tightening.

His wife turned in his arms to face him and take his lean face between her hands. "As I love you," she whispered.

*   *   *

Jack Reade presented himself at Number Seven, Keppel Street, promptly at the time appointed two afternoons later. He was feeling a little more in charity with the world now, for Lady Arbel had danced with him twice the previous evening, and promised to send him a card to the ball her father was planning in her honor. Still, he hid a grimace as the maid admitted him to the respectable rooming house where the Reades were residing.

Martha Reade opened the door to the private sitting room for him herself, loud in her delight at their reunion. As she hugged him, Jack could tell she had put on even more flesh since their last meeting, as had her husband, with his rotund body and round, florid face.

Just as he had suspected, Clorinda Reade was also present, dressed in a youthful gown of pink muslin that proclaimed the virgin. As they exchanged greetings, she batted her eyelashes at him, looking coy, and he had trouble keeping his expression neutral. Someone should tell dear Clorinda that flirting was not her forte; in fact it made her look ridiculous. And the idea that she might be setting her cap for *him* was horrifying. Half an hour, he told himself firmly. Not a minute more.

As the little maid brought in the tea tray, the Reades asked about his voyage, but he could tell that none of them really cared to hear about it, and his remarks were brief. All too soon, Cousin Martha changed the subject, and began to tell him of their plans for the Season.

"We do so hope you will join us often, dear Jack," she said as she passed him a plate of macaroons. "Oh, do take more than one! They are so small. And perhaps a slice of queen's cake?

"Yes, it will be so much more comfortable for dear Clorinda to have your escort," she went on, striking fear in Jack's heart. "As you know, we have little acquaintance in town, but I am sure as the current baronet, you have the entrée everywhere."

"Not quite everywhere, ma'am," Jack said firmly. "Indeed, I doubt I will be much help to you. I have been away for such a length of time, I know few people in town myself."

"Indeed?" Robert Reade asked, his voice disbelieving.

Jack sipped his tea, noticing over the rim of the cup that Cousin Martha had flushed and was looking militant.

"That cannot be due to your journey, Jack," she said. "Oh, no, it is all your *mother's* fault. I knew the consequences of her precipitate marriage to that madman would come home to roost someday! No doubt the *ton* looks at you askance because of her wanton behavior! I only pray that our relationship with her will not destroy all dear Clorinda's chances!"

"I beg your pardon, ma'am? Have I heard you correctly?" Jack asked, his turquoise eyes blazing. He looked quite dangerous, and behind his napkin, Robert Reade coughed a warning to his wife.

"I am sorry if I have upset you, Jack, but I am known to call a spade a spade. And Camille's hasty marriage was sure to offend the highest sticklers. They will not forget, and now you have been tarred with the same brush. It is too bad!"

"I do assure you that the Earl and Countess of Granbourne move in the best circles, ma'am," Jack said through clenched teeth. "What a few old biddies think of my mother does not bother them, nor does it bother me. I know her fineness too well."

"How very forgiving of you, dear Jack," Clorinda said. He shuddered at her loud, raspy tones. "But both Mama and I did not wonder when you chose to leave the country for such a long time as soon as you were grown. Indeed, no."

"I did not leave for the reason you suppose, Clorinda," Jack told her. As he turned those angry eyes toward her, she shrank back in her chair, looking a little frightened.

The three Reades stared at him until he felt compelled to add, "I am very fond of the earl. And he has made my mother a happy woman."

Clorinda tittered, but it was Martha Reade who said, "No doubt. But I have wondered about her ever since your father brought her home to Hythe. Surely it was unusual for Sir John, old bachelor that he was, to take a wife at all. And surely it was unheard-of for such a young girl to marry a man well over twice her age. Of course, I thought she had done it for the title and his wealth, but when you came along so quickly, I had my answer. A woman like that . . . But I suppose we should not be surprised that she contracted another alliance so shortly after poor John's death. You have my sympathy, dear boy."

Jack set his cup down on the table before him and rose. "I must beg you to excuse me, cousins," he said. "I cannot remain and hear my mother maligned. She is a wonderful lady, good and kind, and nothing at all like your insinuations."

"No, no, you must not rush off this way, Jack," Mrs. Reade said, rising to take hold of his arm. "I can see you are angry, but you must allow me my opinion. After all, we are family and we may speak plainly. However, I shall say no more of Camille Reade that was. Come now, do sit down and let Clorinda refill your cup. And tell us what is happening in town. We quite rely on you, you know."

Against his better judgment, Jack was forced to take his seat again. He had promised himself only half an hour's ordeal. He could not rush off after fifteen minutes, no matter how ghastly and insensitive the Reades were.

He managed to get through the remainder of the visit by refusing to speak of anything but the current plays and other public amusements available. He was adroit at refusing any further invitations, and he did not issue any of his own, or make note of future meetings.

When Martha Reade inquired where his rooms were in town, he was glad to be able to tell her he was residing at Granbourne House. Since the lady had been so vehement about cutting any ties with the former Lady Reade, she could not hope to gain admission there.

"Ah, yes, Granbourne House," Robert Reade said in the disappointed silence that followed this revelation. "Most impressive. I was walking by there yesterday, and saw the earl as he was leaving. It was startling how much he resembles you, Jack."

Jack's brows rose. "Resembles me, sir?" he asked, his voice incredulous. "How can that be? I am sure it is only our comparable height that made you think so."

"Probably," Robert Reade admitted. "But that is strange in itself. My cousin John was only a man of average size, and your mother is a small woman. Yet you . . ."

"What are you implying, sir?" Jack asked, his voice steely.

His cousin threw out his pudgy hands. "Why, nothing, my boy, nothing at all. I do assure you, it was merely idle speculation."

Jack's leave-taking shortly thereafter was formal and final. As he ran down the steps, he told himself that no matter what, he would not go anywhere near his only Reade relatives again. And if that meant he was considered rude, so be it. Nothing he could do or say could possible match their bad manners.

He hailed a hackney, and as he traveled back to the West End, he began to consider the visit. He was sure Martha Reade's remarks could be put down to spite and envy of his mother. But Cousin Robert's were more difficult to dismiss. He shifted a little on the old leather squabs, feeling uncomfortable. Here was someone else mentioning his resemblance to the earl! He knew it was true he had more in common physically with Alexander Maxwell than he had had with his late father. Sir John had had light brown hair before it turned white, gray eyes, and the stooped posture of the scholar who took little exercise. And it was also true that he had always felt an uncommon rapport with the earl, almost as if he were his father in truth. But surely that was only because they had always been such fast friends—because the earl had gone out of his way to be kind to him, listen to him, and understand him these past years.

He had been fourteen when his mother had married again. For a time he had been uncomfortable with her and her new husband, and secretly glad he was away at Eton most of the time. And he, too, like Cousin Martha, had been indignant that she had mourned his father such a short time. Why, it had been only a short two months, as he recalled. He had had to fight several of the boys in his form for sly remarks about her.

But in only a little while he had come to accept the marriage. How could he not, they were so happy together, so complete. And when Constance had been born, he had even felt a pang that he did not really belong to this new family his mother was part of. But the earl had not allowed him to separate himself in any way. Jack came to feel that he was their son, and the little girls' brother, in spirit, if not in name.

He told himself he would forget the disagreeable visit

he had just endured; put it from his mind. His Reade
cousins were not pleasant people. Why, look how they
had seemed to enjoy poisoning the conversation.

Fortunately, it was easy to replace his brooding with a
mental image of Lady Arbel. Her ball was in a week's
time. Jack smiled a little, wondering if he could persuade
her to let him speak to her father then. Or would it be
better to wait a little longer? If only Tony Emerson were
not becoming so friendly with her! It was creating quite a
rift between the two old companions, for Tony, encouraged by Arbel's flirting, was pursuing her with more
ardor than Jack liked. And, he reminded himself, Tony
was the son of a marquess, not, he was sure, that anyone as
fine as Arbel would take that into consideration. But
there was always her father, the duke. He knew very
little about the man.

The evening of the Stanton ball, Jack was not at all
pleased when Lady Arbel stood up with Lord Weil first,
after the required opening dance with her father. Angry
that he must wait for the following dance to claim her,
Jack almost decided not to dance himself. But then he
saw Kate Hathaway with her chaperones, and he made
his way to her side. As he bowed, he thought how pretty
she looked this evening, in a primrose silk gown that
almost matched the golden freckles on her nose. She also
wore such a delighted smile to be singled out by him, that
it made him feel much better. Suddenly he remembered
that a friend of his from Oxford had emigrated to Bermuda, and he asked her for news of him and his bride as
they began to dance.

"Farley Williams, m'lord?" Kate asked. "Why, yes,
indeed I do know him. Bermuda society is small. We all
know each other there."

"How is he? What is he doing now?"

"He has started a shipyard," Kate told him. "I believe
he also has plans to engage in trade with the colonies.
Several Bermudians do so, you know. They harvest salt
from the salt ponds on the Turk Islands and transport it
north to trade for fish and other goods. Hardware from
England, clothing, that sort of thing."

"And Mrs. Williams? Maryanne? How is she?"

"She seems happy. Of course, I do not know her very

well. They live at Tucker's Town, and my home is in St. George Town. Then, too, she is busy with her children."

"Children?" Jack asked with a white grin. "Why, they have only been married such a short while."

"You forget you have been gone for two years, sir. A lot can happen in that time," Kate told him with an answering grin. Then she blushed. Lordy, Lordy, she thought. Aunt Mary would have hysterics if she could hear me!

To her delight, Jack laughed down at her. She was most disappointed when the dance ended. Why was it, she wondered, that her few dances with the baronet seemed so short, yet one with Mr. Farnsworth took forever?

"Who was that girl you just partnered, Jack?" Sir Dudley Cowdin inquired when his friend joined him a moment later. Jack explained, and Sir Dudley lifted his brows. "Not in your style at all, dear boy. Too tall, too slim, too ordinary."

"But she is amusing and intelligent, Dudley, and clever as well," Jack retorted.

"Surely a most remarkable female. I must meet her," his friend replied, not sounding at all anxious to do so. Jack chuckled. Dudley had nothing but scorn for the feminine sex, all of whom he considered pea-brained and shallow. Jack was sure he would die a bachelor, he was so hard to please.

"I see your mother and your stepfather are gracing the ball this evening," Dudley remarked next.

"Yes, I knew of it. The earl is an old friend of the duke's," Jack replied, his eyes going to where they stood chatting with the Hanovers. "As you know, they rarely attend social evenings. Strange, neither of them seems to miss them much."

"Sensible people, rather. I begin to think the Season vastly overrated. I swear I hear the same conversations on each and every occasion."

He sounded so gloomy that Jack clapped him on the back. "Bear up, old man. Before long you can return to rusticate in Suffolk and have fascinating conversations with your farmers."

Sir Dudley began to talk then of a house party he intended to give, and to beg Jack's attendance. Jack agreed easily. Dudley might not care for the ladies, but his home was well run and there were all manner of country amusements—fishing, hunting, and horse racing, to say nothing of gambling, prizefights, and fairs.

Just before the two parted, Jack glanced at his step-father again. "Tell me, Dudley, do you think the earl and I look alike?" he asked.

Sir Dudley stared at him, the brown eyes under his dark brows narrowing. "What an extraordinary question to ask!" he exclaimed. "I have never considered it."

"Do so now, if you would be so good," Jack ordered.

His friend stared at him even harder, noting his thinned lips and serious mien. Then he turned to study the earl. There was silence for a long moment before he said slowly, "Well, you are much of a height, of course, and your builds are similar. And well, yes, I would say your jawline is the same, and your cheekbones as well. You are certainly not his twin, however! Now, you tell me, Jack, why did you ask such a singular question?"

Jack tore his eyes from the tall, elegantly dressed man across the room. "It is only that lately I have heard it remarked more than once," he said. "It . . . it has begun to bother me."

Sir Dudley frowned. "Put it from your mind! It was no doubt just easy chitchat, and nothing to the purpose. I suppose it was a woman who mentioned it? Just the sort of thing the silly ninnies would say to try to make them-selves seem clever."

To Sir Dudley's relief, Jack smiled and changed the subject. But as they chatted, Jack told himself he had no intention of mentioning that one of the people he had been referring to had been a relative, who was neither silly nor simple, only vindictive.

Like Kate Hathaway, Jack thought his two dances with Lady Arbel much too short that evening. And the lady was so elusive, she was driving him mad! It was not her teasing smiles and conversation; he found those ador-able. It was because he never knew when he came to her side if she would be warm and welcoming or coolly disinterested. He began to think women were more com-plicated creatures than he had given them credit for. Or perhaps it was just that he had never loved one before. He did not know, but later, as he was being driven home, he decided to ask the earl for advice. Alex was so worldly, so knowledgeable, he would be sure to give him the hint as to how he should go on. He had taken many problems to his stepfather before, and he did not think Alex would fail him now. Surely not when his whole future happiness hinged on the outcome of his campaign to win the lady.

When he reached Granbourne House, the butler told him that although his mother had gone to bed, the earl was relaxing in the library with a snifter of brandy.

"Ah, my boy, do join me," Alexander said, gesturing to the decanter as Jack entered the room.

He saw the little frown that creased Jack's brow as he poured himself a tot, and he went on, "How pleasant this is, after an evening spent among the great. I cannot tell you how glad I am that the portrait of Camille and the girls is almost finished, and we can leave for Willows soon. I hear your miniature is coming along too. Your mother is so pleased with it! Of course, we must have you pose for a full-length portrait as well."

Jack took the seat across from him as he said, "Yes, Sir Joshua is working at a great rate, and I am assured it is a perfect likeness. It is hard for me to tell. I did not think I looked quite that . . . young."

Alexander smiled at him over the rim of his glass. "You will be glad to have it someday when you are old," he said.

Jack swirled the brandy in his glass, his frown back, and the earl waited patiently.

"Sir, if I may ask you something?" Jack said at last.

"Of course, you know that. Anything."

"Then I must tell you that I have found the one woman in the world for me. She is so beautiful, so charming, so sweet, that I fell in love with her at first sight."

Jack was leaning forward in his urgency now, a little smile playing over his handsome mouth, his eyes dreamy as he spoke. Alexander felt a pang, remembering how first love had been for him. And he felt a pang as well for the handsome young man across from him. The young were so sure of themselves and their power. They dreamed dreams the old could no longer aspire to, and they believed implicitly that those dreams would come true. But perhaps the fact that they did believe it was what separated them from their elders. Not for them any doubts.

Not for them contingency plans or uncertainty about their course. No, in their ardor, they could not envision anything but success. Life would, naturally, show them the error of their ways, for life had a way of doing that to everyone. But for now, Jack was invincible. He prayed the boy would have an easier path through life than he had had himself.

". . . name is Arbel Stanton," Jack was saying, and the earl realized he had missed a great deal of a fervent hymn to the girl's wonderful attributes.

"Does she love you too, Jack?" he asked.

Jack shrugged his shoulders. "She has never said so in so many words. Of course, I have told her of my love, even kissed her once. And I have begged her to let me speak to her father. But . . . but Arbel says it is too soon, she cannot be sure. Well, I know she is young, and loath to give up her Season, but . . ."

"She sounds prudent," the earl remarked. "You must remember that just because you fell in love with her at once does not necessarily mean she felt the same way. For some people, love is a slow growing process, not an instant flash of emotion."

Jack nodded eagerly. "Yes, what you say is true. I have tried not to hurry her, sir, tried to be patient. But . . . but it is more than that . . ."

His voice died away and he took a sip of brandy. Again, Alexander waited patiently.

"It is just that since that day when I told her I loved her, she seems to have changed. Sometimes she is as gay and smiling as ever, teasing me with a quick wit, and seemingly happy to be at my side. But there are other times. Times when she flirts with other men, turns her back on me, or refuses even to dance with me. I . . . I never know which Arbel I will find when I approach her."

Privately Alexander recognized the ways of an immature girl reveling in her power over a handsome man, but he did not say so. "As you have said, Jack, she is very young. Perhaps love . . . marriage, frighten her, and she acts as she does to discourage you. Or maybe it is because she fears her own love for you."

Jack's frown was back. "I do not understand," he said. "Why would she be afraid of loving me?"

"Sometimes it is hard for girls to accept marriage. They are afraid of giving the control of their lives into another's hands. Or they fear lovemaking, childbirth—any number of things. You must be patient."

Jack rose then to pace the library, and Alexander's gaze followed him. It did not sound to him as if Jack's love was returned, and he was afraid that eventually the boy would be hurt. He hated to think of that. Jack had every attribute the good fairies could bestow. He was handsome, sure, intelligent, kind, and steadfast. A fine catch in every sense of the word. Was there something about him this Lady Arbel could not like? He did not see how that was possible, although he was quick to acknowledge his prejudice. Then another thought occurred to him, and he added, "Has there been any discussion of your disparate rank? The girl is a duke's daughter, after all, and you a mere baronet. That would not be important if true love were present, but perhaps it weighs with her."

Jack's answer came as swift as a hurled lance. "She is not like that, I know it! She is fine, good."

"I am sure she must be. One so fine as you could not love her otherwise," the earl assured him in a quiet voice. He was glad to see a little smile of thanks replace Jack's frown.

"But before she met you, Lady Arbel no doubt spent many hours dreaming of the man she would meet and marry someday. Perhaps she even dreamt of a prince, or a duke like her father. It would be hard for her to give up her illusions, although I am sure you will be able to convince her to do so, my boy. If she loves you well enough, that is."

"So you advise perseverance, do you, sir? I shall try to curb my impatience! But before the Season is over, I must find a way to make her love me. I must, for without her, my life will be nothing but an empty husk."

Wisely Alexander did not try to refute this dramatic vision Jack had of his future. He knew, however, that if the lady did not now, or ever, return Jack's love, he would find another woman someday. It was only when true lovers were separated that such a disaster could occur. Besides, what Jack was feeling now, although very real to him, was not love. It was the merest beginning of

it, rather like a bud enclosed in a tightly wound sheath of
green. Only time, the sun and the rain, would permit that
bud to flower to its full promise and splendor.

"Were you ever in love like I am now, sir?" he heard
Jack ask, and his brows rose.

Jack flushed, and said quickly, "Excuse me! I do beg
your pardon! That was much too personal a question,
and none of my concern!"

The earl rose and stretched, and came to clap him on
the shoulder. "No harm done. And to answer your question, let me say that I have never loved another woman
as I love your mother, and that I fell in love with her
many long years ago."

"But it was not that long ago that you married her,"
Jack reminded him. "What do you mean?"

The earl's face darkened, and it was a moment before
he said, "I only mean that even though ten years ago I
was much older than you are now, I felt as if I were a
boy. Love can do that, especially to older men."

His voice was wry, and Jack chuckled. Then he asked,
a little hesitantly, "But had there been no love in your
life earlier?"

"I was married before; of course you know that. But
no, that was only an arranged match, done for heirs for
the glory of Granbourne."

Jack finished his brandy before he said, "Well, I am
very glad I don't have to marry someone that way. I
cannot imagine it."

He looked at Alexander almost in pity. The earl's eyes
were cold now, his mouth a thin line, and he wondered at
it.

"No, that is something you will never have to face.
You are fortunate indeed."

The clock struck three then, and he turned toward the
door. "I'm off to bed. I wish you well with your campaign, Jack. If there is anything further you wish to
discuss, at any time, I will be here."

"Thank you, sir. You have always been 'here' for me,
and I appreciate it. I do not think I have ever told you
how much it has meant to me to have you to come to for
help and advice—a thousand things."

The earl's arm was warm around Jack's shoulder as the

two strolled to the stairs. "I do assure you it has been my pleasure," he said, and then, as if he felt the emotion of the moment was becoming too strong, he released him and went to have a word with his butler.

4

MR. Franklin Farnsworth called on Viscount Pelton on a misty morning in early May. After much careful reflection, he had decided to honor the viscount's niece, Katherine Hathaway, by asking her to become his bride. He liked the young lady very well; in fact, he found her shyness and reticence intriguing and her unsophistication attractive. And he was pleased that since her family lived in Bermuda, she would have no one but himself to love and to care for. He was sure she would make him happy, for he would have the exclusive molding of her, teaching her how to go on, and leading her along those paths that would make her a proper wife for him. He rather fancied the picture of him doing so, and her subsequent gratitude.

Of course, her dowry was sure to be less than outstanding, or he would have heard whispers of its size long before this. And it was disappointing that she had no lands in England to bring to him, but he would not allow that to deter him. He had decided on Miss Hathaway, and once his mind was made up, he never changed it.

His mother had often been heard to remark that her dear Franklin was as stubborn as a pig, and always had been even as a child. It was true, he rarely deviated from an opinion once he had decided on it, no matter how much in error he might find himself later. One of the many things about him that had irritated Kate was his calm assumption that the correct name for Bermuda was Somers' Islands, in honor of the Sir George Somers whose ship, the *Sea 'Venture*, had been shipwrecked off its coast in 1609. In vain did Kate point out that the Spaniard Juan Bermúdez had discovered the island a century be-

fore. Mr. Farnsworth refused to accept her argument.
What, name a British colony after a foreigner? Ecod! Of
course the correct name had to be Somers' Islands. And,
it was implied, there would be no further discussion
about it. He was, as always, right.

Unfortunately for the eager suitor, the viscount was
unable to bestow his niece's hand. He admitted he had
no jurisdiction over the girl and suggested Mr. Farnsworth
apply to her mother, Olivia Hathaway.

On learning that the lady was at home, Farnsworth was
quick to do just that. He was ushered into a cheerful
morning room, where Mrs. Hathaway was sitting with
her hostess. Both ladies heard him out without comment.
He noted that Lady Pelton wore a delighted smile, and
nodded to him encouragingly throughout his declaration,
but he wondered at the little frown Katherine's mother
sported.

"I do not know what to say, sir," she remarked when
he fell silent at last. "I do not know my daughter's mind
in this matter . . ."

"And what has her opinion to say to anything, Olivia?"
the viscountess demanded. "As her mother, and in the
absence of her dear father, Katherine must accept your
decision. You have only to tell her the match has your
sanction, which I am sure is the case."

"Yes . . . well, perhaps you are right, but . . ." her
sister-in-law remarked, still uncertain.

Farnsworth was delighted anew at the watery miles
that were going to separate him from this dithering female who did not even see how condescending he was to
honor her provincial family with an offer. And there was
his wealth, his noble relatives as well, he reminded himself.

"I shall call again at three this afternoon," he said,
bowing slightly in turn to both ladies. "That will give you
time, Mrs. Hathaway, to prepare your daughter for her
good fortune. Good day."

As soon as he was out of earshot, Mary Townsend
clapped her hands in glee. "Oh, it is famous, just famous, isn't it, Olivia? To think that my plans have borne
such satisfying fruit! All thanks to my assistance, Katherine is to be envied, for she will become the wife of such a
prominent man. I am sure your dear husband will be
grateful to me, as I know you must be too. No, no, do

not thank me, if you please! I was glad to help, indeed I was.

"Now, let us send for the girl so we might apprise her of her glorious future at once."

Thus admonished, Olivia Hathaway did as she was bidden, but she could not help sending up a small prayer that the antipathy she had sensed in her daughter for this particular man had been only in her imagination.

To her distress, she discovered she had not been wrong after all. At first, Kate had only laughed helplessly at the very idea. And when chastised by her aunt for her levity, she had been quick to say in a positive voice that she had never cared for Mr. Farnsworth, that she never *would* care for him, and that she had no intention of marrying him.

"But of course you will do as your mother tells you!" her Aunt Mary had exclaimed, her eyes bright with indignation. "Who are you to set yourself up to decide your future, you silly, willful girl?"

"Yes, Kate, my dear, perhaps you are being too hasty," her mother said, intervening quickly before her daughter could distress the viscountess further. "Perhaps it is only that you need more time to become accustomed to the idea. I do assure you Mr. Farnsworth said everything that was polite. He seems to want you a great deal. And he is such a wonderful catch too! Do, *do* say you will think about it, and not be so precipitate. Indeed, if you cannot like to receive him until you have had a chance to do so, I shall explain it to him myself this afternoon when he comes to call on you."

Mary Townsend sniffed audibly. "I have never heard of such a thing, to be leaving an eligible gentleman dangling! I begin to think that manners in the colonies leave a great deal to be desired. The very idea!"

"Mama, would you like to be married to Mr. Farnsworth?" Kate asked, quietly now. "Would you like to be told what to think and how to behave by such as he? Would you like to live with him, sleep in his bed, and bear his children?"

"*Katherine!*" Lady Pelton gasped, groping for her salts as she did so. Olivia Hathaway looked stunned as well, and was most effectively silenced by her daughter's questions.

"What happens in the bedroom is not a matter for discussion, especially by young ladies. Have you no delicacy of mind?" Lady Pelton demanded. "Oh, I think I am about to suffer a spasm!"

"I am sorry for it, ma'am," Kate told her, watching her aunt lean back in her chair, her hands to her breast. "But what I spoke of is a part of any marriage, is it not? And I cannot like Mr. Farnsworth as a husband. Ugh!"

She turned to her mother then and said, "No, I do not need time to think about it, Mama. Kindly inform the gentleman that although I am honored by his offer, I cannot accept it."

"Ungrateful hussy! Oh, serpent in my bosom," Lady Pelton moaned. "After all I have done, the time and effort I have expended, to be repaid this way by ingratitude."

She opened her eyes then and sat up straight as something occurred to her. "Olivia, perhaps a period spent locked in her room with nothing but bread and water would bring this tiresome girl to a sense of her responsibilities."

"I should tell you at once, Aunt Mary, that you could lock me up for years, and I would never change my mind. In fact, it would be preferable to marriage with Mr. Farnsworth. And furthermore, I have my father's promise that I don't have to marry any man I don't care to. It is my decision, no one else's."

"Your father promised that? Is he insane?" Lady Pelton asked, her eyes bugging out in shock again.

"No, he is not. He is good and kind, and he loves me."

Kate turned to her mother again and held out her hands. "Mama, do let us go home! I have been here for some months now, and I have seen no man in that time that I would care to wed."

A flitting vision of Sir John Reade's face came to her mind, but she was firm in putting it aside. He was not for her, he never would be. Besides, she knew he was in love with the Lady Arbel. Ever practical, Kate did not chase impossible dreams.

"Please, Mama, may we?" she asked. "I do so long to be back in Bermuda!"

Lady Pelton rose and shook out her skirts with a decisive snap. "I think that is an excellent idea, Olivia," she said coldly. "You daughter sadly lacks decorum, and she has been badly disciplined all her life. Knowing what I know now, I do not care to house her anymore."

Her guest rose as well. She had been about to try to make peace between the two combatants, but now that Kate had been insulted—and she herself, as well—all the conciliatory words died on her tongue. "Of course, ma'am, I understand," she said as coldly as her sister-in-law had spoken. "I shall make arrangements to take the first available ship. I beg you will excuse us."

As the two went up to her room arm in arm, Kate's eyes were shining, but she waited until the door was closed behind them before she said, "Oh, that was famous, Mama! You were so dignified, so proud in your set-down! And now we can go home—*home*!"

Mrs. Hathaway shook her head at her daughter's delight. "Yes, we must go, of course. But I feel such a failure! I meant to find you some young man who would make you happy, Kate, indeed I did. You do not think how hard it will be for you in Bermuda, where there are few suitable gentlemen for you to marry. And believe me, my dear, marriage and children are what make a woman happy."

"We shall see about that, now, won't me, Mama?" Kate said, coming to hug her. "Perhaps I am destined to be a spinster so I can care for you and Father in your old age."

Her mother shook her head again, her lips twisted in a grimace. "What a marvelous future you paint! Nurse-maid to a pair of doddering elderlies! Rather, I would like to welcome your husband to the family, see you settled in your own establishment, cuddle and spoil your babies. And I would like knowing that you are secure and happy in some good man's love."

"Well, perhaps I will be someday," Kate told her. "But never with Franklin Farnsworth! Even as a son-in-law he would be impossible, and you know it!"

"He is a little pompous and stiff, that is true, but marriage might change him. Why—"

"Not another word, Mama! I do not like Mr. Farnsworth, and that is that!"

"Yes, that is that," Mrs. Hathaway said sadly. "Excuse me now, dear. I must see the viscount, set him to searching out passage for us. I fear living here with his wife is going to be most unpleasant from now on, and the sooner we can leave, the better. And I must prepare for a most difficult interview with your suitor; try to find some way to soften the blow of your refusal."

She left the room, and a smiling Kate went to the window. London stretched out before her, as noisy and dirty as it always was. The fine rain that was falling made it even grayer and more depressing than usual, but Kate did not notice. Instead, her eyes sought the direction of the southern coast. Bermuda was waiting for her many miles away, all green and fragrant and warm. The turquoise waters of its shoals, the gentle breezes she remembered, were still there. And soon she would be on her way back, yes, very soon.

Clorinda Reade had been quick to see that her cousin Jack had no intention of smoothing the path for her in London this Season. For one thing, he had refused all her mother's invitations, claiming prior engagements. And only recently, when the Reades had been walking in Hyde Park, he had crossed the roadway rather than be forced to stop and acknowledge them. Oh, of course he had joined a group of friends in doing so, but Clorinda was not fooled. She was furious—furious, and more than a little insulted. Why, it was not as if they were not perfectly presentable, she thought, as wellborn as he was. And they were his only close relatives, too, for her Aunt Camille had never spoken of her background, nor her family.

How very strange that was, Clorinda thought as her abigail brushed out her hair one evening just before bed. I wonder if there is a reason for it? Surely she is not an orphan, or we would know of it! She made a point to speak to her mother about it at breakfast the next morning, but Martha Reade could shed no light on the subject.

"I believe Camille was originally from another part of Kent, and I seem to remember her maiden name was Talbot. But she never visited her birthplace, nor did her mother and father—any of her relatives—visit her. That was singular, now that I come to think of it. I wonder why not."

Clorinda wondered too, but she changed the subject then to fashions and the theater they were to attend that evening. Later that morning, accompanied by her abigail, she made a point of strolling through Berkeley Square. She thought Granbourne House most impressive, and she passed it slowly, hoping her cousin would come out. The door remained closed, however, and she was forced to admit defeat. But the following days, she was often in the square, and at last her vigilance was rewarded.

She was across the park when a sporting tilbury pulled up before the house she had been watching so carefully. Her cousin Jack was driving it, and he was accompanied by an older man she had no trouble recognizing as his stepfather, the earl. She was about to pick up her skirts and hurry around, hoping to intercept them, when suddenly she stopped dead in her tracks, her mouth falling open in astonishment.

The two men, one in his twenties, the other middle-aged, were in profile to her. But surely her father had been right! she thought. They did look somewhat alike. Those firm jaws and high cheekbones set in identically lean faces . . . The more she looked, the more she marked the resemblance.

And when a groom came running to hold the horses, and they climbed down to the flagway, she could see they were the same height as well.

She watched them mount the steps, talking together, and she saw the earl turn sideways, laughing at something Jack had just said. Why, even his laugh was similar!

A stab of excitement swelled her large bosom, and she waited, hardly breathing until they had been admitted to the house and the door had closed behind them.

Later that afternoon, Clorinda sat down at the desk in her mother's sitting room in Keppel Street to compose an anonymous letter to Sir John Reade. Her lips were wreathed in a contented smile as she did so. Let us see how Sir High-and-Mighty takes this, she thought as she dipped her quill in the pot of ink. Vindictive by nature, and quick to take umbrage at any slight, imagined or real, she was pleased she had this way to repay Jack for his lack of interest in her, and his discourtesy. She had long had a *tendre* for him, and she had spent many hours daydreaming of his kiss and his embrace. Remembering this made her especially bitter, and writing the letter eased her somewhat. How it would hurt, and she was glad it would!

Of course, she had no intention of telling her parents what she was doing, for she saw it did not put her in a very good light. And, of course, she had no proof of what she was claiming, none at all. Most probably it was nothing but conjecture. But Jack would not know that, and she didn't care about its veracity. She wanted revenge, and this was the only way she could get it.

She had employed this same method only a few years ago, when a friend of hers, a Harriet Booth, had captured a young man she, Clorinda, considered her beau. Thwarted of taking any direct retaliation, she had done a great deal of harm to the young couple's new marriage by her insinuations and lies. Poor Harriet learned that her adored Mr. Beaton had fathered a child and then refused to marry the girl he had ruined. Her husband also received an anonymous letter claiming his bride was a secret tippler, one, moreover, who had insanity on her family tree.

It was only when Clorinda went too far and sent even more outrageous missives that the two had sat down and compared notes. Clorinda could still remember Harriet's visit to her; the things she had said! Needless to say, the letters had stopped abruptly.

But this time she would not overstep the bounds, she told herself as she covered the page with a disguised handwriting. No, she was sure only one letter would do the trick, and make Jack begin to wonder about his sainted mother, his dear, *dear* stepfather. And that will serve him right for treating me so badly, she thought.

Jack received the letter early that evening. It had been left at the front door by a shabby individual who never spoke a word, and who hurried away as soon as the butler took it from his hand.

Thinking it might be urgent, Kemble had sent a footman with it to Jack's rooms at once. He knew the baronet was dressing to go out later, and he wanted to be sure he had the letter to hand before he did so.

Jack looked puzzled as he broke the seal. He did not recognize the handwriting, and his eyes went quickly to the bottom of the page. Seeing there was no signature, he frowned.

He was scowling a few moments later as he crushed the letter in his hand, shaking his head in disbelief as he did so.

But who could have written such filth? he wondered. Who could have told such lies, implied such vile doings? Was it possible that someone hated him to this extent, and he had never even suspected it?

He went to sit down before the fire, glad he had not called his valet as yet. The evening ahead, to be spent at his club with Tony and Dudley, having dinner and playing cards, was forgotten.

Carefully he smoothed the letter out and read it again, more carefully this time. The writer claimed that he was not the son of Sir John Reade after all. That his real father was Alexander Maxwell, Earl Granbourne. According to the writer, he had been conceived before his mother's marriage to the unsuspecting baronet who had married her so innocently.

"Why do you think you look so much like the earl?" the writer asked. "Your mother is no better than a whore and your real father a dissolute rake, for all they finally married ten years ago. And even though you bear the title of baronet, it does not belong to you. If you doubt my words, ask the earl for the truth if you dare, but be warned. If this comes out, you will be discredited and ruined. For you, sir, when all is said and done, are nothing but a bastard."

Jack scowled again. Of course it was all lies; he knew that. To even imagine for a moment that his pure, good mother would . . . But no! He would not even think of it. It was all hatred and spite and evil—despicable stuff!

He felt a cold shiver on the back of his neck, in spite of the cheerful sea-coal fire in the grate. He was not so naive that he thought the world was made up only of good, kindly people. No, there were plenty of others who would find this kind of slander amusing or exciting. But for the life of him, he could not understand it. Why him? He had no enemies that he knew of, certainly no one he had injured so badly that he would go this far, besmirching his good name, accusing his mother and Alex of . . .

He rose to pace the room. He would forget it. It was not worthy of any consideration. But somehow he could not bring himself to throw the letter on the fire, nor did he ring the bell to summon his valet and prepare to go out as he had planned. Instead, he wrote a short note to his friends, excusing himself from joining them, before he left the house. For even though he knew what he had read was lies, he did not think he could sit down to dinner here either. No, he could not look into his mother's blue eyes with this . . . this obscenity in the back of his mind.

He was tired when he returned home much later. Tired, and even more confused than when he had left the house. He had walked until he could walk no more, and then he had hired a hackney to drive him around town.

As he traveled through the London streets on an aimless journey to nowhere, he had thought and thought again about that letter. He realized that in all probability he would never discover the sender, so he did not waste time wondering about his identity. Instead, he tried dispassionately to consider the information he had been given so he could refute it and put it away from him.

It was true his mother and Alex had known each other when they were young; he had their acknowledgment of that fact. But then his mother had gone to Bath and met Sir John, marrying him a short time later. Jack wondered what she had been doing in the spa town; whom she had visited there. And he was forced to concur with the writer that her lack of family was unusual. Camille Reade had never mentioned her parents, nor any brothers or sisters—even long-dead grandparents. He had never thought to question that, and now he wondered why. People, after all, did not spring from the heads of the gods. She had a family somewhere, or she had had one at one time. Who were they? Why had there been such a rift that she never saw them, or even spoke of them?

It was then he remembered all the times people had remarked on his resemblance to the earl since his return to England. Yes, they did look alike, and in more ways than one. And he remembered, too, how much he liked the earl, how close he felt to him, almost as if he were his father indeed. Could that innate rapport speak truth that he had never suspected?

At last, when the hackney driver pulled up and announced he was going off duty, Jack directed him to Berkeley Square. It was hours after midnight. The streets were emptying now, with only a few late-night revelers still abroad.

Kemble admitted him to the house. Jack did not notice

the butler's frowning concern for the despair he did not realize was etched on his face. Uncharacteristically, he brushed by the old servant without a word, to climb the stairs. He would have to see Alex tomorrow, he told himself. He could not bear this burden alone. Perhaps there was some perfectly logical explanation, and Alex would tell him of it. Perhaps together they could lay this dark shadow to rest, once and for all.

He did not sleep well, for his dreams were troubled, and he woke early. Still, he waited in his rooms until he knew his mother and Alex were at breakfast. Then he sent a note down asking the earl for a private interview as soon as it could be arranged.

The footman who delivered his message came back shortly to tell him the earl was waiting for him in the library. Jack did not hesitate. He knew if he stayed too long, he might change his mind about the coming confrontation, and he could not do that.

Alexander Maxwell's eyes narrowed as Jack entered the room and closed the door carefully behind him. He had never seen the young man look so taut, so unwell. He wondered if the sweet little Lady Arbel had refused him, and perhaps been unkind about it besides. He wished he had that young lady alone now, if she had, he thought as he made himself smile a greeting.

"I have received a most unusual letter, sir," Jack said as he came to stand before the earl's desk. "It was anonymous, and the things it claimed have troubled me ever since first reading. I thought you might be able to help me."

"Certainly, Jack, you know I am glad to do so," Alexander said. "But anonymous letters . . . well, surely you know enough not to put much credence in them?"

"Yes, I do. However, I cannot ignore this one so easily, just toss it on the fire with a grimace. Tell me, if you would be so good, sir, are you my father?"

The silence that filled the library was so pregnant and weighty, it seemed almost a third living presence there. Jack never took his eyes from the earl's face, and he was filled with dread when he saw how it paled and stiffened.

"Do you have that letter, Jack?" Alexander asked at last. "If I might see it?"

Jack took it from his coat pocket and extended it. As

the earl unfolded it and began to read, he sat down across from him. His thoughts were bleak as he did so, for Alex had not denied the charge. Surely if it were nothing but a vicious lie, he would have done so at once, wouldn't he?

He watched the earl's face grow even colder and more stern as he read. It seemed to take him a very long time. At last he put the letter down and wiped his fingers on his handkerchief, as if just touching it had soiled them.

"It is obvious that someone hates you very much, or, more possibly, perhaps, hates me," Alexander said, his voice rough with anger. "I refuse to believe anyone could hate your mother that way. It would be impossible. You were right to come to me. We must talk about this."

Jack's eyes never left the earl's frozen face. "But you do not refute it, sir," he said slowly. "Why is that? Is it true after all?"

Now the earl looked away to stare out the window beside him. His face was very pale, and a muscle clenched for a moment in his lean cheek. "I made your mother a promise years ago. I cannot break it. Do not ask it of me."

He turned back then and said, "This letter is best forgotten. It is damnable, but there is no proof. You are the same Sir John Reade you have always been. Try to forget this, put it from your mind."

"Could you?" Jack asked swiftly. "Could you go on in my place as if nothing had happened, without knowing the truth or falsehood of it?"

There was another pause before the earl replied, "Yes, if it was the only thing I could do, I would. I have had many terrible things said about me, those accusations of madness, for example. I have been forced to watch old friends cut me, heard the whispers, faced the caricatures and doggerel, and I know how that hurts. But you will not have to deal with any of that. The writer can do nothing more without proof, and there is no proof. This need go no further if you are wise."

Jack still stared at him, his unusual eyes as cold as the earl's hazel ones now. "I cannot do that. I must know. I do not ask you to break a promise, but if you will not tell me, you do see I have no choice but to question my mother."

"No!" came the swift retort. "You will not do that, Jack! It would hurt her so!"

Suddenly Jack knew of a certainty that he was facing the man who had given him life twenty-four years ago, and he rose so quickly his chair tumbled over. "You are my father," he said.

It was not a question, that cold, flat statement, and the earl did not answer him.

"You-are-my-father," Jack repeated slowly. "Everything in that letter is true. If you do not tell me about it, I will go to my mother with the story, whether she be hurt or not. I must know the truth!"

The earl ran two trembling hands over his face. Jack waited, his heart pounding in his chest, his breathing shallow in his distress.

"Very well, I will tell you, but only to spare Camille. I pray she will find it in her heart to forgive me," the earl muttered at last. There was a long pause, and then he looked straight at the young man before him.

"Yes, you are my son. My son and hers. If you knew how it has hurt me not to be able to acknowledge you all these years!"

He ignored Jack's muffled curse and went on, "Sit down, my son. In order to understand what happened to us, you must hear the whole ugly story."

"Sit down? When you have just ruined my life?" Jack demanded, leaning on the desk, his eyes blazing. "I am a bastard! I am not Sir John Reade, I never was! I am not anyone. Why should I listen to you, hear a story that no doubt you will invent to make me feel better and excuse you both from your iniquity? I tell you I shall not, sir!"

He turned quickly to leave.

"Wait, Jack!" Alexander called after him. "Where are you going? Stay, I beg you, and let me speak. There is a perfectly good explanation for what happened . . ."

Jack paused at the door of the library. When he spoke, his voice was tortured, thick with emotion. "The letter was right. You are despicable, and my mother is . . ."

He paused for a moment to control himself, and then he said, "I am leaving your house, and I shall never return or have anything to do with either of you again."

The earl hurried toward him as the door slammed shut. A moment later he heard the front door slam as well, and he knew Jack had made good on his word. He grasped a chair back for a moment, feeling such a bleak pain that he thought he must die from it. And what of Camille? Dear Lord, what would this do to her? He must go to her and tell her. He must try to comfort her, even though he had no idea how, when he was in such dire need of comfort himself.

Before he went up to her room, he had a word with his butler. A footman was to be sent to Sir Joshua Reynolds' studio, canceling the countess's sitting that morning. Furthermore, Kemble was to instruct the nursemaids that both Lady Constance and Lady Grace were to be kept either in the nursery or outside in the park. Under no circumstances were they to be brought to their mother or allowed to disturb her in any way.

Kemble bowed and nodded, but his eyes were thoughtful as he watched the slow way the earl climbed the stairs, the slump of his shoulders. There was something wrong in the house, something very wrong. And if he were not mistaken, it had to do with Master Jack, as he still thought of him. Kemble shook his head. They were such a happy family, it was a joy to serve them. He prayed that whatever the trouble was, it would be cleared up shortly.

Alexander was as gentle as he could be when he told his wife that Jack had discovered the secret they had kept safe for so many years. But he saw that it made no difference. Her eyes filled with tears, and as she began to sob, he took her into his arms.

"Sssh, love," he whispered. "I will find out where Jack has gone, and I will go after him. Once he understands, he will forgive us, I know. You must not worry."

"But you know Jack!" she said in a broken voice. "Idealistic and moody! He is so sensitive, this will hurt him even more than it would another young man."

The earl nodded, his face grim. "If only we had not come to town this Season, this might all have been averted," he said. "It was seeing us together that made it possible for someone to connect us. But we have only to deny it, and persuade Jack that he must do so as well, and it will all pass over. There is no proof, none at all. Legally, he is still Sir John Reade. Only if he insists on renouncing the title will there be a scandal. I do not think he will do that to you, my love. He cares for you too much."

He bent to kiss her hair before he went on, "At the moment he is angry, distraught. But when he has had a chance to calm down, a chance to think about the future and what dire consequences there would be to all of us if this came out, he will be sensible. I only pray he keeps his tongue between his teeth until reason triumphs."

"Yes, of course you are right," Camille said, drawing back in his arms so she could wipe her eyes. "Do go after him at once, find him, and make him see reason, Alexander! I could not bear it if his life were to be ruined by this!"

The earl kissed her before he left her. At the door, with his hand on the knob, he turned and said, "When do you suppose it will be over, Camille? When will the evil my father did stop? Even from the grave he touches us with it. Surely we have suffered enough for his treachery! And now Jack must suffer too. Will it follow us all to our own graves?"

The countess put out her hand to him, he sounded so distraught, but he had gone. She shook her head, and then she went to her writing desk. When Alexander found Jack, he would have a letter of hers to give him. Perhaps her words, her honesty at last, would help. For what she had done, she had done for his sake, and because she had been desperate. Jack was a man now. He must understand.

It was much later that afternoon when a carter came to remove Jack's trunks. There was a bustle in the hall while they were being brought down, and Lady Grace, who had escaped the supervision of her nurse, stared from behind the nursery door.

Her blue eyes widened as she saw the strange men in the hall below, and feeling uneasy, she put her thumb in her mouth. Then she crept down a flight to peek over the banister to the front hall. Her father was there, and Kemble, and although they were two of her favorite people, they were not the one she wanted now.

"Want Jack!" she said loudly. "Where is he? Want Jack!"

The faces of the men as they looked up to where she was standing frightened her, and she began to wail. The earl ran up the flight to pick her up. She cuddled against him, feeling safe, as she always did in her big strong father's arms.

"Hush, lovey," the earl said, rocking her a little and cradling her head. "Yes, you want Jack. We all do. But Jack has gone away."

5

WHEN Jack bolted from Granbourne House to hurry through the streets, he had not noticed he cut less than a dashing figure without his tricorne, his gloves, and his sword. But his mind was a chaotic jumble of disconnected thoughts, and it refused to function normally. Oh, somewhere in the back of his fevered brain he knew he would have to find a place to stay, and send for his servant and his clothes, but he could do that later. His first impulse, the need to escape the earl's presence, was still too compelling. It was true, everything in that damnable letter was all true! Alexander Maxwell was his father. He was not John Reade. He had no claim to the title of baronet, nor the estate, nor the wealth it brought. He was suddenly . . . no one. A man of no more importance than the chimney sweep strolling toward him, or the hearty farmer making deliveries of fresh milk from the cart beside him on the cobbles. His hands curled into fists then as he realized that it was possible that he was of less value, for they might well be honorable men born in wedlock, and not the bastard he now knew himself to be.

Jack fought a wave of nausea as his stomach tightened in revulsion, and he paused for a moment until it passed. It was then he noticed he was in Grosvenor Square. He took a deep breath to steady himself. There was the Duke of Stanton's town house, and inside—ah, inside! —was the girl he wanted to marry. The girl who was now forever lost to him. For a moment he wanted to cry out at the injustice of it all, and it took him several moments to compose himself. And then he straightened his shoulders and nodded. Yes, he must call on the Lady Arbel. Not only did he long to see her in his hurt, he owed her an explanation.

Fortunately, the butler admitted him without question, only looking a little perplexed that the accouterments of a gentleman were not there for him to receive. But the butler knew the young baronet was one of Lady Arbel's suitors, and he smiled as he led him to the morning room. Young lovers were so often forgetful, and he himself could be the soul of tact.

Arbel was alone, idly flipping through the latest copy of *The Spectator,* when Jack was announced. She was astonished he had come to call so early, and when she saw his tortured face, the agony in his turquoise eyes, she wondered where her chaperone, Miss Hanrahan, could possibly have gone to.

Jack bowed to her as the butler's footsteps faded away. "Arbel, I came to you at once! I had to see you," he said, his voice rough.

"La, what on earth?" she asked. "You look quite wild, sir! Is anything wrong?"

Jack's laugh was harsh, bitter. "You might say that. Oh, yes, you might say that indeed! I have just discovered that I am not Sir John Reade after all. I am nothing but the bastard son of the Earl of Granbourne."

Arbel gasped, her hands going to her face in shock. "Have you been drinking, sir?" she asked, for it was the only thing she could think of to explain such a wild statement.

"No, I have not," Jack said quickly, shaking his head in his impatience. "I received an anonymous letter yesterday telling me of it, and when I confronted the earl only moments ago, he could not deny it. Arbel, Arbel, what are we to do? How can our marriage ever take place now?"

"Well, of course it can't, if what you say is true," she replied, for the lady was ever practical. Secretly, she was feeling relieved. Jack Reade had become very demanding, and she had not cared to be pressured into a decision she was not at all sure she wanted to make. But now, of course, that decision had been taken out of her hands. Seeing the despair on his face, she made herself say kindly, "Indeed, I am sorry, but it is not as if we were ever promised."

"Arbel! Is that all you can say to me, who love you so much?"

She tossed her black curls. "La, sir, what would you have me say? Of course I feel for your plight most sincerely, for I have always liked you very well."

"*Liked* me? *Liked* me?" Jack echoed, and then he put his head back and gave that discordant laugh again. "She likes me," he told a brocaded armchair. "And to think I love her even until death!"

"You are not fair!" Arbel exclaimed, stamping her little foot. "I never said I loved you, not once! It was all your imagination that there was any more between us. You, sir, have been building castles in the air, dreaming dreams that had no foundation in fact. I have no patience with you. I think you had better leave me."

For a moment she regretted those sharp words, for Jack took a step closer, and what she saw in his eyes made her shiver. Then she drew a shaky breath of relief as he stopped, and the anger she had seen a moment before was replaced by a cold mask, impossible to read.

"Yes, I shall do so. But before I go, allow me to thank you, m'lady. You have shown me very clearly how I shall be regarded from now on. A salutary lesson for me, although a most painful one at this particular time. Beg you to excuse me. Of course a bastard such as I has no right to be in your dainty presence. Give you good-day."

Lady Arbel's rosy mouth fell open as he bowed and left her. And when her father came in a few minutes later to question her about her unusually early caller, she had worked herself up to a fine state of indignation that Jack had spoken to *her* in such a way.

Charles Stanton's brows rose when she told him the news that Jack had brought. He said nothing until she had finished, and then he led her to a sofa and waited until she was seated.

"Does anyone else know of this, Arbel?" he asked sternly.

She shook her head. "No, he said he left the earl only moments ago. But, Papa, is it not dreadful? And he was so angry because I told him I could never marry him and didn't love him. But truly, I never intended to marry a

mere baronet anyway, so do not fear he has broken my
heart! It was just . . . dalliance."

She watched the duke pace the room, his brows knit.
At last he said, "Of course I am delighted your heart is
intact, my dear, but I very much fear today's doings have
broken that young man's heart. It is too bad."

His daughter's blue eyes widened, but he raised a hand
and continued, "I must see Earl Granbourne, and at
once. Perhaps there is some way we can keep this quiet,
or at least diffuse it."

He turned then and said, "Arbel, I charge you on your
honor to say nothing of what you have learned this day,
no, not even to Miss Hanrahan. Do you understand me?
For everyone's sake, this must be kept secret."

Arbel looked a little mutinous at being forced to conceal the most delicious bit of gossip she had heard for a
long time, but her father came and leaned down to take
her shoulders between his hands, and his deep-set eyes
bored into hers. "Admit no one to your confidence,
Arbel. I would not have that young man ruined."

"Very well, Papa. But it is bound to come out sooner
or later, don't you think? After all, whoever wrote that
letter knows the truth, and they will not keep it to
themselves!"

"Perhaps not," the duke admitted as he let her go and
straightened. "But not a word concerning it will come
from these doors. And if I do not have your promise on
it, I shall be sending you down to the country within the
hour."

Lady Arbel looked wounded, for her doting father had
seldom taken that tone with her. At last she rose and
curtsied, her black head held high. "Certainly, Papa.
You need not fear any indiscretion on my part," she said
with dignity.

The duke smiled as he left her, and while he waited for
his tricorne and sword to be brought to him, he made his
plans. He would go round to Granbourne House immediately. Between them, he and his good friend Alexander
Maxwell would discuss how best to handle the situation.
And pray God, Jack Reade, the young fool, would do
nothing precipitate before that time. Still, he thought as
he left the house, he could not but wonder at the tale.
Could it be true indeed?

* * *

On finding himself in Grosvenor Square again, Jack paused for a moment to think. He was coldly furious, but he refused to consider what had just passed between him and Arbel, for he knew if he were to do so, he might lose the somewhat precarious control he was maintaining. Someday soon, he would have to review their meeting, learn to put his dreams of the lifetime together with her aside, but he could not do it now.

He heard a friend driving by in a tilbury hail him, and he made himself smile and bow. It was then that he realized that he must go to ground. He was sure the earl would be searching for him shortly, and he had no desire to see him again. Nor did he wish to meet his friends, for he knew his face must betray him. And he had to think, think hard about what he was to do now that the world as he had known it had disappeared.

As he began to walk away, he considered his friends. There was Lord Weil, of course. But Tony resided with his parents when he was in London, so he could not go there. Jack's face brightened slightly as he remembered Sir Dudley Cowdin. Of course! Since he had reached his majority, Dudley had always kept his own rooms, for although he loved his mother dearly, Lady Cowdin was overprotective of her only son, and he could not stand being fussed over.

Pray Dudley was home, Jack thought, looking about for a hackney. Then he remembered he had no money to pay the fare, and his mouth twisted in a grimace. Not only did he not have the few coins he would need in this instance, he had no money at all. The grimace deepened as he thought of his sudden poverty. He supposed he was still Jack Reade, since his mother had been wed at his birth, but never again could he touch any monies from Hythe. That wealth belonged to a baronet who did not exist.

Fortunately, when he had walked to St. Martin's Street off Leicester Square, he found his friend not only at home, but still at breakfast. The smile Dudley greeted him with faded when he saw his face, and he was quick to dismiss his butler.

"Ecod, man, you look terrible! What has happened to you?" Dudley asked as he came to take Jack's arm and lead him to a seat. "No, don't tell me yet. Sit down, have some ale, or perhaps a brandy?"

Jack shook his head, and Sir Dudley's good-natured face hardened. He had been Jack's friend since Eton days, and admired him even then, but never, even in danger or distress, had he seen him look quite so bad. That handsome carefree face of his was set in hard lines, and his unusual turquoise eyes were bleak and stormy.

He hurried to pour Jack a mug of ale, even closing his fingers around the handle of it, before he took his seat again.

"What is it, Jack?" he asked quietly. "Why do you look that way?"

Wearily Jack told him about the anonymous letter and what he had learned since. As he spoke, Sir Dudley listened intently, only the startled uplifting of his brows betraying his amazement. When Jack concluded with a brief summary of his meeting with the Lady Arbel, his friend's generous mouth tightened in disgust.

"You told Lady Arbel?" he asked. "Lord, man, might just as well have told the crier! It will be all over London in less than a day!"

"What does that matter?" Jack asked, his voice despairing. " 'Tis the truth."

"Try not to be such a noddy, Jack!" Sir Dudley admonished him. As Jack's startled eyes swung from the depths of his mug to his friend's face, he went on, "If you had kept it quiet, no one would ever have known. For even if this malicious correspondent of yours did voice his suspicions, where's the proof? You had only to laugh it off, ignore it as unworthy gossip. You are still Sir John Reade. There can be no doubt that your mother was married to the man at your birth."

Jack frowned down into the foamy ale. "It is a surname I do not deserve, and a title I will not use."

Dudley threw out his hands in disgust. "What will you call yourself, then, idiot? Jack Nobody? I tell you, you are Jack Reade!"

"Yes, for my sins, I suppose I am. But I shall be *Sir John* Reade no more. Nor shall I touch a groat of the money from the estate."

"Well, here's a pretty kettle of fish, I must say! It's not that all your friends won't help, Jack, but what do you

intend to live on, then? Of course, I'll put you up here as
long as you like, but . . ."

"I would not ask that of you, my friend, but I thank
you," came the swift rejoinder. "No, I quite see I must
make my own way in the world now."

"How?" Dudley demanded.

Jack rubbed his hand over his eyes. "I don't have the
slightest idea, but I think I must leave London, perhaps
quit England entirely. Yes, of course. There is no place
for me here now. I am but one of a host of poor bastards,
and to remain would only serve to remind me of that
fact. I shall have to go away and start again. And mayhap, in doing so, I will be able to forget."

"Well, you can't leave today, in any event," Dudley
said briskly. "This must be thought on, Jack, long and
hard."

Jack could see that Dudley meant to try to get him to
change his mind about emigrating, and a ghost of his old
smile touched his eyes. "You'll not talk me out of it, you
know," he warned. "I cannot remain in England any
longer."

"What of your mother, Jack?" Dudley asked, a little
diffidently. "This will go hard with her, for I know how
she loves you. And your little sisters, what of them?"

Jack stared at him intently. "What do you mean? What
have Grace and Constance to do with this?"

"Everything, I should think. True, they are but children now, but they will be grown soon enough. If you go
tearing off, do nothing to stop the rumors that will de-
velop, aren't you condemning them to scandal? The *ton*
have long memories. And they *are* your sisters. You must
have a care for them, even if you have none for yourself."

"I had not thought of that," Jack said slowly, moving
his mug in aimless circles, and frowning again.

"No, nor a great many other things, I'll be bound. But
let us put our heads together and see what we can con-
trive. If both you and the earl deny the charge, what
further can this vicious letter writer do? There is no proof
that you are not Sir John's son, after all, and he is dead
now. For even if you feel you have to renounce the title,
you must see that for the little girls' sake, and for your
mother's, you cannot do that, no matter how keeping it

pains you. Go away, if you must, Jack, but leave them something more than shame."

Jack was impressed by Dudley's reasoning, and he nodded. "I wish I had not seen Arbel," he said. "I accomplished nothing but pain for myself, and perhaps even worse for the others."

"I'll go out, by and by, and see how things lie," Dudley promised him. "Think you Lord Granbourne might come here in search of you?"

"It's possible. Alex will not let this rest. But I will not see him. I refuse!"

The two decided that Jack would remain sequestered in Dudley's rooms for now, and that no one would know of it. Dudley assured him his man was the soul of discretion, and not even a haughty, demanding earl would be able to break his composure. Furthermore, Dudley claimed to know the perfect carter to fetch Jack's trunks, a carter who had been born dumb. Even if the earl tried to bribe him, he would not be able to divulge Jack's whereabouts.

Jack nodded wearily, and Dudley insisted he go and try to rest. "I am sure you didn't sleep well last night," he said as he showed him the spare bedchamber. "Try not to brood about this, Jack. If there's any way to make all right and tight, we shall find it."

He left shortly thereafter, to call on various members of the *ton,* beginning with his cousin, the Lady Arbel. To his relief, the young lady never mentioned Jack or his early call at all, although Dudley thought she seemed very conscious, as if she were concealing some momentous secret. As he left her, he wondered why she had not blurted it out to him, silly female that she was. Was it possible that the earl or her father had managed to still her wagging tongue? If they had, Dudley could only applaud.

It was late the following day when the earl's card and request for a moment of his time were brought to Sir Dudley in his study. Jack was in his own room, making his plans, and Dudley steeled himself for a most unpleasant interview. He had always had great admiration for Earl Granbourne and for Jack's lovely mother, and remembering that did not make what he was about to do any easier.

The earl did not waste any time on pleasantries. "I,

have come to try to discover where Sir John Reade is,
m'lord," he began, even before he took the seat Dudley
indicated. "You are his good friend. If anyone knows his
whereabouts, I am sure it is you."

Dudley had meant to lie, but staring into that hard, set
face and seeing the misery that lay deep in those steady
hazel eyes, he found he could not. "Yes, I know where
Jack is, sir, but I cannot tell you," he said instead. "He
has my pledge."

The earl stared at him for a moment longer. Dudley
was very conscious of the ticking of the mantel clock and
the beat of his own heart.

"I see. I cannot force you to break your promise, of
course, much as I regret it. Jack is well?"

Dudley nodded over the lump in his throat. "As well
as can be expected. He has cut up hard over this, sir."

"I am aware. Did he tell anyone else besides you and
the Lady Arbel?"

"No, he did not, nor does he intend to."

"Thank God for that," Alexander muttered. "Lady
Arbel has been sworn to secrecy, and I know I need fear
nothing that would hurt Jack from you."

He reached into his pocket and withdrew two bulky
letters. "May I ask you to see that Jack has these to
hand, sir? It is important."

"Certainly," Dudley said, taking them and putting them
in his desk.

The earl rose and bowed. "I thank you. You are most
kind, and my son's good friend. I appreciate it."

"I shall always be a good friend of your *stepson,* m'lord,"
Dudley said.

The earl nodded, a muscle high in his lean cheek
twitching for a moment as he took his leave.

Dudley sat quietly for a moment, waiting for his fast-
beating heart to slow, before he went to give the letters
to Jack and leave him alone to read them.

When they met at dinner later, he studied his friend's
sober face. The despair and wildness that had been on it
two days ago had been replaced by a calm determination.
But Dudley thought he saw something more now, a lightening of his expression and a kind of resigned acceptance.

Jack did not speak of the letters until dinner was over
and the butler had left them to their port.

"I thank you for seeing the earl for me," he said then.
"And for accepting those letters. They have explained a
great deal I did not know before. But it is still hard for
me to understand how one man could be so evil!"

"What man, if you don't mind my asking?"

"The earl's father. You see, Alexander fell in love with
my mother many years ago. But Giles Maxwell, who was
then the earl, would not hear of his son marrying a mere
vicar's daughter. He sent Alex away on an errand to
London and forced my mother to leave the village and go
to Bath. Her family disowned her, told her she must
never return. Alex tried to find her, and when his father
saw how determined he was, he had an empty coffin
buried in some small village, and put her name on the
stone. Thinking she had died in a carriage accident, Alex
had to try to forget her."

"Damme, how terrible!" Dudley exclaimed.

"Mother writes me that she learned she was with child
after she reached Bath. She met Sir John there. She
knew him, for she had helped him through an illness that
summer. When he learned of her predicament, he offered for her. She says she told him everything."

Dudley seemed to hear the little doubt in his friend's
voice, and he said quickly, "But of course she did! I have
never known a finer woman than your mother. There is
no way she would try to conceal something like that!"

"That is what I tell myself, even though I find it hard
to believe that Sir John would agree to raising another
man's child as his own son and heir. Yet I remember,
too, how dearly Sir John loved me."

"You were the son he never thought to have. But it
was a generous gesture even so. He must have loved your
mother very much."

Jack nodded, his eyes suspiciously bright. "My mother
said she was desperate, for she did not know what she was
to do or how she was to raise me alone, and so she
accepted him. But she tells me she came to love Sir John
for himself, and could never have left him even after she
discovered why Alex had never come after her. What a
tragedy they have suffered!"

"And should suffer no more," Dudley said firmly.
"Forgive them, and go back to Granbourne House, Jack.

Do not be the instrument of more pain for them. They could not help what happened."

To his regret, Jack shook his handsome head. "I cannot. Oh, I forgive them. It was not their fault, what that evil man did to them. But I cannot go back to them, see them, remain in England. I can never be Sir John Reade again. On that I am adamant."

"You're proud and stubborn, is what you are," Dudley told him, exasperated. "So, you are still determined to emigrate, in spite of what you have learned?"

"Yes, and as soon as I can. I have been thinking of Bermuda. Do you remember Farley Williams, Dudley? He's out there now, you know, in the shipbuilding trade. I'll go to him, ask to captain one of his ships, or if not that, work in his yard for wages."

"Work for wages?" Dudley asked, as if he had never heard of such a thing. "You can't!"

Jack had to smile at the indignation in Dudley's voice. "Oh, yes, I can. There are worse things than that, my friend. Starving, for example. But I must ask you for a small loan for my passage. I'll return it with interest as soon as I can."

Dudley waved his hand before he poured them both another glass of port. "Glad to stake you, of course, but where's the need? Sir John wanted you to be his heir. He even agreed that you should bear his name. Use his money, man! He would have expected you to."

Jack frowned again, deep in thought now. At last, to Dudley's relief, he nodded. "Very well. But I have no intention of touching anything from the estate. I shall use only the money that he left to me directly. I remember the figure well. It will be more than enough to start me off in the New World."

"And what is to become of Hythe? The monies that will accumulate from it?"

Jack shrugged. "I care not," he said. "Let them accumulate as they will."

"Perhaps someday your son will return to Hythe and be glad of them," Dudley remarked.

"Never!" Jack said. The one word was spoken quietly, but with such intensity, Dudley shivered.

"I shall never marry, for I cannot give a wife and children a clean name. Do you know, I feel as if I have suddenly become invisible? I am neither the gentleman nor the baronet I supposed. That person has been . . . obliterated, and all that is left for me is a faint impersonation. But I will not be like a poor player posturing on a stage, pretending to be someone he is not, to act a part. I could never do that. I intend to see what simple Mr. Jack Reade, Englishman, can become."

Before Dudley could comment, Jack rose. "Beg you to excuse me, my friend. I must write to my mother and Alex, and to bid my man of business call on me tomorrow. I would put all in train without delay, for the sooner I am gone now, the better."

Dudley watched him leave the room, and he shook his head. Jack had always been proud, high-minded, but he had not realized how proud. What Jack had learned had changed his world completely. And knowing him as he did, he realized it was not Jack's way to pretend he was someone he was not, even though legally he was still the same Sir John Reade he had always been.

Still, Dudley wished there was something he could say or do that would change Jack's mind about the course he intended to take. But as he drank his port and reflected, he knew there was nothing he could do after all. For good or evil, Jack Reade was ready to sever all ties with home, and sail away to make his way alone in the New World.

Then Dudley grinned to himself and chuckled. He was sure that when the initial pain wore off, Jack would have a fine time doing so. Perhaps in some small, ashamed part of him, carefully hidden, that part that had always beckoned him to adventure, he was even looking forward to it.

Clorinda Reade never saw her cousin again after she sent him her poisonous letter. She wondered where he was, but only several days later did she learn that he had not only left London but also the country. And one morning as she strolled through Berkeley Square, she saw that the shutters were up on Granbourne House as well. Careful questioning of a maid scrubbing some nearby steps elicited the information that the earl and his family had gone to their estate, Willows, in southern Kent.

Clorinda pondered all this for a long time. Was it possible that the random deadly dart she had flung had spoken truth after all? Was it possible that Alexander Maxwell *was* Jack's real father? If this were so, then Jack should never have inherited the estate. Suddenly her heavy features brightened as she remembered that her father was next in line to inherit. How wonderful if it were true! They could move to Hythe, enjoy all the wealth and privilege that came with the title. And she could have her choice of any number of eager beaux, for as the daughter of a baronet, she would be sought after and admired.

The only thing that made her uneasy was that if she voiced her suspicions to her mother and father, she would have to admit what she had done. They knew of her earlier letter writing and its almost tragic consequences, and she hated to reveal she had stooped so low again. It was only a few more minutes, however, before she decided that with something so momentous, she really had no choice. And she did not think she would be punished, not for this priceless bit of news.

She spoke of the letter the very next morning, only waiting until her father had eaten his hearty breakfast and had his customary two cups of strong tea. His disapproving eyes as she confessed made her uncomfortable, but when she stole a glance at her mother, she could see that lady was sitting on the edge of her seat, a little smile of expectation playing over her thin lips. Encouraged, Clorinda did not falter in her tale.

"Of course I know that what I did was wrong, and I am truly sorry for it, but his indifference and rudeness to us made me so angry, I forgot myself," she ended, twisting her napkin and trying to look properly contrite. "However, I have to wonder if perhaps I hit on the truth somehow. For why else has Jack left the country, and the Maxwells deserted London in the middle of the Season? And no one seems to know why! I overheard two of his friends in the park yesterday afternoon. They were speculating on his sudden disappearance, the very day after he received my letter, mark you."

"My word," Martha Reade whispered. "Can it be? . . . Do you think . . . ? Robert . . . ?"

Her husband frowned, but there was a light gleaming in the back of his eyes now that told Clorinda she was in no danger of being chastised for her naughtiness.

"This must be investigated," he said slowly. "It does

seem very singular. And you both remember how I remarked Jack's resemblance to the earl some time ago? I believe it to be entirely possible. Camille only had that one son, after all. Perhaps Sir John was impotent."

"Yes, that could be. And John never did treat Camille as his wife," Martha Reade said. "Sometimes I thought he acted rather as if she were his daughter. Oh, he doted on her, silly old fool, but he paid her none of those little distinctions a man generally does that show how he honors his cherished wife and the mother of his child."

"Perhaps we can find out exactly where Camille was born and brought up," Robert continued, for he placed little credence in signs of passion, or the lack of them. Sir John had been a scholar, not a lover. And he himself could not remember the last time he had treated his wife, the mother of his seven children, to anything but a civil respect.

"But how are we to do that?" Clorinda demanded. "All we know is that her maiden name was Talbot. We know nothing of her family, her background."

Her father smiled suddenly. "But we do know that Alexander Maxwell was raised at Granbourne Hall in Kent. We have only to discover whether there was a family named Talbot in the vicinity twenty-four years ago, and if this family had a daughter named Camille. Such an unusual name, is it not? That, I think, will be more than enough proof that the title was bestowed falsely, especially since Jack looks so much like the earl who married his mother in such indecent haste after my cousin's death. Poor man! To think he was cuckolded so!"

"The very thing!" Mrs. Reade crowed, clapping her pudgy hands. As her husband rose, she said earnestly, "Do go at once and see what you can discover, my dear!"

But it was a further two weeks before the Reades had proof positive that Camille Talbot had been the eldest daughter of the vicar of the church in Saxford, a village that was huddled close to the very walls of Granbourne itself. Robert Reade had discovered other things as well—how Camille had left the village so suddenly, never to return, and how her family had removed shortly thereafter to what was rumored to be a grander life elsewhere.

He wondered if the late earl had bribed them to go after he had found out that Camille was with a child of his own son's begetting.

The Reades wasted no time trying to discover more. In great glee, they made plans to go to the country to confront the earl and his countess. And to be sure that it would all be done legally, and noted as well, they engaged a solicitor to accompany them as a witness. Even if they could not find out where Jack had gone, the solicitor could strip him of his title in the courts, *in absentia*.

Kemble announced Robert Reade to the earl one afternoon a few days later. Alexander frowned. The Reades had ceased to acknowledge Camille after her marriage to him, not that the loss of their company had been anything but a relief to both of them. He wondered what the man wanted now.

Kemble cleared his throat. "Mrs. Reade and a Miss Clorinda Reade accompany him, m'lord. And there is another . . . er, *person* as well."

Alexander stared at him, his brows still furrowed. The return of his old severity and abstraction since Master Jack had left the town house had bothered Kemble, as had the sadness that etched the countess's face. It seemed about to become a permanent feature. The only time she smiled now was when she was with her little daughters, and then it was a fleeting, bittersweet thing.

"Where is the countess?" the earl asked.

"She is resting in her room, m'lord."

"Wait," Alexander told him as he went to his desk and penned a few lines. "Admit my . . . er, guests now, and when you have done so, see the countess gets this note at once."

Kemble bowed and went to do his bidding.

Alexander stared at his unwanted visitors with hooded eyes as they entered the library. He saw the intent way Robert Reade was peering at him, the excitement in the pudgy daughter's face, and the avid way the equally pudgy Mrs. Reade was assessing everything of value that the library contained. The man with them—short, thin, and middle-aged—wore a watchful air as he clutched a worn leather case in both hands. Alexander drew a steadying breath. He would be willing to wager anything you liked that the man was a member of the legal profession.

There was something about that trade that branded its devotees. How glad he was now that he had told Camille to remain apart. He would never subject her to the unpleasant scene he was sure was coming.

"Good afternoon," he said, rising slowly from his desk and managing to look slightly incredulous. "And to what do I owe the . . . er, honor of this unusual call?"

Robert Reade looked around, waiting for the earl to indicate chairs for the ladies, offer them all some refreshment. But when no such offer was forthcoming, he frowned a little and bowed.

"I am afraid we are here on a most serious matter, m'lord," he said. "Where is Lady Granbourne? I command her attendance!"

"Command her attendance? In my house?" Alexander drawled. Before the gentleman could revise his words, he went on, "I am desolated to have to deny you her presence, sir. My wife has been ill. We left London for that reason. She is still not strong enough to receive afternoon callers, not . . . er, even from the bosom of the family, so to speak."

His hazel eyes swept over Martha Reade and her daughter, and although his gaze did not so much as brush their prominent busts, both ladies flushed.

"We are sorry to hear of it," Reade said. "But we have come because we are concerned about my cousin Jack. He left town so precipitately, and without even bidding us—any of his friends—farewell. Most singular, that! Do you know where he is at this moment, m'lord?"

Alexander stared, and then, as if wearying of the game, he asked everyone to be seated. "I have no idea of Jack's exact whereabouts," he said. "He should be in mid-Atlantic by now, I suppose."

As Martha Reade glared, he continued, "But you know my stepson yourself, sir. Jack decided that London was not amusing, and when he heard of a ship sailing almost at once for the colonies, he was quick to take passage. We had hoped he might remain in England longer, but . . ."

His shrug, and the way he spread his hands, spoke volumes.

Suddenly he turned to the stranger in the somber coat and old-fashioned periwig. "But you must forgive me, sir. I have yet to learn your name. Have you come to find out the whereabouts of my stepson too? And for what reason, I wonder? Debts? A disgruntled papa? It sounds most unlike Jack!"

Before the solicitor could speak, Robert Reade said in a loud, blustery voice, "This is Mr. Andrew Jones, m'lord, a respected solicitor in London. He is here at my behest to see justice done."

The earl's brows rose a fraction, and his lips curled in a sneer. Martha Reade cringed back in her chair, and even Clorinda looked frightened.

"I must admit confusion, sir," Alexander said. "What justice? And what have the likes of—oh, I do beg your pardon—what have *you* to reveal that demands justice of me?"

Robert Reade was growing steadily more angry, and he blurted out, "We have good reason to believe that Jack Reade, the current baronet, is not my late cousin's son after all. That he is a bastard son of yours, sir! Can you deny it?"

The earl stared at him in what appeared to be total astonishment. "Have you been troubled with hallucinations lately, Mr. Reade?" he asked softly. "I cannot imagine any other reason for such a preposterous accusation."

"Do you deny that you knew Camille Talbot some twenty-four years ago, m'lord?" Martha Reade spoke up in her strident tones. "Do you deny she lived in Saxford village, hard on the very gates of Granbourne itself? Do you deny begetting a child on her, deny that your father sent her away and bribed her family to leave the county as well?"

"Easily," the earl replied, leaning his elbows on his desk and making a steeple of his fingers. Even to the solicitor's intent gaze, he showed no sign of guilt or discomfort.

"Oh, I certainly do not deny knowing Camille when she was young. She was our vicar's daughter. But the rest of it is a fairy tale of your own imagining, instigated, I have no doubt, by your avarice. But now, I think it is time for you to admit defeat, acknowledge that the estate and the wealth that you crave so badly will never be yours. Jack Reade is Sir John's son and heir, and so he named him. And Sir John has been dead for ten years; you cannot question him."

"But Jack looks nothing like my cousin! Indeed, he might have been spit out of your own mouth, m'lord," Robert Reade shouted.

"Not everyone favors his parents, isn't that so, Mr. Jones?" the earl inquired, his voice gentle. As the solicitor nodded, he went on, "As for your other remarks, madam, sir, I find them insulting in the extreme. I would remind you, and I am sure Mr. Jones will be quick to agree with me, that there are severe penalties for slander. Especially for slandering a peer."

There was silence in the room then, and Alexander waited for a long moment before he went on, "If there is any more of it, even the veriest hint of gossip about it, I shall have to take steps. Steps, I can assure you, that will be financially painful to you, to say nothing of how your reputations will suffer."

His voice grew colder and harder then, and his lined face more severe as he leaned forward and said, "No one is allowed to slander my beloved wife and go unscathed for it. *No one.* Do you understand?"

"Then you deny the charge, m'lord?" Robert Reade asked, blustering still.

"Of course I do. It is ludicrous!" Alexander retorted. "Still, I wonder where you had this fantasy. Could it have anything to do with a certain anonymous letter my stepson received shortly before he left England? He showed me that letter, you know, and we shared a good laugh over it. Some spiteful, shabby person had accused him of just what you have represented today. My, my. Could it have been one of you who was so unscrupulous?"

He looked at each of the Reades in turn, and he was not surprised to see Miss Clorinda's florid face pale, nor the way she swallowed suddenly.

"Ah, so it was you, was it, Miss Reade?" he asked, strolling toward her. "You should be ashamed of yourself. And how very unfortunate it is that you will be named in the suit I may bring."

"You have no proof!" Clorinda exclaimed in her loud, raspy voice.

"No more than you do of the lies you have told," he replied in quick riposte.

He turned then to the solicitor. "I shall leave it in your capable hands, Mr. Jones, to disabuse your clients of any visions they might have had of suddenly coming into my stepson's title. Be sure to point out to them that since Sir John is dead, and my wife and I shall both deny these wicked charges absolutely, there is no recourse for them."

"Pretty words, but not conclusive, m'lord," Robert Reade said. "There is the matter of your hasty marriage to Camille only two months after Sir John died. Why were you in such haste?"

The earl stared at him, his hazel eyes cold. "But surely if what you have been saying is true, it was hardly hasty, indeed, fourteen long years after the fact. But I never saw Lady Reade after she left Saxford until she visited London that spring Sir John was away. It was there that we renewed our childhood acquaintance. As for the haste of our union, you have seen the countess for yourself. Can you doubt any man would want her as soon as possible? But our marriage has no bearing on your charges."

"We will find the Talbot family and ask them!" Reade shouted. "Then you'll sing a different tune, m'lord!"

"Where do you intend to look?" Alexander asked with another sneer. "My wife lost track of her family years ago. You see, they did not approve of her marriage to Sir John, and they cast her off. And Talbot is such a common name."

He moved to the bellpull before he continued, "No, there is nothing you can do, even if you are prepared to spend a fortune on the quest. I do assure you it would be in vain at the end. The Talbots could tell you nothing to the point, for there is nothing to tell."

The butler entered the room then, and he said, "Show these . . . er, people out, Kemble. And at once, if you please."

"Certainly, m'lord," the butler said, staring straight ahead as he held the door wide.

The Reades looked from one to the other, confused. As they hesitated, the solicitor rose from his chair.

"I give you good-day, m'lord. As you have stated, there is no proof, nor any likely to be found at this late date."

Although they were the first words he had uttered

throughout the interview, Alexander was sure he had never heard any he welcomed more, although he did wonder if Mr. Jones believed him, or was just accepting the inevitable. But it did not matter. Camille was safe, and so was Jack.

He stood where he was until the library doors closed behind his furious, unattractive visitors, and only then did he put his hands over his face for a moment in relief. Jack might not be Sir John's rightful heir, he thought as he poured himself a needed tot of brandy, but he could certainly see why the late baronet had preferred him over his greedy, unpleasant relations!

6

AS soon as the morning breeze came up, Kate Hathaway was on her way to the *Sea Sprite,* looking forward to this day on the water by herself. Her brothers Gregory and George were offshore themselves, and had been gone for some time now on a trading expedition to Charles Town. And although her mother still worried about her sailing alone, and had begged her to take Hiram with her, Kate had escaped her strictures today. Hiram was much too busy at the wharf, for one of the Hathaway sloops had returned from the Turks Islands yesterday, with a cargo of salt. Her father was overseeing the loading of fresh supplies, so the sloop could sail to Nova Scotia, where its precious cargo was in great demand for preserving fish.

As Kate rowed out to the little sloop she had inherited from her brothers when they had outgrown it, she smiled. Salt from the Turks and Caicos Islands, cedar from Bermuda forests, fish, whale oil, and the occasional hunk of ambergris were Bermuda's lifeline. For from the proceeds of these valuable commodities, the islanders were able to purchase food, clothing, and machinery. It was a never-ending circle of trade.

Nathan Tucker waved to her from the deck of his own,

larger sloop anchored nearby, and Kate remembered there
was also treasure. Nate was famous for finding that, in
long-forgotten Spanish galleons lost to the reefs that
guarded Bermuda's shores. His two Portuguese divers
had brought up many a gold doubloon.

Climbing aboard the *Sprite*, Kate thought of the other
kind of treasure—salvage from ships sinking offshore on
the reefs. Often, Bermudians saved many lives, as well as
valuable cargoes.

As she made the painter of the rowboat fast to the mooring line, Kate remembered that there were rumors that
some of the islanders did not hesitate to lure ships to their
doom with lanterns. Well, she knew nothing about that! But
it was true that very little went to the bottom that could be
brought ashore and divided among the salvage crew, sometimes even before the customs men were notified.

Kate stowed her packet of food in the shady cuddy,
and began to make sail. As she looked around St. George
Town harbor, she could see that not many sloops were
still at anchor. It was early October now, and there had
been the threat of a hurricane only last week. Fortunately, the storm had veered off to the east, but at this
time of year hurricanes were a fact of life here, as were
the deadly waterspouts. Whenever they came ashore,
they became miniature tornadoes, and caused more damage than the worst hurricane.

She glanced idly then at the little town hugging the
waterfront. Next to her own house, the Tuckers' stood
white amidst its flower gardens and the green lawn that
stretched to the water's edge. Mrs. Tucker was in the
garden, cutting a bouquet. Beyond were other homes of
the native white aeolian limestone, their dazzling whitewashed roofs waiting to catch any rain that fell, to fill
their large water tanks. A few of the older cedar houses
with their plaited palmetto roofs still survived as well. Up
the slight rise, Kate could see St. Peter's Church and
cross, imposing behind the long flight of stairs that led up
to it and its graveyard. The wharves near King's Square
and the State House, the four small shops, were busy this
morning, and all manner of people strolled the narrow
streets and lanes, carrying baskets and parcels, or rolling
hogsheads from ship to shore. Two little boys with fishing
poles were perched on the end of the Customs House

dock, patiently waiting for a bite. It was all just as she had remembered it in London. It was home.

As Kate climbed to the deck to hoist the sails, she cursed her confining skirts. She had already abandoned her leather shoes and her hose, and as soon as she was out of sight of the spyglass set in the window of her father's library, and all the inhabitants of St. George Town, she would discard the calico skirt she wore over her breeches as well. Sometimes she wondered if her mother was really so unsuspecting about those old nankeen breeches of Greg's, or whether she had decided to ignore them if Kate would preserve her decorum when she was on land.

The mainsail and jib slatted idly to and fro as Kate cast off the mooring. Soon, in her capable hands, the sails were hauled in and cleated down for the long reach to the mouth of the harbor.

Kate sat on the windward seat, the tiller under her left arm as she raised her head to check the set of the sails. It was a glorious day, and she prayed it would continue. Not that they did not need the rain when it came, but since today was the first time in almost two weeks she had been able to escape her duties as daughter of the house, surely the gods would smile on her and give her the sunshine she craved.

Once clear of the harbor, Kate tightened sail to tack. She had decided to sail down the southern side of the islands, perhaps even going to the little settlement of Tucker's Town. She had not been there since her return from England this summer. She would have to keep a sharp eye out for reefs, but with the sun so bright, she was not worried about them, not when the *Sea Sprite* responded so quickly to the helm and danced with such grace between the darker patches of water that showed the coral outcroppings clearly. It was not long before Kate, her calico skirt and her bonnet discarded, became a completely happy soul, her bare toes enjoying the warmth of the smooth cedar deck.

Well, as happy as she could be, she told herself stoutly, watching a pair of longtails fishing nearer the shore. They were such beautiful birds. As one after the other dived, she realized that somehow, home had not been as wonderful as she had thought it would be when she had been yearning for it in dreary, chilly London Town. Oh, the benevolent sun, the clear aqua water, and the land-scent laden with flowers were the same. It was just that things were different now. Or maybe it was because *she* was different, she admitted. This strong feeling of malaise she had been suffering was one of the reasons she had gone off by herself today, to try to sort it out.

She and her mother had been welcomed home with glee and affection, not only by her father and brothers but also by the slaves. Keza had given Kate one of her most encompassing hugs, and cooked a festive dinner to celebrate their return. She had even sacrificed two of her bantam hens, and made Kate's favorite, a spicy cassava pie. And her husband, Daniel, and Hiram and Tully, their sons—all the slaves—had beamed at her so, tears had come to her eyes.

But in the weeks that followed, as Kate returned to her former pursuits, she had been dissatisfied and unsettled. But why? she wondered now. How could she be so perverse, she who had longed so for home?

Was it because on the westward passage, her mother had managed to turn Mr. Farnsworth into such a paragon? All his many faults were forgotten, and his good qualities polished to a high shine. Even now, Olivia Hathaway never stopped bemoaning the loss of such a desirable husband, with his wealth and noble relations. Kate had borne it as best she could, and her brothers' lighthearted teasing as well, and tried not to give a sharp disclaimer whenever her mother began to sing Mr. Farnsworth's praises. Instead, she had turned the subject as soon as she could, persuading her mother to speak of the parties they had attended, the other people they had met, the shops and theaters and parks.

For, to her, distance had not enhanced Mr. Farnsworth's image. She was delighted she never had to see him again.

But it was more than the memory of that pompous little man. No, it was that life now seemed too tame here, too ordered, too quiet. Her friends had been as affectionate as ever, including her in all their doings, and she had gone sailing many times with her brothers, enjoyed picnics and tea parties, resumed a mild dalliance with her old beaux. But sometimes, even while sitting reverently in St. Peter's in the box pew the Hathaways had used for so many years, she would feel a twinge of doubt. Was it because she had seen the larger world? Come to realize how tiny Bermuda was, how constrained? Perhaps when she went to Charles Town later this fall to visit her eldest brother, Matthew, and his wife, Alicia, she would be more herself.

Kate altered course slightly to avoid a reef ahead off the port bow, and another to starboard directly beyond. Suddenly she was too busy sailing to think about her problem. Or, she scolded herself, to remember a certain handsome face with soaring black brows and eyes exactly the color of the water beneath the *Sprite*'s hull.

She had eaten her lunch by the time she sailed into the capacious reaches of Castle Harbor. Tucker's Town lay ahead of her in Stoke's Bay. Perhaps she should call on Sir John Reade's friends Mr. and Mrs. Williams? Mayhap they had even heard from him and could give her word? Of what, his marriage to Lady Arbel Stanton? she scoffed, her soft lips tightening. What a fool she was!

The shores around the quieter water were empty except for the birds that had nested there, the plentiful cahow, the petrels, terns, and boobies. Kate steered the *Sprite* along, laughing as a school of little fish jumped ahead of the sloop, turning the aquamarine of the water into a flurry of diamond drops.

As she neared the village at Stoke's Harbor, and the few buildings there, she could see that the Williams shipyard was thriving, and alive with busy men. A sloop of some sixty feet in length was taking shape in one of the larger cradles, and next to the careening wharf, another was getting her bottom scrubbed clean of barnacles and grass. There were men carrying tar buckets and wielding caulking hammers, others intent on their planes and saws.

Kate looked beyond the yard then, and when she saw Maryanne Williams standing before her house, her eyes shaded against the sun, she waved. It was then she remembered her skirts, and hurried to scramble into them. Maryanne was a very proper young lady, and it would not do to sail in, barefoot and in breeches, not under the eyes of so many men.

She was fastening the ties of the skirt around her waist when the *Sea Sprite* came to a sudden shuddering halt. It threw Kate to her hands and knees in the well of the boat, and she scrambled up, cursing her carelessness. But

surely that little snag reef had not been there on her last
trip to Tucker's Town, she thought as she used the long
sounding pole she always carried, to push off. She prayed
the *Sprite* had not been holed as she settled down to steer
clear. She could hear no ominous gurgle of water under
the floorboards beneath her feet, but that did not reassure her. And then, as the little sloop showed her stern,
the reef exacted a final payment. The rudder scraped hard
and caught. Kate thought she would never work it free,
and when the reef let the *Sprite* go at last, she could tell by
the play in the helm that the rudder had been damaged.
Dammit! she muttered, heading directly for shore now.

As a man in a wide-brimmed palmetto hat waded out
to catch the bow for her, she could see Maryanne was
coming down to watch. She had a baby in her arms, and
another one toddling around her skirts.

And then Kate forgot her as her breath stopped in her
throat. She stared speechlessly at the man who had reached
the *Sprite* and was running an expert hand down her bow.

"Lower your sails," he said, not even looking up at
her. But what was Sir John Reade doing here? she wondered as she made herself obey his command, her fingers
clumsy in her shock.

"I can't tell for sure she's not sprung a leak," he
muttered, still bent over inspecting the hull.

"Why . . . why, it's you, Sir John!" Kate exclaimed as
the mainsail tumbled down around her feet. "What a
surprise!"

His dark head came up quickly then, and the expression on the handsome face she had been remembering
today startled her. Under the brim of his island hat, it
was stern and unsmiling, and his unusual eyes were mere
slits in his tan face.

"But what is wrong? What is the matter?" she whispered, the sails forgotten in her distress.

She could see how he tried to brighten his expression
then, the small smile he forced himself to assume, and
she wanted to touch him, comfort him, for whatever had
changed him so.

"Mistress Kate Hathaway," he said, bowing slightly.
" 'Tis plain Jack Reade now. Only *Mr.* Jack Reade."

Kate did not understand, but she made herself nod.

"You have an anchor?" he asked.

Kate hurried to fetch it from the cuddy and hand it to him. Then, as he cleated it down and set it, she turned her attention to the sails.

"It's not the hull I worry about so much," she told him when she saw his hands go there in inspection again. She was not averse to changing the subject in any case; to speak of innocuous things. "I fear I have damaged the rudder. But I do not remember that reef. Surely it was not a danger when last I was here."

"Coral grows steadily, as you should know," he said, wading toward the stern. Kate stared at his hands, so big and capable as they grasped the rudder and lifted it from its pins. "Aye, you've split it finely," he said. "I think Farley has another, though. I'll see to it. And I'll have those floorboards up as well. You've a long sail home."

"Thank you," Kate said, because suddenly she could think of nothing else to say. She yearned to ask him what he was doing here, and why she had not heard of his arrival, to ask how long he was going to stay . . . Lady Arbel's whereabouts . . . a hundred things.

Yet still she stood and stared at him, as dumb as any cedar tree or hunk of coral. A genuine smile creased his face as he looked up at her. "And how did you intend to get ashore, mistress?" he asked.

"Why, like this," Kate told him, coming to perch on the gunwale and swing her legs over the side. She held her skirts up as she lowered herself into the warm shallow water. As she peeked up at him, she saw that he had looked away, as if to spare her any distress in her immodesty, and a white grin escaped her.

She had forgotten he was used to the belles of London, who, although they might reveal far too much of their shoulders and bosoms, were careful to guard their lower limbs from view. Kate had often wondered at such misplaced priorities.

She waded to shore, his hand beneath her elbow to steady her. Every inch of her body was focused on that one commonplace spot, and how wonderful his fingers felt there.

"Mistress Hathaway, how delightful to see you after such a long time," Maryanne Williams welcomed her. Kate forced herself to smile in return.

"Prithee, tell me, is your sloop all right?"

"Except for a damaged rudder, ma'am," Kate said, curtsying to the plump little blond with her wide brown eyes. "I beg you will forgive my coming like this, all unexpected, but it was such a lovely day to sail, I quite forgot the distance."

"Beg you to excuse me, ladies," Jack interrupted. "I'll see to that rudder at once."

With an effort, Kate forced herself not to turn and watch him as he strode away.

"Oh, no, I am so glad you came," Maryanne Williams said, taking Kate's hand to lead her to the cool veranda that fronted the house. "I so seldom have company except for the slaves, for we are isolated here. And I have been longing to hear all your tales of home!"

As Kate looked around, a little confused, Maryanne said quickly, "I meant the tales of your journey, of course. I always think of England as home, you see. Ah, there you are, Sukey! Take the baby and Master Farley inside, please. And have Polly bring us a cool drink."

Kate was glad the children were leaving. She had no expertise with them, and she had a number of questions to ask her hostess, better uninterrupted by childish prattle. As the slave girl nodded and disappeared with the children, her bare feet slapping on the cedar floor of the veranda, Maryanne Williams indicated two rustic chairs set near a small table.

"Please be seated, Mistress Hathaway," she said.

"Do call me Kate, if you would be so good," Kate begged. She did not know Maryanne Williams very well, but now that she had learned Sir John was staying here, she intended to become a much better friend of hers. At the young wife's shy nod, Kate went on, "Yes, I spent some months in England and in London this past year. It was very . . . festive."

Maryanne's eyes glowed and she leaned forward to say eagerly, "Tell me all . . . oh, all of it! Is it still so grand, London? What is playing at the theaters? Were there a great many parties and balls? And did you see the king, Queen Charlotte? Our handsome boy prince? I miss home so much!"

Kate made herself talk of London then, much as her mother was wont to do. Whenever she faltered in her tale, her hostess had another question to ask, and they passed the time thus engaged. Kate was growing weary of the discussion when she saw Sir John coming along the shore, another man by his side. He carried a new rudder, and the two only waved before they waded out to the *Sprite* to fit it.

"Tell me, ma'am, what is Sir John doing here?" Kate asked, finally having a reason to ask the one question she had wanted answered so badly. "I was so surprised to see him, for when we last met, it was in London."

To her astonishment, Maryanne Williams did not reply at once. Instead, she frowned as she set her empty lemonade glass down beside her. "He does not call himself Sir John anymore, indeed, he gets angry if one forgets," she said at last. "He wants to be known only as Jack Reade here."

"But why?" Kate asked, confused.

"I have no idea," the other girl confessed. "He arrived in August, and he told us he had to make a fresh start here. Farley, Mr. Williams, that is, was delighted to welcome him, for overseeing the yard is time-consuming, we have so many orders for boats. And then too, I believe Jack intends to begin trading. That sloop in the cradle is his. No doubt he'll be gone to sea as soon as she is finished."

With an expert eye, Kate inspected the naked keel and futtocks, delighted that so much time must pass before this boat could slide into the harbor, be masted and rigged.

Both girls turned then to watch the two men busy at the *Sprite*'s stern. "I do not know Jack very well," Maryanne confessed. "He is a strange man, so quiet and cool. And he refused to stay with us here in Tucker's Town. Instead, he built a house further out on the point. I cannot imagine why. He has to carry all his water out there, and it cannot be very convivial with only a pair of slaves to talk to. But Farley says he has changed into a man who shuns society. Mayhap you know why, Kate?"

Kate shook her head, her eyes never leaving that broad-shouldered, narrow-waisted figure. He wore no wig, and his black hair under the palmetto hat was tied back by a plain leather thong. His white shirt was wrinkled and none too clean, and the sleeves were rolled up above his elbows. He was barefoot, without hose, and as he climbed aboard to inspect the hull for leaks, she could see that the plain canvas breeches of a sailor fit his slim hips and thighs closely. And yet, even dressed as any common seaman, he was still the handsomest man she had ever seen, one who would draw every eye, no matter what he wore. And he was here, in Bermuda!

She saw the questioning way Maryanne was regarding her for her strange silence, and she hurried to say, "It does seem very strange. He was much feted in London— why, he was the life of every circle. And he was so gay, so sure of his place there, that I envied him."

She paused then, wondering if she should mention his attraction for the Lady Arbel, before she decided better not. Perhaps she would have a chance to ask Sir John—no, Jack!—what had happened to bring him to these tiny island specks far at sea, and so very far from his home.

The two men were wading ashore now, and she was quick to rise. "This has been so pleasant, Maryanne. I am glad I came, in spite of the mishap to the *Sea Sprite.* But I must not linger, for I have a long sail back, even going by way of the reach between St. David's and St. George's islands. Do you ever come to St. George Town? Perhaps you could come and call on me? My mother would be so happy to talk to you of London."

Her hostess was quick to accept the invitation, proffering a return one of her own, that Kate must not think herself a stranger at Tucker's Town. Kate was happy to assure her she would not.

She was introduced to Maryanne's husband then. Farley Williams was a stocky young man with an engaging grin, bright red hair, and a fierce sunburn. As she said good-bye, she prayed Jack would walk her to the shore, and she was delighted when he did so. Of course, it was merely to tell her what course she would be best to steer leaving the harbor, but at least she had him to herself for a moment or two.

"Maryanne tells me you have built a house on the point, sir. Dare I hope that means you intend to remain here?"

Glancing sideways, she saw his grim little smile at her eagerness, and she hastened to add, "You have yet to tell me about your adventures in China and the South Seas, you know. I intend to hold you to that promise!"

"I shall be at sea most of the time," Jack said, his eyes

cold again. "But, yes, I intend to make Bermuda my home now. It is as lovely a place as you claimed, mistress. And the weather is a delight."

"It seems strange you would choose to do so, even so," Kate mused, carefully not looking at him now. "It is such a long way from your estate, after all, and—"

"I have no desire to live in England any longer," he interrupted her, his voice harsh. Then, as if he feared he had revealed too much, he changed the subject. "You can reach the sloop yourself? I must get back to my work in the yard."

"Of course," Kate said, holding out her hand. Reluctantly he took it as she continued, "But I must pay you for my new rudder. Unfortunately, I do not sail with my purse. Please call on me in St. George Town so I might reimburse you."

He nodded, bowed, and left her. Aware of the wide brown eyes watching her from the shaded veranda, Kate waded out to her sloop without another glance in his direction. But she remembered to wave to her new friend Maryanne after she raised the sails and anchor and started for home.

And as Tucker's Town grew smaller and smaller behind the stern, she did not even wonder that her mood now was so very different from the one she had had this morning when she set out. He was here, he was really here! And on islands so small, with so few people inhabiting them, surely she would see him soon again.

But it was early November before Kate even laid eyes on anyone from Tucker's Town. She had waited almost breathlessly those first days for Jack to come to town and call on her, but he did not appear. Careful questioning of her brothers when they returned from Charles Town revealed that although they had met the new immigrant in August, they seldom saw him, for he rarely left the shipyard where he worked. Kate was tempted to rage at this entire impossible situation. She knew she could hardly begin to visit Tucker's Town on a regular basis without calling down on her head all kinds of censure for immodest behavior.

But there was still that matter of payment for the new rudder. Just when she had convinced herself, however, that it was only right she go and discharge the debt, the

Williamses came to town and called on the Hathaways. Kate's heart sank when Farley Williams left his wife to visit while he went to seek Roger Hathaway at the State House and present the bill.

Maryanne and Olivia Hathaway were instantly compatible, as Kate had known they would be. For well over an hour, she busied herself with some sewing while the two chatted of the one subject they both found so fascinating—London and England. Since she was not required to make any more than an occasional comment, Kate was free to ponder yet again how she was to solve the problem of seeing Jack Reade.

And she knew she had to see him. The men here who had pursued her, Aaron Evans and William Younge, could not compare to him in any way. Jack Reade attracted her without even trying. And she could not seem to get him out of her mind. Several times a day she would remember how he looked, that smooth black hair gleaming in the sunlight, the way his eyes could change from pure turquoise to stormy green with his moods, his narrow hips and broad shoulders. And she would picture that tanned, capable hand; even wonder how it would feel touching her. She would have to think of something else then—anything!—for she knew it was dangerous to linger on such a delicious mental image. Besides, it made her tingle in a way she had never experienced before. She knew such thoughts were wrong, sinful, but she kept thinking them anyway. She couldn't stop.

Kate wondered if this was what being in love was like. If it were, she was only too ready to surrender to it, lose herself in its power. But how could she when she never saw him? And how could she make him love her in return?

Putting aside plans for a picnic or a dancing party, since she knew very well he would not accept her invitation to either, she began to plot. Perhaps she would see him someday when she was out sailing? Perhaps he liked to stroll along the broad southern beaches of Bermuda Island in his spare time? Or maybe he went fishing occasionally? He could not work in the yard all the time, she told herself.

"Kate, are you woolgathering?" Olivia Hathaway asked sharply, interrupting her musing. "Here I have asked you twice to have Keza prepare a tea tray for us, and you are lost in a dream!"

As Kate put her sewing aside, she apologized. And as she left them, she was not at all reluctant, for from the London Season they had progressed to child care and the best way to deal with Master Farley's teething problems.

Kate could tell her mother was enjoying herself very much, playing surrogate parent to the young wife and imparting all her hard-won wisdom. Kate smiled as she crossed the yard to the kitchen house. By next summer her mother would have her own grandchild to coddle. Alicia Hathaway's discomfort during the early months of her first pregnancy had given Kate all the excuse she needed to avoid making her planned visit to Charles Town lest she miss seeing the man she longed for so.

After that day, Kate did see Jack Reade a few times, although always at a distance. Once, while sailing with her brothers, she had spotted him in a small dory. He was accompanied by an elderly slave, and engaged in rowing among the reefs. She had asked her brothers what he was doing, hoping they would alter course so she could speak to him, and George had said carelessly, "Clever man! I see he's got old Samuel with him, and no one knows the local waters better. No doubt he's charting the reefs of the approach to Castle Harbor. I hear his sloop is coming along at a fine rate. It won't be long now before she's ready for her maiden voyage."

Although it was a lovely day, and Kate had been looking forward to fishing, she felt very low for the remainder of the afternoon, and hard put to hide it from her brothers.

Another time, two weeks later, while walking with friends at St. Catherine's Point, she had seen Jack diving offshore near a reef. Once again he had the old black sailor with him, waiting patiently in a dory nearby. Kate wondered at it. Very few people swam in November.

But although she waited and watched, Jack never came to town, nor did he seek any female company that she knew of.

With three older brothers, Kate was very well aware what men were like, and she had to wonder if Jack had found a woman here to warm his bed. It was impossible that he had been celibate all this time. And perhaps he had come to love the woman, considered marrying her? But that could not be. Men might employ whores for their purposes, but they did not wed them, no, not even a plain Mr. Jack Reade would stoop that low. And since Kate knew there were no unmarried young ladies of good family living in or near Tucker's Town, and Jack never came to St. George Town, she was not worried about a rival. Still, when he did put to sea in his beautiful new sloop, now nearing completion, he would be sailing to many different places, with all kinds of unattached girls onshore to entice him. Kate knew she had to do something, and soon!

She also had to wonder sometimes how he had lost all his money. Was it from bad investments or gambling debts? Because surely the reason Jack had left England and come here at all was because he was poor now, and had to work for his bread. And maybe that was why he was avoiding her, because he did not feel worthy even of Viscount Pelton's niece anymore? How she longed to disabuse him of that notion!

As for the mystery of the abandoned Lady Arbel, Kate did not waste any time pondering it. It was enough that that particular miracle had occurred, and she was still in England. For no matter how lovely and accomplished the lady was, no matter how much Jack had thought he cared for her, she was now far, far away.

And Kate Hathaway was right here.

7

THE following Sunday afternoon, Kate announced her decision to call on Maryanne Williams. She told her mother it was because she had never returned the girl's call, and Olivia Hathaway nodded and agreed. She even made Kate feel worse by congratulating her on her thoughtfulness, when, in reality, Kate had planned the trip because she was so desperate to see Jack.

It was a hot day for November, and curiously still, so

she could not sail to Tucker's Town. Instead, wearing the habit she had bought for use in London, she took her father's horse and rode to the ferry between St. George and Bermuda islands.

When she reached the little village at last, and inquired at the house, she discovered that Mr. and Mrs. Williams had taken the children to visit friends at Crow Harbor that morning. The slave girl, Sukey, did not know when they would return.

Disheartened, as well as hot and uncomfortable in the heavy habit, Kate went back to her mount. She was not sorry to miss Maryanne, but she had hoped to see Jack working on his sloop, now planked and decked. But the shipyard lay quiet and deserted under the hot sun.

So Mr. Reade observed the Sabbath, did he? Was he at home, then, out on the point? Feeling daring, as well as desperate, Kate rode out that way, searching for him. She spotted him a few minutes later, walking along the shore on the ocean side, and her heart beat rapidly as she cantered to intercept him.

"Sir John . . . er, Mr. Reade!" she called while still some distance away. She hoped she was only imagining the little frown he wore as he turned toward her.

Kate had not imagined that frown. Jack was impatient at seeing the girl again. He had sensed that she was interested in him, and he had no intention of allowing their slight acquaintance to deepen even into friendship, never mind love. He must avoid the young ladies of Bermuda at all costs. And if he gained the reputation of being a confirmed bachelor, well, that was all he was ever going to be anyway, wasn't it?

And yet now, in spite of all his good intentions, here she was with him on this deserted beach. He would have to find a way to get rid of her without hurting her feelings, he thought. For he liked Kate Hathaway, he always had. She was as appealing and saucy as a shiny new penny, and quick-witted and amusing as well. And her fine-featured face, her generous soft lips and steady gray eyes, even those golden freckles dusting the bridge of her nose, were endearing. He had found himself sometimes remembering how shapely her legs had been in the one flash he had seen of them the day she waded ashore from her sloop. But such thoughts would not do.

Contrary to Kate's surmises, Jack had been celibate since he left England. At first it was because he was still so heartsore over his loss of Lady Arbel that he could not contemplate even a casual bedding. Since his arrival here, and his isolation at Tucker's Town, he had met no one. He was smart enough to realize that any pretty young girl would appeal to him in his present state. Kate Hathaway deserved better than that. Indeed, if he so much as kissed her, her father would have every right to insist he marry her.

"Give you good-day, sir," Kate was saying now with her bright smile as she slid from her mount to stand beside him.

Jack thought he had never seen anyone who smiled so completely, not just with her lips and eyes, but with every inch of her being. He could not help smiling back at her, forgetting his good resolutions.

"A good day to you, too, mistress. But I am surprised to see you here so far from home, riding in such heat. Surely it would have been better to have stayed indoors, where it is cool?"

Conscious of her shiny face and the limp curls under her straw hat, the way her clothes were sticking to her, Kate sighed. "Yes, it is a real Sarah Bassett day, isn't it?"

"A Sarah Bassett day? Whatever do you mean?" Jack asked in spite of himself.

Kate laughed and wrinkled her nose at him. "That's an old Bermudian term for a weather breeder. It seems some years ago there was a slave by that name. She was tried and found guilty of attempting to poison her master and being one of the ringleaders in a planned slave revolt. On the day she was to be executed, while she was being brought to the gallows, she saw a number of people rushing along so they wouldn't miss her hanging. Legend has it that she laughed at them and said, 'Don't hurry! The fun doesn't start till I get there!' It was a very hot, still day, just like this one, and so now we always call days like this by her name."

As Jack put back his head and laughed in much his old way, Kate's heart lightened. She had amused him, made him forget whatever it was that was troubling him.

"May I walk the beach with you?" she asked somewhat shyly. "Perhaps I can tell you other things about Bermuda. We have a number of funny old tales."

Jack hesitated before he nodded almost reluctantly, she thought as she set off by his side, the horse trailing along behind them.

"Have you been in any of our caves yet?" she asked, determined to keep the conversation going. "Some of them are very large, and very beautiful. I am not fond of them, however, for I dislike being underground. But my brother Gregory could show them to you. He has inspected any number over the years."

Before he could reply, Kate's eye was caught by something far ahead of them, washing to and fro in the waves. "Oh, look!" she cried, grasping his arm tightly. "Hurry!"

To Jack's astonishment, she dropped the reins she held, picked up her skirts, and ran away from him down the beach as fast as she could. Jack thought her much like a wave herself, all fluid, graceful motion. When he reached her, she had removed her shoes and hose and was already wading into the surf.

"Whatever do you think you're doing?" he asked.

Kate's gray eyes were shining as she pointed to a large shapeless gray mass floating several feet from shore. "Do you know what that is?" she whispered, as if afraid someone might overhear. Since there was no one about for miles, Jack could only doubt her sanity.

"It's ambergris!" she said, still whispering. "Oh, and such a huge piece of it, too! What luck!"

His face cleared then, for what sailor had not heard of ambergris, that waxy substance produced by sick whales? He knew that in London an ounce of it was worth a great deal of money for its value in making perfume.

Kate was advancing into the surf now, her habit held up to her knees. Jack quickly removed his own shoes and stockings to follow her. "Let me get it, Mistress Kate," he said. " 'Tis not seemly for you, and you may fall and get thoroughly wet."

Kate was about to refuse such a tame role with scorn, when a scheme formed in her mind. "Of course," she said. "I'll just wait here until you can move it closer to shore."

She watched him wade in to his waist. A moment later, he had reached the ugly gray mass lying so sluggishly in the waves, and was pushing it ahead of him back to shore. Kate's eyes widened even more at the size of it. But there must be at least fifty or sixty pounds, she thought.

Between the two of them, they hauled the ambergris above the tide mark. Kate sniffed its sweet, musky odor appreciatively. While Jack began to calculate how much it weighed, she went to search up and down the sands nearby, and it was only a few minutes before she had discovered two much smaller pieces and brought them to add to their loot.

"Oh, what a wonderful discovery!" she cried, picking up his hands in her delight and doing an impromtu jig on the sands. As she stumbled a little, Jack's arms went around her to steady her. He let her go as soon as she had her balance, but she was so excited, she did not notice the quickness of his retreat. Instead, she flew into his arms again, to give him a hearty hug. "Isn't it grand, Jack?" she asked, her gray eyes blazing. "Now you will have a fortune, be rich again!"

He put her away from him, but held her tightly by the shoulders as he demanded, "What do you mean, be rich again?"

Kate did not notice the sudden coolness of his voice, his watchful expression. "Why, the fortune you lost before you left London, sir!" she exclaimed. "But when you sell this ambergris, you will be a wealthy man once more. And you will not have to sail the seas trading, nor work in a shipyard like a common laborer."

His face was grim now, and Kate gasped. "I work in the yard because I choose to do so, Mistress Kate," he said, sounding as if he were biting off his words between his teeth. "I am not destitute. Indeed, I cannot imagine where you ever got such an idea."

"Oh, I do beg your pardon . . ." Kate faltered, her face turning rosy in her embarrassment. "It was just that . . . well, I could not understand why . . . I mean . . ."

"Besides, you saw the treasure first," Jack went on, more kindly now that he saw her distress. "It was your discovery, not mine."

"But I could never have brought it to shore, it is too heavy. And I insist you take it, truly I do."

He saw her mouth was set stubbornly now, and he

sighed. Kate Hathaway was a revelation; he had never met another woman like her. Then he reminded himself she was not a woman. She was only a girl—a girl who was more tomboy than young lady. Even her hug had been nothing more than an innocent expression of joy. And she sailed and rode, wore breeches, waded into the surf—why, she probably even knew how to swim! And he did not need to ask her if she baited her own hook when she fished, for he was sure she did. Probably cleaned the fish as well when she caught them.

He began to tow the ambergris back to the water then, and Kate grabbed his arm. "Stop! What are you doing?" she asked.

"I'm putting it back where we found it," he said. "Since I won't accept your find, and you don't appear to want it, what else is there to do?"

To his amusement, Kate stamped her foot at him. "You are the most impossible man!" she exclaimed. "Are you always so difficult to help?"

Jack straightened up then, wiping his hands on his tight damp breeches. Kate was resolute in keeping her eyes on his face.

"I'm sorry you find me difficult, mistress," he said in a meek tone that did not fool his listener in the slightest.

She stood there glaring at him, hands on hips, until he chuckled a little and threw up his hands in defeat. "Very well," he said, "I'll tell you what we'll do. I'll take the ambergris to St. George Town and ship it to London. When the money for it arrives, we will split it. Does that meet with your satisfaction, ma'am?"

Kate sighed. "I suppose so," she said slowly, telling herself that half a loaf for him was better than none. "How are we to get it off the beach, do you suppose? We can't leave it here unattended. Someone else might come along."

Jack looked around to where Roger Hathaway's old horse was waiting patiently, switching his tail against the flies. When he told her of his plan, Kate clapped her hands. And while he was gone, fetching the cart from his house, she quickly removed her petticoats and habit, to enjoy the coolness of the water clad only in her shift.

Jack saw her from a distance when he came back with the cart, and he stayed where he was until she had finished and donned her clothes again. Unfortunately for his peace of mind, his eyesight was excellent, and he had to turn aside when he saw how shapely she was, how gracefully formed. It appeared that he must be a friend of Kate Hathaway's now, no matter how he had tried to avoid it, for they were partners in a business venture. But that was all he would be, he promised himself as he started toward her at last, dragging the cart through the loose sand.

When they reached the little house Jack had had built for him facing the ocean, he would have said good-bye, for he knew it was not at all the thing for a young unmarried girl to enter a bachelor's house. But although Kate understood the predicament as well as he did, she had no intention of leaving him, not yet. It was not late, and she meant to stay with him as long as she could.

As he put the cart carrying its valuable burden away in an outbuilding and covered it up with an old tarp, she asked him to show her his sloop.

"I noticed her when I rode in to Tucker's Town, sir," she said. "She has such lovely lines."

Jack was proud of his boat, proud of some of the innovations he had built into her, and he agreed at once. Besides, he told himself as they set off together on foot, trailing the patient horse, it solved the problem of having to avoid asking her into his house.

Tucker's Town was still drowsing in the late-afternoon sunlight when they reached it. Not even chickens stirred in the heat. Jack wondered where everyone had gone. Or were a great many pairs of eyes peering at them even now; people nodding and making their own assumptions about why they were together and what they had been doing?

But he forgot the possibility of gossip when he saw Kate's delight in the sloop. She picked up her skirts to skip up the ladder ahead of him, as agile as any boy.

As she gained the deck, her hands caressed the cedar railing, carefully sanded now to a satin smoothness. "She'll carry a lot of sail," she remarked, assessing the length of the deck. "She's to be Bermuda-rigged "

"Yes, she'll be faster that way. And speed can be important," Jack told her.

"When will the mast be stepped?" Kate asked as she

strolled toward the stern, her knowledgeable eyes missing nothing. She peeked below into what would be the stern cabin, the captain's quarters, and then her fingers grasped the large wheel.

"After she's afloat in two weeks or so. There's a certain amount of finishing to be done, both on deck and below."

Kate looked forward in inspection. "I see she's to carry cannon," she said, pointing to the gun ports already cut, and the prepared mounts. "Do you expect trouble, sir?"

"I may have need of a letter of marque one of these days," he said, his voice grim. "The world is rumbling again—France and Spain, even Holland, to say nothing of the colonies. And if there is to be a war, there'll be a need for fast privateers. I intend to be ready."

Kate nodded, a tiny frown creasing her brow. Jack wondered what she was thinking about. But she did not tell him. Instead, her gray eyes took on a dreamy cast, and she tilted her head to one side as she said, "There is something about a boat like this, isn't there? She is so new, so untried! And yet it is as if she is just waiting—waiting anxiously to slide into her natural element and show off her paces." She flushed a little then, and tried to laugh. "No doubt you think me fanciful, sir?"

"Not at all," he reassured her with a little smile. "Sometimes, after the workmen have left her for the day, I stay aboard and have that same feeling. I confess I even talk to her sometimes—oh, in a whisper, of course, lest others hear and think me daft. She has come alive to me."

He noticed her warm smile, her eager nod, and he looked away.

"What will you call her?" Kate asked in the little silence that fell between them.

"She is to be the *Camille*. That is my mother's name. Pray she has smoother sailing than that lady has had."

"What a beautiful tribute!" Kate exclaimed. "You must love your mother very much."

She saw the familiar shadow pass over his face, and she wondered at it. Before he could be lost to her in brooding again, she pointed to the bow. "Now, why does that look so different to me?" she asked, perplexed.

Jack took her arm and led her to the rail. "To see why, we must disembark, ma'am. Shall you go first?"

Kate nodded, after one last look around. She wanted to memorize everything, so she could picture him here after he left on his voyaging.

When they stood beneath the bow, towering above them in the cradle, Kate's eyes widened. "Why, I have never seen one like that before," she told him.

Jack knelt then and picked up a stick nearby. After smoothing the sand, he drew the top of a half-circle. Next to it he drew the sharper two sides of a triangle, very like the shape of the *Camille*'s bow. "Doesn't it stand to reason, mistress, that a bow like this one will cut through the water faster than the old stubby design? Allow a ship to tack closer to the wind?" he asked.

Kate put her hands on his shoulders as she bent down to inspect the simple drawings. "Why, yes, I would think so, but it is most unusual. What did the old sailors say when they saw it?"

Jack was chuckling as he rose to dust off his hands. "Some of them predicted disaster and an early watery grave for all hands. But Samuel Simpson agreed with me. And soon we shall see who is in the right of it, now, won't we?"

"It is a risk," Kate said. "But very like you to try it, I think. And after all, someone has to be first."

Jack stared down at her, wondering why he felt so attuned to this slip of a girl. She was as comfortable to be with as any of his male friends had ever been. Then he heard voices coming from the village, and he frowned.

"Best you be on your way, mistress," he said. "It grows late, and you should not have spent all this time alone with me."

Kate shrugged, and was about to protest when she saw the position of the sun. "It is getting late," she agreed. "Thank you for showing me your lovely lady. I wish you good fortune sailing her. Perhaps you could let me know when she is to be launched?"

She saw his obvious hesitation, and she added quickly, "Since I missed Maryanne today, I could plan to see her at the same time. And perhaps my twin brothers will come. A launching is always a festive occasion. Besides, I will want to hear if our ambergris has been sent safely on its way."

Jack nodded, defeated. As he walked with her to her

mount, Kate remembered something. "On no account must you tell anyone of our discovery, sir," she warned. "There are many poor people on the islands, people who would not hesitate to kill to wrest such wealth from you. Be sure I shall be silent as well."

He agreed as he tossed her to the saddle, his hands impersonal. But even so, Kate had to swallow hard at the touch of them on her waist.

"Good-bye, Mistress Kate," he said. "And my thanks for the good luck you have brought me."

"Let us pray it continues on water as well as land," she said with a last brilliant smile.

Kate was not surprised that she did not hear from anyone at Tucker's Town until two days before the sloop was to be launched. She had not expected to, not that that kept her from thinking of Jack almost continually.

He was so different now from the handsome, assured young man in London whom she had admired. What had caused such a change? Why were his smiles so few and so fleeting now, his demeanor so solemn, his laughter so infrequent? And why had he left his homeland, his estate, and the girl it had been obvious he loved, to come here and work in a shipyard?

He had said he was not poor, but if that were true, what reason did he have for doing it? Because the whole thing was incomprehensible. No wealthy peer would turn his back on everything he cherished without a very good reason.

Kate was determined to find out that reason—one day. And when she understood it, she would understand him, be closer to him, be able to make him love her. Sometimes she wished she might talk to her mother about Jack, but she did not dare. Knowing her daughter was interested in a baronet might still Olivia's Hathaway's constant references to Franklin Farnsworth, but even so, Kate did not speak to her. Nor did she tell anyone about the ambergris, not even her father.

A brigantine had sailed from St. George Town for England four days after their discovery, and as Kate watched her go, wishing her a safe voyage, she wondered if she carried that valuable cargo.

When a note came from Maryanne, announcing the launching of the *Camille* and begging Kate to join them for it and stay overnight afterward, Kate was quick to tell her family of it at dinner. Her father nodded his permission after a glance at his wife's face. All the family was gathered around the shining mahogany table under the handsome Waterford crystal chandelier that Olivia Hathaway had brought back with her from England.

Both Gregory and George agreed to accompany their sister.

"We can go in the *Sprite*," George said as he helped himself to a platter of fish fillets in lemon sauce. "Greg and I can sleep aboard her. It will not be the first time we have done so."

"Aye," his twin agreed, sprinkling salt from the trencher on his heaped plate. "I'm anxious to see this sloop. I've heard all kinds of rumors about her radical design."

"She is very lovely," Kate told them. "And so graceful!"

"Perhaps we should all go?" her mother suggested, putting fear in Kate's heart. Her casual twin brothers were one thing, her mother's all-encompassing eye another. And she had planned to see Jack alone somehow, spend more time with him. If her mother was there, she would have to be more circumspect.

"But no, I don't suppose Mrs. Williams would have room for all of us," Olivia Hathaway was saying now. "She is such a dear little thing! You would like her, Roger. But she is very young. I would not fluster her for our sakes, not when she has those two babies to care for."

The subject changed then to Alicia Hathaway's condition, and how strange it would be for George and Gregory to be uncles, and Kate an aunt.

"And I must become a grandfather," Roger Hathaway complained. "I am not at all prepared for that august role, you know!"

Kate laughed at him, relieved that her parents were to remain in St. George Town. She had already decided on the gown she would wear, a pretty blue cambric with white lace fichu and elbow cuffs. And with it, her best lacy palmetto straw hat with its matching blue ribbons, white stockings, and her blue velvet shoes on the slender Italian heels. It was only too bad, since it was almost December now, she could not decorate the brim of her hat with fragrant flowers.

And since the twins were going, and would do the sailing, she would not have to bother with breeches. Instead, she would be the perfect lady in honor of the occasion. Perhaps when Jack saw her all dressed in her finest, he would be attracted to her.

The *Sprite* sailed in to Tucker's Town early on the morning of the launch. Kate's eyes went first to the *Camille*, glad she was still on land in her cradle. Someone had decked her with red-white-and blue bunting, and she looked very festive. Kate spotted Jack, surrounded by a crew of workers near her stern.

"Quite a crowd has gathered, I see," George remarked as he steered to avoid the snag reef Kate had warned him about.

"A lot of people are as curious as we are about her design," Greg told him as he studied the other boats assembled, the people onshore. Then he stared at the new sloop, and his eyes narrowed. "I say, George! Look at her bow! Have you ever seen one like that before?"

Kate had no eyes for anyone but Jack, and her brothers had to call her attention to Maryanne Williams, who was standing on the shore before her house, waving her apron to them.

When the *Sprite* was anchored close in, the twins jumped over the side to form a chair with their arms so they could transport their sister to shore. When Gregory threatened to drop her, claiming she was too heavy for him, Kate promised to drop the shoes and hose she was carrying for them if he tried it. All three were laughing as Kate was set carefully down on dry land.

Maryanne was delighted to have company, and a delicate rose flushed her cheeks. "Do let us repair to the shade of the veranda," she said, whirling to lead the way. "And you shall have some punch and some of my special cakes. It will be a long time yet before the launching."

The twins excused themselves as soon as they could. Kate knew they were anxious to get closer to the new sloop, inspect her for themselves. She wished she might join them, but she made herself sit quietly and listen to Maryanne's prattle.

"Jack has been just like a cat with one kitten," Maryanne confided. "Farley says he has never seen anyone so anxious, and so proud! Of course it is a worrying time until she is safely afloat. So much can go wrong."

Kate shaded her eyes to watch the men generously greasing the ways with tallow, while others stood ready to strike the shores, those heavy timbers stuck in the ground in support, that prevented the sloop and her cradle from sliding into the sea.

It seemed to take ages before Farley Williams called to them and waved. And then, instead of being able to run to join the others as she wanted to, Kate had to stroll at a snail's pace to accommodate Master Farley's short little legs.

The shores were being struck one by one when they arrived. Kate could see how carefully Jack was watching the operation, how he seemed to be everywhere at once in his anxiety. At last, when only the two dog shores remained, there was a sudden silence in the assembled throng.

Jack stepped forward, holding a bottle of port and a glass in his hands. He had no eyes for anything but his boat as he poured the wine and drank it down, as was the custom. Then he recorked the bottle and swung it hard at that narrow bow. A sigh went up as the bottle shattered, and he shouted, "I name this boat *Camille*! Sweet sailing and successful voyages to her!"

A hearty cheer went up as the men struck the dog shores. For a moment the sloop did not move, almost as if she were hesitant now to take to the sea she had been built beside. But then the weight of her, and that of the cradle, began to move her down the greased ways.

Kate's throat was tight as the *Camille* slid into the water, softly and deftly as a gull. The workmen waded in after her to remove the cradle, while Jack fastened a long line from her bow to a ring bolt ashore.

Master Farley was jumping up and down in his excitement, and even the baby was crowing. "Mama, Mama, did you see?" the little boy demanded, swinging her hand. "Unca Jack's boat went swoosh!"

Maryanne smiled. "She went swoosh, all right," she agreed.

"Make 'em do it again!" he demanded, and both girls laughed.

Kate could hear a fiddler tuning up behind her, and smell the rich aromas of roasting pig, chicken, and a caldron of spicy fish chowder. She was glad it was such a bright blue day. It seemed a good omen for the *Camille*.

As she followed Maryanne and the children back to

the house, she wondered when she would see Jack again, and then she had to shake her head at herself. It would be a long time before they would be able to drag him away from the boat, of that she was sure. Even now, he was surrounded by a crowd of men, all listening carefully as he explained the unusual bow, the amount of canvas *Camille* would carry, and how she would be rigged.

By late afternoon, sated by the large dinner that had been prepared in honor of the occasion, and the numerous rum punches they had consumed, they all sat around the veranda in idle conversation. The children had been taken away by Sukey for a much-needed nap, and the grown-ups were alone.

"She's a beauty, sir," Gregory told Jack, admiration in his voice. Of the Hathaway twins, he had been the more fascinated by the sloop, and had asked Jack innumerable questions. "Who will you get to crew her?"

Jack thought for a moment. "Well, I'll be the captain, of course. But the only hand I have at the moment is Samuel."

"Simpson?" George inquired in a lazy voice. "Isn't he a bit past the life?"

"Perhaps he'll not be much use physically, but I have come to trust his good judgment and knowledge of the sea. And this is my first command. I rely on him to keep me out of trouble."

"We will miss you, Jack, when you are gone," Mary-anne told him.

Silently Kate agreed with her.

"Aye, it's too bad you've decided to make your fortune as skipper, Jack," her husband agreed. He was leaning back in his chair, a pipe in his mouth. "You've been such an invaluable help to me here. Sure I can't persuade you to find another captain for her?"

Jack's eyes went back to his boat, and he shook his head. "No man but me will be her captain," he said softly.

Farley shrugged. "It doesn't do to get too attached to any one ship," he warned. "So much can happen to them, and you can always build another."

"Oh, no," Kate said without thinking. "There can never be another like the *Camille*, even if one were to be built to her exact specifications."

The others laughed, but Jack nodded to her, as if in approval for the way she understood. Her answering smile for him was dazzling.

Kate had only a few moments to talk with Jack alone much later. All the other guests had returned to their homes in other parts of the island long ago, for night was coming on. Kate could hear her brothers talking and laughing as they arranged their blankets in the *Sprite*, and the murmurs of the Williamses as they put their children to bed. Uneasy at being alone with her, Jack announced he was leaving as well, and Kate put her hand on his arm.

"The ambergris?" she whispered. "Is it safe?"

He nodded, looking down at her and thinking how pretty she was today in her blue gown and broad-brimmed hat. "I decided not to send it to England from here, if that meets with your approval, partner," he told her.

Kate looked surprised, and he added, "There is no guarantee it would arrive safely if everyone knew what it was. Instead, as soon as the *Camille* is rigged, I'll transport it to Charles Town myself, ship it on from there in a large crate marked with different contents. My man of business in London will see to its sale for us. It will take longer that way, but it will be surer."

"It seems an elaborate scheme," Kate said. "But whatever you think best, of course."

"What will you do with your new wealth, Mistress Kate?" he asked idly, lingering in spite of himself.

Kate listened to the sleepy chirps of some birds in a nearby olivewood bark tree, and then she shrugged. "I have no idea. I've never had any before. And what will you do with your share?"

"Build other ships, perhaps even a brigantine, and put it to good use buying goods and food in the colonies. I can see Bermuda needs them badly. You have little to trade here, besides salt and fish and whale oil. I had not thought Bermuda so poor."

Kate ruffled up in defense of her beloved islands. "Well, it is true we cannot grow the sugarcane Jamaica does, nor the tobacco and cotton of Virginia, but a man can make a decent living for himself here even so. Look at my father, sir! He not only has trading ships, he also serves as one of the governor's councilmen!"

Without thinking, Jack squeezed her shoulder in rough camaraderie. "No need to be on the defensive with me, mistress. I like it here, and I agree with you. But it grows late. I must be gone."

"Yes," Kate said reluctantly. She wondered what he would do if she put her arms around his strong tanned neck and begged him to kiss her.

As she stared up at him, her parted lips and lucent gray eyes told him what she was thinking as clearly as if she had spoken.

Jack found himself reaching for her, the excitement and triumph of the day, and all the rum punches he had consumed, making him careless. Only at the last moment did he remember that he must not touch her, and with an effort he stepped away and bowed.

Kate curtsied in return, and held out her hand. "Good night, sir," she said. "I am so glad I was here. I would not have missed the launching for the world!"

He took her hand only briefly, his fingers cool, before he nodded to her in farewell. In a moment he was gone. Kate lingered there in the soft dusk, watching him until he was lost from sight among the dark lush foliage at the edge of the lawn.

8

AFTER the *Camille* had been masted and rigged, Jack assembled his crew. To the Hathaways' surprise, their son Gregory signed on as mate. The evening he apprised them of this startling news, his twin had gone out to visit a friend.

"Oh, Gregory, my dear," Olivia Hathaway had mourned, looking most distressed at the news, " 'tis not that you and George have quarreled, is it?"

Greg laughed at her and shook his head. "Never, Mama! When have we ever quarreled? But I'm almost twenty-five now. I've a mind to strike out on my own. Besides, a ship can have only one captain. It is more than time for me to try to make my fortune, and George his as well, unhampered by even a compatible twin."

Kate wondered if perhaps the little vignette she had observed after church last Sunday had had anything to do with this sudden decision. Both George and Gregory had lingered to talk to Cecily Lunne, one of the town's prettiest girls. To their sister's critical eye, Cecily had not appeared to favor one brother over the other, but obviously she could marry only one of them. Perhaps Greg was allowing his brother a free field? He could not care very much about Cecily, then, she thought.

"I do not know this Jack Reade," Roger Hathaway said with a frown. "What manner of man is he?"

"He's a fine sailor, Father. As you know, I've been spending a lot of time with him since his sloop was launched. He told me he had but recently returned from a voyage that took him as far as China and the South Seas."

Olivia Hathaway frowned a little, her head tilted to one side as if in thought, and Kate held her breath.

"He may call himself plain Jack Reade now, but he has a title," Greg boasted.

"Never tell me he is the baronet Sir John Reade!" his mother exclaimed, turning to her daughter.

"Indeed he is, Mama," Kate said as evenly as she could. "But I thought you knew of his arrival here, that Maryanne had surely mentioned him to you."

Olivia Hathaway continued to stare at her, but her husband wanted to bring the conversation back to more important matters than a man's standing in the world. It was all very well to be a lord, no doubt, but you wanted something more to rely on than that from a man who might hold your life in his hands on a dirty night in strange waters.

"We're to go to Charles Town first," Greg went on before he could speak. "Jack has business there, although he is most reticent about it. From there, who knows? But no doubt when we return, we'll have some needed goods to sell, as well as exciting tales to tell."

His gray eyes, darker than his sister's, sparkled at the thought. "And Jack has other plans as well, including building more sloops. Perhaps I'll captain the next one."

"What will he use for money, a man who has been

employed as a common laborer in a yard?" his father demanded.

Greg waved a dismissing hand. "Never fear. He's well-to-do, Father. He chose to work in the yard, for he wanted to oversee the building of his sloop. We take old Samuel with us, and a fine crew. Henry, the Symons' slave, and the Bartons' slaves Babur and Tom—you know them all—and Edward and Christopher Abbott as well."

Roger Hathaway nodded. "Good men. But I am surprised this stranger to Bermuda was so successful in his quest for top hands."

"Everyone likes him," Greg explained. He paused for a moment, and then he said, "There's something about Jack that makes a man trust him, want to follow him. I can't explain it well, it's just a fact. He's a quiet man, not given to levity or easy smiles and casual conversation, but he's different from most men in other ways too. He is unique."

As his voice died away, Kate agreed with him in her heart. She said nothing, however, for she sensed her mother was still uneasy at what she had learned. And that was most strange, she thought. She had imagined that her mother would be ecstatic with a possible replacement for the absent Mr. Farnsworth.

The *Camille* sailed from Tucker's Town early in January 1773. Greg had packed his trunk the afternoon before, kissed his tearful mother and quiet sister, shaken hands with his father, and slapped his twin on the back before he left to make that fortune he had been talking about so incessantly.

There was no reason for Kate to be there when the untried sloop slipped between the reefs and headed for the open water. Indeed, she had not spoken to Jack since the evening of the launching, and she felt he had been avoiding her. The morning after the launching, when she had gone to call her brothers to the breakfast Maryanne had prepared for them, she discovered Jack had gone to Crow Harbor to see a man about joining his crew, and she had had to leave before he returned. Since that time she had seen him only briefly—once while on a visit to Maryanne Williams, and once in St. George Town, when he had been summoned by Governor Bruere to be questioned about his journey and wished good fortune. Neither time had she exchanged more than a few words with him.

Kate was awake very early the morning the *Camille* sailed. She dressed and went out to walk down the green lawn to the harbor's edge, trying to picture the scene at Tucker's Town: the crew, busy with sails and anchor, old Samuel stationed at the bow to watch for reefs, and at the helm, Jack Reade, his face raised to the peak of the mainsail, surely a breathtaking sight at the head of that tall, raked mast. Was he smiling now? she wondered. Were those turquoise eyes of his ablaze with excitement and accomplishment that he was free of land at last, sailing a boat he had designed, brought to life?

She was sure Greg was beside him, his brown hair blowing in the breeze and his dark gray eyes warm. And as clearly as if she were there, Kate could see how his generous mouth was stretched in a wide grin. She wished him well. She wished them all well. She would pray for them, all those long dreary months they would be gone.

As she trailed up to the house again, her slippers now wet with dew, Kate realized for the first time how hard it was for the loved ones who must be left behind. And how many ships had never returned to Bermuda? Samuel's elderly mistress, Mrs. Simpson, had lost her husband that way. Granny Bessie, as everyone called her now, had only been middle-aged then. But months had turned into a year, and then two, with no sign of the vessel her husband captained. At last she had been forced to accept his death, and that of all hands. The sea was a hard mistress, for so many things could go wrong.

Kate refused to dwell on such depressing thoughts. Jack would be all right. He *had* to be! And Greg too, she reminded herself quickly, ashamed at how easily she had forgotten him.

The new sloop had an easy reach to Charles Town, with the prevailing westerlies. Jack was delighted with the way she handled, her grace and speed. The new pointed bow proved to be everything he had hoped it would be, after he deliberately changed course one blustery day to tack as close to the wind as he could. He smiled when he saw how well the *Camille* held the line, and old Samuel, standing beside him at the wheel, laughed out loud. The old man had taken over the cooking chores in the galley, and Jack was pleased at how his crew was all getting on together. It had rather amazed him, this easy camaraderie between black and white, slave and free, that was so common with Bermudians. Perhaps it was because they were all such superb seamen, and that was all that mattered on an ocean voyage.

When they reached the magnificent harbor that Charles Town boasted, Jack could see that it was alive with ships of all sizes. Greg had told him it was a major port of the southern colonies, and now, as he pointed out various things of interest ashore, including his older brother's house facing the Battery, Jack hoped one of those ships was about to sail for England. For on that ship he intended to place a large, heavy wooden crate securely nailed shut and plainly marked "Personal Property of Sir John Reade," with his agent's name and address below. He had disliked using the title, but in this instance it was most necessary. Other cargo might be searched by the customs men in Plymouth; he did not think Sir John Reade's belongings would be disturbed.

He anchored the sloop near the mouth of the Cooper River and had the small boat lowered so he and Greg could go ashore together. Greg had told him that if anyone would know about a ship to transport his crate, it would be his brother Matthew.

"And he'll treat us to a fine dinner as well," Greg confided as the two rowed themselves ashore. "Not that Samuel's not a good cook, but Alicia has a way of dressing chicken. And won't some fresh vegetables taste fine?"

Jack reminded himself to set Greg to provisioning the *Camille* with the abundance that could be found in Charles Town, and to arrange for the crew to go ashore as well. He hoped he did not have to linger here too long, but he knew it might take a while before the ambergris was safely on its way to England and he could decide where he wanted to go next. There were the New England colonies, of course, but unless he picked up a cargo here, there would be no profit in the journey. And then there was all that unrest in the North. Did he want to get involved in it? He had heard that the Boston Assembly had even gone so far as to threaten secession, and that one of their leaders, a Samuel Adams, had formed a Committee of Correspondence to take action against the crown.

Perhaps he would go to the West Indies instead, with rice or indigo to trade for molasses. He did not have to worry about money on this trip, but he knew he would feel easier when he had more, from the sale of the ambergris. Until then, he would have to be careful, try to make each leg of the journey profitable.

When he was introduced to Matthew Hathaway, Jack saw he was a vastly different man from his younger brother. The elder Hathaway was taller, for one thing, and yet more slightly built, and whereas Greg's eyes were more often than not sleepy and content, his brother's were full of purpose. Of course, there were five years between them, and Matthew was a married man, with a child on the way. Jack had learned he had a successful trading business of his own here, and a large plantation several miles west of the city. Clearly he was a man of some account.

His wife, Alicia, was a tall woman with soft brown hair and a lovely smile that made you forget her lack of beauty. She seemed delighted to provide dinner for two more gentlemen, and hurried away to see to it. The talk at the table was mainly about Hathaway business and Bermuda, until Alicia left them all to their wine, carefully closing the doors to the dining room behind her.

"Beg you will forgive us, Captain, for our preoccupation with family matters," Matthew Hathaway said as he poured his guest another glass of port.

Jack waved a careless hand. "My business could wait, sir. You and Greg have not seen each other for some time. But if I may, I would like to ask your advice. I am very new to this trading business, after all."

At his host's nod, he went on, "First I must find a ship to transport a very important crate to England for me. But when that is done, I've a mind to go adventuring. I thought of the Massachusetts Bay Colony, for a cargo of rum, cloth, and machinery, but I'm concerned about the disorder there. Would you advise that for the *Camille*'s maiden voyage I head for the Indies? And if I do, what cargo would I be best to carry?"

Matthew Hathaway was frowning now, staring into the wineglass on the shining table before him. Jack waited, but it was Greg who said, "I say, what's to do, Matt? You look very harsh!"

"I was just thinking," his brother said, rousing himself from his abstraction. "Yes, there is unrest and disorder in the colonies. And not just in the North, for all some Englishmen claim Boston to be a very rat's nest of traitors."

"Indeed, I heard how Governor Bruere protested when the troops on Bermuda were sent there to reinforce the crown's authority," Jack remarked.

Matthew suddenly looked straight at both men in turn. "I very much fear that war is coming."

"But that can't be, Matt," his brother protested. "Surely 'tis but the actions of the few, not the many."

"No, it is more than that, although I do not wonder you have not heard in Bermuda, where such things are far away and unimportant. But all these acts and taxes, the stifling of our trade by embargo! Everyone in the colonies wearies of them. And yet all our protests bring no change at all. Sometimes I doubt anyone in England is even listening to us. But the king and his ministers had better heed what is happening, lest they find themselves with a revolution on their hands."

"From loyal Englishmen?" Jack asked doubtfully.

"There are those who say that since we are not treated as the English freemen we are, we have every reason to fight for what is ours by birthright."

He turned his palms up then, and smiled. "But you asked me what cargo would bring you the most profit, Captain Reade. My last remarks were not a digression, as you will see. What the colonies need most, and what bring the highest prices here, are arms and ammunition."

Greg whistled softly, and even Jack looked startled.

"We have no way of manufacturing such things, and those in power in England have kept us short of supply. No doubt it is deliberate, to prevent the very war I have been telling you about. Still, powder, shot, rifles—all are being delivered to us, one way or another. At present it is only a dribble, for few colonists look that far ahead. But I intend to accumulate as much as I can. Just in case."

"Where would be the best place to buy such a cargo?" Jack asked, his steady voice noncommittal.

"St. Eustatius, without a doubt. It's Dutch-held and neutral; a free port. There's a man there, an Isaac Van Dam, who is willing to help us in this matter. If you

should go, you might look him up. And I'll give you a
letter to Governor De Windt as well. I believe there is
every need for haste."

"But why?" Greg asked, looking puzzled. "I can't
believe we're that close to revolution!"

"Is haste important because when the authorities realize what is going on, they'll move to stop the practice?"
Jack asked.

His host raised his glass in a tribute to his guest's
acuity. "But of course they will," he said. "In a year,
perhaps two, arms and ammunition will be forbidden
imports, considered contraband.

"But it may be you have a moral problem with this
type of cargo, Captain? Many men do," he went on.
"For carrying it, in effect, is an act of civil disobedience.
Some might even say treason, and no doubt the world
would agree with them."

Jack stared at him, deep in thought, and Greg found
himself wondering what was going on behind those hooded
turquoise eyes.

At last Jack stirred and said, "Oh, surely not, sir. Men
on the edge of such a wilderness as the colonies are, have
much need of weaponry, to deal with the savages and
wild beasts and to provide meat for their tables, isn't that
so? I would consider it a patriotic act, rather, done to
ensure the success of our holdings here."

Matthew Hathaway rose then, to extend his hand,
although his brief knowing smile was ironic. "As you say,
Captain. I am sure you have a most exemplary motive. I
applaud you for discovering it."

The *Camille* sailed from Charles Town ten days later.
In that time, Jack had come to know and admire Matthew Hathaway a great deal. They had talked at length
about the temper of the colonies, the restrictions that had
driven them closer and closer to open rebellion. And
Jack was thankful as well when his new friend instructed
him on trading matters, everything from dealing with
customs men to privateers. After the handpicked ship
Hathaway had chosen to carry Jack's crate had sailed, he
had provided him with a cargo of indigo at fair prices,
and been instrumental in easing a stranger's way in buying
supplies and foodstuffs.

Greg had not been glad to leave. He had met a little blond beauty at one of the small parties his sister-in-law gave for them, and he was much in her thrall. Only the thought of the Dutch and French and Spanish women who surely awaited him in St. Eustatius allowed him to retain his good spirits.

Fighting the prevailing wind now, the *Camille* sailed southeast, tacking day after day. Jack had set a course for her that would permit them to avoid the Bahamas and the other islands below them in the long Indies chain that stretched from North to South America. He had yet to acquire the cannon for the sloop's deck, and he knew he had to avoid trouble.

At last they dropped anchor in Gallows Bay. The crew was astounded at the number of ships in the roadstead, the different flags at their sterns. St. Eustatius was truly an international meeting place, for here, even those currently at war swung at anchor peacefully beside each other. What could happen to them after they left the port was of no concern to the merchant Dutch, intent as they were on accumulating a fortune in trade.

Above the town, Fort Orange guarded the harbor. To Jack's searching eyes, it looked remarkably unwarlike. And yet, only eight miles away, the British island of St. Kitts loomed against the horizon. In the lucent air, it seemed very close.

The town fronting the harbor was not much better than two large untidy villages, an upper and a lower. There was, however, a lot of building going on. Several warehouses, probably filled with goods, stood waiting for trade, and in spite of the eternal lassitude so common to the Caribbean, there was an air of purpose to be discerned.

Jack rowed ashore with Greg after the *Camille* had been anchored. He intended to find this Isaac Van Dam as soon as possible. There was something about the port that made the hair on the back of his neck rise. It seemed so innocent, so peaceful, and yet . . .

First, of course, he must pay his respects to the governor, and present Matthew Hathaway's letter. But when that was done, he would locate Van Dam, and make all haste to sell his indigo, buy powder and shot, and the cannon he needed, and sail away from here.

The governor was properly welcoming, and offered his

aid if they should have need of it. And the Dutch merchant, when they found him next, was even more so.

He was a short, stubby-legged man with a huge stomach and a rich chuckle. Almost bald, his head was covered with brown blotches, the result of too much time spent in the sun without a hat. He struck a hard bargain for the indigo, smiling and chuckling as he did so, and when Jack bargained in kind over the price of the guns, he did not lose his good humor.

When their business had been concluded, Van Dam invited them both to his home for dinner. Greg was disappointed when Jack accepted with every sign of pleasure, for he was anxious to investigate the taverns, filled with all those luscious females of every color and nationality.

After the first day, Jack set up watches so that all the crew could go ashore in turn. He put Greg in charge of one, while he took the other. A Spanish ketch was anchored near the *Camille*, and only a short distance away were a New England merchant ship and a French cutter.

The shape of the *Camille*'s bow drew a lot of attention, and several sailors rowed over to ask questions about it. Jack was cordial and open with everyone, but he invited no one aboard, and told the crew to keep to themselves.

One afternoon, as he was getting ready to row ashore, he noticed Samuel Simpson leaning against the rail, his pipe in hand. He realized that the old man had not gone ashore as yet, not once, and he called to him and suggested it.

Samuel's face was wreathed in a smile as he ambled over to join his captain.

"No, thank you, suh," he said. "Ah been ashore 'nuff times in mah life. Dere's rum here on board, and what else's dere for an ole man lak me in Statia Town?"

As Jack shook his head, he grinned again. "But you ain't old, Mistuh Jack, no indeedy! Have a fine time, suh. No need to come back till dawn, iffen you don't care to. Ah'll keep an eye out."

Jack smiled at him as he lowered himself down the rope ladder to the small dory. As he rowed ashore, he realized Samuel was right. There was little to do in Statia, unless you frequented the taverns. For some reason, Jack had no desire to sit in a smoky, close room swilling rum, not today. The blue and turquoise and golden afternoon

was soft and fair. Perhaps he would take a walk instead,
find a deserted beach where he could swim. Or maybe he
would scale the larger of the two steep peaks that formed
either end of the island and, with its reputation for trade,
gave it its nickname, "The Golden Rock."

As he walked along the road out of town, the noise
faded behind him, and he took a deep breath of the
sweet-scented air. Ahead of him, a cordia tree was in
bloom, its reddish-orange clusters of flowers pretty with
their frilled edges.

Just beyond the tree, he spotted a large white stone
house set in an extensive garden. Its appearance here
surprised him. Most of the inhabitants of Statia lived in
town; this place was isolated.

As he drew nearer, he spied a blond woman kneeling
among the flowers. She was wearing a pale green gown
and a large straw hat, and he paused to watch her. She
made an attractive picture, for a host of butterflies danced
around her, the shafts of sunlight turning them into brilliant, living jewels.

As if she sensed his regard, she turned and rose, and
her eyes widened. It seemed to a bemused Jack as if they
stared at each other for a very long time. He saw her
eyes were a bright blue, and for a moment the memory
of Lady Arbel that he thought he had banished forever
invaded his mind. He frowned then, his lips tightening.

The woman wiped her hands on her skirts as she came
toward him. When she was closer, Jack could see she was
older than he had thought originally, and she bore no
other resemblance to the lovely Arbel. She greeted him
then in Dutch, to which Jack was forced to respond in
English.

"*Ach*, I should have known," she said, switching easily
to that language. "Your hair is too dark for a Netherlander."

Her voice was a husky drawl, and her slow smile for
him, intriguing. Jack smiled in return.

"Won't you come and sit down in the garden?" she
invited, gesturing to a pair of cane chairs set near a table
in the shade. "It is a warm day for walking, and I would
like to get to know you."

Jack nodded, aware from his physical reaction how
much he would like to get to know her too.

As he took a seat, she poured them drinks from a

pitcher set on the table. **An**d when she gave him his glass, her hand touched his. Jack never took his eyes from hers as he sipped the citrus punch.

"I am Greta Dreeber," she told him. "And you?"

"My name is Jack Reade, captain of the Bermudian sloop *Camille*."

She raised a languid hand to brush away a hovering insect, and the gold of her wedding band flashed in the sunlight.

Jack's frown returned. "Mrs. Dreeber," he said, his voice noncommittal.

She shrugged her round shoulders, and the corner of her mouth lifted a little. "Yes, Mrs. Dreeber. But I am a widow now."

"My sympathy, ma'am."

"There is no need for it. My husband was lost at sea. It happened a very long time ago."

"And yet you remained here in Statia?" he asked. "I wonder you did not return to Holland."

"Oh, I intend to one of these days. I have just not got around to it as yet."

"How long have you been widowed?" he asked, curious.

She thought for a moment. "Why, it is ten years in September. How time passes."

She looked at him then, her hands folded in her lap. Jack thought her one of the most restful women he had ever met. She exuded serenity, and everything about her was languid—her voice, her movements.

"You must be newcome to Statia," she said. "I have not seen you before, and I know I would remember you. You are such a handsome young man, and your eyes are so unusual, just like the water here."

Jack nodded and finished his drink, somewhat at a loss as to how he was to reply to such a compliment, the open admiration in her eyes.

He rose then and bowed. "Thank you for your kindness, ma'am," he said. "That was most refreshing."

"You are leaving?" she asked, rising and coming to stand beside him. He noted she was almost as tall as he was. Slowly she reached out to touch his arm. Through his linen shirt, Jack could feel the warmth of her hand, its soft caress as it moved slowly over his muscles. He stood very still, his intent eyes asking a question.

"Don't go," she said, and her heavy eyelids almost closed. "Stay with me. I am lonely today, and so, I think, are you. And I sense, too, that you have been hurt somehow. Hurt badly. Let us be together. Let me comfort you."

Jack had never had such a direct proposal from anyone but a whore before, but somehow he knew that this Greta Dreeber was not a member of that profession, for all that her invitation had been natural and easy. And he knew how he wanted to accept it.

Before he could frame a reply, she moved closer to put her arms around him and kiss him. And suddenly there was no need to say anything. Anything at all.

She led him without haste through the high-ceilinged dim rooms to a large bedroom that overlooked the ocean. Vaguely Jack was aware of slaves' voices in another part of the house as he closed the door behind them. In his impatience, he was undressed long before she was, and he watched her as she removed the last of her clothes. She was a full-bodied woman, with breasts as round and heavy as ripe fruit. Her skin was a creamy white, and somehow more opaque, thicker, than most people's. He could not wait to touch it.

When she joined him at last on the high-posted bed behind the mosquito netting, he was in a fever. It had been so very long since he had had a woman. Disillusioned by his fate, and stung by Lady Arbel's callous rejection, he had isolated himself in Tucker's Town and worked until he fell into bed exhausted. But he was very conscious now of all those celibate months.

His lovemaking was hurried, and in spite of his efforts to slow the pace, over much too soon.

"I'm sorry," he whispered several moments later, after his breathing quieted. "That was not good for you."

"Shhh," she said, smoothing back his black hair. As he stared down at her in doubt, she smiled at him. "My turn will come. There is plenty of time."

Jack did not return to the *Camille* until dawn. Greta Dreeber was a revelation to him. He discovered in those hours he spent with her that she was perfectly content to sleep beside him, or make love again and again—whatever he wished. And when he mentioned he was hungry, she rang a bell and had a slave bring a tray of food and drink for them both.

He was with her as often as he could manage it in the days that followed, and he forgot how boring a place Statia was. Sometimes they sat in the garden and talked in a desultory way, or dined on the broad terrace that fronted her bedroom. It was a completely private place, enclosed on all sides but the ocean with thick flowering vines.

He told her only a little about himself, and, to his surprise, she did not appear to be at all curious about those things he never mentioned. She did not even ask what had hurt him, or why it had happened. She would listen when he talked, and answer his questions, but she never questioned him in return, or volunteered anything about her past life. It was as if this moment in time was enough for her, and she required nothing more.

Somehow, she reminded him of a contented cat, one that has been well-fed and pampered all its life. She even moved and stretched like a cat, slowly and sinuously.

They had five days together. And whereas Jack had been impatient before at the delay getting the indigo unloaded and the new cargo of powder and shot put aboard, because the *Camille* had to wait her turn in this busy port, now he did not care. The warm-scented golden days, the velvet-blue nights, became his reality. Everything else faded into insignificance.

One night he woke to find her shaking him. Rubbing the sleep from his eyes, he heard the drumming of a sudden tropical rainstorm striking the terrace just outside the long doors.

"Come," she said, sliding off the bed and beckoning to him.

He rose and followed her, somewhat bemused. She went behind the screen that concealed the washstand and chamber pot, to return with towels and a bar of soap.

His mouth curved in a grin as she opened the door and stepped outside. The rain was a deluge, and in moments her whole body was streaming with it. It darkened her blond hair, and she turned her face up to meet it, smiling in pleasure. As she began to soap herself, he was quick to join her. He had not expected the rain to be so cold or to strike his bed-warmed nakedness so sharply, and he shuddered. Greta laughed at him, as she slid behind him to soap his back for him.

Her touch on his buttocks excited him, and he spun around to take her breasts in his hands and kiss her open mouth. Her soapy skin was slippery, smooth, erotic.

But even as his hands tightened, Greta pushed him away. "Greedy boy!" she scolded. "Later, when we are clean. Besides, I want to wash my hair. You know these sudden cloudbursts never last long."

Jack subsided, resolved to be patient. At least for now.

It was good to step inside at last, feeling clean and fresh, to towel-dry and climb back into the big bed and pull up the covers. Idly Jack propped himself up on the pillows to watch Greta drying her hair. She had donned a loose wrapper, so he knew she was feeling the chill too, for she seldom bothered with clothes here in her room. She was the most unself-conscious woman he had ever known. Naked or clothed was all the same to her.

"Why did you ask me to stay that first afternoon?" he asked her now, wanting her complete attention.

The hairbrush she held continued its slow movements. "Because I liked you. And I wanted you," she told him, her face hidden behind the curtain of her hair.

"Do you do that often?" he persisted. Somehow he wanted to know that now, although he had never asked her before. Perhaps, he mused, it was because he wanted to be special to her.

"Do what?" she asked idly. "Wash my hair?"

Jack grimaced. "Of course not! I meant, ask men to stay here."

Greta lowered the brush and tossed the damp hair back from her face. Her heavy-lidded blue eyes regarded him seriously.

"No, not often," she told him, her voice steady. "I am not a promiscuous woman. Mainly, I suppose, because it is so much trouble. I have grown to like living alone, answering to no one but myself."

"Is that why you never married again?"

She shrugged in that now familiar gesture. "When Johann died, he left me a wealthy woman. I did not have to marry if I did not choose to. And I found marriage, mmm, very fatiguing."

"And our lovemaking is not?" Jack teased, remembering all those breathless, athletic hours they had spent.

She smiled at him, that slow, mysterious smile. "Ah, but afterward, you go back to your ship, and I can sleep all day, while you must scurry about, being the decisive captain again. But I like to eat when I am hungry, drink when I am thirsty, sleep when I am tired. I am a simple woman with simple desires, satisfied by simple pleasures, is it not so?"

"I will be leaving soon," he told her, perversely trying to upset her serene equanimity somehow. "Will you miss me?"

"Of course," she told him, her voice unchanged. "For a while."

Jack climbed out of bed then, and came to take the brush from her hands. As he ran it through the thick tresses in even strokes, he whispered, "Only for a while?"

She was holding up her looking glass now, and her blue eyes regarded his reflection dispassionately. Feeling hurt, even challenged, by her nonchalance, Jack bent to nibble her earlobe, kiss her throat and shoulders.

"Perhaps for quite a long while," she admitted. She knew very well what he was about, but she had no intention of revealing how much she did care for this handsome young man. She was a wise woman, well-versed in the ways of the world. And in that world, there was no chance of any permanent liaison between them. No, for two so disparate, there could be nothing but this one passionate but ephemeral meeting.

"You are too young for me, Jack," she told him. "You would be too young if we were the same age. And I am thirty-five now. No, this can be only an interlude, as I knew very well when I invited you into my garden—and my bed."

"You are ageless," he argued. "And so very beautiful."

Her wry smile mocked his compliment. "Now I am, perhaps. But later? Ah, well. Some women mind getting older. I do not."

Again came that eloquent shrug. "Why rail against the inevitable? And in a few years, or next month—whenever Statia begins to pall—I shall move on. Perhaps I will go to another island here in the Caribbean. The snows and icy winds of winter in Holland do not appeal to me any longer."

"And you will forget me?" he persisted in a rough voice, as if to dare her to say she could.

She studied his reflection, her blue eyes calm. "In time, of course, I will," she told him evenly. "Nothing lasts forever. But I will also remember you sometimes, and that memory will give me joy. I would you remember me the same way."

"You are a unique woman, Greta," he said. Then he dropped the hairbrush and grasped her shoulders to turn her toward him. "Your hair is almost dry."

She heard both the plea and the order in his voice, and she smiled, admiring the blazing turquoise in his eyes. Then she rose to shrug out of her wrapper. It fluttered unheeded to the floor.

Two days later, the *Camille* left Statia. Her departure had not been unmarked; indeed, while she was being loaded, Jack had noticed some intense interest in the cargo she was to carry. He debated long and hard about the best time to slip from the harbor, for he wanted no trouble he could avoid. And he had his doubts about the Spanish ketch, that French cutter. Old Samuel had told him how their captains had tried to find out when they were to sail.

Greg argued for cover of darkness, but Jack did not want to risk the unknown and unseen reefs. Instead, he chose the early-morning hour just before sunrise. No one kept a very good watch here in this neutral port, especially in the gray hour before dawn. He might very well be able to ghost through the fleet unnoticed.

Everything went as he had hoped. Using hand signals instead of shouted orders, Jack had his crew raise the sails and anchor, so as to fall off and catch the wind.

As silently as possible, the *Camille* threaded her way through the anchorage. When a loose rope end chattered against the mast, Jack had no need to raise his hand. Christopher Abbott was there in a flash to secure the noisy line. Jack noticed he seemed nervous, unlike his younger brother, Edward, whose whole tense posture betrayed his excitement. To Edward, this was all a game. But then, he, unlike his brother, had never had to fight pirates or privateers.

Jack turned the wheel slightly to starboard then, to avoid the broad stern of an American schooner. He frowned when he saw a man leaning against the rail

watching them. If he should shout a greeting, all would
be lost!

But the American merely raised his cap and waved it
in salute, a broad smile creasing his sunburned face. Jack
grinned back in relief. Obviously the American had heard
of the cargo they carried, and probably the *Camille*'s next
port of call as well, and he would do nothing to hinder
her safe arrival there.

They were well clear of the harbor, and Jack was about
to set the course to Charles Town, when Greg gripped
his shoulder and pointed astern. His eyes were glittering
with excitement.

Jack saw that the French cutter, the *Otarie*, was making sail as fast as she could. Greg almost looked as if he
were trying to speed her along, and Jack laughed before
he called out, "Ready about . . . hard alee!"

The *Camille* came about to head back to the port
again.

"Beg pardon, sir, what are you doing?" Christopher
Abbott asked. "We were clean away!"

"But what a poor sport you are, Chris," Jack said. "I
mean to dally about, give that greedy Frenchman a fair
chance to catch us."

Abbott shook his head, looking worried, and Jack
smiled at him. "Nothing to worry about, believe me.
We'll show them a clean pair of heels when the time
comes for it."

"And we'll fight if we have to!" Greg vowed, as old
Samuel came chuckling from the galley, so as not to miss
the fun.

As the French cutter loomed closer and closer, it seemed
an age to at least one of the crew before Jack gave the
order to tighten sail. Obediently the *Camille* settled down
to a hard, businesslike tack in the fresh trade winds, her
pointed bow cleaving the waves.

"Now we shall see how fast she is," Jack told the crew.
"I'll wager you anything you like that we escape without
a fight."

Greg's air of exhilaration grew as the distance between the
two ships widened, and soon he was laughing in delight.

"Why, we'll be hull down over the horizon long before
Monsieur Français," he boasted. "What a greyhound we
have here!"

Jack nodded, and handed over the helm, stifling a yawn as he did so. He had stayed with Greta until the last moment, and now he felt exhausted.

The salt air was making him drowsy, and he looked forward to his hammock. He never slept so soundly as he did at sea, lulled by the slap of the waves against the hull, the soothing motion of the sloop as she slid through the water. Even the small sounds of the sails, the hum of the rigging, were a lullaby to his ears.

But even as anxious as he was to sleep, he paused for a moment to stare back over the stern. Statia lay in sight still, as it would for hours in this clear air.

He wondered if he would ever see Greta Dreeber again. Perhaps she would be gone when next he called there. He had no hold on her, had never had. And as attracted to her as he had been, he knew that what she had told him was correct. They did not love each other, not that way. Still, he was glad to have this memory to keep. Silently he thanked her for it, and for something else as well. For Greta had exorcised the ghost of Arbel Stanton once and for all. That silly little doll-like girl, concerned only with her high rank in society, the delights of a Season, and the number of beaux she could attract, had been banished forever.

9

FROM Charles Town, the *Camille* sailed south again, to the Turks Islands this time, to collect a cargo of salt. Matthew Hathaway had suggested this be taken to the Massachusetts Bay Colony, and showed Jack how gunpowder could be hidden in the barrels so customs men would never even know it was there. He gave Jack the name of a merchant in Boston to see, asked him to find out the lay of the land there, and report on it.

Once arrived, Jack was quick to note the unrest, the enmity between the colonists and the British there. The harbor was full of Royal Navy shipping, and over two regiments of red-coated soldiers patrolled the busy streets to keep order. They had been stationed here for five long years, and it did not appear they intended to leave in the foreseeable future.

If Jack had been uneasy in sleepy Statia, he was even more on edge in this brisk northern town, where tension was so rife it was almost palpable. No longer could he doubt that war was coming.

Mr. Winslow, the Boston merchant, bought his salt and gave him suggestions for further cargoes that might prove profitable. He also told him of a smaller harbor on Cape Cod where the *Camille* could unload at night in the future, unhampered by British customs men. The cargo could be transported overland to Boston from there. It was all an elaborate web, but Jack discovered that few Bostonians were directly involved, even now after the Boston Massacre and other punitive acts by the government. As adamant as they were about their rights, few foresaw an open rift with the crown. They were Englishmen first, last, and always. But as Englishmen, Jack knew they would fight for those rights when the time came.

It was late one afternoon in September when the *Camille* returned to St. George Town harbor. The crew was excited about being home at last, and Jack, casting a knowledgeable eye at the sky, was glad to escape the gale he sensed was coming. He refused Greg's offer of supper at his home, claiming he could go nowhere until he had had his hair cut and his clothes cleaned. Besides, he wanted to remain on board until the cargo was unloaded, and he could not like interrupting a family reunion. He paid the crew their share of the profits, which were considerable, and told them he would let them know when the *Camille* would sail again.

Old Samuel was the last to get his wages. As he put the guineas safely way in an old purse, he nodded with satisfaction.

"Miz Simpson surely be glad to see dis, suh," he said, his faded eyes twinkling. "Ah jess hope she ain't suffered none while Ah been gone."

"Suffered?" Jack asked as he put his money chest away. "Why ever would she?"

"Ah be her last slave, suh," Samuel explained. "She

old now. Older den me, even, and she got nobody else. What I kin make is all she got to live on."

Jack stared at him, horrified. "But why didn't you tell me that, Samuel?" he demanded. "I could have given her some of your share in advance, to see her through the time you were gone."

The old man shook his head. "Miz Simpson, she wouldn't be takin' it. Dat'd be lak charity to her, and she cain't 'bide charity. She proud, dat lady. S'pose we never come home? S'pose we lost at sea, lak she done lost her husband? Dat money wouldn't be hers den."

Jack did not know what to say, and he waved the old sailor away. "Best you hurry along, then, Samuel—see to her. And do let me know if there's anything I can do to help, hear?"

Samuel nodded, his creased face serene. He'd do for Miz Bessie, jess lak he always done, he thought. But it was kind o' Cap'n Reade to offer. A good man, the cap'n, in every way.

Bessie Simpson *had* suffered those long months her slave had been at sea. She had thought he might come back sooner, and as time passed, she began to worry that he was lost. She grew some vegetables in her small garden, although she was not strong enough to work it as she should, and she stole out sometimes at night to try to catch some fish when others could not see her. But her supplies had dwindled away, and if it had not been for Kate Hathaway, she might not have been alive to welcome Samuel home when he came weaving up the alley, trying to get his land legs back.

Kate had noticed the old lady had stopped coming to church in her one threadbare "good" dress that summer, and she had called on her to see if she were in ill health. She was shocked at how emaciated and worn the widow looked, even as she smiled and said she was sorry she could not ask Kate to step inside. She claimed she was about to make a call, but Kate knew that was not true. No, the reason she was not welcome was that Granny Bessie had nothing to offer her in hospitality, and was ashamed of it.

Since that time, Kate had often brought her a loaf of bread, claiming Keza had baked too many for the family, or a mess of fish that the Hathaways could not eat before they spoiled. Once she had brought a packet of tea and some cakes, saying her mother wished the older woman's opinion of this new recipe. She helped in other ways too. She alerted others in town to Granny's predicament, and the vicar as well. But no one was as successful as Kate in gaining her trust.

On the pretext of making her mother a special birthday gift, Kate asked the old lady to help her design and embroider a light silk stole. Granny Bessie was famous for her needlework, so it was a good way to provide her with money, for her help could not be considered charity. Since Kate hated to sew, it was a real sacrifice on her part. But she liked the old woman, her gallantry in the face of such crushing odds, how she continued to fight in her own genteel way for survival. And as they sewed, they talked of many things.

"Never marry a sailor, Mistress Kate," Mrs. Simpson had admonished her one afternoon. "Not if you can avoid it, that is. The woman who does so must be strong, a special kind of person, for it's a terrible life."

"How so?" Kate asked, her needle stilled as she remembered Jack Reade's handsome face.

"Well, for one thing, a sailor is gone more than he's home. And then, whether he ever *comes* home again is problematic. The wife he leaves behind can only pray."

Suddenly she snorted and shook her head. "Not that there's all that much time for praying! No, for now that wife must see to everything alone. The household, the children, any crisis of health or storm, and whatever business her husband left her to take care of. Well I remember dealing with it when the roof of this house was blown away in a hurricane! Oh, 'tis a thankless chore, a sailor's wife has! Better for you, my girl, to find some nice young man who always gets so seasick he won't even step into a dory!"

"And wherever would I find such a man in Bermuda, ma'am?" Kate asked demurely.

The two chuckled at the impossibility of such a thing.

Later, after they had enjoyed a pot of tea, Kate helped her hostess do the washing-up. She had tried to get her to accept the help of one of the Hathaway slaves, at least part of the time, but this the old lady would not hear of.

"No, no, indeed, Mistress Kate," she had said indignantly. Kate subsided, knowing this was a battle she could not win.

"I shall do very well alone, as always. I'm set in my ways, you know, and can't abide interference. And soon, pray God, my slave Samuel will return. He's a good man, Samuel. I pray for him as much as I ever did for my Will."

Kate asked her then about the old slave, whom she had known since childhood. She learned the Simpsons had bought him, and his wife and daughters, when they were first married. Now his wife was dead, and his daughters, too, and there was only Samuel left.

"We get on very well," Mrs. Simpson told her. "He knows my ways, and I know his. And he's such a help to me. I don't know what I'd do without him."

"Jack Reade said he trusted him above all others," Kate remarked. "And he wanted him on this voyage from the first."

Mrs. Simpson stole a quick look at Kate. She was in profile, and as she bent over her sewing, a stray sunbeam lit her chestnut curls. What a dear, dear girl! the old lady thought. Pretty as a picture, and so straight and true! She was very much afraid that her lecture on the evils of marrying a seafaring man had done no good at all. There was something in the girl's voice when she spoke Captain Reade's name that gave the game away.

She sighed then in regret, and Kate looked up. "Are you tired, ma'am? Oh, yes, I see I have overstayed my time! You should have reminded me of it!"

In only a few minutes she was gone, promising to return in a few days to work on the stole again. Behind her, in a handkerchief, she left the coins for her lesson. Mrs. Simpson sighed again as she put them safely away. She hated to take money for doing a favor for such a nice girl, but she had to admit it was comforting to be able to eat regularly now.

When Samuel called out and knocked on the door, her welcoming smile and general well-being relieved his mind. It was not long before he learned how she had been getting along, all thanks to Kate Hathaway's kindness. Samuel resolved to thank the young lady some way, as soon as he had a chance.

Mrs. Simpson was thrilled at the amount of money

Samuel had earned; thrilled and relieved. She planned a
festive supper and sent him hurrying back to the harbor
for fresh fish and supplies, while she set about making a
loaf of bread. It did not matter that this was the last of
her flour. Now there was enough money for everything
she needed. Why, she could even buy some material for
a new gown, and begin going to church again when it was
made up. God was very good, she decided as she dusted
the bread board with flour and begin to knead the dough.

When Kate reached home and saw her brother Gregory, she flew into his arms to kiss him and exclaim. Tears
welled up in her eyes at the sight of his dear face, while
their parents watched the two indulgently.

"Here, now, belay that, Kate!" Greg growled at her,
putting her firmly away from him. "Only been gone nine
months, and yet you act as if it were nine years!"

Kate demanded to know all about his journey as the
four trooped in to supper. George was dining with the
Lunnes today. He had recently become affianced to their
daughter Cecily, and so must miss the homecoming.

As they ate, served by a beaming Keza and her husband, Daniel, Greg told them of his adventures. Well,
most of them anyway. On Jack's advice, he did not
mention the cargo of powder and shot they had carried,
nor why they had done so. Matthew had warned him that
their father would not approve such a blatant preparation
for war against their rightful king, and Greg had had to
agree with him. He had heard Roger Hathaway rant too
often about traitors and rabble rousers to doubt where
his sympathy lay.

At last he was silent and fell to his dinner, and Olivia
Hathaway said, "We have some exciting news too, dear
Gregory. While you were gone, your sister became a
wealthy young woman."

Greg stared at Kate, and she wrinkled her nose at him.

"Now, how is this?" he asked. "How could Kate become wealthy?"

"Only by the sale of some sixty-two pounds of ambergris, that's all," his father told him with a twinkle in his
eyes. "The sly puss found it last year, along with that
captain of yours, and they shipped it to England. Sir
John's man sent us half the proceeds only a while ago.

You can imagine how astounded we were to suddenly receive almost four thousand pounds!"

"Indeed we were," Olivia Hathaway echoed, but a little frown creased her brow for a moment. She had still not entirely accepted Kate's explanation of that chance meeting on the beach. No, she was sure there had to be something more to it that Kate would not tell her, but she put it from her mind for now.

"By all that's holy!" Greg exclaimed. "So that was what was in that precious crate of Jack's! My word, Kate, what will you do with all that money?"

"I do not feel that it is only mine," Kate said. "It is for all of us, of course."

"Do not be so silly, old girl," her brother told her in much his old way. "You found it. It is yours."

"Yes, and what a marvelous dowry it will make," his mother pointed out. "And now Kate and I can travel to England again, dress as fine as we wish, and your sister may have her pick of any number of men to marry."

"I have told you, Mama, I do not want to return to England," Kate said evenly, for this was an argument they had had many times since the ambergris money had arrived.

Olivia Hathaway sighed till a glance at her husband's face silenced her. But as much as she loved her daughter, she did wish she was not so stubborn! It must be that chestnut hair, she thought as she served the pudding. What a shame Kate is not more malleable, for then I could guide her better. And she is twenty now, twenty years old! If she did not marry soon, she would be on the shelf, and what a horrid prospect that was!

Greg asked about the other Hathaways then, and in telling him all about his new niece—such a dear, darling baby, Greg! you will love her!—Olivia Hathaway was able to forget her problems with her difficult daughter.

As Greg learned all about the baby, named Rosemary Katherine, and his brother and sister-in-law, Kate ate her pudding quietly and tried to calm a heart that had beat unevenly ever since she learned the *Camille* was home at last.

He was here! He was really here, less than a mile away, instead of thousands distant! His absence had been a long and dreary time for Kate, although she had contin-

ued her usual life in spite of it. She had made calls with
her mother, gone walking and sailing with her friends,
attended church, and celebrated George's betrothal to
Cecily Lunne with every sign of delight. Only Kate knew
the envy she felt in her breast for their happiness. And
she had called on the Williamses often. It was not that she
felt that great a liking for Maryanne, with her constant
prattle of either England or her children, but it was there
she found she could remember Jack best. Sometimes she
even strolled along the beach where they had found the
ambergris, trying as hard as she could to recall every
word he had ever said to her.

She had also traveled to Charles Town with her mother,
just before Alicia Hathaway had had her baby early in
June, and spent a month there. Her mother had pro-
moted first one and then another young gentleman as
suitable husbands, but all of them fell far short in Kate's
estimation, to a tall raven-haired man with turquoise eyes
and a deep tan.

Kate had learned from her brother Matthew of the
Camille's call at Charles Town, and that she was currently in the Turks Islands after salt. Matthew also mentioned that the salt was intended for Boston, so Kate
knew she could not hope to see Jack for months yet. She
had set herself to a further spell of patience, telling
herself how good an exercise in discipline it was, even
though she could not help missing him more and more.

And the springtime passed, and the long hot summer,
and still he did not come back.

But he was home now. When Greg had mentioned that
Jack remained on board alone, it was all Kate could do
not to excuse herself from the table, rush from the house
and down the broad lawn, and row herself out to the
Camille then and there. Her lips curled in a secret smile
as she tried to imagine what Jack's reaction to such a
bold act would be!

She was recalled to present company when her mother
asked Greg his future plans.

"I imagine we'll stay in Bermuda for a space," Greg
said. "The *Camille* has to be careened, have her bottom
scrubbed. Then too, Jack plans to build another sloop,
her sister ship, and he wants to oversee at least the start

of her building. And I'm to be the new captain, just as I had hoped."

"How grand!" Kate exclaimed. "And how grand that you will remain here for such a period. We have missed you so!"

It was then that Olivia Hathaway had the wonderful idea that they must have a party to properly welcome their sailor home. As the talk swirled around Kate about the guests they would ask, the food and drink and music to be provided, she tried to control the joy she felt. For surely Jack must come to such an affair, and then she could see him at last. And since the *Camille* was unloading here in St. George Town, she might even see him as soon as tomorrow.

A shutter banged just then in a gust of wind, and Roger Hathaway got up to pull it down and latch it. "Weather's changing," he said to his son as he took his seat again.

"Aye, there'll be a handsome gale before morning, I think. We were all glad to make port before it struck," Greg replied. "Not that the *Camille* has not weathered some mighty blows since we left here. There was a storm off New York, Father, that sorely tried us. Why, the wind . . ."

Kate's mind wandered again. Should she wear her primrose gown tomorrow? she wondered. Or perhaps the blue? It was the one she had worn to the launching, and she knew how it became her.

Much later, she left the house and wandered down the lawn to the harbor. The wind had risen, and there wasn't a star to be seen among the thick, scudding clouds. When she reached the water's edge, she could tell by the unusual height of the tide that this would be a mighty storm. It wouldn't matter what she wore tomorrow, for she would be confined to the house. And the *Camille* could not be unloaded.

Her eyes searched the harbor till she saw where the sloop was anchored. There was a light in the stern cabin, and she clasped her hands tightly together. Was Jack lying in his hammock reading? she wondered. Or was he perhaps adding up the profits from his journey or drawing plans for his new boat?

She was still there leaning against the trunk of a cedar

tree to shelter from the wind when the twins came home.
For after supper Greg had walked over to the Lunnes' to
fetch his brother, and as all the Hathaways had expected,
he had stayed to regale that family with the same tales of
his adventures as he had just told them.

Kate would have stepped out of the shadows to join
them, but Greg's words, borne to her clearly on the
freshening wind, held her motionless.

"Aye, there were some fine women on Statia, twin,
but not a one to compare to Jack's widow! He has the
devil's own luck with women! I suspect 'tis that handsome face of his, his distant, mysterious air that attracts
'em. Whatever, this Dutchwoman was putty in his hands.
He spent every moment he could with her, for five long
days—and nights."

"What did she look like?" George asked, curious.

"She was tall, a bit older than Jack, and built like a
goddess," Greg told him, his voice awed. "And she was a
fair blond with skin like milk, and blue eyes the color of
deep water. To be sure, a most handsome woman. I only
saw her once, you understand. She was not often seen in
town, nor was Jack. One does not have to wonder why.
I'm sure I wouldn't have come there at all if I'd been
lucky enough to be asked to share her bed. 'Swounds!"

He chuckled then, and George echoed that chuckle a
moment later. Shrinking back in the shadows, Kate felt a
terrible foreboding. Had Jack fallen in love? Was he
planning to return to Statia to marry this woman? She
could not bear it!

She waited until her brothers went into the house, and
then, to avoid the family, she made her way around to
the back, to enter through the dining-room door. Keza
was still there wiping the gleaming table, but when she
saw Kate's face, she dropped her cloth to hurry to her
side.

"Miz Kate! Y'all done seen a ghost, girl?" she asked,
her hands warm on Kate's chilled arms.

Kate bent and kissed her, and gave her a quick hug.
"No, indeed, Keza," she made herself say. "I must have
eaten too much of your wonderful dinner, for I feel a
little queasy. I think I'll go right up to bed. Please tell my
mother, and beg her to excuse me."

With a frown on her broad black face, Keza watched

as Kate went to the stairs. There was a slump to the girl's shoulders now, and there had been a lost look in her eyes that upset the slave. Keza had taken up the baby Kate the moment she had been born, cut the cord, washed her, and wrapped her in a blanket. From that time, Kate had been as much her daughter as she ever had been Olivia Hathaway's. And whatever it was that was upsetting her baby, upset Keza as well.

She gave her mistress Kate's message before she went back to the kitchen house to sit before the dying fire and think. Her sons, Hiram and Tully, were playing at dice at the rough table, while their father looked on, but Keza brooded into the coals and thought her own thoughts.

Upstairs, Kate fastened the shutters over her windows securely before she lit another candle. The wind was beginning to howl now, and little gusts came through the barely open windows to stir the curtains and rustle the bed hangings. It was warm and muggy, and the air smelled of sulfur. Hurricane weather.

Slowly Kate undressed for bed. Before she put on her white bedgown, however, she went to stand naked before the pier glass. Her gray eyes were troubled as she regarded the tall, slender form reflected there.

Her mouth twisted in a grimace of despair as she did so. Not by any stretch of the imagination could she be considered a goddess! Her breasts were much too small, her waist too slim, her hips too boyish. And her legs were miles too long, and as thin as a new colt's. Turning a little, she observed her narrow back and neat bottom. Compared to that Dutch widow in Statia, she could see she had little to offer a man. Certainly not one who preferred women who were lushly ripe.

Miserable now, Kate pulled the bedgown over her head in a hurry, so she would not have to see her inadequacies anymore. Then she went to the basin to wash her hot face in cool water.

But as she climbed into bed and adjusted her pillows, Kate thought of something, and felt a little better. For after all, she reminded herself, Jack had not married that woman in Statia. No, he had left her there, and he hadn't returned to the island again. Surely if he were as mad for her as Greg had claimed, he would have found some way to do so before now. Wouldn't he?

Reassured by this thought, Kate closed her eyes, said a prayer of thanksgiving for Jack's safe return as a bachelor, and fell fast asleep.

The storm veered off to the east during the night, and the islands escaped the main force of the gale. Still, it was a nasty, windy, rain-streaked dawn that greeted Kate when she opened her eyes at last. She lay in bed, a little smile curling her lips as she tried to picture Jack in his hammock. Was he now opening his eyes too? Was he yawning and stretching before he threw his legs over the side and rose to brush the black hair back from his face? Or did he hear the drumming of the rain on the deck over his head and turn over for another nap?

It was two long days before the rain abated. Kate knew she should be delighted, for now everyone's water tank was brimming again with clean, fresh water. But all she could feel was impatience. Indeed, it was hard for her to sit still, or settle to anything, and finally her mother spoke to her sharply.

"Do cease that pacing, Kate!" she said with a frown on her face. "If you go to the window one more time to peer out, I swear I shall scream! Sit down and finish that petticoat for baby that you were working on, and stop being so restless!"

Kate begged her pardon and took up her sewing again. She tried to interest herself in her mother's chatter about little Rosemary, and how dear she would look in the dainty gown her grandmother was smocking for her in palest pink embroidery thread.

Kate was out early when the sun finally shone again, and as she strolled along Water Street to King's Square, dressed in a new green gown and a snowy white fichu, she breathed deeply of the clear air. It was often like this after a storm, as if the rain had cleansed everything so the world showed its brightest, freshest face. The morning glories falling over a stone wall were a riot of color, and the scent of the oleanders and hibiscus was piercing sweet. The grass was so emerald it hurt the eye, and to her right the water of the harbor glistened as well, each little wave sporting a cap of white lace. Over all, the soft blue of the sky smiled a benign benediction. It was hard to believe there were such things as gales on such a baby-fresh day.

Kate paused to speak to Mrs. Tucker and Mrs. Kempthorne, both ladies out to assess the storm's damage to their gardens. In the square, Kate's eyes went immediately to the *Camille*, anchored some one hundred yards out in the harbor. She ignored the other pedestrians and the shrill cries of some small boys who were taunting Wilcox Hinson, in the stocks again for public drunkenness. Hinson was there so often, he was almost a permanent feature of the square, and no one but the children paid him much attention anymore.

Making her way to the Customs House, Kate kept a keen lookout for that tall, distinctive figure she sought. But Jack Reade was nowhere to be seen, not ashore, nor on the *Camille*'s deck. And careful questioning of the Bartons' slave Tom, who had been one of Jack's crew, only elicited the information that the captain had gone ashore earlier and had not said when he would return. Tom told her he himself had come down to see the fun, for Frank Norwood's wife was to be put on the ducking stool later, her punishment for being a scold.

Kate thanked him gravely for the information, but declined to remain for the treat. She did not like the pillory or the stocks, but she hated the ducking stool. For even though the harbor water was still warm from the summer, any woman's public humiliation was painful to watch. As she walked away, she wondered why Priscilla Norwood did not mind her tongue. This would be the second time this year she would be ducked.

Since there was no point in remaining in the square, and not wanting to call attention to herself loitering there, Kate walked up the hill to Broad Alley to visit Granny Bessie. She had missed her embroidery lesson yesterday because of the rain. And she decided she would see how the old lady was doing, and congratulate her on the return of her Samuel.

Samuel himself opened the door to her knock, a white smile creasing his black face. "Come in, come in, Mistress Kate," he said with a little bow. "Miz Simpson be glad to see you, 'deed she will!"

Kate smiled at him and entered the neat little parlor. And then her breath stopped in her throat, and her heart began to pound. She barely remembered to curtsy to the widow before she turned again to Captain John Reade.

"Why, Captain, what a surprise! Welcome home, sir
. . . welcome home!" she cried, extending both her hands
and giving him her best smile.

Jack was forced to take those hands, and once again
that encompassing smile demanded a return one of his
own. He even smiled more broadly when he spied the
little golden freckles on her nose, though he knew he
should not encourage the girl. Her delight in their meeting was too heartfelt, and the way her gray eyes were
shining with her joy, too blatant.

Squeezing her hands only a little, he released them and
stepped back. "Thank you, Mistress Kate. It is good to
be back," he said.

"I understand your voyage was most successful, sir,"
she persisted. "La, Greg has not stopped speaking of it
yet!"

Jack nodded, but before he could answer, she hurried
on, "My parents are planning a festive evening to celebrate. Of course we shall expect you to join us."

He nodded again, but she noted he did not say that he
would come. Before she could say anything to ensure his
acceptance, he turned to their hostess.

"I shall not take up any more of your time, Mrs.
Simpson. Thank you for allowing me to hire Samuel to
watch the *Camille* while we are in port. It will relieve my
mind to have him there when I cannot be, and it is good
of you to spare him to me."

Mrs. Simpson smiled and nodded. When Captain Reade
had appeared to beg her for Samuel's hire, she had been
delighted to comply, for the money he was to pay would
add to her newfound prosperity. She did not know that
Jack had purposely suggested the scheme for just that
reason.

He bowed then and said, "Give you good-day, ladies."

Kate wondered how she could possibly delay him, or
leave with him, even though she knew there was no way
she could accomplish this without slighting her elderly
friend. Why, she had just arrived! Such rudeness would
not go unremarked.

To her relief, Mrs. Simpson refused to hear of it. "No,
no, you must not be so precipitate, sir!" she scolded.
"Please stay and have a cup of punch with us, and some
of my special cherry scones, new-baked this morning. I

know you sailing men! Don't eat proper, not a one of you! You shall let me fatten you up a bit, if you please. And it would be a kindness to me if you remained. I seldom have company, and I want to celebrate your safe return, as well as Samuel's. Samuel, pour us all some punch, and fetch the scones. We shall have a party!''

Defeated in the face of such hospitality, Jack took his seat again. Immediately the little parlor seemed both bigger and brighter, and Kate sat down where she could watch his face without being too obvious about it.

The four of them spent a merry half-hour. Mrs. Simpson had a number of questions to ask about the voyage, and since she had once sailed to Statia with her husband, was able to discuss that island knowledgeably. A certain handsome blond widow was not mentioned, however, nor had Kate expected her to be.

Samuel told them about the race with the cutter when they left Statia, and how Jack had tarried at the harbor's mouth to give the French a sporting chance of catching the *Camille*. Kate thought such a move irresponsible and dangerous, but she could see both Jack and the slave considered it a wonderful joke.

When Jack rose at last, she was quick to join him, for now it was perfectly permissible for her to take her leave as well. And when they had said their good-byes and were out in Broad Alley again, Jack was forced to offer her his arm for the walk back to the harbor.

He fell silent as they strolled along, and a peek at his face showed Kate he had retreated into moodiness again. She wondered why, and what she could possibly do to regain his attention. But the harsh lines of his face, his tight-set lips and cold eyes, caused her to fall silent as well.

Jack was not thinking of her. Mrs. Simpson—Granny Bessie—had reminded him in so many ways of his dear godmother, dead these many years. Lady Virginia had been like her in her concern for him, her graying blond hair, and the merry twinkle in her eyes. He realized then how much he missed Lady Virginia still.

And how much he missed Hythe. For some reason it had become precious to him in a way it had never been before. Was it because he had lost it now, forever? Could never go back to it?

And then there was his mother, and Alex as well. Thinking of them brought an even deeper ache to his heart. He hoped they were well, and his little sisters too. Why, Constance was eight now, and darling Grace five. He wondered if she had stopped sucking her thumb.

For a moment a longing for England swept over him, and he almost groaned. Would he never be able to forget? Would he never stop regretting what had happened to isolate him from everyone and everything he loved, held dear? Would he never come to accept his new place in the world, be able to go forward without these painful backward glances?

He was recalled from his memories when his companion suddenly stopped walking. He looked around, bemused, to see that they had reached King's Square again. Before he could say anything, Kate released his arm and curtsied to him.

"I beg you to excuse me, sir," she said with quiet dignity. "I must return home now, and our ways lie in different directions."

As he bowed, Jack apologized. "I beg pardon for my abstraction, mistress. Seeing Mrs. Simpson brought back memories of someone I once loved very much. I fear I have not been good company for you."

The little hurt look in her eyes disappeared in a flash. "Do not regard it, sir," she said. "I understand."

She smiled at him and turned away. Jack watched her for a moment as she made her way past the crowd that had assembled to see Mrs. Norwood's punishment. As Jack strode back to the wharf, he ignored their excited chatter and laughter, for he didn't like the ducking stool any better than Kate did.

10

THE preparations for the Hathaway party kept Kate very much at home in the next few days. She had to help her mother write the invitations, then deliver them, and she and Keza had to polish all the silver and see to the washing of the chandeliers in both the dining room and the parlor. Then the furniture had to be waxed, and some special baking done—a thousand things to ensure a successful evening.

On the afternoon of the day before the big event, Kate was finally able to escape for a few hours. She had begged Greg to go sailing with her, and when he saw the brisk breeze ruffling the harbor waters, he had agreed.

After they left the mooring, their course took them near the *Camille*. Kate's heart leapt when she saw Jack leaning on the rail high above them, watching them. She knew his sloop had been unloaded earlier and that Jack only remained in St. George Town until the evening of the party. Then he would sail the *Camille* to the boatyard near Tucker's Town, and she would have little chance to see him. How glad she was Greg had persuaded him to attend the party, overriden all his protests!

She waved, and Jack waved back. Suddenly Greg brought the *Sea Sprite* up to the side of the bigger boat and called, "Can we lure you out for a sail, Captain? I realize the *Sprite* is nothing like your lovely lady, but she's yare enough in this fresh breeze."

Silently Kate prayed Jack would accept, and when she saw something like denial in his eyes, she added, "Yes, do say you will come, sir! We could use the ballast!"

Greg laughed uproariously, and Jack grinned. But still he hesitated, until Samuel Simpson came to stand beside him.

"Why not go, suh?" he asked. " 'Tis a good day for a sail, and Ah'll stand watch heah."

Jack threw up his hands in defeat, and a moment later

he was climbing down a rope to the *Sprite*'s deck. Kate scrunched over to make room for him, so happy she was sure she must die from it.

"Ballast, is it, Mistress Kate?" Jack growled in mock anger. "And how am I to take that, I wonder? Should I stop eating for a while, or only forgo Granny Bessie's scones from now on?"

Kate did not even look at his trim waist and flat stomach. She did not dare. "Well, you do weigh more than I do," she pointed out.

Jack gave her a lazy smile, and she relaxed.

The breeze freshened once they left the shelter of the harbor. Jack watched, a little bemused, as Kate eyed the set of the sails and made a small adjustment to the sheets. Her chestnut curls were tied back with a ribbon, and she was wearing a faded calico skirt and cotton jacket. He noticed she had discarded her shoes and hose, as had her brother. At ease now, and feeling somewhat carefree, Jack rolled up the sleeves of his cambric shirt and took off his own shoes and stockings.

Suddenly Kate grasped Greg's arm, before she pointed ahead to port. "Oh, Greg, look! Isn't that a turtle in the net out there that I see?"

Jack followed her gaze, and his eyes widened. Some distance away, a small schooner appeared in distress, the collar of white water around her indicating the reef she had somehow stumbled on.

"Lord, and in broad daylight, with not even a storm as excuse," Greg muttered. "Was there no one on watch?"

"Dammit!" Kate exclaimed, causing Jack's eyebrows to rise. Neither she nor her brother noticed. "There's Aaron Evans and his crew ahead of us! And isn't that the Bartons' boat as well?"

"You're right, old lady," Greg told her. "Shall we race them for it?"

Kate nodded, her eyes blazing with excitement. "I'll take the helm—Greg, you tighten sail. And, Jack, move to leeward if you please."

"It will be sloppy," Greg warned, sliding around her to the main and jib sheets. "You're sure to get wet!"

"What of it?" Kate demanded, busy bringing the *Sprite* closer to the wind. The boat heeled over, and, startled, Jack stared down at the water racing so close to the coaming he was leaning on. He wanted to warn her against the loss of speed when the rail was under, but before he could speak, she had made the necessary adjustment to the helm.

A wave hit the bow then and sprayed them, and Kate laughed. Jack thought he had never heard anyone laugh with so much gusto and simple pleasure.

"Aaron's gaining ground on us, Kate," Greg warned her.

Leaning forward in her eagerness to speed the *Sprite*, Kate stared ahead at the rowing boat filled with straining men.

As Jack wiped his streaming face, he asked, "Why did you call the schooner a turtle in the net?"

"Any boat caught on the reefs is considered such," Kate told him absently. "Either that or a lame duck. Those rowing boats you see are racing each other—and us—for salvage rights. First to get there wins all."

"Oh," Jack remarked mildly. "And here I thought we were merely going to help them, perhaps even save lives."

"Never fear, Jack, we'll do that as well," Greg told him, never taking his eyes from the edge of the mainsail. "Watch it, Kate, she's beginning to luff!"

"I know, I know! I was trying to point too high," his sister admitted. "What I wouldn't give for the *Camille*'s bow right now, Jack!"

"Do you think we're gaining on them?" she asked next.

"Coming up nicely," Greg assured her. "There's a reef to starboard, Kate, and beyond that, one to port."

"I see them. We'll split them. Get ready to lift the fin keel if it scrapes, Greg."

"Somehow I feel I have fallen in with dangerous company today," Jack murmured. "And to think how aghast you looked at Granny Bessie's the other day when Samuel told you about racing the French cutter!"

Kate spared him a tight smile, but he saw she was completely absorbed in the job at hand. He settled back on the bench, lending his considerable "ballast" to the trim of the boat. He realized that Kate Hathaway was a superb sailor. Like the best of them, she seemed to become one with her boat, able to sense instinctively what would give the *Sprite* the fastest speed. She was

quick to ease the helm or hold it firm to take advantage
of any extra gust of wind. He wondered how she would
do on an uncertain day, full of puffs and calms, and
wished he might see her at it.

Suddenly he turned to Greg. "But why did you let
Kate take over, my friend, when you were sailing before?"

Greg stopped watching the sails for a moment to stare
at him in amazement. "Why, because the *Sea Sprite* is
Kate's boat to command. She's captain here, and has
been for years."

Jack looked back up at their "captain," high on the
weather side. She had braced her bare feet against the
opposite bench, and her soaked jacket and skirt clung to
her slender form. One chestnut curl had escaped from
the ribbon, and he saw her blow from one corner of her
mouth, to get it out of her way. For a moment Jack's
mind went to a London ballroom, crowded with the *beau
monde*, all posturing and simpering in their finery, and
he laughed to himself. No wonder Mistress Kate had
found them a trifle insipid!

They reached the distressed schooner at almost the
same moment one of the rowing boats did. As Kate
brought the *Sprite* up into the wind, a man in the stern of
the other boat grabbed an oar to push the sloop away.

"Stand clear there, Kate Hathaway!" he bellowed. "We
were here first!"

"What a chivalrous beau you have, sister," Greg
muttered.

Kate ignored him, to rise in the sloop and shake her
fist at the other boat. "That's a moot point, Aaron, and
you know it!"

"You haven't the hands to salvage—I do!" he yelled.
"Stand away, there!"

Kate looked so furious that Jack felt she was about to
dive overboard, swim to the rowing boat, and do murder
with her bare hands. He almost reached out to grab her
skirt to prevent her from such a dangerous course.

"He's right, you know, Kate," her brother reminded
her. "We don't have the hands. And what could Jack and
I do alone?"

Kate shrugged as she took her seat again. Her gray
eyes were still stormy as she watched Aaron's crew swarm-
ing over the helpless schooner. Some of her crew had

gathered at the rail now, begging them to save them, although Jack did not think the ship in any imminent danger of sinking. But then, he reminded himself, he did not know how much water she was taking on, or the condition of her bilges.

The second rowing boat had arrived by now, its men slumping over their oars and looking disgusted that they had lost the prize. Still, instead of taking the crew off and heading back to St. George Town, they continued to hold their place. Jack shuddered a little. The scene reminded him of vultures he had once seen circling high above a dying calf in a meadow.

Kate's head came up as a baby's cries rose faintly over all the other noise. A moment later a heavyset bearded man appeared at the rail, a small bundle in his arms.

"For the love of God, save my wife and baby son!" he cried. "Please, I beg you!"

Kate signaled to Greg, and he hurried up on the *Sprite*'s foredeck to grasp a dangling line and hold the sloop steady against the holed schooner's side.

"Thank you, thank you!" the bearded man said. "Here!"

Jack had risen now, and being taller than Kate, held up his arms. He looked more than a little startled to be taking the squirming, screaming bundle he was handed, and in any other circumstances, Kate would have had to giggle.

But when he turned and thrust the baby hastily into her arms, she did not feel like laughing. Instead, she sat down carefully, cradling the baby's head instinctively.

"Where is your wife, Captain?" Greg demanded. "Tell her we can take her as well."

"She's unconscious," the captain said. "I'll get her!"

He disappeared from sight. Already the first crates and kegs were being loaded into Aaron Evans' boat, his crew forming a line to pass them up from the hold. They were laughing and joking as they did so, and to Jack they seemed a strange contrast to the frightened, depressed crew of the schooner.

The captain appeared again with a woman in his arms. She was bleeding from a long gash on her forehead, and she was so pale and still that Kate gasped, thinking she was surely dead.

It was an awkward business lowering her into the sloop,

and Jack was perspiring when he had her safely stretched out on the port bench. Quickly he sat down to take her in his arms and support her.

Kate saw the worried face of the captain peering down at them, and she said, "Don't worry, sir! We'll see them safe to St. George Town, and in a doctor's care. Er, does the baby have any other clothes? He is very . . . damp."

The man disappeared again, returning in a few moments with a blanket and a small satchel. "God bless you, mistress, and all my thanks," he said as he handed them down. "Take good care of them!"

"You intend to stay with your ship, sir?" Greg asked. At the man's grim nod, he gave him a smile of encouragement. "She seems all right and tight for the moment. I don't expect she'll founder now, since she hasn't already. Our name is Hathaway. When you get to St. George Town, just ask anyone to direct you to our house. We'll keep your wife and baby safe there."

He let go the line then and pushed the *Sprite* clear before he scrambled to the stern.

"Move aside, there, Kate. I'll sail now, since you have your hands full," he told his sister.

"I'd rather sail and *you* have your hands full," Kate muttered. As the baby continued his relentless howling, she tried jiggling him up and down in her arms, but since that only seemed to raise the intensity of his wails, she subsided.

"Does she still breathe, Jack?" she asked, looking anxiously at the ashen woman stretched out on the bench across from her.

"Yes, but it is thready," he told her. "Have you anything to staunch the wound, bind it up perhaps?"

Kate looked down at her calico skirt before she remembered the satchel. Rummaging through it with one hand, she found a clean cloth and handed it to him. "Can you reach that blanket, Greg?" she asked. "Perhaps the baby is cold, and if I wrap him more securely, he'll stop screaming."

But the baby did not stop; indeed, his howling seemed to be growing in intensity. Kate stared down into his ugly, distorted red face in despair, wondering how it was possible for anything so wee to make so much noise.

"Come now, Kate, can't you do something to stop that infernal racket?" Greg demanded, sounding impatient.

"What?" Kate demanded. "I don't know anything about babies! Do *you* know how to make them stop?"

"I believe I have heard they cry when they are hungry or wet," Jack volunteered from where he sat across from her, holding the cloth tightly to the mother's head.

Kate looked up, furious at the hint of laughter she was sure she heard in his voice. Then the whole ridiculous situation made her begin to laugh helplessly. As soon as she got her breath again, she said, "Obviously *I* can't feed him, and as for changing him, his mother is using what appears to be his last dry diaper. But perhaps, since you know so much about them, you'd have better luck, Jack? Yes, do let's try it! I'll hold his mother safely while you mind the baby."

As she had known he would, Jack was quick to object to this plan, saying that if she had little experience with infants, he had none at all. He would probably drop the child, or lose him overboard.

They all began to chuckle then, but when the wounded woman groaned, Jack was quick to turn his attention to her. "Yes, shh, shh," he said in a gentle voice. "It is all right now. We have you safe, and your baby too."

The woman subsided in his arms, a little smile on her pale lips, and a few moments later the baby fell asleep. Kate was sure it must be from exhaustion, and she did nothing to disturb the blessed quiet. Instead, with some relief she watched the harbor coming closer and closer.

Her brother chuckled suddenly. "I was just thinking of the party tomorrow night. Is it safe to say Aaron Evans will have a time of it claiming a dance with you, Kate?"

"Huh! He'll not get any!" his sister told him. "You know we reached that schooner together, and so does he! And if the cargo is valuable, I'll be furious!"

"I must admit I was surprised he treated *you* so rudely," Greg went on.

"But why wouldn't he?" Jack asked. "It was obvious how keen he was to claim the salvage. Or did you mean because Kate is a woman?"

"Aaron's been hot for my sister for years—always trying to persuade her to wed him," Greg explained. "But I imagine he'll have to start courting elsewhere after this day's doing."

"He had better," Kate said darkly. "Pirate! Lying opportunist! I'd rather marry a lizard!"

They had reached the harbor now, and Greg had to bring the *Sprite* to her new course. For a moment, everyone had his hands full, until the boat settled down in the sheltered water and they could relax a bit.

"I'd better go right to the Customs House dock," Greg told them. "Dr. Webb lives very near the square."

As they approached the dock, Kate could see it was crowded with people, all come to see what salvage had been taken, and to help any of the survivors. Willing hands helped them tie up, and lifted the unconscious woman from the sloop. Kate was delighted to hand the baby ashore as well. He had woken and was crying again, and her lap was sopping, and not entirely from seawater either.

Greg explained to everyone what had happened, and a boy was sent running to warn the doctor. Then Mrs. Simpson pushed forward.

"Mistress Kate," she called, "I'll take the baby to my house, and after the doctor sees to her, I'll care for that poor woman as well. I have a spare room, and I'm glad to help the shipwrecked."

Kate smiled and thanked her, for she had wondered what her mother would say if she were to show up with this noisy, most unattractive infant in her arms the day before the party. Besides, with the Williamses planning to stay overnight tomorrow, there wouldn't be a spare bed in the house. As it was, George and Greg were to sleep aboard the *Camille* tomorrow night.

"Let's hope Granny Bessie has a goodly supply of cloth, Kate," Jack murmured as he pushed off.

The three of them laughed together, feeling a real sense of camaraderie now that their adventure was successfully concluded. Before he climbed to the *Camille*'s deck, Jack thanked the Hathaways gravely, in his most formal manner, for a delightful afternoon's sail.

His matter-of-fact statement set them all to laughing wildly again, and Kate was still chuckling as she and Greg left for their own mooring.

Jack stayed on deck and watched them go, a broad smile on his face. He suddenly realized that today was the first time he had laughed heartily in a very long time.

And then that smile faded, as he also realized that some-time this afternoon—exactly when, he could not tell—he and the chestnut-haired girl waving good-bye to him now had become "Kate" and "Jack" to each other. And that would not do. No, not at all.

Kate wore her primrose silk gown to the party. It was much too elaborate for Bermuda, but it was the prettiest one she owned, and she had worn it in London the evening Jack had asked her to dance with him. Perhaps he would remember.

While dressing, she had experimented stuffing hand-kerchiefs in the bodice of the gown to make her more shapely, but she had given up in disgust when she discov-ered they had a tendency to slip, and no matter what care she took, could not be made to match each other. Better too little than lopsided, she told herself with a grin as she threaded a primrose ribbon through her curls.

Jack had completely forgotten the gown, although when he greeted her later, receiving guests with her parents, he told her how very pretty she looked. Kate smiled at him, but she was a little confused, for his compliment had been de-livered coolly, and he had not lingered, going away almost immediately afterward to greet Farley Williams and his wife.

As the party wore on, it seemed to Kate that he was determined to remain either with the twins or with other young men. She wondered what had happened to change him so from the gay, teasing companion she had been sailing with yesterday. And he looked so outstanding this evening, too!

Dressed in a long-tailed coat of navy brocade, he wore dazzling white linen and smallclothes, and his black pumps were adorned with shiny silver buckles. Lace peeped from beneath his cuffed sleeves and foamed at his throat, and he had powdered his black hair in honor of the occasion, and tied it back neatly with a blue velvet rib-bon. With his dark tan and brilliant turquoise eyes, he was, to Kate, purely and simply breathtaking.

When the fiddlers struck up the first dance, Kate looked around. Greg was smiling as he came toward her, and she forced herself to smile in response, even as she saw the back of a navy brocade coat disappearing into the dining room.

Everyone mentioned what a wonderful party it was, and they did seem to be enjoying themselves, either dancing or talking and laughing together, strolling the broad lawn for a breath of air, drinking Roger Hathaway's potent punch, or devouring all the delicacies Keza had made. Indeed, everyone was having a marvelous time except the daughter of the house. She was hurt—hurt and bewildered. Whatever was the matter with Jack? Why did he treat her so? And surely it was most impolite not to honor his host's daughter with a dance or a few minutes of conversation about the adventure they had shared? She wondered if he knew the captain's wife and baby were going to be all right, and that all hands had been saved, and the schooner as well?

And it didn't make any difference that Jack was ignoring all the other young ladies present, in spite of the many languishing looks he received. Kate thought Anne Chamberlain's smiles for him very obvious, and as for Mercy Barton and her deliberate maneuvering so as to be in his vicinity every chance she got, well, she was disgraceful! But still, the only ladies Jack asked to dance were his hostess, old Mrs. Tucker, and Maryanne Williams.

True to her word, Kate had refused to dance with Aaron Evans. The young man had looked a little wary when he suggested it, and, as Greg whispered to her later, more like a puppy who has disgraced himself on the best carpet than the victor in a struggle.

"But, Mistress Kate," Aaron had said when she refused his company, "you know that salvaging is a competition! And anyway, I don't know what your brother was thinking about, to bring you out there in the first place. Not at all suitable for a lady!"

Kate merely sniffed and turned away.

As she left him, her head held high, she heard him add from behind her in a disconsolate voice, "Besides, it was mostly just lumber. Nothing of real value at all!"

Kate had looked around then, surprising a little smile on Jack Reade's handsome face, and she had smiled in return, knowing he had overheard and was enjoying the joke. But still he did not ask her to dance or seek her company for a chat.

Later, Kate went outside, fanning herself as she did so. The house was growing warm from the press of people and the many candles, and she felt she had to be alone. She had been very busy, after all, fetching shawls, plates, and cups of punch. And she had had to help Mrs. Barton find her misplaced handkerchief, and spend a lot of time with Maryanne Williams, who seemed to be suffering under a cloud of pique this evening. Kate wondered if she and her husband had quarreled about something, but of course she could not ask. Escaping Maryanne at last, she wandered down to the harborside.

It was just the same as always, with the usual boats at anchor. Kate checked the *Sprite*'s safety first, and then her gaze went further, to where the *Camille* was anchored. There was a light on her deck. Old Samuel, no doubt, keeping watch while Jack was at the party. But Jack and the *Camille* would be gone tomorrow, back to Tucker's Town.

Greg had told her that he would be moving to Tucker's Town as well, to live with Jack while the new sloop was being built. She knew having her brother there would give her more excuses to visit, but even that happy thought could not raise her spirits now. She felt so leaden, so miserable! Perhaps Jack's behavior this evening was his way of telling her he was not interested in her or ever would be. If so, all her dreams would come to nothing.

For Kate was a realist. She knew that if Jack didn't want her, there was nothing she could do about it. And even if she tricked him into marrying her, she would be settling for a great deal less than she wanted. No, better not to marry him at all, in that case.

She was still there staring out at the harbor when she heard a step behind her. Turning, she saw Aaron Evans approaching, and she stiffened.

"Please, Kate, I must talk to you!" he said, coming closer and putting his hand on her arm.

She twitched it away impatiently. Aaron was not a bad-looking suitor, and in the past she had enjoyed his company. He was of medium height with sandy hair and dark brown eyes, and she knew he had loved her from childhood. In fact, his devotion had often pleased her in the past. But now, of course, everything was different.

He grasped her arm again and turned her toward him. "Stop that at once!" he ordered, reminding her of the way he had spoken to her yesterday. "You will listen, do you hear me?"

"I imagine most of the guests at the party can hear you," she said coldly. "Very well, say what you have to, and then let me go."

"Kate, Kate," he moaned, but more softly now. "You know how I love you, and yet you would ruin everything, all because of a stupid salvage job! Please, darling, say you forgive me! I . . . I know I spoke to you harshly yesterday—the heat of the moment, you see—but it did not mean that I did not love you still. No, that was business, business you should never have been involved in. But the way we feel for each other is different. And you do love me—yes, yes, I know you do! It is only because your pride is hurt that you treat me so now. But someday soon, we'll be wed. Don't you see that the more money I can save, the more salvage I can take, will only speed that happy day? That's why I was out there, for *our* future!"

"I have never given you any reason to suppose we had one," Kate snapped. "You take too much on yourself, sir!"

"What nonsense is this?" Aaron demanded roughly. "Of course you will marry me! I have been waiting for you all my life!"

The anguish in his voice stirred Kate's sympathy suddenly. Yes, Aaron did love her. And no one understood better than she what he was feeling now, for didn't she feel the same helplessness in her love for Jack Reade?

She took his hand and squeezed it. "Aaron, I am sorry, indeed I am. And it has nothing to do with yesterday. But I have come to see that I don't love you, not that way, and I never will. I would not hurt you if I could avoid it, but I fear it is only right to tell you now, lest you continue to plan a future that can never be."

He stared down at her, bending closer to search her face in the dim light. "No," he said. "I don't believe you. I won't."

Before Kate knew what he was about, he had pulled her into his arms and was kissing her cheeks, her eyelids, her lips. His strong hands held her captive, and she could do nothing to escape him. His mouth was warm and passionate on hers, and it should have been thrilling, but Kate felt nothing but despair. She knew there was nothing Aaron could do to wring a response from her, and her pain for his disappointment made her weep.

As the hot tears coursed down her face, they touched his as well, and he lifted his head at once.

"What is it, Kate?" he whispered. "Why do you cry, love?"

"Because I don't want to hurt you, and yet I must," she told him, groping for her handkerchief. "Aaron, believe me. I do not love you. Oh, I am so very, very sorry! I wish I could!"

She buried her face in her handkerchief and wept, and he inhaled sharply. There was silence for a long moment, broken only by Kate's little sobs.

"I see," he said slowly in a completely different tone of voice. "Here, then, Kate, dry your eyes. I see I must accept what you have told me. I must, no matter how I wish to dispute it. Yes, it does pain me, for I have loved you dearly for a long time. But know that I love you enough to do nothing that might give *you* pain. And I cannot bear to see you cry!"

Kate made a valiant effort to stem her tears, and when he saw she was more composed, he bowed to her. "I shall take leave of you now. Kindly give my excuses to your mother and father, and thank them for their hospitality. I find I am not in the mood for further festivity."

She watched him stride across the lawn and around the house to the lane. And she shook her head a little, even as she straightened the gown that he had disarranged in his passion.

A small sound nearby caused her to whirl suddenly. "Who is it? Who is there?" she demanded.

Jack Reade stepped out of the shadows of the oleander hedge. "I had hoped to escape without your seeing me, mistress," he told her as he came to her side. "Believe me, I would not have listened to such a private conversation for the world, but I was trapped there in the shadows and could not call attention to myself without embarrassing you and your young man."

"I know you would never have done so, sir," Kate told him in a broken little voice.

"May I commend you, however, for the way you handled the situation?" Jack asked. His voice was suddenly colder, more remote. "Some girls, in refusing a man's love, are nowhere near as kind, or considerate of his feelings."

Kate sensed he was remembering the Lady Arbel, and she said quickly, "I have always had a great fondness for Aaron. I think I always will. We played together as children. But what I felt was never more than fondness."

"Perhaps one day you will change your mind," Jack suggested, staring out at the harbor.

Kate took a deep breath as she studied what she could see of that strong profile. "No, Jack, I will not," she said.

She wanted so badly to tell him of her love for him then, that she had to turn away and clench her fists. As she did so, tears began to flow again, and she could not restrain a tiny sob.

Jack stepped closer, to raise her chin with one finger. "Here, now, what's this?" he asked, his voice concerned. "But there is no need to weep so, Kate. The young man will recover someday and learn to love another. Believe me, I know."

Kate shook her head, and when he saw how useless her damp little handkerchief was, he reached into his pocket to get his own. He mopped her face carefully, but his care only made her weep harder.

"I'm sorry. I never meant to . . . indeed, I cannot understand why I . . . Oh, *dammit*!"

Her exasperated wail for her incoherence and weakness made Jack smile. Without thinking, he took her in his arms to cradle her head against his chest and rock her to and fro, for all the world as if she were a small child, no older than Lady Grace. Kate's tears stopped abruptly, and after a moment she leaned back in his arms to stare up at him, wondering. Suddenly he began to frown, and his eyes grew cold. Kate reached up to smooth that frown away.

As her fingers touched him, Jack stiffened. Her gray eyes were steady on his, steady and true and honest, and he had no trouble reading the message they conveyed. He made a quick move to put her aside, even though he knew in his heart that what he really wanted to do was pull her closer still. She was so slender, yet shapely, and so very dear now that he held her in his arms.

Before he could step back as he knew he should, she

took his face between her hands and stood on tiptoe so she could kiss him. Her lips were soft on his, and tentative, and she was trembling at her daring. Her kiss was so sweet that Jack groaned, and, losing a struggle he did not want to win, he captured her in his arms. The light, fresh scent she wore was all around him, and as his lips grew more demanding, her eager response told him that she was just as affected by their embrace as he was.

It was a long time before he could bear to end their kiss. Yet when he opened his eyes and saw how hers were shining, the all-encompassing smile of joy she wore, he cursed himself for his folly.

"Forgive me, mistress," he made himself say. "That was unforgivable of me. I beg you to forget what just happened, put my lapse down to your loveliness, your spirit. I promise it will not happen again."

"Not happen again?" Kate echoed, looking confused now. "Why ever not? I quite long for you to kiss me! The sooner the better, in fact!"

She held out her hands to him, but he ignored them. "No," he said, his voice cold now, controlled. "There are reasons, very good reasons, why I will not."

"I don't understand," she whispered. Then she raised her chin, her eyes sparkling as she said, "I think you owe me an explanation, do you not?"

He turned away from her then and drew a deep breath. "Very well, you are right," he said, showing her only his profile. "But I cannot tell you all. Suffice it to say that I never intend to marry. I cannot, in good conscience, ask any woman to share my life. I knew that when I took you in my arms and kissed you, but I could not help myself. You are so sweet, Kate, so true and dear. And I am growing much too fond of you. I shall endeavor to stay away from you from now on, my word on it."

"But what if I do not want you to?" she asked, trying to keep her voice steady. I will not cry again! she told herself fiercely. "And what could possibly be this reason you speak of? You are a worthy man—why, you are Sir John Reade . . ."

Jack swung around to stare at her, and her words died in her throat when she saw how bleak he looked.

"No more, if you please," he said. "I cannot speak of it."

He bowed to her then. "Beg you to excuse me, mistress. Like Master Evans, I find I have lost my taste for any more festivity. Thank your parents for me, and tell Greg and George I await them on the *Camille*."

Speechless, Kate watched him stride away even as Aaron had. How ironic it was that both of them should take the same path, she thought. She noticed that somehow she had acquired Jack's handkerchief, and she put it to her face. It smelled faintly of the lotion he used, and it brought back all those wonderful sensations she had just felt, held close in his arms. She closed her eyes to remember them more clearly, and she was able to smile a little then. He had kissed her as if he loved her, wanted her. And he had told her she was sweet and lovely . . . spirited and true.

Kate shivered then, and she realized it was growing late and chilly. She had been out here too long; her mother would be wondering where she was. But as she hurried back toward the lighted house, she told herself that no matter what it was that was forcing Jack to avoid marriage, she would find a way to overcome it. Nothing, *nothing* could be that bad. And now that she knew from his words, his ardent kiss, that he was not indifferent to her as she had feared, she would convince him he was wrong if it was the last thing she ever did!

11

WHEN Kate came down to breakfast the next morning, she found her mother and father before her. She asked their pardon for her tardiness, blushing a little as she took her seat. The reason she had overslept was that she had not been able to fall asleep last night for hours. No, instead she had lain in bed and dreamed of Jack, reliving every moment they had spent together—how his arms had felt, his warm strong hands on her back, his wonderful mouth. And then she had tried to picture him in his hammock on the *Camille*. Was he wakeful too—was he thinking of her? she had wondered.

Now, as she peeled a banana and sliced it, her mother looked up from the letter she was reading. A brigantine from England had anchored in St. George Town harbor early this morning, and it had brought her a letter from her brother, Viscount Pelton. "Oh, my," Olivia Hathaway said softly. "Oh, dear."

"There is something wrong at home, Olivia?" her husband asked as he stirred his tea.

"No, not exactly, but . . . Oh, my," his wife replied.

Kate chuckled. "Out with it, Mama," she said. "Father and I cannot even begin to guess what is making you look so conscious, but the suspense is awesome."

"William writes me that Franklin Farnsworth intends to travel to Bermuda in the near future," Olivia Hathaway got out all in a rush. Then she peered at her daughter almost fearfully, as if concerned about her reaction to this startling news.

"Why would he want to do that?" Kate asked, not sounding very interested. "He knows I don't want to marry him, doesn't he? Mama, you didn't let him think I was *undecided* about it, did you? That I might change my mind?"

"Oh, no, of course not," Olivia Hathaway said quickly, trying to forget that she had not been as decisive as she should have been, in an effort to spare the young man's feelings.

"It does seem unusual that he would come, then," Roger Hathaway said mildly. "It is quite an arduous journey, and a long one. I wonder why he undertakes it."

Kate had been thinking, thinking hard. "Mama, did you write to my aunt and uncle to tell them about the ambergris? Did you?"

Her mother hung her head, seemingly intent on the pleats she was making in her napkin.

"Oh, Mama, how could you?" Kate demanded. "I have no doubt that Aunt Mary told Mr. Farnsworth, and now he is coming to try again, since my dowry has grown so substantial."

"I hardly think four thousand pounds *that* much an enticement, my dear. I understand from your mother that Mr. Farnsworth is a well-to-do man," her father pointed out.

"But he thinks it is eight thousand," his wife admitted in a little voice. "I . . . I never mentioned Sir John's share."

"Why ever not?" both her husband and her daughter demanded in unison.

"Why, because I knew Mary would be horrified, think me much too lax a mother to be letting Kate wander the beaches alone with a strange man. She never did approve of me! And you remember how she did not consider Sir John or his family quite respectable, Kate?"

"Aunt Mary is a stuffy old prude," Kate announced, her gray eyes darkening. "But now just see what you have done, Mama! In no time at all, we'll have Mr. Farnsworth here a-wooing, and I tell you again, I'd rather die a spinster than marry *him*!"

"Especially now you have proof he persists only for your new wealth," Roger Hathaway remarked. "I don't blame you in the slightest, daughter. In fact, I myself begin to feel quite an antipathy for the man, and I don't even know him. But never fear! We'll put him to the right-about in short order. And if he returns on the ship that brings him, he might not even have to acquire his land legs until he steps ashore in England again."

Kate laughed at the picture he painted, but her mother shook her head. "But perhaps you might like him better now, Kate," she suggested in an eager voice. "Such a good catch he is, and you're not getting any younger, you know. And after the way Aaron Evans tore off last evening—yes, it was much remarked, as was Sir John's abrupt departure as well—it appears you are bent on estranging every single male who crosses your path. Surely you *want* to marry someday, don't you?"

There was a little silence in the dining room then, and both elder Hathaways stared at their only daughter. Kate's eyes had grown dreamy, and a little smile played over her lips. Startled, Olivia Hathaway looked a question to her husband, but he only shook his head, warning her to be silent.

"Of course I do. Someday," Kate said at last. "When the right man appears, that is. But he is not Franklin Farnsworth!"

Keza came in then with a plate of muffins, and nothing more was said. Still, as she finished both her letter and her breakfast, Olivia Hathaway wondered if that right man had not already appeared. She had been watching her daughter closely these past days, and she suspected that Kate thought herself enamored of Sir John Reade. It was true he was a handsome young man, and titled as well, but still, Olivia Hathaway could not like him. There was something about him. She had pondered long on his inexplicable arrival here. Why had he come? Why wasn't he at home seeing to his estate? She felt deep in her bones that something had forced him to emigrate, and it was something dire. Besides, there was Mary's assessment of his family. They were not quite "nice" with their hasty marriages, their wanton destruction of a noble seat. Why, that bordered on madness, something she did not want to touch her darling daughter.

Completely unaware of her mother's reservations about the man she was determined to have, Kate asked if the *Camille* had sailed.

"Yes, she left just after dawn, much to your brother's disgust, I'm sure," her father told her. "George came home very early to tell us, still yawning. He's gone back to bed now. It appears the twins made quite an evening of it last night."

"Perhaps it was fortunate that Mr. Williams persuaded his wife to sail back on the *Camille*, rather than going by ferry," Olivia Hathaway remarked. "I had hoped to have a chance to speak to Maryanne privately, but there was no time. There is something wrong there, and I would help her if I could."

"Yes, I noticed it too," Kate said. "Maryanne was almost angry last evening, and she had little to say to her husband. Perhaps they have quarreled."

Her mother sighed. "It is entirely possible. I must try to get out to Tucker's Town soon. She is such a sweet girl! And then there are those little boys. I quite long to kiss the dears!"

Kate finished her breakfast as her mother's light conversation eddied around her. He was gone again, but she did not despair. Tucker's Town was not that far away. She would wait a few days, and then she would go there herself, not to see Maryanne's adorable babies, but an older, much more intriguing specimen of the male sex.

When she excused herself from the table, she said she planned to call on Mrs. Simpson. Her mother nodded, and told Kate to be sure to find out if there was anything the Hathaways could do to assist that poor shipwrecked family.

Kate stayed at Granny Bessie's only a short time. The old lady was very busy caring for her guests—the sewing could wait until another time. While she was there, others came in with clothing and supplies—a bag of flour, some cheese, a little gown too small for the baby now, a second-best petticoat. Kate knew all the callers. They were good neighbors, kind to anyone who had fallen victim to the sea. As she walked home, she realized it was probably because they themselves knew only too well how quickly your life could change for the worse when you were at the mercy of wind and wave and reef. Why, even Aaron's father had come, with a pair of knee breeches and a linen shirt for the captain. The irony of his providing clothing for the man who had lost a valuable cargo to his son did not occur to him. Kate knew he would have stared if she had mentioned it. Christian concern was one thing, but salvaging was a business. Let the sailor beware!

Kate's eyes searched the harbor when she reached the square. The ship from England had anchored very close to where the *Camille* had been, and as she inspected the brigantine, she frowned. How she wished Mama had kept the news of the ambergris between her teeth! For now Mr. Farnsworth might be coming on the very next ship. And he would bother her, and, by his very pompousness and calm assumption that as a man, he knew best, try to wear her down. But he will never do that, Kate told herself. Suddenly it became all-important that she resolve her dilemma with Jack before Farnsworth arrived. For even someone as dense as he was would have to admit defeat when he learned she was betrothed to another man.

Later, busy helping Keza in the kitchen house, Kate wondered about this problem that Jack claimed he had. All kinds of possibilities occurred to her, to be discarded one by one. He had said he had not lost all his money, but had he been telling her the truth? But why would even poverty stop him from marrying? He was well on the way to making a tidy fortune with his ships, his trading, the sale of the ambergris. Perhaps he had discovered something dark on the family tree, and hesitated to perpetuate it? No, that was too farfetched, like something in a novel. Could he have killed someone in a duel, and been forced to flee England, his life at stake? Perhaps even a duel over Lady Arbel? Kate sighed heavily, and Keza looked up to stare at her from where she was peeling potatoes across the table.

"Y'all got sumpin' on you mind, child?" she asked. "Y'all is mighty quiet today."

Kate grinned at her, and Keza's face brightened. "Yes, I was thinking, and I do have a problem. But it's nothing I can't solve," she told the black woman she had loved from babyhood.

She sounded so sure of herself, Keza chuckled. "When y'all talk like dat, Miz Kate, honey, Ah shudders for dat problem, Ah surely do!"

Olivia Hathaway had a slight cold and remained at home when Kate sailed to Tucker's Town two days later. In the *Sprite*'s cuddy she carried a basket of Greg's favorite food, some clean shirts, and a message to him from his father. She had a perfectly legitimate reason to go, she told herself stoutly. Greg was her brother. She was sure no one could question her visit, not even Jack.

When she waded ashore near the Williamses' small house, she looked eagerly toward the yard. She could see Farley Williams busy near the keel of the new sloop, but there was no sign of Greg or Jack. She wondered where they were, even as she waved to Maryanne.

"How good of you to come!" Maryanne said as Kate climbed the veranda steps. "Prithee sit down. I have been feeling low lately, and I am glad of your company."

Maryanne looked so woebegone, that Kate put Jack and his whereabouts from her mind. "But what is troubling you, Maryanne? Can I help?" she asked.

Maryanne began to cry helplessly then, and Kate put an arm around her and hugged her. At last the girl wiped her eyes on the edge of her apron and said, "Please wait. I'll just tell Sukey to bring us a cool drink and keep the children inside. There's really nothing you can do, but mayhap it would ease my mind to speak of it."

Several minutes later, when they were alone again, Maryanne appeared to be having second thoughts about the wisdom of baring her soul. "Perhaps it is wrong of me to burden you, Kate. You are not married, and . . . well, 'tis not exactly seemly."

"I am not a child," Kate reminded her, her gray eyes steady.

Maryanne considered her gravely before she nodded. "That is true enough, I guess. No doubt you'll be married yourself soon. And I only wish someone had warned *me* about what was ahead of me!"

She sighed then and sipped her lemonade, her brooding gaze seeking her husband's bright red head down at the yard. Her lips twisted in a grimace when she spotted him. "The reason I have been so sad lately is that I have discovered I am with child yet again," she said.

She sounded so morose, Kate was not even tempted to tender her congratulations.

"And it is so soon after Baby's birth, too!" Maryanne went on. "It seems ever since I have been married I have been in that condition. And it is just disgusting bearing children here! There isn't even another Englishwoman to be with me—a midwife—only the slaves. And Polly is always so full of foolishness, trying to make me walk about the room while I am in labor, even suggesting I squat down on the floor for the birth. How revolting! So primitive!"

She shuddered and paused, but Kate was speechless, for she knew nothing about childbirth. It did occur to her, however, that if she were to give birth, there wouldn't be another woman in the world she'd want helping more than Keza. Yes, Keza, not her mother.

"I have begged and begged Farley to sell the yard and take me home, but he won't listen to me," Maryanne went on in her complaining voice. "He likes it here in this horrible backwater!"

Kate stiffened as she always did when Bermuda was being maligned, but her hostess did not notice as she rushed on, "Oh, I am so homesick, I am like to die from it! I am used to genteel company, a lot of it—tea parties, afternoon calls. And many shops, all full of wonderful things! Everything you need in profusion! And I am used to proper English servants dressed neatly in aprons and caps. And wearing shoes! Servants who speak the King's English. Do you know, little Farley is beginning to sound just like Sukey—to say 'dis' and 'dat' and 'lak'?

"And oh, how I miss a real spring that follows a real winter, with snow for Christmas and a Yule log. And a real house that doesn't have spiders as big as my palm living in it with me. And being able to go to sleep without a noisy chorus of those ghastly tree toads chirping all night! I am so unhappy!"

She buried her face in her apron and sobbed. Awkwardly Kate rose to pat her back and smooth her blond curls. She was almost sorry her mother had not come after all. Surely she would have been of more use in this situation, for Kate felt helpless.

Maryanne raised her streaming face then and said, "And to think I have nothing to look forward to but spending my life here being miserable and having to bear a baby a year! *Men!* Just you wait, Katherine Hathaway! Your turn is coming!"

Kate made soothing noises, even gave her a hug. "Perhaps it won't always be like that, Maryanne," she said. "And maybe someday you will be able to go home."

"Huh!" Maryanne scoffed. "And pigs will fly! They'll do that long before my obstinate husband changes his mind!"

She looked up then and jumped to her feet. "But no more now! I see he is coming for his dinner. I wonder where Jack and your brother are."

As she fled into the house, Kate was recalled to her real reason for visiting. She thought Farley Williams looked a little uncomfortable, almost as if he suspected what the two girls had been talking about.

She indicated the basket at her feet. "I have brought a few things for Greg, sir," she said. "He is not at the yard?"

Farley smiled at her then. "No, he went off to Crow Harbor this morning on an errand. Is . . . is Maryanne all right?"

Kate nodded. "I think she is feeling homesick, sir," she said. "But where is Jack? I could give him these things for Greg."

"Oh, Jack left the yard a short time ago. He said he wanted to spend the rest of the day going over plans for his next voyage," Farley told her as he leaned against the railing.

Kate wondered if Jack had left before or after the *Sprite* had sailed in, but she did not know how to ask. Instead, she smiled and said, "Well, I would not disturb him, but I think I will walk over there and leave the basket. I cannot linger today, for my mother is not feeling well."

"What, not even stay for dinner?" Maryanne asked, coming to the door. "Oh, Kate, I wish you did not have to go!"

"I am sorry," Kate said, coming to kiss her. "Perhaps you could come in to St. George Town soon, my dear? My mother has missed you, and I think talking to her would do you good."

Plans were made for a visit a few days later, and Kate was glad to see Maryanne looked a little more cheerful as she waved good-bye. She herself was delighted to be able to take her leave. There was nothing she could do, and sitting there eating her dinner between a stubborn husband and a disgruntled wife did not appeal to her at all.

She reached Jack's house a few minutes later. He was not in sight, and when she questioned the slave who answered her knock, she discovered he had gone out to walk the beach. Kate left the basket and prepared to follow him. For even if he were avoiding her, as she now began to suspect he was, she could not go home without seeing him.

But when she reached the broad beach, it was empty.

A little disconsolate, Kate decided to walk for a while; perhaps Jack was walking back toward her even now. She made her way down to the white sand, to sit and take off her shoes and hose. When she reached the water's edge, the waves washing over her feet and ankles were cool and refreshing this hot day. And as she strolled along, always searching the empty beach ahead of her, she thought about what Maryanne had told her this morning. Poor girl! she thought. I never realized she was no unhappy here. But why anyone could want to trade Bermuda for cold, dismal, formal England, she could not fathom.

At length, she reached the end of the beach, still without a glimpse of Jack. Ahead of her lay a high barrier of jutting limestone, and it prevented her from going any further, unless she took to the water. Kate smiled then, and looked around. Only a few seabirds disturbed her solitude, and she began to unbutton her gown. She was warm from her trudge through the sand, and even if she had missed Jack, at least she could have a swim before she had to sail home again.

Moments later, her clothes discarded on the beach, she waded into the water, wearing only her cotton shift.

To be cool all over felt so good, she lingered for a long time, riding the waves as George and Greg had taught her. Once a wave caught her unawares, and she came up sputtering and laughing.

Above her, hidden in the foliage that marked the edge of the beach, Jack Reade watched her playing. A little smile curled his lips as he did so. Kate was as much in her element in the water as she had been on her sloop. He was not worried about her.

But then he heard voices, and he whirled to see a group of men walking up the beach. Dressed as sailors, they were laughing and shoving each other in rough horseplay until they paused for a moment to drink from a dark bottle one of them carried. Jack could see they were having an argument about whether to go on, or back to the small boat they had left behind them, pulled up on the beach. He prayed they would go back, before they saw Kate. Suddenly one of them pointed to her, a wild, loose grin on his face, and they all began to run. They were clumsy in the loose sand, and none too steady from the rum they had consumed, but he was afraid. He could hear their ribald shouts clearly now; it was obvious they had rape in mind. Cursing them under his breath, Jack left his concealment to go and help her.

He tore off his shoes and hose and threw them aside when he reached the water's edge. Behind him, the drunken sailors were gaining ground, still calling lewd suggestions to the "mermaid" they had found.

Kate heard them then, and she looked around. Jack saw the fear in her eyes as he waded in, to dive under a wave and swim to her as fast as he could. He reached her just as the men came to a halt on the sands behind them.

"C'mere, wench! C'mere!" one of them called. "We won't 'urt ye! We'll pleasure ye!"

" 'Ey, man! We seen 'er first," another added. "She's *our* prize!"

"Quick! Swim for the cliffs," Jack ordered. "There's no way to reason with them, not the state they're in. And I'm no match for so many."

Kate nodded, and set off with a long, steady stroke, Jack just behind her. He risked a glance back to the beach and saw two of the men were stripping off their clothes to follow them, and he wondered if the plan he had concocted had any chance of success. Pray they were indifferent swimmers! The others were lolling on the sand now, waving Kate's petticoat as encouragement to their mates. Jack looked for Kate again. She had not faltered, nor slowed, and he was relieved.

As soon as they were around the headland, he caught up to her and touched her shoulder to point to shore. Kate looked confused, but she nodded and followed him in. To her, the limestone there looked impenetrable, and much too steep to climb.

As they reached the shallows, they could hear the splashing of their pursuers, although they were not in sight as yet. Without hesitating, Jack grabbed her hand and waded to shore. Closer now, Kate could see that the face of the limestone cliff was pocked with holes, and she shuddered a little. She hated being in small, enclosed places underground, and those holes meant caves. But when she considered what awaited her if she remained exposed, she took a deep breath and followed him willingly.

She had to get down on her hands and knees to enter the cave he chose, and when they were safely inside, her face fell. From what she could see from the light that came through the entrance, it was very small. The water was not very deep either. It looked like a trap, and she turned to Jack in despair.

"But there's no place to hide here!" she whispered, a little out of breath still. "They'll find us in no time!"

Jack's hand on the small of her back urged her forward. His face was grim as he said, "There's another cave beyond this one. It's much larger. You'll be safe there."

They had reached what appeared to be a solid limestone wall, and Kate stared at him as if she thought him mad. "But there's no way in!" she exclaimed.

He pushed her down until she was on her hands and knees in the water. As he did so, he said, "See there, right in front of you, that hole. You'll have to take a deep breath and swim underwater, but it will not be for long, I promise you. I found this entrance some time ago. I've been in there many times."

He noticed she looked terrified now, and he squeezed her wet shoulders. "We must hurry!" he warned her. "They will be here anytime now!"

She nodded and closed her eyes for a moment and swallowed. Then he saw her take a deep ragged breath before she went under. He watched anxiously until her hips, then her long legs and kicking feet, disappeared. Only then did he follow her.

Jack came sputtering to the surface beside her in the deep-bottomed cave moments later. In the uncertain dim light that filtered down from above, he saw she was about to speak, and he put his hand over her mouth. When she nodded, he led her to one side of the cave and pulled her up on a ledge there, beside him.

Kate was shivering. As he wrapped his arm around her, he wondered at it. It wasn't cold in here. Then he realized she was shaking from fright, and he remembered her telling him once that she did not like caves—being underground. Still, she did not make a sound, and he admired her courage.

Kate stiffened then as a voice boomed all around them. The two sailors had found the first cave and entered it.

" 'Swounds, Alf! Ain't that a sight now, all them pointy rocks 'angin' from the roof?" the voice demanded. "But there ain't no wench in 'ere."

"Then mebbe she's in another one. I seen lot o' 'oles! Tallyho, 'Arry! We'll get 'er, me boy, and then the fun will start. An' you 'n me, why, we'll 'ave first go o' the lot o' em!"

Both Kate and Jack heard them stumble from the cave, but neither spoke until it was very quiet again.

"Thank you for saving me," Kate whispered at last, looking around in terrified awe. She could not see the back of the cave. It was huge. She wondered where the light was coming from, even as she thanked God for it. To have been here in blackness would have been more than she could bear. Perhaps there was another way out, up to the clifftop. She told herself she would climb anything to avoid that horrifying narrow underwater passage again.

"And what did you think you were doing?" Jack demanded, his whisper rough with his anger. "To take off your clothes and go swimming! Are you daft? You might have drowned, to say nothing of the unpleasant fate that was in store for you at those sailors' hands!"

"But I often do so!" Kate protested, remembering to keep her voice down. "And no one's ever bothered me before!"

"You should have remembered the brigantine anchored in St. George Town harbor," he said. "Obviously, some of her crew were exploring the islands, drinking themselves to a fine state as they did so. They've been at sea a long time, and you are much too tempting."

Kate hung her head. Briefly Jack looked down at her, and his lips tightened. The diffused light that filtered from above to play over the water of the cave turned the stalactites hanging above them into strange icicle forms, but he was not thinking of the eerie beauty of the cave right now. For that same light revealed only too clearly how her wet, almost transparent shift clung to her high pert breasts and nipples, her narrow waist, as if it had been pasted on her body. The sight left little to the imagination. He felt a sudden warmth deep in his loins, and he released her to move further away on the narrow ledge.

He saw her color up then, as if his retreat had reminded her that she was practically naked. She bit her lip as she wrapped her arms over her breasts. Since that left her hips and belly and her long, shapely legs exposed to his gaze, the chestnut V of hair between her thighs clearly evident, he could not say her modest gesture was much of an improvement. It had been easier when they were busy escaping the sailors and immersed in the ocean, but he could not suggest they slip into the deep pool again. For one thing, Kate had been in the water for a long time already and she was probably tired, and for another, he had no idea what might be swimming in the cave. A small barracuda had surprised him on his last visit here, too small, fortunately, to dare to attack him. But there might be more of them, sharks even, that had been swept in on a floodtide and were unable to escape now.

"How will we get out of here?" Kate whispered, as if the silence between them was making her uneasy. "I do so pray there is another way!"

He saw her glance hopefully to the roof of the cave, high above them, and he was sorry he had to shake his head. "No, there is just that one underground conduit. But in any case, we must stay here for a long time. There's no telling how long those sailors might hang about, waiting for you to come back for your clothes."

He fell silent then, brooding about the situation—and about Kate. He had been thinking of her a great deal since the night of the Hathaways' party, remembering the tender eagerness of her lips, the feel of her in his arms, all pliant and loving. And he had come to see that he was not just attracted to her, as he would have been to any pretty girl. No, he knew he cared for her.

Even he had wondered when his feelings for her must have changed from liking to love, and in his mind's eye he had seen her sailing her sloop again, with the salt spray on her face, and her damp clothes clinging to her lithe, slender body. But what had set the final seal on his downfall had been her artless wail the night of the party, cursing whatever it was that was making her weep. She was truly a revelation. He had never known another girl even remotely like her.

But someone so good, so unique, was not for the likes of plain Jack Reade. Kate Hathaway deserved someone better than a bastard who sported a title he did not own and who was forced by circumstance to continue to use it to protect his mother and sisters' reputations.

He stole a glance at Kate then, and saw that she was shivering again, but trying valiantly to suppress it. Since he himself was comfortably warm, even in his wet shirt and breeches, he knew she must be thinking of the cave again, and the weight of all those rocks above them. Perhaps she was even imagining they were hanging there precariously, and might tumble down any minute, leaving her entombed here.

To keep her from contemplating it, he made himself say, "It is too bad that you missed your brother today. Farley had heard of a couple of schooners that put in to Ely and

Crow harbors lately, with cargoes of marine stores. He sent Greg to see about them. Of course, no custom was paid on the cargoes, so it had to be done in secret."

She turned to him in relief and smiled, but he saw it was not one of her better efforts. "Yes, it was too bad, but I do not repine," she said. "I left the basket I brought for him at your house. But are you so short of supplies in the yard?"

He shrugged. "We're always short. A certain size line or enough anchor chain, particular brass fittings. Bermuda is not like England, with all its rich abundance. Here we have to make do sometimes, or we wait. I am glad I did not go into shipbuilding after all. Sailing and trading are more to my liking than waiting. I have never liked waiting."

"Where will you go next? And when will you leave?" she asked.

"Not for a while yet. Farley needs my help with the new sloop, for Greg has never built a ship before. But when she is well along, decked, I'll gather the *Camille*'s crew together again and head for Charles Town. Your brother Matthew and I have become friends, and I trust his judgment. I'll probably go wherever he suggests."

"My father says the colonies are in a disgraceful state, that rebellion against the crown is rife there. Won't it be dangerous for you?" she asked, sounding worried.

He smiled a little for her concern. "Any voyage is dangerous, mistress. But we are not at war—not yet."

"Do you expect one?"

"I feel it is inevitable, and so does Matthew. But I doubt Bermuda will be involved. The people here remain loyal almost to the man. Even those who use Ely Harbor and the others to avoid the Customs House at St. George Town would scorn open revolution. And of course Bermuda is not truly a part of the colonies, sharing their concerns, but a separate entity, far at sea."

They continued to talk, fall silent, and talk again for a long time. Once Kate heard a fish jump somewhere in the cave, and she started. To distract her, Jack told her more of his last journey, the flat salt ponds on the Turks Islands, the heat there that was like a heavy blanket pressing on the skin at certain times of the year. He also told her about the port of Boston, the red-coated regiments stationed there, the colonists' unrest. But for all their conversation, he never asked her why she had been on the beach, because he already knew the answer to that question all too well. And Kate did not know how to get him to talk about their kiss—the things he had said to her—not in the face of his determined formality. Why, she thought, he acts as if it never happened at all! But a small part of her was relieved as well. He was so matter-of-fact, so normal, it made it easier for her to forget her lack of clothing. It was almost as if they were seated together at a London party, exchanging chitchat. She thought of what her Aunt Mary would say if she could see her now, and a vision of her horrified face just before she would most surely swoon away into a dead faint almost made Kate giggle. Only the amplitude of her fear, trapped here underground, made her able to control herself.

It was much later before Jack felt it was safe enough to leave. As he slid into the water, he said, "I am sure we have tarried long enough. And if those men are still waiting for you, we will hear them and continue along this beach. There's a place about a half-mile ahead where we can climb to the top. Come!"

He saw her little hesitation, the way she caught her breath, and he said, "Since there is only one way out, isn't it best to get it over with quickly, Kate? And you know how it's done now, how easy it is. Besides, in a few minutes there will be nothing over your head but brilliant blue sky."

As he had hoped, her face brightened at the thought of such wonder, and she joined him in the water at once. The tide had been dropping while they were in the cave, and she saw when they reached the entrance hole that she would be able to raise her head in the narrow passage for air if she needed it. Once again, Jack made her go first, still not at all sure she might not panic and freeze if she were left here alone. And there *was* that barracuda, and his possible fellows.

He watched her as she swam underwater and the cotton shift she wore floated up to her waist. He could see her hips, her rounded bottom clearly beneath the pale green water. He could not help admiring how lithe and graceful she was, and, for all her slenderness, curved as sweetly as any woman could ever be. He grimaced at how intensely he yearned to hold her tightly against his own body and caress every one of those curves.

As he followed her to freedom, he realized there was a great deal more to her, however, than just a lovely body, a fine-featured aristocratic face. She was bright and intelligent and braver than many men. For hadn't she just conquered an awful fear without a single whimper? A rare woman indeed, Kate Hathaway.

12

"OH, dear, I am so worried about Kate! Whatever could have happened to her?" Maryanne moaned as she twisted her damp handkerchief in her hands.

Her husband patted her shoulder, but he looked just as concerned as she did. And Gregory Hathaway's pacing up and down the main room in Jack Reade's house, his face drawn, showed his anxiety as well. Two slaves hovered together near the doorway, their eyes big in their dark faces.

"You say she was only going to leave the basket here?" Greg asked the Williamses. "That she told you she had to return home quickly because my mother was not feeling well?"

Maryanne nodded. Although she had been asked this same question many times in the past hour, she was patient with the man's nervousness. "She would not even stay for dinner," she told him. "But it was not until later that I noticed she had not returned to the *Sprite* and sailed for home. I ran to tell Farley at once, sir. And by the time you came back from Crow Harbor, we had set the men to searching between here and the yard, and then on to the point."

"Tatum, Annie," Greg said, and the slaves edged closer. "She left here as soon as she had delivered the basket? You're sure?"

They both nodded, but it was Annie who spoke up.

" 'Deed she did, Massa Greg. Ah was makin' a pie for your supper, so I din't see which way she-all went. An' Tatum here, why, he wuz fetchin' water from Tucker's Town. He din't see nothin' of her, no suh."

"But where could she have gotten to, then?" Greg demanded. "What could have happened to her?"

Maryanne sniffed and sobbed a little as she shook her head. " 'Tis most unlike her, to disappear like that. And where is Jack?"

Just then the door opened and Kate Hathaway stepped into the room. Jack, naked to the waist, was right behind her. Kate was wearing his damp shirt over her shift now, and although she was decently covered to her thighs, she still blushed at the horror in everyone's eyes and at Maryanne's startled gasp.

"Kate! What the devil?" Greg exploded, coming to take her arms as he yelled over his shoulder, "Get a blanket at once, Annie!

"Where have you been, Kate?" he demanded, shaking her a little. "And what does this mean, the two of you coming in almost naked?"

"Your sister ran into a bit of trouble, Greg," Jack told him, his turquoise eyes cold and wary. "She went for a walk on the beach and decided to have a swim down by the cliffs. Unfortunately, a band of sailors from that newly arrived brigantine spotted her there. They had been drinking heavily, and they decided on a little sport."

"Gracious heaven!" Maryanne exclaimed, looking horrified. "Never tell us they . . . You mean . . . ? Dear God!"

"It was fortunate for me that Jack was nearby and saw them before I did," Kate hurried to say. "Together we swam around the cliff and hid in a cave until they went away."

"But it has been hours!" Greg exclaimed as Annie wrapped a blanket around his sister. "You've been alone in a cave all this time? Without any clothes on?"

Even though she was now draped in the blanket and covered from head to toe, Kate paled, the golden freckles on her nose standing out in bold relief. "There . . . there was nothing else we could do. There were six of them, and Jack was alone," she whispered. She put her chin up then and said in a louder voice, "I do not know what you are thinking, Greg, but I can assure you nothing happened in that cave. Nothing at all. You shame both the captain and your sister for even imagining such a thing!"

Maryanne's hissed indrawn breath and Greg's look of disbelief angered her further. But before she could speak and upbraid them for not believing her, Jack said, "It is just as your sister said, Greg. And when it was safe to leave the cave and swim around the point again, we saw that the sailors had taken all Kate's clothes with them when they left. No doubt it was done purely from spite, to pay her back for successfully evading their rape. But come now, Annie, Tatum. Didn't you see the boat they came in? Hear them? Even though they landed a distance down the beach, they were drunk and loud enough!"

Both slaves shook their heads. "Never heered nothin', suh," Annie told him. "Nor seed nothin' neither. Ah wuz busy in da kitchen house, an' Tatum here, wal, he wuz out searchin' wit de others."

"I am sure there is no need for such drama," Kate told them, her voice annoyed. "It was unfortunate, of course, but there was no harm done!"

"No harm done?" Greg repeated. "No *harm*? This will be all over the islands in a day! For even if we agree to keep quiet about it, there are all those men in the yard who have been looking for you these past two hours. You are naive indeed, Kate, if you think you can avoid censure."

Jack saw Kate's gray eyes widen with shock. He thought she looked almost regal standing there so straight, even dressed in the rough blanket that trailed behind her in folds on the floor. In the little silence that followed Greg's impassioned speech, he moved to her side to put his arm around her waist. "There is no need to lambaste your sister, sir," he said. "I shall, of course, call on your father tomorrow. And Kate and I will be married as soon as the banns can be called. There is no need for any of you to remind me of my duty as a gentleman."

"But that's not fair!" Kate wailed. "No, not that way! *Dammit*, I refuse!"

Maryanne came forward then to take her hands. "You cannot refuse, my dear. Jack honors you just as he should. For you'll never live down the stigma, and your reputation will be ruined if the two of you do not marry at once. And even then, people will be counting the months till your first child. It is the way of the world."

Kate didn't dare to look up at Jack, so close beside her. His comforting arm around her waist steadied her, but she could tell from its rigidity how tense he was, and her heart sank. To marry him had been her fondest dream, but not this way! Oh, no, not coerced into it by convention and the possibility of gossip. She drew a deep breath, but before she could speak, refuse again, he said, "Maryanne is right, Kate. I promise you I shall do my best to be a comfortable husband for you."

He withdrew his arm then, as Greg came to take his hand, a look of profound relief on his face as he did so. For not only would Kate's good name be saved, he would be saved as well, from calling out his friend for insulting and misusing his sister. And he would not have to explain such a terrible matter to his parents either. As he grasped Jack's shoulder hard, he thought they might make a very good match of it, these two, after all. For some time he had suspected Kate was sweet on Jack. And although he had never seen any answering affection for her on the quiet, moody captain's face, he had noted how easy Jack had been with her the day the schooner had been caught on the reef, even the way the two had laughed together. Yes, it might be all right at that. But Lord, to think this was the way Kate got to be a "lady"! It really was something!

"Now, you must come with us back to our house, Kate," Maryanne was saying. "I've a spare skirt and jacket you can borrow. And tomorrow you can return home with Jack to confront your parents. I pray your mother will not worry overmuch about your absence tonight, for surely it is too late for you to leave now. There is only an hour or so to sunset, and the reefs to consider. No, it is not to be thought of! Come along now, my dear. Let me see to your care . . ."

Kate let herself be led away, her mind spinning like a top. Still she did not look at Jack. She did not dare. What might she see in his eyes?

She longed to cry out, protest again, but suddenly she was so tired she was like to die from it. All she really wanted to do was sleep, after a good soaking cry, she realized. For her heart's desire should not have to come to her like this. And Jack's voice, when he had made his offer to call on her father, had been cold and leaden in his determination to do the right thing. Ah, but she could not fathom it all out now, she told herself as she left the house with the Williamses. Her head was throbbing, her feet sore from climbing the rough path from the beach.

Tomorrow, before she went back to St. George Town, she would talk to Jack. And maybe they could find another way out of this dilemma. And maybe by then she would dare to look at him, not be so afraid of what she might find on his face, in those handsome eyes. She shivered, and Maryanne tucked the blanket more closely around her and began to talk of hot cups of tea and supper, even a hot bath to wash away the salt.

It was a strangely subdued Kate Hathaway who took her place in the *Sprite* the following morning. Jack was quiet as well, his face shuttered and cold. Only Greg's cheerful chatter broke the uneasy silence as Kate remembered to wave good-bye to Maryanne.

Outside of a few terse comments, Jack did not say much until they reached the *Sprite*'s mooring. Kate realized he had spoken up only once, after Greg had twitted her about having to mend her ways now.

"My word—Lady Reade!" Greg had chortled, hoping to lighten the atmosphere. "Here's a new come-out for you, sister! Shall I have to address you as 'milady' in future?"

"Kate will be known as Mrs. Jack Reade, and only by that name," Jack had said then, his voice harsh.

Kate had stolen a glance at him, but he had been looking out to sea and she could see only his stern, immobile profile. She had wondered why he had said that, and in quite that way, and she remembered she had yet to discover a great deal about this man.

"Of course, if that is your wish, Jack," Greg agreed easily. He did not like the undercurrents in the air, but he was sure his mother and father would take care of whatever was bothering Jack, and Kate as well. He had never seen his sister so quiet, so inhibited.

Mrs. Hathaway was much relieved when Kate entered the house, but she wondered at the clothes she was wearing. And Kate's feet and lower legs were bare. It

was most immodest, for as large around the body as the
jacket and skirt were, the skirt was much too short.

Concerned as he had been for his daughter's safety,
Roger Hathaway had not gone to the State House that
morning, and now he took both young men away to his
own room after a quiet word with Greg. His wife bustled
Kate up to her room, determined not to ask a single
question until they were alone.

As she changed her clothes and did her hair, Kate told
her in a flat voice what had happened. Outside of a few
shocked gasps, her mother let her speak without inter-
ruption to the end.

"And that is all that happened, Mama! You must
believe me! But Greg and the Williamses were so horrified! And Maryanne said I must marry Jack as soon as
possible! Oh, why did it have to happen this way?" she
wailed.

"Can it be you do not want to marry him?" her mother
asked, her eyes shrewd. "Yet here I have been so afraid
you were forming a *tendre* for the young man."

Kate threw herself into her mother's arms and wept.
"Of course I want to marry him! I have wanted to from
the first moment we met in London! And I have been
intent on capturing his love ever since I knew he was
here in Bermuda. But not like this, Mama! Not to *force*
him to it! I wanted him to love me as I love him. Instead,
now he must marry me because he has to! It is too bad!"

Olivia Hathaway patted her back as she rocked her in
her arms. "Yes, it is too bad," she said sadly. "You
know, Kate, I did not want you to marry Jack Reade,
and yet now you must. How strange life is!"

"Not want me to?" Kate echoed, drawing away to
stare at her. "Why ever not?"

Her mother made herself smile. "There is no need to
discuss it, my dear, since it must come to pass after all.
At least you will be Lady Reade, and that is something.
And we must hope that all my suspicions are nothing but
a mother's skepticism."

Kate would have insisted she tell her what was in her
mind, but Keza knocked and came in then. Her eyes
were intent on Kate's face as she told her her father
wished to see her at once.

Kate hugged the old slave to reassure her before she

hurried downstairs. As she crossed the wide hall, she could see through the open door that Jack had gone out to stand beside the harbor.

Roger Hathaway took her in his arms and stared down into her eyes before he bade her take a seat. "Well, here's a pretty kettle of fish, Kate!" he said. "For it is plain you must marry the young man now, after what has happened."

"But do I have to, Father?" Kate pleaded. "I would not have him trapped like this, all for my carelessness and stupidity."

"Don't you care for him, my dear?" her father asked as he took his own seat. "Strange, that. I was so sure you did."

She looked at him squarely. "I love him to distraction, and I have always hoped to wed him. But not like this, Father! Not like *this*!"

Roger Hathaway's face cleared a little. "Unfortunately, it must be like this," he told her. Kate had heard that implacable tone in his voice only a few times in her life, but it made her subside at once.

He went on, "Yes, no doubt it would have been better if he could have come a-wooing, but such niceties must be disregarded now. It is Friday. By the time the vicar reads the banns in St. Peter's this Sunday morning, there won't be a single member of the congregation who is not waiting to hear them, and knowing full well the reason they are being called. For if they are not called, all kinds of censure would come down on our heads."

Kate sighed, her eyes troubled, and he rose to draw her to her feet. "I suggest you go out and speak to your Jack now, my dear. Perhaps you can make all right. I do assure you, he is the complete gentleman, and he reveres you, honors you. He is waiting for you now."

Kate hugged him for a moment before she went to do his bidding and wander down the broad green lawn to where Jack was standing alone, staring out at the harbor. Was he wishing he were on a ship leaving Bermuda for good? she wondered. Was he sorry he had ever come here? She wouldn't have blamed him for it if he were.

He turned just before she reached him, and for a moment the two stared at each other. Then, seeing the trouble in her eyes, her hesitation, Jack made himself smile at her.

"You look vastly more suitable now than you did yesterday, Kate," he told her as he bowed. "And I have always liked you in that blue gown. It becomes you."

Silently she curtsied, and as he drew her up, he did not release her hand. Instead, he covered it with his other big one and said, "There is no need to look so glum, my dear. No doubt you would have preferred a different inception to married life, but it was not to be. And I meant what I said yesterday, you know. I will make you the best husband I know how. You will always have my respect and admiration."

But I don't care for that! Kate cried inwardly. I want you to love me! She swallowed hard, and then she whispered, "I am so very sorry, Jack. All this is my fault. And I know how trapped you must feel, how helpless, unable to avoid this fate you never sought. If there were anything I could do to change it, believe me, I would!"

She paused for a moment, but when he had no comment, she went on in a rush, only just then raising her eyes to his dear face, "I hope you know how much I . . . I revere you, how much I will always try as well to be everything you might wish for in a wife. Indeed, sir, you have only to tell me your desires, and I shall do my best to see to them."

Her abnegating pledge lightened his expression a little. Of course she would, the valiant Kate Hathaway! He did not deserve her, no, not at all. And yet a mischance had given her to him, and now he must make the best of it. But he would not tell her why he had planned never to marry anyone. And if they remained in Bermuda, never visited England, she would never learn his reason. Instead, she would accept being plain Mrs. Jack Reade. None of it was fair to either of them, but perhaps it was less fair to Kate. For no doubt she had dreamed of having children someday, and now she would never know that joy and fulfillment. But he had no intention of telling her why that must be so either.

"Your father asked me to stay for dinner, but I made my excuses," he said now. "I shall, however, return early Sunday morning to attend church with the family, and have dinner with you as well. Till then, Kate . . ."

She stared at him, her gray eyes puzzled, and he bent
to kiss her hand. Before she could speak, he had bowed
and left her, his long strides covering the grassy sweep of
lawn quickly. In a moment he was gone.

True to his word, Jack accompanied the family to
church that Sunday, taking his place beside Kate in the
Hathaway box pew with graceful ease. Kate bowed her
head in prayer, trying to ignore the whispers she heard
all around her. It was hard for her to concentrate on the
service. Indeed, she felt as if she had been lost in a thick
gray fog ever since the day in the cave.

The brigantine had sailed for England at dawn on
Friday, so none of the crew could be questioned. Her
clothes had never been found. Kate wondered what those
randy sailors had done with them.

All through the lessons, the collect, even Holy Commu-
nion, Kate was aware only of Jack's lean hard body next
to hers. She could not seem to keep her eyes from the
hands holding his prayer book. And when she thought
how soon those hands would be caressing her, she had to
swallow and pray that God forgive her such thoughts in
church.

At last the moment Kate had been waiting for, with a
mixture of dread and anticipation, arrived. The vicar smiled
down at her for a moment before he said in his deep,
carrying voice, "I, Alexander Richardson, by divine permission, rector of St. Peter's, to our well-beloved in
Christ, Sir John James Reade, of the parish of Hythe,
Kent, bachelor, and Katherine Allegra Hathaway, of the
parish of St. George's, spinster, sendeth greetings. Whereas
ye are, as is alleged, determined to enter into the holy
state of matrimony, by and with the consent of . . ."

Kate stopped listening. It was done. There was no
escape now for either of them. Unwittingly her hands
formed tight fists, and to her surprise, Jack took one of
them in his and smoothed it open. She knew she could
not turn and look at him, but it did comfort her to be
able to look down at their clasped hands while the final
words were said in this, the first calling of the banns.

After church, she had to listen to a great many good
wishes from all her friends and acquaintance. Jack remained close by her side, and although his mood was not
ebullient, he smiled often and accepted the congrega-

tion's congratulations with his usual aplomb. And at dinner later, he kept up an easy flow of conversation about any number of subjects. Kate was relieved. She could see her mother was feeling better about the situation now, and her father was softening as well. By the time they rose from the table, it seemed to Kate that a stranger observing them would assume that her marriage to Jack Reade would be an occasion of great joy all around.

Jack asked her then if she would care to stroll to St. Catherine's Point with him before he took the ferry back to Tucker's Town.

Wearing her best palmetto straw, Kate took his arm a little shyly. They were alone now. Perhaps Jack would tell her more about himself, his family? Why he had left England, and whatever had happened to the Lady Arbel?

But he did not speak of the past, not once, and there was no way she could introduce the topic. Instead, he told her about his trading business, and the addition he was planning to his house, now that he would be bringing a bride to it. And he told her if she did not feel the two slaves he owned were adequate, she was to purchase another, or bring one with her from home.

When he left her at last, standing on the steps before her house, she was not surprised he did nothing more than kiss her hand. Mrs. Tucker was out on her front steps next door, all smiles for the happy couple, and beyond her, Mrs. Kempthorne was leaning way over her garden wall so she would not miss a single thing. In the face of such wholehearted interest, it was hardly likely that Jack would care to kiss her.

As she went up to her room to change into an older gown, Kate realized that Jack had never touched her if he could help it since their one and only kiss, and she wondered at it. They were betrothed now. No one, even the highest stickler, could take offense at an embrace. She had been waiting rather breathlessly all afternoon for him to take her in his arms so she could know the same joy she had had the evening of the party. But he had not, not even when they were quite alone and far from interested eyes. A little disconsolate, she reminded herself that there were only three more weeks before the ceremony, and then, alone in the little house that was to be theirs, she would find out what men—and one man in particular—were like. She could not help but wish Jack loved her, though. It would make all the difference. But she told herself stoutly that her love for him more than made up for that little discrepancy. And she would do everything in her power to make him love her at last. No matter how long it took.

The three weeks seemed to fly by. Kate was busy altering the aqua silk gown she had worn in London so it would be suitable for church rather than a ballroom. Sometimes, as she sat and stitched, Keza kept her company. She had told the slave of her love for Jack, and Keza had beamed in relief. And one afternoon she had done a great deal to explain what went on between a man and a woman, the pain and bleeding the first time. Kate was glad to hear it, for she knew it was something her mother could never have brought herself to discuss.

Mrs. Simpson came to call on her one afternoon. She had brought Kate a pretty lace-trimmed petticoat threaded through with pale blue ribbon as a bride gift. And just before she left, she pressed a fragile lace handkerchief into her hands.

"This can only be borrowed, my dear girl, for I carried it the day I wedded my Will," she said, her eyes misting slightly. "I would like you to carry it as well. Perhaps it will be a talisman, ensuring that your marriage will be as happy as mine was. For even if a sailor's wife has a hard road ahead of her, her life can be filled with wonder and joy. You'll see!"

Kate kissed her and thanked her. Dear Granny Bessie! she thought as she waved good-bye. But Granny didn't know the circumstances. No one did. Sometimes it was so hard for Kate to preserve a calm, smiling front when her friends came to whisper to her about her love for Jack and his love for her.

Kate's wedding day dawned bright and clear. It was still warm in late October, and Olivia Hathaway had stripped the gardens of their last blooms to decorate the house. Several people were coming back after the ceremony for wine and bride's cake. And Roger Hathaway had won special permission from the governor for the bridal party to be escorted from the church by a band of Gombey dancers. These slaves, dressed in fantastic costumes, masks, and headdresses, had been forbidden to assemble after the troubles in 1761. But today, Kate would be led by a whirling, foot-stomping group, complete with their drums and whistles.

When she met Jack at the altar, Kate's knees were trembling. She blessed the wide hoops she wore that made her weakness impossible to see. But only after Jack drew her hand into his arm and smiled down at her was she able to smile in return. Ah, he looked so handsome today! she thought. He was wearing formal London clothes, and he had powdered his black hair in honor of the occasion.

When the ceremony was over, and they turned to walk up the aisle, Kate looked up to the western gallery first, where she knew Keza was seated with the other slaves. Her eyes filled with tears when she saw her dear face and broad smile. And then there was Aaron, looking pale but resigned, and Granny Bessie, right on the aisle, resplendent in her new gray cambric, and all the others whom Kate had known all her life. And all of these people were smiling to wish her well. Except one. At the very back of the church, Kate came face-to-face with the newly arrived Franklin Farnsworth. She had not known he had taken passage on the schooner that had dropped anchor late yesterday afternoon.

Mr. Farnsworth was wearing a most disgruntled expression that clearly proclaimed his high dudgeon, and his bow to the newlyweds was very shallow.

Kate could not quite stifle a giggle as they passed him, and when Jack leaned down to ask her why she was laughing, she could only shake her head at him, her eyes dancing with mirth. And then she could not have answered anyway, for they were at the top of the long flight of stairs that fronted the church, and below them in the street, the Gombey dancers had begun their noisy serenade.

Kate and Jack had decided to sail the *Sprite* to Tucker's Town that afternoon, so Greg had taken her trunks and belongings there earlier. Besides her clothes, Kate had a large chest of linen and blankets, and the household items her mother had collected for her over the years as well. She had a dozen silver spoons and a handsome silver tea service, and a great many pewter dishes and porringers. For even though Kate brought a dowry of well over four thousand pounds with her, Olivia Hathaway had made sure she came equipped with all the necessities any bride brought to her husband on her wedding day.

For some time Kate moved among the guests, serving them her cake and chatting, while Jack was kept busy accepting the congratulations and toasts of the gentlemen present. But at last Mrs. Hathaway whispered to Kate that it was time to change her clothes for something more suitable for sailing. Shortly afterward, when she had kissed all her family and Keza as well, she and Jack walked down to the water, the guests trailing behind.

The Gombey dancers continued to celebrate in Water Street, and from the noise, Kate could tell they had been joined by a great many other slaves as well. It seemed to her as if everyone in the islands had come to wish her well, to be happy for her on her wedding day.

As Jack handed her into the skiff, the guests set up a cheer, and they were still cheering and waving as the sails were raised and the *Sprite* left the mooring.

Suddenly Kate could think of nothing to say, but Jack would not allow her to be silent. Instead he growled, "And now, madam wife, you will be good enough to tell me exactly what you found so amusing right after our solemn ceremony. I am sure, as your husband, I have a right to know!"

Kate saw that he was smiling at her, and remembering Mr. Farnsworth's face again, she laughed out loud. Jack was sailing the *Sprite* today; she had nothing to do but sit back and take her ease.

" 'Twas only that Franklin Farnsworth must have just arrived from England. La, the look on his face in church!" she confided.

"Farnsworth? Farnsworth?" Jack mused, looking puzzled.

"I doubt he moved in your circles in London, sir. But my Aunt Mary was delighted when he offered for me, and very angry indeed when I refused him."

She chuckled again as she told him how her mother had let her Aunt Mary assume that all the money from the ambergris belonged to her daughter, which was no doubt why Mr. Farnsworth had decided to come such a distance to try his luck again.

Now Jack was chuckling too. He had changed from his formal clothes, and in his tight breeches and open-necked white shirt he looked much more the Jack Reade she was used to. Of course, his hair was still powdered, but soon that would be gone as well.

"But the poor man! How he is to be pitied," he said now, his turquoise eyes merry. "Such a distance to travel, only to find out he was too late by a matter of minutes. And I do remember the gentleman, I believe. Stuffy, pompous, conceited, opinionated? Have I drawn him right?"

Kate nodded. "Perfectly. Why, he seemed to feel in our short acquaintance that I needed to be instructed in everything. I often wondered sometimes when he was going to tell me how to breathe, and walk, and cut my meat!"

"I am surprised, though, that you were able to escape him," Jack remarked. "Surely it was not your place to refuse, if your mother and your relatives approved his suit."

"It made no never-mind what they thought. I had my father's promise that I did not have to wed anyone I did not love," Kate told him.

A little silence fell between them then, until Jack pointed out a school of small silver-green fry jumping frantically to avoid some larger predator, and bade her keep a sharp lookout for reefs.

Jack carried his bride ashore after he had anchored the sloop in a small cove near his house. Kate was glad they had not put in near the yard and had to face all the workmen's knowing smiles. Instead, she felt as if they were the only two people in the world in this isolated spot, and she was glad to have it so.

When she saw the well-trodden path that led up from the cove to the house, she questioned Jack about it. He told her he often swam there first thing in the morning, or when he returned from the yard in the late afternoon.

"I would like to do that too," Kate said, grasping the hand he extended to help her over a large chunk of limestone.

"You would be safe enough there," he said. "I've never seen another boat in the cove, and there are no other houses nearby."

Jack's two slaves were at the house to welcome them, and Jack gave them instructions about supper before he showed Kate the bedroom where her trunks had been placed.

Kate tried to keep her eyes from the large tester bed against the wall as he explained he had emptied the chest so she might unpack her things.

"Call Annie if you need anything, Kate," he told her. "I have a few things to see to. I will join you for supper in an hour."

Kate's heart was beating rapidly now, and a tiny pulse in her throat seemed to have taken on a life of its own. She wondered if he could see it, but he only nodded to her and smiled a little before he went away.

For the next hour, she took her gowns, petticoats, and shifts from the trunks and folded them carefully before she stored them in the big chest. As she did so, her eyes strayed often to the bed. At last she went and inspected it, behind its netting. It had been made up with fresh sheets, and it looked inviting. She had a pretty blue-and-white quilt she would put on it tomorrow, to cover the practical blanket Jack had used. And she had a pair of goose-feather pillows too. They would be an improvement over those sacking-and-straw ones.

When she heard the slaves bringing supper to the front room, she washed her face and hands and smoothed her curls. Then, smiling a little, she picked up a neatly folded garment she had laid aside and went to join her husband.

He was waiting for her at the table, and as she curtsied, she said a little shyly, "I have something for you, Jack."

He looked at her, his face shuttered, and she hurried to put a white shirt in his hands. "It is yours, sir," she told him. "I only . . . borrowed it, if you recall. And the least I could do was wash and iron it for you after you were so chivalrous."

She was delighted to see Jack smile then. "It also needed a button, and there was a rip in the band that I repaired," she said as she took the seat he was holding for her.

"I can see that having a wife is going to add to my comfort," he said as he put the shirt on a small table nearby. "Do you, er, enjoy sewing, Kate?"

She wrinkled her nose at him. "Not particularly, but of course I know how. My mother saw to that. But what is that delicious aroma?"

"Annie made us a fish chowder and some cassava bread. I have found her an excellent cook."

After she had served Jack, Kate ladled some of the chowder into her bowl. She felt very domestic as she did so. But deep inside, she could not help wishing that this was tomorrow night. She felt so strange. So breathless and anxious, and yet somehow uneasy. And Jack's mood seemed to have changed. He was unsmiling now, somber as he ate his supper.

"Should you mind very much if we use some of my dowry to buy additional furniture, Jack?" she asked, determined to keep the conversation going. "And we will need material for curtains, and a carpet for this room."

"Do whatever you wish, my dear. I realize this has been but a bachelor's house, and looks it. It was never anything more to me than shelter, a place to eat and sleep. But now, of course, all that must change. Yes, come to think of it, I could use a desk. I have had to work at this table for lack of one.

"And there are those two rooms I planned to build. We do have the kitchen house, but Annie and Tatum sleep there. And this house only has this front room and two bedrooms. We could add a library for my use, and perhaps a small morning room for you, facing the ocean."

Kate smiled at him. "I trust you will remain here long enough to enjoy them," she said.

He wiped his mouth on his napkin before he answered. "As to that, we shall see. I cannot make my fortune sitting here in Bermuda. And it pains me to see the *Camille* at anchor day after day."

Kate took another piece of cassava bread and buttered it, her eyes lowered. She did not want to think about the day that Jack would sail away. Not now. Not on her wedding night. Time enough to face that pain when she had to, and not a moment before.

13

AFTER supper, they went out to walk the beach until dark. As they strolled along, Kate stole many a glance at her husband's strong profile. He was silent now, much as he had been the day they left Granny Bessie's together. She wondered what he was thinking about, what had happened to change him so. But she would know soon, she was sure.

Still, she was confused. Jack had done nothing more than touch her hand, and when he had carried her to shore from the *Sprite*, he had set her down on the sand without a word or a caress. Would he never kiss her? Hold her close?

They came back to the house at sunset. Jack lit some candles, and after asking her if there were anything he could get for her, he settled down at the table with his ledgers. Kate wanted to shake him, but she made herself go and fetch her sewing box. Somehow she was sure that most newly married couples did not occupy themselves this way on their first evening together, but she did not know what to do or say to change the situation.

The room was quiet except for the ticking of the clock on the mantel, the slight sound when Jack turned a page or dipped his quill in the inkwell, and the scratching of that quill as he wrote.

At last the clock struck ten, and Kate put her sewing away. As she rose, he looked up.

"I think I shall go to bed now, Jack," she told him. She had been rehearsing the words in her mind for the past half-hour, but still they came out in a breathless rush.

He rose to bow to her, but she noted he kept his finger in the ledger to mark his place. "Sleep well," he told her, his turquoise eyes bleak.

"Sleep well?" she echoed, coming to stand before him. "But surely . . . I mean, you . . . aren't you coming . . . ?"

He took her hands in both of his to stare down at her confused, rosy face. "I shall be sleeping in the other room," he told her.

"But why do that?" Kate asked, bewildered. "We are married!"

"Yes, that is true. But you are to be Mrs. Reade in name only," he said.

"I don't understand," Kate whispered. Then she straightened her back and said, "I think you owe me an explanation, sir! There is so much I do not understand about you now—not why you are here, or why you left England in the first place, nor why you refuse to use your title. Come, we are man and wife! You can tell me anything!"

"Not quite anything," he said bitterly. "There are things I must keep to myself. You would not care to hear them."

Kate suddenly remembered something. "Is it . . . is it because I am not beautiful enough? And so thin I do not appeal to you as a woman?" she asked, her voice tortured. "Is that it?"

For reply, Jack pulled her into his arms and held her close for a moment. "No, you must never think that!" he said. "You are lovely, Kate—everything any man could want! But you are not for me, not that way."

Kate was reassured by his embrace, his fervent words. Her eyes were flashing as she said, "You told me you would make me a 'comfortable' husband, sir. Well, I am not comfortable! And if you refuse my bed, you will shame me before everyone! And when you keep secrets from me, what am I to think? I am your wife now. I am supposed to share things with you, ease your mind if I can, see to *your* comfort. Besides, I don't believe anything can be as bad as you say it is."

He sighed then, and went to the side table to pour himself a large brandy. Kate stood where he had left her, determined to remain until he explained himself.

At last he turned back to her and said, "Very well, since you insist. But you will remember, after you have heard my tale, that you *did* insist."

He told her everything then, as coldly and factually as he could, while trying to suppress his turbulent emotions. It took a long time, but she did not interrupt him. At last

he said, "You see where all this leaves me. I am neither
fish nor fowl nor good red meat. It is why I promised
myself I would never marry. And I cannot live on the
estate or touch the money from it, nor use the title
anymore, for it is not mine. It would be like living a lie,
and that I will not, *cannot*, do. Well, madam, now you
know my dark secret. Now you understand. Are you
sorry that you asked me to bare my soul?"

"I am only sorry for you, my dear," she whispered.
"How terrible it must have been to discover such a
thing!"

"Terrible indeed," he agreed, his handsome face distorted with pain. "I felt as if the world I knew had ceased
to exist, as if everything—everyone—I had ever believed
in had proved me false. In that one blinding moment of
revelation, I had become only an empty shell of a man,
with nothing that belonged to me truly but my next
breath."

"But . . . but you are Sir John Reade still! You are *not*
a bastard!" Kate cried, holding out her hands to him.

He ignored their invitation. "Except in my own eyes,"
he told her bitterly before he gulped his brandy.

Kate stared at him, wondering how she was to break
down his awful reserve, get him to see that none of this
mattered to her, no, not one little bit. But before she
could find the words to speak, he said, "Go to bed, Kate.
And sleep well. No doubt we shall grow accustomed to
the situation in time."

He turned his back on her then, and when she did not
move, he said over his shoulder, "No more! Leave me!"

His voice was so harsh and tortured that Kate turned
without another word. In some small way she felt as
helpless and bereft as he had told her he had been when
he learned the truth about himself.

In the room that was to be hers alone, she undressed
by the light of one candle. Her hands were shaking as she
did so. And as she dropped her new white nightrobe over
her head and fastened the tiny pearl buttons at its neck,
she felt like weeping. She had made the robe herself,
of the softest cotton she could find, smocked the bodice
of it, and added the dainty white lace to the collar, all the
while dreaming of Jack's hands taking it off her. And
now she would never know that joy—never.

She lay there alone in the big bed, unable to sleep. Much later, she heard him moving around the adjoining room, heard the creak of the bed as he climbed into it, and still she lay there, her eyes wide as she stared up at the tester far above her. The soft scents of Bermuda drifted into her open windows, and she could hear the tree toads chirping. In the distance there were the ever-present waves as they curled up on the shore below, the hissing sound they made as they retreated. And she thought—thought hard for a very long time.

Jack had had several brandies before he felt it was safe to go to his lonely bed. He only hoped they would help him sleep. Strangely, he felt better now that he had told Kate his story, as if he had been relieved of the terrible burden of carrying the secret alone. He had never intended to reveal it, but he had come to see that she deserved that much consideration, since she must live with the situation from now on. He had had no intention of touching her, but when she had asked him if the reason he would not consummate their marriage was that he did not find her attractive, he had been unable to refrain from taking her in his arms.

Dear God! he thought, rolling over. Not attractive enough? Even now he could remember the feel of her in his arms, the fine bones of her back and shoulders, her soft skin, the gentle swelling of her breasts against his chest. Holding Kate was like holding something infinitely precious. And all through supper, especially when she had wrinkled her nose at him in that familiar gesture, he had longed to kiss every one of those golden freckles.

He rolled over on his other side. He had known this would be difficult, but he had never imagined to what degree. Just to know she was only a room away from him was agony, and it was a very long time before he slept.

The door to his room was opened slowly, cautiously. From the little moonlight that came through the window, Kate was able to tiptoe up to the bed without making a sound. Holding her breath, she climbed in and lay down beside him. And then she wondered what she should do now. It was all very well to have told herself that it would be easy to resolve the problem once she was with him, but now she was not so sure. Jack was sleeping deeply. His breath came in slow waves, and he did not stir.

Well, you're here, do something! she chastised herself. If you don't, you'll fall asleep yourself, and you know how much more difficult all this will be in the clear light of morning!

Biting her lip, she moved closer to him, to cuddle against his back a little tentatively. Then she closed her eyes. How wonderful he felt! she thought. How warm he was, how big and hard and strong!

Now what? she asked herself. She had hoped he would wake up once their bodies were touching, but he had not moved. Steeling herself, she reached up to stroke his back, and she gasped a little when she realized he slept naked.

Her touch, and that gasp, woke Jack in an instant. For a moment, foggy with sleep, he lay there savoring the feel of her curled up next to him. And then he rolled over and grasped her shoulders.

"Whatever do you think you are doing here?" he asked, his voice ragged.

Fumes from the brandy he had consumed swept over her, and she felt light and giddy, almost as if she were intoxicated. "I'm seducing you," she whispered. "Well, I'm trying to, anyway. I've no experience at it, but it occurred to me that since you won't do anything about this, it was up to me to see to it."

Her hands trailed down his chest, to catch in the black hair there, and he tried to put the sensations that hand evoked, away from him. He had to think clearly!

"Kate, this is not right," he said, trying to speak kindly, calmly. "You know my mind, and I am determined—"

"Yes, I heard you, my dear," she told him, fitting her head under his chin while her arms crept around him to hold him close. He could feel her breath against his skin, and he shivered.

"But I am just as determined as you are, you see." She drew a deep breath then. "Jack, I love you," she said, all in a rush. "I have loved you since first meeting, but so much more now. And none of what you told me tonight matters to me in the slightest. I don't care about being Lady Reade. I never did. I just want to be your wife."

He could feel the nipples of her soft breasts against his chest, and as if he had no control over them, his hands left her shoulders to brush the sides of those breasts softly. Kate sighed.

As his hands wandered down to her waist, her hips, urgent in their exploring, she said a little breathlessly, "Do you believe me? Oh, you must, for I never lie!"

"My God, you should be whipped for this, Kate!" he muttered. "I am not made of iron, you know."

"I do hope not, sir, for I am running out of things to do next," she said, her voice a breathy whisper. "But . . . but maybe if I kiss you . . . ? Does that help a seduction?"

He was not even tempted to laugh at her naiveté. How inexperienced she was! And yet she had come to him, even though he was sure she must have been frightened. He wondered if anyone had told her about the act of love. Yet she had come anyway, barefoot and in the dark, even though he had not kissed her or caressed her, not once, to awaken her. And she had told him she loved him. Could that be true? Could she love him enough so that even his being a bastard truly did not matter to her?

He pulled away from her then, to reach for his flint to light the candle. When he turned back, he saw by its light that she was sitting up in the narrow bed. She was wearing a virginal white nightrobe that buttoned to the chin, but he was not tempted to smile. Her long chestnut hair had been brushed smooth, and it fell over her shoulders. He stared into her gray eyes as if trying to see into her soul. Those eyes regarded him steadily.

And then, as if she knew why he had lit the candle, why he had to see her, she said, "I do love you, Jack. Know I will always love you."

She lowered her eyes for a moment to her tightly clasped hands and whispered, "Can't you love me? Just a little?"

"Oh, Kate," he muttered, reaching for her to hold her close again. And as his mouth came down on hers, her lips opened beneath it and he gave in to pure sensation.

When he carried her back to the bigger bed, Kate hid her face in his shoulder and smiled. It was going to be all right now. She had done the right thing.

Once the netting had been pulled down around them, Kate felt as if they were inside their own private misty cocoon. Jack had left the candle burning, set on the chest, and although it felt strange to be undressed by him in its flickering light, strange to be able to see his face, watch his hands on her body, Kate did not protest. Indeed, she wanted to see him clearly too.

She had never realized that she could feel like this, never imagined a man's hands and lips could be so magical, could move her to such sensation as she had only dreamed of before, and then imperfectly. He murmured to her all the time he caressed her, telling her how beautiful she was, how precious; telling her of his love and homage. And when she did not think she could stand the tide of feeling sweeping over her another minute, he paused and whispered, "Forgive me, sweet. This is going to hurt you, but it will be over very soon."

"I know. Keza told me," she said, her eyes glowing. "But she said it would make me your woman. I want that!"

He closed his eyes then and lowered himself, being careful to keep most of his weight on his arms, lest he crush her. He moved slowly and carefully now, keeping his desire for her under tight control until he felt her maidenhead resisting him, and he hesitated. To his delight, Kate was quick to move her hips to meet him, her hands urgent on his back. Her little cry was quickly gone, and, intoxicated by her now, he quickened his thrust until he came to a shuddering release.

A moment later, he lay panting by her side. He reached out to pull her close to him and caress her until he could speak again. So giving she was! So full of love and warmth! He realized his Kate made love the way she smiled—with every fiber of her being—and he knew he was the luckiest of men after all.

"Are you all right, my love?" he asked. "I am sorry I hurt you, but it could not be helped. And I promise it will never hurt again."

"Sssh. I am fine," she said, smoothing back his black hair from his face. "Oh, my! To think of the wonder of it, and I never even knew!"

He grinned down at her then. She was lying on her back, her eyes closed, and she was wearing such a satisfied, beatific smile that he had to chuckle before he bent and kissed those golden freckles on the bridge of her nose. For some reason, he had neglected them up to now.

They spent a week completely alone, except for the slaves. Every morning they went down to the cove to swim naked before they dressed for breakfast. And they walked the beaches, sailed the *Sprite*, and talked of everything under the sun—their childhoods, their dreams, even their disappointments and sorrows. And they made love—wonderful, passionate, consuming love—at all hours of the days and nights.

One day Jack took her out to dive on a reef he had found that contained the remains of a long-sunk caravelle. He told her he was sure there was treasure there.

Kate quickly discovered she did not like diving and being deep under the water, any more than she liked caves. The only part of it she enjoyed was watching the shy, deep-blue angelfish, with their yellow fins and piping, or the parrot fish and striped sergeant majors. Still, she preferred to loll in the boat, keeping an eye out for sharks, while Jack did the diving.

It was almost time to head back to shore when he surfaced, holding a coral-encrusted gold doubloon in each hand. His turquoise eyes were blazing with triumph. "One for each of us, love!" he told her as he climbed aboard to take the huckaback towel she handed him. "Pray they bring us good luck! I've a mind to build a diving bell, get a crew together, and really explore the wreck. What say you?"

Kate smiled at him, he seemed so young, so boyish in his enthusiasm. And she didn't need the doubloon. Her "good luck" was toweling his black hair dry now. Since his face was covered by the towel, she looked her fill at his strong body—those broad shoulders and muscled arms, his firm chest and flat stomach. As her eyes went lower, he tossed the towel down and shook his finger at her.

"Caught in the very act, madam! Have you no shame?"

"Where you are concerned, none at all," she told him. "How can I help admiring you, when you are so beautiful?"

"Huh! Men are not supposed to be beautiful," he

instructed her. "Men can be handsome, seemly, well-set-up, attractive maybe, but not beautiful!"

"You are," she retorted in a voice that brooked no argument. Then she got up to raise the sails while he pulled on his clothes. When she turned back to him, she caught his intense gaze, and she knew he had been staring at her figure in the tight nankeen breeches she wore. "Aha!" she said, shaking her finger at him. "So that is what they mean about what's sauce for the goose being sauce for the gander, is it?"

Jack grinned at her, his eyes admiring. "What else can I do when your brother's breeches fit you so well?" he asked. " 'Sblood!"

And the brilliant days of sun and shower, the long nights spent in each other's arms, were like a dream made up of sensation and of memories carefully stored—of moments so precious they almost made Kate cry when she recalled them. And slowly, slowly, these two began to learn each other—what pleased and what did not, when to speak and when to remain silent, how to amuse or delight or comfort, and how to turn two separate parts into one whole. How to love.

But of course, such an idyll could not go on forever. Farley Williams came one morning just as they were having a last cup of coffee and discussing how they would spend the day. There was a problem at the yard, he told them. Perhaps Jack wouldn't mind coming over and help him see to it? And that evening, Greg came back with Jack for supper. He had been staying at the Williamses' ever since the wedding, and he carried a message to his sister from Maryanne, asking her to call.

"I suppose it was too good to last," Kate complained as she undressed for bed later. "But still, I wish our solitude could have continued longer. And I never did get to go sailing on the *Camille*, as you promised me I might one fine day."

"We've plenty of time for that, love," Jack told her easily. He was already in bed, lying propped up on his goose-feather pillow so he could watch her. Kate had lost any feeling of embarrassment before him days earlier. Jack was so matter-of-fact about his own nakedness that she could hardly disappear behind the screen to undress herself. Besides, he had told her how much he enjoyed watching her, when he was not undressing her himself, that was.

But when she came to bed after using the chamber pot and washbasin behind that screen, she was scowling. *"Dammit!"* she muttered as she climbed into bed beside him.

"You are very free with your cursing, for a lady, madam," Jack scolded as he pulled her down close beside him. "And tell me why you are wearing this large, encompassing nightrobe, when you know I'm sure to remove it."

"But you can't," Kate grumbled, tucking her head under his jaw and nuzzling the warm skin of his shoulder. "I . . . I have started my menses."

There was silence for a moment, and when Jack spoke again, Kate was puzzled. There was something in his tone of voice she could not place. Was he—could he be—relieved? But why would that be so?

"I see it really is time for me to go back to work. But don't grumble, sweet. It doesn't last that long, and no doubt you could use the rest. We have been . . . ah, how shall I phrase it?—very *assiduous* this past week, have we not?"

Kate was still grumbling under her breath, but he only laughed at her before he gave her a tender kiss and a hearty hug and rolled on his side away from her.

After that, they never did completely recapture the halcyon days of their first week together. They were free to spend only Sundays alone together, when Jack did not work at the yard. And sometimes they did not even have that day, for the Hathaways, or George and his bride, often invited them to St. George Town for church services and dinner. Kate wished she might refuse their invitations, much as she loved them all, for she missed having Jack to herself. Now, it seemed, she must share him with the world.

But there were still the nights, she reminded herself, her eyes growing soft as she thought of them. And sometimes, when Jack came home for his dinner, they stole a precious hour in the tester bed then as well.

She wondered if Jack missed their time alone as she did, but she never asked him. She was afraid he might stare at her in amazement if she did. For it appeared to Kate he seemed perfectly content to reenter the world of men—to work on the sloop, search the islands for supplies, plan his next voyage, or oversee the new additions that were being built. She realized that men were very complicated creatures, and difficult to fathom.

Why, just look how excited he had become about building what he called a moongate. It was to face the sea, and it was his bride gift to her. He had first seen a gate like it when he had been in China, and he assured her it would be a breathtaking sight when the full moon rose over the horizon, to shine across the waves, its perfect circle framed by the large circular stone gate.

By Christmastime Kate could tell Jack was growing restless. Sometimes, while they were walking the beach, or just sitting together in the front room in the evenings, she would look up to see him staring in the direction of the ocean, his turquoise eyes distant, shuttered. And the alert way he held his head, as if he were listening to something audible only to him, made her want to cry out, do something to bring him back to her. And sometimes, when he did not realize she was watching him, his face would become so bitter, it made her want to weep for what she knew was bedeviling him still. And weep because all her heartfelt love could not erase the stigma he carried with him always.

He was gone right after the new year, sailing away one pearl-gray dawn in the *Camille*. After he had kissed her good-bye at the house, Kate had walked out to the point to see him go, her eyes as bleak as his had ever been. He had promised to return by springtime, but she knew a great many things might delay him. The chance of an especially lucrative cargo, storms, blockades, or repairs to the sloop.

She sat down on a flat stone, turning over and over in her hands the gold doubloon she wore now on a long gold chain around her neck. And she brooded as the *Camille* grew smaller and smaller in the distance. Pray God he would come back safe! She could not live if he did not.

When the *Camille* was only a distant speck on the horizon, she rose and turned her back. She knew it was bad luck to watch any vessel out of sight. Instead, she made her way back to the house. There were the builders to oversee, and curtains to be made. And she herself had plans to go to Charles Town soon to visit Matt and Alicia and baby Rosemary. While she was there, she would purchase the furniture that she and Jack had decided they needed. Oh, yes, she knew there was a great deal to do that would keep her busy. Busy, yes. Not happy. Never happy—until he returned.

She went to stay with her parents for several days, but although she was glad to see them, even comforted by their company, somehow she felt a stranger there. She knew then she could never return to being the daughter of the house, not that she had any wish to do so. And even if it was lonely out on the point past Tucker's Town, that was where her memories of Jack were strongest. And she could fall asleep in their own bed beneath the netting, and dream that he was beside her.

She had been disappointed when she discovered she was not with child, as she had hoped to be before Jack sailed. But at least now there could be no stigma attached to their hasty wedding, no whispering behind raised hands as she grew larger and larger. For she knew the women of St. George Town were watching and waiting. Sometimes their glances at her narrow waist were so obvious that Kate wanted to laugh in their avid faces.

The elder Hathaways came out to stay with Kate for the launching of the new sloop. Greg was euphoric about her, so graceful and tall-masted, so much his own! Kate did not know what the sloop was to be called until the day of the launch, for Greg had told her it was a secret that he was pledged to keep.

So when he drank down the glass of port, corked the bottle and flung it at the bow, and cried, "I name this sloop the *Lady Sprite*," Kate's eyes filled with tears. That was Jack's secret name for her, what he whispered when they were making love. It was a lovely tribute, and her heart ached, wanting him there so she might tell him how touched she was by his gesture.

It was late February when Greg sailed away. He took Samuel Simpson with him in the *Lady Sprite*. Jack had explained to Kate that he would feel better if old Samuel went along with her brother, for Greg had a reckless streak sometimes, and often made decisions too quickly, without considering all his options. Jack himself had made

Christopher Abbott the new mate of the *Camille*, and hired another seaman to take his place in the crew.

And now there were two Reade sloops plying the shipping lanes between Bermuda, the Caribbean, and the colonies. Kate wondered if they might not come across each other somewhere on their journeys, and envied them the encounter if they should.

One day in April, right after she returned from Charles Town with the new furniture and carpets, Kate made a call on Granny Bessie. She was concerned for the old lady, left alone again. But Granny seemed perfectly content. There was enough money now so she did not have to worry, no matter how long her slave might be gone, and the prospect of even more wealth when he returned.

As they sat drinking tea, Granny eyed her young visitor carefully, noting how quiet Kate had become, the loss of sparkle in her gray eyes, and the absence of her heartfelt smile. She set her cup down on the table so she could lean forward and take the girl's hands in hers.

"You are missing your husband, are you not, my dear Kate?" she asked, stroking those hands softly. "I know what you are feeling as a bride. But remember what I told you. A sailor's wife must be strong. It it a hard life."

Kate sighed. "Yes, I know. But I miss him more every day. And he has been gone for almost four months now, twice as long as the time we had together. Sometimes I cannot sleep for wanting him home, and I worry about him so! Granny, does it ever get easier? Does there ever come a day when you stop worrying and praying? Even accept the separation?"

Granny Bessie shook her head, her faded eyes sad. "No, I don't believe it ever does. Sometimes you can forget for a while, if you are busy, but the feeling always comes back, because you sense that half of you is missing. I lived with it for years. Do you know, the time I used to miss Will the most was at mealtimes? Eating alone, without him across the table from me, seemed the worst thing about it of all! But every one of us has our own special bugbears. And you must remember, Kate, he is missing you just as much."

"Huh! No, he's not," Kate said. "I don't believe it, for I know Jack. He's busy and happy, sailing and trading and making plans. I don't expect he thinks of me more than once or twice a day—if that!"

Granny Bessie laughed long and hard, and Kate looked surprised. "Oh, my dear girl," the old lady said as she wiped her eyes on her apron, "but you are describing all men, you know! They don't feel things as intensely as we do, and they have a world we can never enter. A woman's life is a seamless garment; a man's is divided neatly into different compartments."

"But maybe right now he is in port and someone is smiling at him, flirting," Kate whispered, suddenly deciding to bare her soul and reveal one of her most persistent nightmares. "Someone lovely, full-figured, who will attract Jack. And I am so far away!"

Granny shook her finger at her woebegone guest. "Now, you listen to me, young woman," she said in quite the sternest voice Kate had ever heard her use. "You must accept the fact that men are different from us in that way too. If your Jack takes another woman while he is gone, it is only male nature that drives him to it. It will not mean anything to him, beyond the simple gratification of the flesh. For he will sail away from her to return to you. You are his wife.

"And if you are wise, you will never, never ask him about it, for to do so will put him in a terrible position. If he has fallen from grace, he will either have to admit it, which will damage your marriage in an irretrievable way, or have to lie to you. No, you must keep your tongue between your teeth, do you hear me? Some things are better left unknown. For how will you feel if he does admit a lapse, from either loneliness or need? Best not to know at all. Best to pretend he has been faithful, and let it go at that."

Kate nodded, but still, as she walked back to her parents' house, she wondered if she could be so wise. She worried about so many things: pirates, privateers, fights at sea, even Jack's being killed or maimed, or lost overboard on a stormy night. But of all her fears, the picture of him in some other woman's arms was by far the worst, the most painful. He wouldn't do that to her, would he? Could he?

She nodded to Mrs. Kempthorne a little absently as she passed, for she was wondering if Jack had called at

Statia again; if that Dutchwoman he had spent so much time with on his first trip was still living there. Would he take up with her again, just as if he were not married, as if there were no Kate Reade, wife, waiting for him at home? She could not bear it!

But she promised herself she would heed Granny Bessie's advice. She would not ask him anything.

And so, of course, being Kate, it was practically the first thing she did ask when he came home at last.

14

ONE beautiful early May day, when there was a fresh breeze blowing off the ocean, Kate decided to turn out the bedrooms. It had been a rainy April, and she had had to put off this housewifely chore. But today, with Annie and Tatum's help, she could see to it. Tatum dragged the carpets, blankets, and mattresses out in the sun to beat them, and Annie washed the curtains and sheets. Kate spread them on the bushes to dry. She had just stepped back to admire their pristine whiteness when she sensed someone staring at her, and she turned.

And there, as if conjured up by some benevolent fairy, was her long-gone husband. He was smiling at her, his white grin and turquoise eyes a brilliant contrast to the dark tan of his face.

"Jack! At last!" she cried, dropping the basket she carried, to run and throw herself in his arms.

He caught her up and kissed her soundly, much to the slaves' delight. Kate put her arms around his neck and snuggled as close to him as she could get, almost delirious with joy. When he lifted his head at last, he murmured, "How I have missed you, my Lady Sprite!"

"And I have missed you, love, so much, so much," she whispered. "It has been such a long time! Promise me you won't go away again—not for ages, anyway!"

He kissed the bridge of her nose lightly before he set her down to greet the slaves. As Tatum took his portmanteau inside and Annie scurried away to prepare a festive dinner in honor of his homecoming, Jack inspected the domestic scene in his yard.

"Is that our mattress I see there, Kate?" he asked, his arm tight around her. "And our sheets and pillows? Even the mosquito netting?"

"Oh, why did I choose today of all days to freshen everything?" Kate mourned. "I had hoped to have it all done by the time you came home!"

"It is unfortunate," he agreed. "But then, we have waited all this time for each other. A few more hours won't matter, I guess."

She stared at him, and the color rose in her cheeks. Then she took his hand. "Let's swim," she suggested.

She sent him ahead of her to the cove, and when she followed him moments later, he saw she was carrying a blanket, as well as their huckaback towels.

They did not swim till much later. Kate was sure she had never been so happy in her life as when she was naked in his arms again, stretched out beside him on the blanket. Her hands caressed every inch of him, and she had tears in her eyes as she silently thanked God for his safe return. Jack made love to her urgently, and with a hunger that reassured her about his faithfulness.

Sated, for now at least, they lay in each other's arms and talked. Jack told her he had just arrived a little while ago, that he had brought the *Camille* to Stokes Bay first because he could not wait to see her.

"But tomorrow, of course, I must sail her to St. George Town to the customs," he told her. "Mayhap you would like to join me, love?"

She nodded, before she demanded to hear everything about his voyage. He told her he had gone to Charles Town first, and then on to Statia for a cargo to sell in New England.

Kate sat up then, her gray eyes stormy. "You went back to Statia?" she asked.

Jack did not notice her ominous tone. "Indeed. There is a Dutch merchant there who is instrumental in getting me the cargoes that bring the most money in the colonies. And, Kate, you will not believe how profitable this voyage has been. Why—"

"Did you see *her* again?" Kate interrupted, glaring at him. "Did you?"

"Who?" Jack asked, looking bewildered.

"Your Dutchwoman!" she snapped. "The one you were so entranced with on your last voyage that you barely left her bed for days and days!"

"However did you learn of Greta Dreeber?" he asked.

"I overheard Greg telling George about her, right after you both returned. Well, tell me! Did you see her?"

"Of course I did. Statia is a small place and she lives there," Jack said easily.

"Were you unfaithful to me?" Kate demanded, sounding quite fierce. "Did you make love to her again? Forget me? . . . Well, answer me!"

Jack rose to tower over her. "No, I will not answer you," he said, his own voice rough with anger now. "What right have you to ask such a thing?"

"What right? I am your wife! Of course I demand to know!"

"You will not know, madam, and let that be the end of it. I am most displeased with you and your accusations. Is this any way to welcome me home, like a testy shrew, loud and shrill? Ecod! I've a mind to teach you a lesson!"

Kate was scrambling to her feet now, and in spite of his anger, Jack admired her slim curved body as she did so. But even as much as he wanted to reach for her, crush her against him again, even as much as he admitted his need for her, he did not. He had not been unfaithful to her, but her assumption that he might have been angered him beyond imagining.

When he had first sailed away, he had thought of her a great deal, relived their short married life together, wondered at the intensity of his feelings for her. She had even made him forget England, Hythe, his mother and Alex. And all the way back from Boston, he had prayed for favorable winds to speed the time of their reunion. And now she had ruined it all.

Anger rose in his throat again, and he snarled, "I beg you have a care, madam! There is still the ducking stool for scolding, recalcitrant wives!"

"No! You wouldn't dare!" she exclaimed, sounding horrified. "If you ever did such a thing to me, Jack, I'd . . . I'd *kill* you!"

Jack was taken aback by her passionate outcry, the way her gray eyes glittered almost black in her fury. She had never looked so handsome.

Suddenly she put both hands over her face, and her shoulders slumped. "Oh, *dammit*," she wailed. "Now I've ruined everything! And Granny Bessie warned me, but I didn't heed her, and . . . and . . . Oh, Jack, please forgive me! You must!"

Her hands dropped then, and he saw the misery in her face, the way she was trying so valiantly to contain her tears. His anger melted away, and he put his arms around her. He was smiling a little now, at that familiar curse of hers. While he had been gone, he had remembered that about her too, and chuckled every time he thought of it.

"I'll forgive you, but only if you get our bed reassembled by nightfall," he told her, tipping her chin up with one finger so he could kiss each eyelid. "The beach is all very well, but, er . . . sandy, don't you agree? I'm for a swim. Are you coming?"

Kate nodded, but he saw her eyes were still troubled. It would be easy to restore her sunny good humor by telling her of his faithfulness, but he did not do so. It had become a matter of principle. And deep inside, he was hurt, and he admitted it. Hurt that she could doubt him, hurt that she thought him so casual, just like a rutting animal in heat. Did she put so little trust in him and his love for her?

As he dived into the crystal waters of the cove and began to swim, he remembered his meeting with Greta in Statia. He had just rowed ashore after dropping anchor, and was striding toward Van Dam's warehouse, when he heard his name called.

Turning, he spotted her standing before a market stall, a basket on her arm. As he went toward her, he saw she was as lovely as ever, with her lush figure and white skin, that gleaming pale blond hair. She was smiling at him, holding out her hand in welcome, but as he took it and bowed over it, she stared at him, her smile fading away.

"What is it, Jack?" she asked softly. "What has changed you?"

"Is it that obvious?" he asked, his mouth twisting in a wry grin. "I'm married now, but I did not think myself a marked man by it."

Greta had laughed, the slow, rich chuckle he remembered from the past. "Perhaps not to everyone, but I am—how do you say it?—more perspicacious than most. Is she nice, this wife of yours? Do you love her?"

"Yes, I do," Jack said at once. "I never thought to love anyone so well, but Kate—it would be impossible not to love Kate."

"I am glad for you," Greta said. "I wish you both happiness."

She saw he looked uncomfortable, this big handsome young man. Uncomfortable, and more than a little ashamed, and her heart went out to him. Loving him still, as she did, she decided to be kind.

"I myself am to be married shortly," she said.

She was glad she had been so magnanimous, for his face cleared immediately.

"But you once said marriage would be too fatiguing," he reminded her.

She shrugged. "This one will not be. My future husband is a much older man. He adores me, but more as a daughter than a wife."

Jack looked dubious now. "But, Greta, he does not sound a fit mate for you. Will you be happy with such a man?"

She made herself smile, chuckle. "Of course I will. It will be . . . restful. And he is kind and good, and very, very wealthy. I shall be leaving Statia shortly to join him in the Netherlands."

"I wish you only the best, Greta," Jack said. "I will never forget you, nor a certain night of tropical downpour."

Her smile was genuine this time. "*Ja*, it is good to have memories like that, is it not? They will warm our bones when we are old. Good-bye, Jack. Take care of yourself. Be happy always."

She had left him then, and as Jack continued on his way, he pondered his new reaction to her. He had expected to have the same physical longing he had had last time, in spite of his marriage. And yet, there had been nothing beyond the little stirring any man felt in the presence of a beautiful, desirable woman. Certainly there had been no rush of hot desire to possess her again. Strange, that. Marriage seemed to have changed him in a great many ways. He remembered now how quickly he had put Greta from his mind, forgotten her completely. For now, just before he went to sleep, only Kate's face appeared in his mind's eye. He could hardly wait to see her again.

And yet, now that he was home with her at last, everything was different, because of her jealousy, her distrust. As he rolled over on his back to float, Jack told himself he must forget that, put it down to her youth, her inexperience, and her love for him.

Nothing more was said about the voluptuous Greta Dreeber, and on the surface, everything was as it always had been in the weeks that followed. But Kate could not quite quell a nagging little doubt that by not denying any adultery, Jack had as much as admitted his guilt. And sometimes, after he had fallen asleep, she would lie beside him staring up into the darkness, to wonder if he had ever compared his wife to the Dutchwoman, to her, Kate's, detriment.

Their lovemaking was as consuming, as ecstatic, as it had always been. But their first quarrel had brought a shadow between them which Kate would have sold her soul to eradicate. Why didn't I listen to Granny? she wondered as she tried to arrange her pillow more comfortably one night. How could I have been so stupid?

Maryanne Williams had a baby girl in June, whom she named Olivia Mary. Kate's mother had come out from St. George Town to be with her for the birth, much to Kate's relief, for she had been afraid Maryanne might ask her instead. But when she herself saw the newborn infant, held her in her own arms, she felt a wave of yearning rise in her breast. She was still not with child, and she could not understand it, not with the regularity with which she and Jack made love. Of course, there were certain times of the month when he seemd preoccupied, almost uninterested in lovemaking, and several times, at the last moment, he had withdrawn from her to spill his seed on her belly. When Kate had asked him why, he had only kissed her freckles and told her he had a good reason for it, and to go to sleep now. Kate did not persist in her questions, although she wanted to. Jack was home now, busy drawing up plans for the brigantine he intended to build, and Kate was determined to do nothing

to upset his peace. But she made plans herself to talk all
this over with Keza. Keza would know, if anyone did.

Jack had made a diving bell, modeled after one he had
seen in England. And after he had tested it in shallow
waters, he bought a Jamaican slave noted for his diving
prowess, and went out with him to plunder the reef he
had shown Kate. The two men brought up a vast number
of gold doubloons, and some gold drinking cups and
plate.

Kate went out to the reef only once. She did not like to
watch Jack sinking lower and lower in the bell, and it was
boring and hot in the sun with only Manfred, the sullen
black diver, for company. And of course, she was not
alone with Jack as before.

One day, when Jack went out diving early, Kate took
the *Sprite* and sailed to St. George Town. She had some
errands to do, but the main purpose of her trip was to see
her beloved Keza.

Kate found her busy with her baking in the kitchen
house, quite alone, and it was not long before she was
pouring out her concerns about her husband and their
inability to conceive a child.

Keza listened as she kneaded the bread she was making, and she had no comment until at last Kate finished
her tale.

"Sounds to me as if Cap'n Jack done decided he doan
want chillun," Keza said then. "Y'all ever axed him iffen
he did, Miz Kate?"

Kate shook her head, looking troubled.

"Iffen he done avoid y'all de middle o' de month, 'n
spill his seed, dat's a sure sign," the cook told her. Then
she dusted her hands on a cloth, and came to put her
arms around her baby.

"Mebbe y'all should ax him, honey. Doan do no good
'tall jess a-frettin' 'bout it by you lonesome. Have it out
wit 'im. He you man now."

Kate's face brightened, but only for a moment. Then
she buried her head on Keza's shoulder and whispered of
what she had done when Jack had first come home.

"Miz Kate!" Keza exclaimed. "Oh, my, chile! Y'all so
'petuous! Why y'all do dat? Now he think y'all a jealous
woman, and mens, dey hate dat kind. An' such a fuss

'bout such a silly thing! You wuzn't dere, an' he all a man, de cap'n.''

"I know, Keza. It was stupid. I have regretted it ever since. However, everything is all right between us now. But . . . but Jack will be gone again soon. It's almost August. I know he plans another voyage soon. And then I will have to stay at home and fret again! Dammit, I hate being a sailor's wife! I *hate* it!''

Keza's rich chuckle echoed off the thick whitewashed walls of the kitchen as she went back to her dough. "It be a bit late fo' dat, honey," she reminded the girl. "You *iz* one now. Got to make de best o' it. But why doan y'all go wit 'im? Lots o' wimmins sail wit dere husbands.''

"Suppose he won't let me come?" Kate whispered, her eyes shining now at such a wonderful idea.

"Den y'all got to stow away, Ah guess," Keza told her, chuckling again at the thought. "Oh, my, chile, y'all brings de sunshine wit you when y'all come! Sho do miss y'all, way over dere in Tucker's Town.''

When Kate finally left, after dinner and a visit with her parents, she had a lot to think about. Could Jack truly not want children? Was it because he still thought of himself as a bastard? she wondered. But that was silly! No one here in Bermuda knew of it, so what difference did it make?

Her gray eyes grew somber as she realized that Jack knew—and could not forget. And if he had decided he would not produce an heir for Hythe, because it was not truly his to bequeath to his son, there was little she could do about it. Unless, by some miracle, she should find herself with child by accident.

She also thought about Keza's joking comment that she might have to stow away on the *Camille*, to enable her to go with Jack when next he sailed. And until she anchored the *Sprite* in the private cove again, she was busy making plans to do just that if she had to.

To her surprise, she found a note waiting for her at the house. It was from Maryanne Williams, and it begged her to come over at once, for she had some stupendous news that could not keep till morning.

Telling Annie where she was going, Kate walked to Tucker's Town, wondering what the news might be. She only prayed that Maryanne was not with child again. But surely that could not be possible, she told herself, not so soon after the new baby. Besides, the note had sounded as if Maryanne was excited, not angry.

Maryanne was more animated than Kate had ever seen her. She called to Sukey to bring them a cool drink before she whirled Kate in a mad jig down the length of the veranda. Farley was at the yard as usual. Kate spotted his bright red head among the other workmen's.

"Kate! Such glorious news! La, you will stare when you hear!" Maryanne told her after the two had collapsed laughing in the rustic chairs. "Farley has had a letter from England! It seems both his uncle and cousin have died in a smallpox epidemic. Isn't that grand?"

Kate stared at her, wondering if she had gone mad to be happy about such a dire event, and Maryanne blushed.

"Of course, I don't mean their deaths were grand," she hastened to say, and then she hung her head. "Except they truly are—for us, anyway. You see, Farley's uncle was Lord Stern. And now Farley, as the next in line to inherit, is the viscount. Oh, Kate, we can go home! *Home!* And I will have an estate to manage, be m'lady, Viscountess Stern! Was ever anything so marvelous?"

Kate congratulated her on her sudden good fortune, and begged her to walk over with Farley for supper later, so he could apprise Jack of the news as well.

"Yes, we'll be sure to come," Maryanne told her. "Farley must find someone to buy the yard, take it over. I suspect he hopes Jack will do that. It would be such a neat solution, and it will speed the time until we can be gone. I confess, I have already begun to pack!"

Remembering Farley's contentment in Bermuda, Kate asked a little shyly, "Does Mr. Williams want to go home, Maryanne? He seems so happy here."

Maryanne tossed her blond curls and looked militant. "It makes no never-mind what he wants," she said. "He must! He is the viscount now, and his inheritance awaits him. Besides, he knows how I feel about it. He'll go all right!"

It seemed Maryanne had not made a vain boast. When she and her husband came to visit that evening, Farley Williams seemed resigned to it, although Kate noticed he rarely smiled, and his usually merry eyes were somber.

To everyone's disappointment, Jack professed no interest in taking over the yard. Kate had thought perhaps it would be a good way to stop his wandering, keep him safe at home, but he was firm in his refusal.

"I am sorry, Farley, Maryanne," he said as soon as the proposal was made to him. "I've no mind to stop sailing and trading, not yet. But I'm sure you'll have no trouble finding a buyer. The yard is such a success. Just spread the word in St. George Town, and you might be surprised."

Farley nodded, his face glum, as Maryanne added, "You must do so tomorrow, husband. That way we can be home by winter, and the voyage will be easier on the children. But I should have called you 'm'lord,' should I not? To think how you have been elevated!"

She laughed and smiled, and she was still smiling when they took their leave. Jack shook his head as he and Kate undressed for bed. "Poor Farley," he said carelessly. "He was truly happy here. It is too bad, for he's not at all cut out for the life of a lord."

"Maryanne will more than make up for any lack of his," Kate told him. "She can hardly wait to come into her new glory. I wouldn't be at all surprised if she doesn't insist the slaves start calling her 'milady' now."

Jack chuckled as he pulled her down on the bed and into his arms. "How glad I am that you have no such pretensions, Mrs. Reade," he said. "When I compare my marriage to poor Farley's, I pity him. He goes only for his wife's sake, for he told me how he loves the islands, how he planned to remain here forever. As her husband, I suppose he could insist on it, of course, but I am sure he knows what a misery his life would become with Maryanne's sulking and pouting. She's already given him a taste of it when she has been displeased in the past. Ah, Kate, you are a jewel in comparison to *that* lady."

He kissed her soundly then. "Mmmm," he said. "How good you taste!"

His hands caressed her arms and wandered to her waist before he shook his head. "No, better not. Manfred and I made a great many dives today. Alas, we found but a few more doubloons."

As he yawned and stretched out in bed, Kate looked at him. He was smiling even so, and seemed in such a good humor that she said a little breathlessly, "Jack, have you ever wondered why I haven't conceived?"

His eyes narrowed, and he propped himself up on one elbow. "It's late, and I'm tired, Kate. Could we discuss this another time?"

Kate stared down at her clasped hands. Then she took a deep breath and said all in a rush, "Is it because you don't want to have children, Jack? Because of Hythe, the inheritance? If it is, I will understand, but . . . but I wanted you to know that I would like to have your baby. Very much."

She sounded so wistful that Jack forgot his weariness, to gather her in his arms and hold her close. "I wish you might, my love, but it is not to be. Yes, it is because of Hythe. That part of my life is over. It took me a long time to accept it—indeed, I often dreamed of returning home again after I reached Bermuda. But I came to see I was indulging in fantasy. My life is here now. As far as my family is concerned, I am dead. It was better that way, that clean break."

"But if you never go back, why can't we have children?" Kate persisted. "We wouldn't have to worry about Hythe then, or the inheritance, not here in Bermuda."

"You are not thinking, madam," Jack told her, his voice growing colder. "Whether or not I use the title, I am still Sir John Reade. And so my son will be after me. I will neither foist an impostor on the estate, nor, someday, have to look into my son's eyes and admit my shame. No! Never that! It was hard enough for me to tell you! There will be no children, Kate."

As he put her away from him and lay down again, Kate's eyes widened. Of course she was disappointed at his ultimatum, but she had been half-expecting it, so it had come as no real surprise to her. What did startle her was learning that Jack did not even correspond with his mother, his father—that they thought him dead.

"Jack, what you said just now. Did you mean that your family does not know where you are or how you are? That they don't know of our marriage?" she asked.

The only answer she received was a little snore. Lying down beside her sleeping husband, Kate decided it was better he had not heard her question after all. For after she said her prayers and composed herself for sleep, Kate told herself she would write to Countess Granbourne herself. Somehow she was sure Jack would not approve such a correspondence. But the poor lady! Not to even know her son was well and happy, and he had been gone for two years now!

It took Kate a long time to compose that letter to her satisfaction. There was so much to tell about Jack and his life here. And she couldn't help feeling a little shy as she wrote, even if she was the lady's daughter-in-law now, for she had never met Camille Maxwell. She only knew what Jack had told her their first week of marriage. He had never mentioned his mother again. But she must be wonderful, and understanding, Kate thought. Jack loved her so, in spite of his anguish over his birth.

When she went to St. George Town again, Kate asked her father to see her letter safely aboard the next ship to England. To her relief, Roger Hathaway did not question this unusual request, when his daughter had a perfectly good husband to see to it instead.

The long sunny days of August passed slowly. In the Williams shipyard the brigantine was quickly taking shape, the naked futtocks that rose from her keel looking massive after those of the smaller sloops that had preceded her.

Farley Williams had found a buyer for the yard. To Kate's delight, her brother George had decided to purchase it and move into the Williamses' house with his wife, Cecily. He claimed he had done enough sailing; it was time he settled down. Kate was delighted they would be so close.

By the end of August, the Williamses were gone, Maryanne sporting an ecstatic smile that was quite at odds with her husband's sad air of resignation. The elder Hathaways had given a small party for them the night before they sailed, and although Kate kissed Maryanne and told her how she would miss her, deep in her heart she knew she would not miss her at all. Maryanne had grown so proud now that she was viscountess! And although Maryanne had suggested it might be more fitting, Kate had not been able to call her "Lady Stern."

Kate knew she would miss Farley, however.

She had chanced to hear him talking to Jack that last evening, and the sorrow and regret in his voice had saddened her.

"How I wish I did not have to leave Bermuda," he had said. "But Maryanne is miserable here. Strange, is it not? I have been happier and more content than I ever was at home, but now I must put that happiness aside."

"But you could have insisted on it," Jack had said even as he sounded doubtful about the wisdom of such a course. "After all, you are her husband. Where you and your family will live is your decision."

"No, there you are wrong, my friend. But you're married yourself now. Could you choose to do something that you knew would make Kate miserable? I don't think so. I've seen the love in your eyes for her when you look at her."

Kate waited breathlessly, but she was to be disappointed. Before Jack could speak, Farley had gone on, "I never wanted to be a lord, you know, never wanted the estate or the responsibility. I love the sea, working beside it, building the ships that sail it. But Maryanne considers shipbuilding a lowly profession, and my becoming Viscount Stern the coup of a lifetime. And I can only shudder at it. And whereas she misses the pomp and cold formality of England, I have reveled in the freedom of the New World, where every man is on his mettle to prove himself, and none are better than others because of name or background. Sometimes I wonder how two so disparate ever came to marry in the first place. Life is strange indeed, my friend."

The two had wandered away then, and Kate had pondered their conversation for quite a while. Yes, Farley did love that silly little woman; loved her enough to put his own desires aside. Kate wondered if perhaps it was like this in every marriage, if one partner always loved more than the other, gave more, *bent* more to assure the other's joy. Surely Maryanne made no concessions for Farley, poor man!

And when she saw his yearning glance ashore the next morning from the deck of the ship the family was taking passage on, a lump formed in her throat. Maryanne was facing the bow and smiling, even though she was standing beside her husband and children. It was almost as if she fancied England was just over the horizon, and they would be there tomorrow, instead of two or even three months from now.

*   *   *

By the first of September, Jack's plans for his next voyage were complete. He had salvaged enough gold from the wrecked caravelle so he could sail directly to Statia, without calling at Charles Town to collect a cargo. It would shorten the trip, and gold, that scarce commodity, would get him a better price. And Jack was in a hurry, although he was careful to keep any signs of it from Kate.

On his last visit to Boston, the merchant Charles Winslow had told him all about the Boston Tea Party, and although Jack had laughed as heartily as his host, he knew the "party" boded no good for the colonies. For in May, an irate ministry in London had hurried a set of laws through Parliament that everyone in America was calling the Intolerable Acts. Not the least of these was the closing of the port of Boston until such time as the East India Company, the owner of the jettisoned tea, had been paid for it in full and customs had been collected for every last wet leaf of it.

What would England do next? Jack wondered. And what would the colonies do in retaliation, for retaliation was sure to come. It always had before. Just last week he had read a speech by Edmund Burke, given in the House of Commons earlier, in which Burke mocked the backtracking that occurred after every new tax was imposed, and the colonists found a way to get around it. "What enforcing and what repealing; what bullying and what submitting; what doing and what undoing!" Burke had said, loud in his derision.

And how long would it be before cargoes such as the one he planned were forbidden? He hoped it would be quite a while, for powder, shot, and rifles were extremely profitable to him, far more so than sugar, rum, and molasses. But once they were declared illegal, once that revolution Matthew Hathaway was so sure of, began, Jack, in good conscience, would stop carrying arms. He was an Englishman and loyal to his country, even though he might never see it again. He only hoped he would have enough saved so he and Kate could be comfortable.

He had had another letter from his agent regarding the monies accruing from Hythe. They were becoming a tidy sum. But he would never touch that money now, no

matter how badly he might need it. It would be like
stealing, and he was no more a thief than he was a rebel
or a traitor.

The day before he was to sail, Kate told him that she
had to go to St. George Town to be with her mother.
Jack was not surprised. At the party for the Williamses,
he had seen how Olivia Hathaway was fretting because
her son Greg had not returned as yet. And Kate had
spent a lot of time with her lately, trying to reassure her.
But although Greg had been gone for only seven months,
Olivia Hathaway could not be comforted. Jack found
himself growing impatient with his mother-in-law, and
tried to avoid her. She was a silly woman, all suspicions
and superstitions, airs and graces. He was glad his Kate
took after her practical father.

He watched his wife pack a portmanteau now, and he
grinned as he said, "Well, I see we have become an old
married couple indeed! And here I was planning a most
energetic night tonight, to say good-bye to you properly,
love."

Kate wrinkled her nose at him. "If I remember correctly, Captain, you did that last night, right after we
watched the full moon rise, to be framed by your
moongate. I think you were bewitched by the sight, but I
cannot tell you how delighted I am that you had it built,
since the results were so . . . hmmm . . . fulfilling."

"You, madam, are a saucy baggage," he told her. As
she nodded in complete agreement, he went on, "Will
you take the *Sprite*?"

"Not this time. I'll row the dory over to the reach. The
ferrymen can watch it for me till I return. I may have to
stay with my mother for quite a while. My father says she
is most distraught, that she has a premonition of disaster."

Jack kissed her long and hard, unwilling to discuss
Mrs. Hathaway any longer. How he would miss Kate!
Yet to his surprise and chagrin, she appeared to be
taking their coming separation with a lot more composure than she had last time. He wondered at it, but then
his mate, Christopher Abbott, knocked on the door with
some questions about supplies, and he was diverted.

Still, early the next morning, as the *Camille* sailed past
the point, he could not help frowning that he did not see

Kate standing there waving her apron to him in farewell. How unbelievably selfish a man could be! he chided himself as he turned his attention to the reefs they must avoid before they reached the open sea and he could set a course for Statia.

Later that day, a storm came up, and he was forced to shorten sail. Some of the crew were troubled with sea-sickness, as they always were after a long spell ashore, and he was shorthanded. Still, he was pleased to be at sea again, the *Camille* responsive to his hand on the helm. Even with reefed sails, Jack knew they were making splendid time.

He had turned the watch over to his mate late that evening, and was relaxing in his hammock in the stern cabin, when he heard a strange sound. He rose, clutching the side of the hammock to keep his balance in the rough seas, and wondering at that alien sound. Suddenly it came again—a stifled groan. He hurried to go and open his large sea chest.

His amazement and anger at seeing Kate curled up inside turned to concern at the green pallor of her complexion, and without a word he hauled her to her feet and hurried her to a basin.

While he held her head, Kate retched for a long time. At last she leaned back against his chest and said weakly, "Dammit! I never thought how I would feel trapped inside there in this weather. I'm . . . I'm sorry."

When he would have lifted her into the hammock, she shook her head. "I must have some air first! I'll be all right then. You are not to worry about me. I'm never sick at sea."

As he took her up the ladder to the deck, Jack muttered, "And then, madam, no doubt you'll be good enough to explain what you are doing here, and how you got aboard in the first place. You lied to me with that tale of your mother! Ecod, I've a mind to come about and take you back right now! For you knew I didn't want you to sail with me, else you would have asked my permission to do so, instead of stowing away. Admit it!"

Kate ignored a flabbergasted Christopher Abbott at the wheel as she whispered, "Yes, yes, of course I knew. But you can't take me back. It would delay you, and truly, there is no need."

She breathed deeply of the fresh salt air, and Jack waited patiently until he saw the color come back in her cheeks.

"Well, Kate?" he asked in a tightly controlled voice. "You were about to explain, I believe?"

"Lots of women go with their husbands," she said evasively. "Why, Granny Bessie told me she went any number of times! And just last month Beth Caswell sailed on her husband's schooner. And then there was—"

"I do not require the name of every woman you know who has done so, madam," Jack interrupted, looking grim. "May I remind you those ladies went at their husbands' *invitations*? In a time of peace and tranquillity?"

"But we *are* at peace," Kate argued. "And if we are not, why then did Captain Caswell allow—"

"We are not discussing the Caswells!" Jack snapped. He grasped her shoulders then and shook her. "Do not try my patience further, wife! Tell me at once why you did such a wild, improvident thing, and against my wishes, as you have just admitted."

Kate stared into his blazing eyes and quickly lowered her own. She had never seen Jack so angry, and she was a little frightened. "I had to be with you. I . . . I could not bear another long separation," she told him. "Besides, I heard you and George discussing the cargo you intended to carry, and I have been so worried! Guns, Jack! Powder! How could you? Surely such a thing is dangerous! Why, the risk of explosion makes me shiver! One well-placed shot from a pirate's guns could blow you all to kingdom come! Besides, my father says delivering guns to the malcontents in the colonies is the act of a traitor. Think, Jack! Those you trade with in the colonies are rebels! And you would aid them in their insurrection?"

She dared a sideways glance at him before she added, more softly now, "I stowed away because I wanted to convince you to change your mind. But even if I couldn't do so, I . . . I thought you might not carry out your plan just because I was aboard."

"You are a meddling fool," he said roughly. "Know that your presence will not deter me from my course, Kate! No, you must take your chances with the rest of us, since you wanted to come so badly. And your father is mistaken. I am not a traitor. The colonies are not at war with England. Powder and guns are not contraband yet. Did you think I would allow my *wife* to dictate to me? Or her family? Fool! I, and I alone, determine the *Camille*'s cargoes."

She would have answered him hotly, but Jack looked around then and saw Babur and Tom staring at them from the foredeck, and he motioned to the hatch. "We'll go below now," he ordered. "I've no mind for my crew to see how I have been defied by you, or for them to have to listen to your silly feminine fears. Come!"

Kate found herself propelled by a large firm hand at the small of her back. Once below, in the stern cabin again, she looked at Jack apprehensively in the light of the lantern, swinging in its gimbals from the deckhead. He looked so furious that she was frightened. Those turquoise eyes were icy now, and his whole body was taut with rage. She noticed his clenched fists, and shivered. Surely he would not beat her! Would he?

To her relief, Jack turned away for a moment, struggling for control. When he turned back to her, he inspected her from head to foot. "Nor do I care for the crew to see my wife—my wife!—wearing those tight breeches. Have you no modesty? No decorum at all, madam?" he demanded.

"But I can't sail in petticoats," Kate protested. "And they've all seen me time without number in my breeches. I don't understand this sudden prudishness of yours, Jack!"

"Men at sea are not like men ashore, especially during a long voyage. Surely *you* should know that," he told her coldly. "Do you have a skirt? Put it on at once!"

Kate recovered her portmanteau from the dark corner where she had hidden it, and rummaged through it, her eyes stormy. As she did so, Jack went on, relentless, "You will be dressed appropriately as Mrs. Jack Reade from now on. There is no question of your sailing."

"But, Jack, this is so silly!" she said as she fastened the ties of her skirts around her slender waist. "Think what a help I could be! Why, I could take a turn at the wheel, relieve the crew. You know I can sail."

"The only thing you will be allowed to do aboard the *Camille* is help Babur in the galley. Furthermore, you will remain secluded here most of the time, and you will not come on deck except at my express invitation. The

Camille is not large. The men need privacy for their
needs. I will not have them looking over their shoulders
every time they need to unbutton their breeches. Do you
understand, madam?"

Kate opened her mouth and just as quickly closed it
before she nodded. It did not take a needle-witted person
to know that this was not the time for further argument.

"How did you get aboard?" he asked her next. "Did
one of the crew help you? 'Fore gad, if that was so, I'll
flog the bastard, whoever he is!"

"No, no! No one helped," Kate hastened to say. "Well,
just Cecily. I told her my plan a week ago, and she
considered it romantic. And yesterday, when you thought
me gone to St. George Town, I was only hiding with the
dory in a deserted cove. Late last night, when everyone
in Tucker's Town was asleep, and only Babur yet aboard,
Cecily rowed me out to the *Camille* with my portmanteau. It took but a moment to gain the safety of this
cabin. I counted on Babur not keeping a close watch in
home port. Why should he? I had food with me, water,
and I only had to hide in the chest when I heard someone
coming. I'm glad of that. It was so dark and confining in
there!"

She shivered, remembering, but there was no answering gleam of sympathy for her fears in Jack's cold, stern
eyes. Not this time.

"Empty the basin you used from the stern port," he
ordered as he rose to search a small chest. "There's
water here for you to rinse it out. You will have to use it
as a chamber pot. We have no such niceties aboard. The
men generally relieve themselves out that port. I shall
have to make other arrangements . . . speak to the crew
tomorrow . . . try to explain your appearance here without seeming a damn fool, one unable to keep his own
wife in order."

As Kate threw the basin's contents to the winds, being
careful to aim it to leeward, she swallowed hard. She
could feel the bile rising in her throat again, at its foul
odor, but she did not wonder why Jack hadn't performed
that task for her. He was much too furious for that.

She turned to see him slinging another hammock across
the cabin from his.

"You will sleep here," he told her. Then he climbed into his own hammock and turned his back on her.

Kate stared at that rigid, unforgiving back. "Jack, I'm sorry, truly I am," she said. "I had no idea you'd take it this way. I thought you might be angry for a minute, but then we could laugh at it together. But won't you even kiss me good night, my love? Are you listening? . . . Jack?"

There was no answer, and she stifled a sob as she got ready to sleep. However she had imagined Jack would react, it had never been that he would be so angry with her that he would treat her coldly, not even kiss her as he always did before they slept.

As she climbed into her hammock, she realized there was a great deal she did not know about this husband of hers. A very great deal indeed.

15

KATE had hoped that Jack's attitude toward her might soften as the days went by and his initial anger wore off, but she was to be disappointed. She obeyed him meekly, wearing her skirts as ordered, and coming on deck only when he told her she might do so, but he continued to treat her coldly, almost as if she were a stranger. It made her feel like an interloper, a disruptive presence in a world of men. And Jack never spoke a word more to her than necessary, or so much as touched her hand.

One night, after an especially hot day when the air in the stern cabin had grown stale and close, Kate heard the crew washing themselves on deck in a sudden rainstorm, and laughing and joking together as they did so. She fumed. Her soiled clothes were sticking to her, and she felt dirty, uncomfortable.

But when she asked Jack if she might not have some water for a bath, he refused, telling her they had no tub on board for her use. Furthermore, such an amount of fresh water must be saved for drinking, in case they ran into a period of prolonged calm. Kate had to make do with her basin, and wash herself piecemeal. It was most unsatisfactory.

Even Babur, generally the most jovial and talkative of the slaves, seemed subdued when she joined him in the galley to peel potatoes for the fish stew they all ate with such monotonous regularity. The fumes of the fire and the odors of cooking in the close quarters of the galley upset her stomach, but she did not ask to be excused from her task. She was determined to show Jack she was no bother, although she had to swallow hard any number of times.

Kate had seen the perplexed stares of the crew, but although she had known them all her life, they took their clue as to how to treat her from Jack. Even the mate, Chris Abbott, a friendly man who had always admired her in the past, ignored her.

She began to think they would never reach Statia. Twice on the voyage there she had heard a great commotion on deck, and Jack's thundered orders as the crew ran to do his bidding. Listening carefully, Kate could tell they had spotted other ships, and were taking evasive action, lest they be pirates or privateers. Miserably, she knew such a course would delay their arrival. If she had not been aboard, Jack would not have hesitated to use his cannon, fight any enemy. He had been prepared to do so before, according to the tales Greg had told her. Now, however, he was forced to run, for *her* safety. No wonder he continued cold to her!

And Kate had never been so bored. There was little for her to do after she had helped prepare dinner. She read the *Camille*'s log and the few books Jack had with him twice over, and tried to teach herself to navigate—a futile chore. She found she was even missing needlework, just to while away the lonely hours she had to spend each day.

She took to pacing up and down the cabin then, feeding the anger she was beginning to feel at her husband for his punishment of her. Late one evening, when he came off watch, she was waiting to do battle, but only a glance at his dark expression told her that any fury she might unleash now would be most unwise. Instead, she made herself say softly, "Jack, must we go on this way? Can't you forgive me? Or at least talk to me? I am so bored!"

He stared at her as he removed his shirt. Kate swallowed hard at the sight of his muscled chest, his narrow hips and strong legs. How many days had it been since they had made love? Didn't he miss her too? Want her?

She went to him then to caress his bare chest. "My love," she pleaded. "Please do not do this to me. I . . . I want you, need you so."

He removed her hands and held them away from him. "I have no time for lovemaking at sea," he said. "And if you are bored, Kate, you should have considered that possibility before."

"I think you are being horrid!" she raged, forgetting her new plan to be as conciliatory as possible. "What difference would it make, now that I am here? Chris has the watch. No one will come below. They never have before!"

"I am not concerned about that. But as captain, I must be ready instantly for any crisis that arises. It is one of the reasons I didn't want you aboard on these voyages. You are too distracting."

He turned her around and pushed her toward her hammock. "Go to sleep, Kate. We'll be in Statia soon, and I'll make arrangements for you to stay somewhere ashore while we're in port."

"Will you stay there with me?" she whispered as she climbed into her hammock.

"No, I cannot," he said. "I must take my regular watch on board."

He turned his back on her then, and Kate swallowed her retort: that keeping his watch had not deterred him when he had been that Dutchwoman's lover. Miserable now, she blinked her unbidden tears away. Keeping him from Greta Dreeber had been one of the reasons she had stowed away. But now she wondered if Jack was not so furious with her that he would go to his former mistress in defiance. She knew she could not bear it if he did.

But she had noticed he had not seemed so angry with her this evening. For one moment there had even been an answering gleam in his turquoise eyes when she confessed her hunger for him. Reassured a bit, she relaxed. Somehow, some way, she would discover the means to bring him back to her bed once they reached Statia, she told herself.

The *Camille* sailed into Statia's Gallows Bay late one afternoon a few days later. Kate opened the stern port, frustrated that her view of the harbor was so constricted.

But her eyes widened as the sloop sailed past all the ships at anchor. She saw English flags, and colonial, Spanish, Dutch, and French ones as well. Just like Jack's first reaction to the port, the hair on the back of her neck rose. It was so incongruous to be here among their past and future enemies, all observing a quiet, precarious peace.

When a French sailor saw her leaning from the port, he shouted to her and made a rude gesture. Sick at heart, Kate turned away.

Jack did not release her from the cabin to walk the deck until well after dark. She did not question this, not after her first reception, but she was sorry, because she couldn't see much of the harbor at night.

Jack was gone early the next morning, to call on the governor and see some man named Isaac Van Dam about his cargo. Kate had little to do but pace the small confines of the stuffy cabin until he returned. Now that they were at anchor, there was not even the breeze of their passage, and she was hot and miserable. She had not been asked to help in the galley, for all the crew were to eat ashore today. She wondered when Jack intended to feed her, and what it would be, now that the galley fire was out.

He came back just before dinner, telling her brusquely to pack her portmanteau and get ready to leave the *Camille.* Kate flew into action, stripping all her clothes off to wash as best she could before she dressed in a pale gray muslin gown. Jack left her to her ablutions abruptly, and went on deck to wait for her.

When he rowed her to shore, Kate looked around eagerly. How large the roadstead was, she thought, how crowded! She asked innumerable questions, and was glad when Jack answered her normally. If only he would not treat her as if she were a nun, she knew all would be well.

Once landed on the broad beach, and putting her portmanteau on his shoulder, Jack took her arm and led her up a steep narrow street to the upper village. "I have secured a room for you at a Mrs. Mayer's. The governor recommended her. She speaks English, and sometimes she takes travelers for short periods. There is no inn here, not that I would want you to stay in one. Statia is a sailors' town, full of rough and rowdy men, as

you can see. You will not leave Mrs. Mayer's house
unless I am with you. Do you understand?" he asked, his
voice fierce again.

"I promise you I won't," Kate told him, ignoring the
sailors' leers and some rowdy catcalls. She knew it was
only because she had Jack's escort, and he was so tall and
competent-looking, that she was not attacked right there
in the street.

"You will come and see me as often as you can, won't
you, Jack?" she asked. "I long to explore the island, to
have a swim if we can find a deserted beach."

His eyes blazed down at her for a moment before he
turned away. "I shall try to be with you when I can. But I
have much to do here, for I want to load my cargo and
fresh provisions and be gone as soon as possible."

"I understand, for I feel so uneasy," she whispered.
"This is a frightening place somehow, yet I don't know
why."

"Statia does that to you," he admitted. "I always sleep
with one eye open here, and insist on alert men on
watch, whatever the hour, night or day."

"Perhaps you will allow me to buy something to read?"
Kate asked. "And some sewing materials? If I don't have
something to do on the next leg of our journey, I think I
will go mad!"

He nodded. "I'll take you to the few shops this afternoon, after we eat dinner. But first I must introduce you
to Mrs. Mayer and get you settled in. Ah, here we are."

He opened a neat gate set into high stone walls, to lead
the way up a narrow pathway of crushed shells. The
pathway was lined with flowers, and more grew in pots
on the spotless white steps. Kate admired a frangipani
tree in the corner of the garden. It was lovely with its
large dark green glossy leaves and fragrant white flowers.
How delicious it smelled, she thought, so sweet and
piercing.

Mrs. Mayer welcomed them, but she did not smile as
she did so, and Kate's heart sank. Her hostess was a
woman in her fifties, short and so spare she was as flat as
a board. Her black gown was as immaculate as her house,
but the deep lines of her face all seemed to run down-
ward, as if she had spent most of her life frowning. Kate
did not think she would be a very convivial companion,

and she was disappointed. She felt it had been an age since she had had a real conversation with another woman, or even a man.

Mrs. Mayer showed them to a small room with a single bed, chair, and wardrobe. Fortunately, it had a door that opened off it, leading to the walled garden.

Jack arranged to return for her in an hour, and Kate almost ran after him to beg him not to leave her here. Then she drew a deep breath, to regain her control.

"I should like to have a bath, if that is possible, ma'am," she said to her forbidding hostess. "I have been sailing for so long, I am in desperate need of it."

She touched her dirty hair and wrinkled her nose in distaste, but Mrs. Mayer did not relax her stern expression.

"I can see you are," she said in her tight, dry voice. "Samantha will bring a bath to you at once. Let her know if you require anything further. She will do your laundry as well. The captain made all the arrangements. Supper is served at seven. If you return after that hour, there will be nothing for you till morning. And every day, breakfast is at eight, dinner at one. Served promptly."

She turned away then, and Kate said, "Have you other guests staying, ma'am?"

"No, you are the only one," the woman told her over her shoulder as she walked to the door. "Few women come to Statia if they do not have to. It is not a place for *decent* females."

Before Kate could reply, she was gone, closing the door behind her with a decisive snap. Kate put her hands to her face. The thought of eating alone with such a cold creature was most unappealing. She began to pray that Jack would be able to have his cargo loaded in a very short time, even if that cargo *was* guns.

The *Camille* remained in Statia for over a week. It was one of the longest weeks Kate had ever spent. Although Jack came to see her every day, and sometimes had time to take her for a stroll or out for a meal, he was often absent. His explanation for this was that there was a problem buying the cargo he wanted. But when she questioned him further, he would not tell her more.

She felt a little better, however, since she had learned from her landlady that Greta Dreeber was gone.

"Left here this summer, and good riddance!" Mrs. Mayer said, compressing her lips tightly.

Since she rarely volunteered a comment about anything, Kate felt brave enough to ask her why she thought so.

"She was a whore, a Jezebel," the older woman intoned, leaning forward now, her pale eyes shining with hatred. Kate tried not to recoil.

"But why do you ask about her? How do you know of her?" Mrs. Mayer asked next, suddenly suspicious.

"My . . . my brother mentioned her after his last visit here," Kate stammered.

"Huh!" Mrs. Mayer snorted. "Was he one of her lovers? For shame!"

"No, no, I . . . I am sure he was not," Kate made herself say. "He only told me of her beauty, and I wondered about her."

Mrs. Mayer snorted again. "Beauty! God will punish her and others like her after death. Then I shall have the last laugh!"

Kate changed the subject abruptly. She did not think Mrs. Mayer quite sane, and it bothered her that the two female slaves in the house could not be cajoled into conversation or smiles. They spent most of their time looking over their shoulders, their eyes rolling with fright. No doubt this horrid creature beat them—or worse.

One afternoon, Jack came to take her for a walk. He seemed more relaxed suddenly, and when Kate learned that they were to leave Statia the following day at dawn, her own spirits revived. They walked quite a distance out of town, far from the noise and bustle of the busy port.

Jack took her to a small deserted beach, and when he suggested a swim, Kate was quick to agree, her heart beating a fast tattoo as she hurried to undress.

Her hands were unsteady, and silently she cursed their clumsiness. Suddenly she felt herself spun around. Jack stood before her naked, and she reached up to grasp his shoulders to steady herself while he undid the lacings of the gown himself. His eyes were intent on the task, and Kate stared at him with hunger in her eyes. She was glad to see that his breath was coming as unevenly as her own.

The discarded gown dropped to the sand, and was quickly followed by her petticoats and shift. The sun was hot on her bare skin, but it was a poor rival to the burning she felt wherever Jack touched her. His kiss seared her, it was so hungry and passionate, and his tongue was none too gentle as it possessed her mouth. His hands cupped her breasts, caressing and molding, his fingers teasing her nipples into taut aching peaks. Kate felt consumed with the fire as her own hands explored the hard muscles of his chest and arms and back. He grasped her buttocks then, pressing her still closer, his aroused manhood pulsing with a life of its own. For a moment she was frightened, frightened as she had never been with Jack. But surely he will not hurt me! she told herself. She willed her muscles to relax as he lifted her off the sand, and she wrapped her arms and legs around the long column of his body for support. She was helpless against his demanding masculine onslaught.

When he made them one, her fears went away, for in spite of his urgency, he was not brutal about it. And then she forgot those fears, and all the loneliness and uncertainty of the past days, in an urgent storm of passion that moved and demanded and consumed. She thought she might faint, and she held him closer still.

As her senses exploded in ecstasy a moment later, and her nails dug into his back, Jack's shuddering cry joined her own. And then Kate knew that her world had come right again. He loved her still! She began to cry, large sobs of abandon and relief. Jack lowered her to the sand at last, and lay down beside her. He was breathing hard, and his turquoise eyes blazed still in the dark tan of his face.

He gathered her into his arms then, and held her tight, rocking her to comfort her. But still he did not speak openly to her as he carried her down to the water later to swim.

They spent the afternoon on the beach, sometimes sheltering from the blazing sun under a large sea-grape tree and talking and making slow love again. Finally Jack admitted his anger had made him cold to her, determined to repay her for her willfulness. Kate promised never to do anything so foolish again. She suddenly realized, even though Jack never said so directly, that the worst part of the whole debacle had been that she had made him look foolish before his men. She should have thought of that. Jack was proud, and she had wounded that pride. Had anyone ever been so stupid? she wondered. She had forgotten that beneath their manly exteriors, their air of assurance and competence, men were just as sensitive as women. And as quickly hurt, even though they could not rail at fate or cry helplessly, as women did. All at once Kate was glad she was not a man.

"I intend to go by way of Bermuda and put you ashore before I head north to sell my cargo," Jack was saying now, and she set her musings aside for another time. "You will not miss seeing New England, now that cold weather approaches. None of us like it. The winter that is coming will be harsh there, with blinding snowstorms, and ice that has to be chipped off the deck and rigging every day. Otherwise, the sloop would grow top-heavy, be in danger of turning turtle."

"I cannot imagine such a thing," Kate said dreamily, her eyes half-closed as she lay sprawled with her head resting on his hard, naked thigh. The relentless sun beat down on her. Its power made her feel flattened, insignificant. It was hard to picture the ice he described, although she wouldn't have minded having a chunk of it in a large citrus punch right now.

"Will you return to Bermuda then, love?" she asked.

"No. I will go to Charles Town, see your brother, get a new cargo there. War will be upon us soon. And when it comes, trading will cease. I must do all I can before that time, if we are to live in comfort."

"I shall miss you," Kate said softly. "But I will pray for you every day you are gone."

Jack sat up and tilted his head to check the position of the sun. "Time we were going, lest you miss your last supper with your gracious old hostess, ma'am. 'Pon my word, we must do nothing to distress such a kind, cheerful angel!"

Kate laughed at his sarcasm. She had told him all about Mrs. Mayer this afternoon, and how anxious she was to leave her. Now she hurried to dress, hoping she would have time for a bath and be able to wash her hair before Jack came for her. It would be such a long time before she would have the chance to do so again.

Kate was a little surprised when the *Camille* sailed well before dawn. Once again she was secluded in the stern cabin, and she wondered at the lack of noise. She heard no orders given, no anchor chain rattling, and Jack had warned her she must be as quiet as a mouse. She won-

dered what all this stealth was in aid of, and she could
not relax until Statia was left astern.

Jack had not cared to enlighten her, for he himself was
concerned. He had heard tales ashore that cargoes such
as his were being intercepted by the British ships stationed at St. Kitts. Somehow, or so Isaac Van Dam had
claimed, the British seemed to know which ships carried
powder and shot, and the time they intended to sail.
Then, Van Dam said, the Royal Navy was ready to
intercept them and take those cargoes.

Jack—all the crew—had made a great noise about putting off their departure till the end of the week, but Jack
was not sure this decoy would serve. It was obvious that
there were British spies on Statia, with the means of
getting any information they gleaned to the authorities
on St. Kitts. He told himself he could bluff his way clear
if the *Camille* was stopped, and say he was taking the
cargo to the British garrison in Boston, but he preferred
to avoid any encounter, even make a run for it if he had
to.

His luck did not hold this time, and when he saw the
two fast ships flying the British ensign, tacking to intercept the *Camille*, he cursed. He could not even turn tail
and run for Statia again, for a large French brigantine
was coming up behind him. Forced to choose among the
three ships, Jack settled for the lesser evil of his own
countrymen. If Kate had not been aboard, he might have
risked a fight. Now he had no choice.

Kate heard the excited comments on the deck above
her, and when Jack came below and told her she was to
remain there until he told her it was safe, she nodded
obediently. But a few minutes later, when one of the
British ships fired a shot across the *Camille*'s bow and
Jack brought the sloop up into the wind to lie motionless,
Kate hurried into action.

Grimly, with narrowed eyes, Jack watched the small
boat that had been lowered, to be rowed over to the
Camille. There were eight men aboard it, all of them
armed. And he had no possible avenue of escape, for the
other English ship now patrolled the entrance to Statia's
harbor. Jack could see her crew standing to the guns, and
he was not surprised that the French brigantine had scurried back to safety.

A grappling iron thrown over the *Camille*'s railing recalled him to present danger as the British marines swarmed aboard.

Their officer, wearing a full dress coat and epaulets, a three-cornered hat, and sword and knot, was a tall thin man in his forties. Even as hot and miserable as he looked in his finery, he still had a pompous air. "Your papers, sir," he demanded.

Jack handed them over. "I am Captain Jack Reade, of the Bermudian sloop *Camille*, sir," he said. "Is there some problem?"

"What cargo do you carry? In the name of His Majesty, King George the Third, I order you to open the hatches!" the officer snarled.

"La, what on earth?" a breathless voice asked from behind them. Jack whirled to see Kate climbing the ladder from the cabin, and his eyes widened. She was wearing her blue muslin gown, pulled down almost to the nipples of her high pert breasts, and without even a kerchief over them. She held a broad-brimmed palmetto hat on her chestnut hair, freed now from the customary braid she affected at sea, and she was smiling. It was the smile that stunned Jack the most. He had never imagined Kate could simper like that, or saunter toward them twitching her skirts in a manner more suitable to a prostitute than a lady.

"Why, Sir John, my love, who is this gentleman?" she asked, pouting a little. "And why did you not warn me we were to have company? La, I would have put on a prettier gown had I but known! Oh, welladay, it's too late now, I suppose!"

"Ma'am," the officer said as he bowed. Jack wanted to strike him for the avid way he was inspecting Kate's half-exposed bosom. Then he looked around at his crew, and if the moment had not been so fraught with danger, he would have had to laugh. To a man, they were all staring at Kate with their mouths ajar. Christopher Abbott looked particularly stunned, as if he had never seen her before in his life. Jack noticed that the British marines were equally impressed.

"I am Katherine, Lady Reade," Kate said, extending her hand with another intimate smile. "And this, of course, is my husband, Captain Sir John Reade. And you are, sir . . . ?"

"Lieutenant Beverly Frobisher, m'lady, of His Majesty's ship *Nemesis*. A pleasure to meet you!"

"Oh, prithee, do not say so, sir! The pleasure is all ours! After Statia and those horrid French, Spaniards, and Dutchmen, it is *such* a relief to see our own countrymen again. May we offer you some refreshment? Such a warm day, is it not, early as it is?"

As she spoke, Kate batted her lashes, and the tip of her little pink tongue caressed her lips. Jack ached to spank her, but the lieutentant seemed entranced by the sight.

"That would be very welcome, of course, m'lady, but I have my duty to do first," Frobisher said reluctantly.

Turning back to Jack then, he hardened his expression. "The hatches, Sir John? And perhaps you might explain what a member of the peerage is doing sailing a small sloop in these dangerous waters."

Jack watched Kate flounce over to his side, showing a great deal more ankle than was seemly as she did so. She trilled another laugh before she said, "It is merely a small conceit of my husband's, sir. La, you men can be so ridiculous! I myself will be very glad to return to London and civilization, but Sir John thrives on adventure. Do you know London, Lieutenant? Have you been there lately?"

On learning that Frobisher had not visited the capital for five years, Kate went on, "It is very gay now. The theaters, the shops, the balls! Strange, that. As Her Majesty said to me once while we were taking tea together, 'These are perilous times we live in, my dear Lady Reade, yet society acts as if England had not an enemy in the world.' So acute, Queen Charlotte, is she not?"

"Babur, Tom, open the hatches," Jack ordered as his suddenly garrulous wife paused for breath. "You will see we are carrying shot, powder, and guns, sir, bound for the port of Boston."

"But that port is closed, sirrah," Lieutenant Frobisher said coldly, even though he had been impressed by Lady Reade's friendship with the queen. He told himself he must go carefully here. He did have his advancement to consider, and he was close to making post.

"Not to me, it isn't," Jack retorted, his voice haughty now. "This cargo is intended for the troops garrisoned there."

Frobisher's brows rose in disbelief. Unable to resist the chance to appear clever, he turned to his midshipman and said, "The tales we are told, Mr. Thomas!"

Turning back to Jack, he said, "But in that case, Captain, you will have the appropriate authorization. I should like to see it."

Before Jack could speak, Kate laughed again. "Oh, dearie me," she said, sounding as gay and unconcerned as her mother ever had. "I fear Sir John cannot show the papers to you, sir. You see, I am afraid I . . . I lost them."

"You lost them, m'lady?" Frobisher echoed. "How very singular!"

"Yes, wasn't it? I must have misplaced them, but I am positive they are *somewhere* on board. I do assure you I have searched high and low. I did not know they were so important—indeed, sir, I did not. Sir John was most angry with me. But isn't that always the way? Momentous papers disappear without a trace, while silly lists and *billets-doux* are constantly under your hand. How perverse life is! But if you *must* see them, I should be glad to search again. My cabin is so untidy, however, I fear it will take an age!"

She pouted then, looking adorable, before she sighed and said, "If only Sir John had permitted my abigail to accompany me, everything would not be at such sixes and sevens! I am *such* a careless girl!"

She gave Jack a fleeting, desperate glance then, and he realized he must take a hand. Kate was doing her valiant best, but she could not carry this game she was playing alone.

"You may be sure I was angry, Frobisher, even with my dearest wife," he said in his most lordly voice. "But truly, you cannot imagine that an English baronet who takes his seat in Parliament and is most fervent in his loyalty to the crown would be carrying arms to colonial malcontents. 'Swounds! That would be impossible!"

Frobisher was seen to pause, somewhat disconcerted

by Jack's sudden blustering. As he considered, Jack went on, "Not that I thought to have trouble, even without the papers. The general—Tom Gage, y'know—is a personal friend. I sail with his commission, and at his request, for Bermudian sloops are seldom stopped. Tom has lost many valuable cargoes before, especially those coming with supplies from England. Ergo, a new approach to the problem!"

The lieutentant nodded, and turned to walk a little distance away with his midshipman. Jack took Kate's arm and smiled down at her, The smile seemed to reassure her, and she pressed his arm.

Frobisher strode back to them then. "If what you say is the case, why did you bring your wife on such a dangerous mission?" he asked sharply. "Most unwise, most unwise indeed!"

Jack spread his hands wide. "Why, for comfort, sir, and because I knew I would be in no danger once I left these waters. This sloop can outrun most vessels. Did you note her bow? And I intended to avoid the other islands in the West Indies chain, head east first for safety. I most certainly never expected any danger from my own countrymen."

"Nor I!" Kate exclaimed, sounding both horrified and haughty.

"No, no, sir, you have nothing to fear from us," Mr. Thomas assured him. "Nor does your lovely lady either."

Kate relaxed and simpered at the young man, wishing she had a fan to complete the picture. Then she had to stifle a giggle at how ridiculous a fan would have been in the stiff trade winds.

She clapped her hands then. "Sir John! I have just had the most wonderful idea! Why doesn't the lieutenant escort us in the *Nemesis*? Just think how safe we would be then, my love! Oh, do insist he does so!"

"Unfortunately, I cannot leave my station, m'lady," Frobisher told her. "It pains me to have to deny you my protection. Such beauty as yours should be carefully guarded. 'Sblood, it should!"

As he glared at her husband, Kate went to hug his arm. "You are such a *dear* man," she told him with her best smile. "I have always been told our navy excelled in every way, but I did not expect to find a gentleman sailor. Oh, I mean *plural*, 'gentlemen,' " she amended, smiling impartially at the avid faces surrounding her. One carrot-topped marine turned the color of his hair in his delight.

Jack realized the ship's company had been stationed at St. Kitts for a long time, and he thanked God their isolation from pretty Englishwomen was making them so careless. But after he had given orders for a rum punch all around, the lieutenant was recalled to his duty once again.

"From whom did you purchase this cargo, m'lord?" he asked.

Jack shrugged. "From that abomination of a Dutchman, Isaac Van Dam. I told him I intended to sell it to the colonial rebels, else he would not have given it to me for any amount of gold. But no, perhaps that is not correct. The Dutch are so greedy, so lost to any sense of honor as we know it, they probably sell to both sides indiscriminately. Just remember how they have abused their treaty with us all these years, sir! No Englishman would act so!"

Frobisher nodded, appeased by this show of patriotism, before he turned away to speak to Kate again. Jack hid a smile as he engaged Mr. Thomas in idle conversation. Learning the youth was from Kent, he mentioned Hythe, and Thomas' eyes grew wide with admiration.

"A most outstanding property, sir! You are to be congratulated!" he said with enthusiasm.

"When next you return home, prithee do me the honor of calling on my wife and me there. We should be delighted to welcome you," Jack told him.

"Yes, the Lieutenant Frobisher must come as well," Kate agreed. "Ah, here is the punch at last! Gentlemen? Shall we drink to our king?"

Jack thought the small boat from the *Nemesis* would never leave, even though nothing in his calm, assured demeanor showed his impatience for it to do so. But finally, after a lingering kiss on Kate's hand, Frobisher disappeared over the side.

Jack gave orders to sail at once, and he did not relax until they were several miles away, and the *Nemesis*— which had almost been *their* nemesis—was safely behind them, an ever-dwindling speck on the vast blue-green waters of the Caribbean Sea.

Kate had stayed topside only long enough for a last wave as the small boat reached her own vessel. Then she had scurried down the ladder to the stern cabin as fast as she could go.

Jack let her leave without the trace of a smile on his face. But as he strode the deck and listened to the men exclaiming over the dangerous confrontation they had just had, he acknowledged how much they all owed their escape to the behavior of his once-again-disobedient wife. He doubted he could have pulled it off without Kate's help. No, to be truthful, it was her appearance and her flirting that had saved the day, and her deliberate use of his title to disarm a man she must have recognized, at once, as one obsequious to any of the nobility. Perhaps she had run across the breed before?

But although he would have more than a few words to say to her about her disgraceful, almost wanton behavior, even to appearing without so much as a kerchief veiling her shapely breasts, he knew his heart would not be in it. And she *had* looked beautiful! He didn't fault Lieutenant Frobisher and his men in the slightest for abandoning their duty.

He looked up then to see his mate regarding him with a questioning twinkle in his eyes. And suddenly the whole ridiculous, farcical performance they had just participated in made him put back his head and give a loud shout of laughter. And he continued to laugh so hard that the rest of the crew were quick to join him, slapping their knees and wiping their eyes as they did so.

Below, in the stern cabin, where she was changing her clothes, Kate closed her eyes for a moment and whistled a heartfelt "Whew!" in her relief that Jack was not angry at her yet again.

The return voyage to Bermuda was much more pleasant than the outward-bound one had been. Although Kate stayed below most of the time, Jack allowed her the use of the deck more frequently, and the crew was as friendly as they had ever been. Henry let her pull in a large fish he had caught, and Babur started singing and telling her stories as they prepared dinner in the galley together.

And only a few days from home, Jack began to make love to her again. The first time they tried it in the hammock, they tumbled onto the deck in an untidy heap, and Kate had had to hold her stomach, it ached so with stifled laughter. But of course, then they discovered the deck itself, so wide and accommodating, or the long stern bench.

Even though he was still firm about putting her ashore, Jack spoke of their coming separation with regret. But the British sailors of St. Kitts were one thing; the beleaguered garrison in Boston, and the Royal Navy fleet in her harbor, were another. He could hardly claim any friendship with General Gage there, or, indeed, anywhere in the New England colonies. And an American captain who had been anchored near them in Statia had told him about a British captain who was terrorizing the shipping lanes from Long Island Sound to Narragansett Bay in the small colony of Rhode Island and Providence Plantations.

Sometimes, when he took the early watch, Jack pondered why he continued to run guns and powder to the colonies. Alone then, at the helm, watching the gray sky on the horizon brighten with the coming of the sun, he wondered why he was doing so. For he was a loyal Englishman, was he not? And yet he had tremendous admiration for the colonists, admiration that in the case of Matthew Hathaway and some others amounted to great respect. And he could sympathize with this struggle with the crown. The colonists had long been engaged in taming a wilderness, and were now intent on forging a new country. Such an ambitious scheme ignited an answering spark in his own heart. They were Englishmen too, but Englishmen who would not permit the mother country to deny them their rights. No, they were prepared to fight for them; fight and die, if that were necessary.

Perhaps it was the air in the New World, Jack mused. Perhaps it was stronger and fresher here, blowing away fusty old ideas and making people feel they could do anything, be anything, they chose. In England, class was all. As rigid and impenetrable as any stone wall, it divided the high and the low very neatly. But in the colonies, you were as good as your own brain, strength, and heart could make you. It was a refreshing idea, equality, and one that appealed to him greatly. Perhaps because he was only plain Jack Reade now?

And maybe that was why he continued to carry these dangerous cargoes, was able to tell himself he was doing no wrong. Not yet, at any rate. He knew the time was fast approaching, however, when he would have to decide one way or the other, for England or the colonies. And when he did so, he told himself, it would be his own decision. It would have nothing to do with Kate's fears for him, or her own slavish devotion to her father's beliefs. He loved her more than he had ever thought it possible to love a woman, but in this instance she would not sway him.

Reminded of her again, Jack scanned the ocean in all directions. There was no other sail in sight, and he relaxed. But he knew he would not rest easy on this voyage until Kate was safe on land. Then, with his mind at ease about her and her welfare, he could give his whole-hearted attention to his ship and the safe delivery of his precious cargo where it would bring the most profit and do the most good.

He must go on alone, much as he would miss his wife. There was a new softness to Kate these days that intrigued him, a fresh beauty and a glow that he attributed to the salt air.

Kate could have told him that the salt air had nothing to do with it, but she held her tongue. She knew Jack would not be pleased to learn she was with child, not after he had been so adamant that there must never be one, and she wanted nothing to distract him on the coming dangerous journey. Time enough to tell him when he returned. Of course, by then she would not have to tell him, she reminded herself with a giggle as she hugged herself in delight. She only hoped he would not consider her ugly, grown so round and unwieldy.

She was sure she had conceived the last time Jack had made love to her in Bermuda—the magical, memorable night that the full moon had shone through the moongate. She knew it was a night she would never forget.

Yes, it had to have been then, for Jack had not touched her again until Statia. And she had not bled since even before she left Bermuda. Counting on her fingers, she saw that the baby would be born in early June. Surely

Jack would be home by then! And when he held his child, either a son or a daughter, in his arms, he would forget Hythe and England, be happy in Bermuda. Kate sensed he was not happy now, even though she knew how he loved her, for he was still moody at times, still far, far away someplace she could not reach him.

But if he grew content in his fatherhood, learned to accept his exile, he would forget his title—that ever-present shame that followed him through his life. Kate was sure of it.

16

IT was late in the afternoon when Jack brought the *Camille* into St. George Town harbor. He asked Tom and Henry to lower the small boat and row Kate ashore, telling her he would be along in time for supper. He himself had to see about getting some fresh provisions first, and he had to call at the Customs House to announce he had nothing to declare, since his cargo was destined for the northern colonies. Jack was sorry he could not permit the crew to go ashore now that they were home, but there was no time for it, since he intended to be under way again at dawn.

Kate ran up the broad green lawn of her old home. The front door was open, and as she reached it, she called out. But where was everyone? she wondered as she entered the parlor.

Her mother was seated there at her embroidery frame, and when she saw Kate, she rose, a hand to her heart. And then, as if she saw some dread apparition standing there, and not her own dear daughter, her thin face paled and she collapsed in an unconscious heap on the floor.

As Kate ran to help her, she called for Keza as loudly as she could. She was kneeling beside her mother, supporting her head, when the old black woman came in.

"Keza! But what on earth is wrong with Mama?" she asked with a worried frown.

Keza reached into her mistress's pocket for her smelling salts. As she waved them under Olivia Hathaway's nose, she said, "Sho glad yo' back, Miz Kate, honey. Yo' mama been bad. Massa Greg ain't come home, an' when y'all went away too, she done go all to pieces. She sho y'all both dead."

"But I left her a letter!" Kate protested as she chafed her mother's hands.

"Miz 'Livia doan take no stock in letters, chile. Yo' cain't *hug* a letter! But dis all 'cause o' her age. She gets nervous, doan think clear-like."

Mrs. Hathaway groaned then, and her eyelids fluttered. Grasping a chair arm, Keza hauled her considerable bulk upright. "Ah'll fetch a cuppa tea for her. She goan need it for de shock."

Kate nodded, still frowning. Her mother did not look well to her, no, not at all. She had lost a lot of flesh, and her thin face had lines on it that had never been there before. For a moment Kate was assailed with guilt. If she had not stowed away, if she had stayed home, all this might have been averted. She could have visited her mother and comforted her. But she had been selfish, concerned only with her own happiness.

Olivia Hathaway opened her eyes then, and sighed. "Oh, my dearest Kate, it *is* you! I thought you were a ghost! Thank the Lord, *you*, at least, are safe!"

"Of course I am, Mama! What are these megrims of yours? I've only been to Statia with Jack, as I told you I was going to do in my letter. But come. Let me help you to a chair. Keza is bringing you a cup of tea. You'll soon feel more the thing."

She was glad to see her mother smile a little then, and nod. And it wasn't long before Mrs. Hathaway was sipping a cup of hot, fragrant brew and pouring out her heart. Kate listened patiently.

"I have been so lonely, darling, so very lonely! You all went away and left me!"

"Now, Mama, that's not true. I was just on a short voyage with my husband, and George and Cecily are here."

Olivia Hathaway shook her head. "I should not complain, I know, for I am only her mama-in-law, but Cecily has not been at all attentive. And on the rare occasions she does come to town, she spends more time with her own family than with *me*. And dear George! Well! He is so busy with his new shipyard, he hasn't a moment for *me*!"

Kate wondered why she had never noticed the self-pitying tone of her mother's voice before, how self-absorbed she was. But did she truly expect her grown children to neglect their own lives to dance attendance on her?

"And darling Greg! Oh, Kate, he has not come home! I fear he is dead, and I cannot bear it!" Mrs. Hathaway moaned, tears coming to her eyes. "And you know how I have always worried the most about him, of all my children. He has such a wild, reckless streak!"

"Mama, Mama! Don't you go borrowing trouble," Kate told her briskly. "It has not even been a year since he sailed. No doubt he's having a fine old time, carrying cargoes from port to port, and making a fortune for himself as he told us he wanted to do.

"And you know Greg, how heedless he is! He is not thinking we might be worrying about him. Why, when he does return, even if it is two years from now, he'll be amazed that we even gave him a thought. I can hear him now. 'But I was all *right*! Ecod! Surely you *knew* that!' "

Her imitation of her brother's indignant denial of any wrongdoing made her mother smile a little.

Suddenly remembering something, Kate went on, "Mama, do you recall that time Greg went exploring when he was a boy, and didn't come home for almost a week because he was having such a grand time at Ely Harbor? And how stunned he was when he learned his absence had upset us? Why, he even protested the caning father gave him!"

As Olivia Hathaway smiled again, Kate took her hands in hers and leaned forward to kiss her lined cheek. "And, Mama, you must remember that Greg is not that little boy anymore. He's a man now, and he has his own life to live. You make yourself ill to no avail, fussing over him—over any of us."

Mrs. Hathaway sighed. "No doubt you are right, Kate, but it is very hard."

Kate saw she was about to start complaining again, and she said quickly, "But you have not heard of my adventure!

Oh, Mama, Jack was so angry with me when he found I had stowed away!"

"You did what?" Mrs. Hathaway asked, her mouth dropping open, for she had not known of this. Successfully diverted, at least for now, she demanded Kate tell her all about it.

Jack arrived at the house with Kate's portmanteau just before supper. He had called at the State House, thinking to walk home with his father-in-law, but Roger Hathaway had already left.

Now, as that man took Jack's hand and welcomed him home, Jack wondered at his stiff, formal tones, the absence of any real smile. As he took his seat across from Kate at the supper table later, Jack inspected his inlaws carefully. He thought Olivia Hathaway much changed, and not for the better either. Her hands were so thin as to appear bloodless, and they were never still. And a little muscle in her cheek twitched almost continually. He also noticed that her voice had become a whine.

As for her husband, now serving himself a piece of chicken, he had aged as well, grown sterner, much more forbidding. Only when his eyes rested on his daughter did his expression soften.

Ah, well, Jack thought as he buttered a biscuit, if I were married to Olivia Hathaway, I might be stern and forbidding too. So many complaints! Such gross self-pity!

He glanced then at his own wife, admiring the young, slim body he loved under the gray gown she wore. Kate's chestnut hair was arranged simply this evening, and beneath the candles in the Waterford chandelier above them, it glowed rich as finest satin. She was in profile to him, listening to her mother again, and he thought how pure, how aristocratic her features were. That broad, smooth forehead, her straight nose and high cheekbones, her round determined chin and generous mouth. He was a lucky man—and he would hate to leave her tomorrow.

"You said you intend to sail at dawn?" Roger Hathaway asked as he passed him the platter of chicken.

"Yes. I only called here to put Kate ashore," Jack told him.

"Roger! You will never guess what this naughty girl did," his wife said, her eyes round with excitement. "She stowed away! Have you ever heard the like?"

"Kate should be spanked," her fond father said. "But perhaps she has been."

"No, just isolated in the cabin and ignored, which was much, much worse," Kate told him, wrinkling her nose at her husband. "I shall not stow away again."

"No doubt you'll think of something else to bedevil me," Jack remarked. "I know you, Kate!"

She chuckled. "Never say so, sir! I intend to be a saint the entire time you are gone. Just don't be too long, Jack. Sainthood is a difficult thing to maintain for excessive periods."

"Where do you sail, Jack?" Roger Hathaway asked.

"My cargo is bound for the Massachusetts Bay Colony, sir."

"Those rebels! That nest of serpents! I beg you to think twice about dealing with traitors!"

Stunned by the venom in his father-in-law's voice, Jack was careful only to remark that as far as he knew, open rebellion had not come to pass as yet.

"Mayhap not, but it will not be long in coming," Roger Hathaway persisted. "Those Bostonians stir up enmity throughout the colonies!"

"Some of the taxes and laws that have been imposed are most unfair, sir," Jack pointed out as mildly as he could.

"Perhaps they have been, but in time they have been repealed. But rather than deal calmly and rationally, send arguments and petitions, the Bay Colony preaches defiance, war, revolution!"

Olivia Hathaway stirred restlessly at the other end of the table. All this talk of dissension was not at all to her taste, and she had heard her husband's views time out of mind.

"Jack, have you heard nothing of Greg?" she asked, changing the subject. "I am so worried about him, for he has yet to come home!"

"Only that he has called in at Statia twice. Van Dam, the Dutch trader, says he is doing well. But I shall inquire at every port I reach, question other ships' captains. I am sure he is fine, ma'am."

His mother-in-law sighed, her mouth turning down again. "You men!" she said, raising her napkin to dab at her eyes. "You cannot understand the tenderness of a mother's heart, her grief and pain when parted from her child."

Kate started. She could tell from Jack's suddenly bleak expression that he was thinking of his own mother, and she tried to think of something to say to change the subject.

Before she could speak, Mrs. Hathaway went on, "And it is no use telling me that Greg is a man now, Kate! To me he will always be my dearest child. Every mother feels this way, and our agony never ceases."

She sighed again, and Jack rose. "I must beg to be excused now, ma'am, sir. I am awaited on the *Camille*."

"You must go so soon?" Kate mourned, rising and coming to take his arm.

"It would hardly be fair for me to stay long ashore, Kate, when I have denied the crew even that privilege," he said.

As her mother and father rose to say their good-byes, Kate nodded reluctantly.

A few minutes later, Kate and Jack went arm in arm to the garden for their own private farewell. Jack's lingering kiss was at first passionate and then so tender that Kate felt tears coming to her eyes.

As one escaped and ran down her cheek, Jack raised his head. "Here now, Kate, belay that!" he ordered gruffly. "You may be sure I'll be back as soon as possible, although I doubt it will be before the brigantine is launched. Your brother Matt introduced me to a good man in Charles Town, an Alfred Griffin. He's to be her captain, and he has my orders. Just be sure to send word to Matt about the launching. He'll see Captain Griffin knows."

Kate nodded, and he kissed her again. "How hard it is to say good-bye," he murmured.

"I know. Well, Granny told me it never gets any easier, and I see she was right. I do love you so, Jack! And you will have a care for yourself, won't you? Especially with that cargo?"

He hugged her close before he bent and kissed the bridge of her nose. "You may be sure I shall be circumspect, now that I don't have a certain wanton charmer to distract those in authority."

Kate giggled. "I was of some use to you on the voyage after all, wasn't I?" she asked smugly.

He gave her bottom a little spank. "In more ways than one," he said, his turquoise eyes full of amusement.

A few minutes later he was gone, striding down Water Street to the King's Square.

The next morning, shortly after dawn, as the *Camille* sailed into the vastness of the Atlantic Ocean, Jack's eye was caught by a speck of white near St. Catherine's Point. He was sure it was his Kate, waving her apron in farewell, and it seemed such a good omen to him that he smiled for the first time since he had left her.

Kate stayed in St. George Town for a week. While she was there, her mother improved considerably, for Kate was able to divert her mind from her worries about her son and from her preoccupation with her health. Kate did not think there was anything seriously wrong with her, for Keza had explained that women around Olivia Hathaway's age often had strange notions at this particular time of their lives.

But all the days she was there, Kate never once mentioned the baby she was carrying. For some reason, known only to her own heart, she wanted to keep it a secret as long as she could. Of course, Keza discovered it almost at once, although Kate couldn't understand how she could have guessed.

The old woman hugged her and chuckled. "Oh, chile, yo' cain't hide nuttin' from me!" she said. "Yo' mama know?"

"No, and I don't want her to, not yet," Kate said. The two were alone in the kitchen house, and so could talk freely.

"Jess as well, Ah guess," Keza agreed. "Miz 'Livia goan fuss over you sumpin' terrible when she do know. An' y'all always did hate bein' fussed over!"

"Yes, there is that. And I'm afraid she'll try to keep me here if I tell her. But I can't stay, Keza."

Kate sighed then, and rubbed her forehead with her fingertips. "I love Mama, but I can't live with her anymore. She is so . . . so trying!"

"Ah knows, honey, Ah knows. Be 'nuff iffen y'all come callin' every once in a while. But yo' be better in yo' own house. Did y'all know Miz Cec'ly bearin' too? Mah, mah! Muss be sumpin' in de air out dere!"

Roger Hathaway had made arrangements for Kate to travel to Tucker's Town on an island sloop that was going that way. Kate was anxious to see her own home, Annie and Tatum, even Manfred, but first she stopped at the little house near the shipyard to visit Cecily.

She and her new sister-in-law had been good friends all the time they were growing up. Cecily had been refreshingly nonchalant about her good looks, and had been as much of a tomboy as Kate when young. Very tall for a woman, she had a wealth of nut-brown curls and a rosebud mouth, but her most startling feature was her big eyes. They were a pure limpid green, and they were framed with ridiculously long, thick lashes.

Cecily was seated on the veranda when Kate approached, and as soon as she saw her coming, she called a greeting and ran down the steps to go and meet her.

"My dear Kate! Sister!" she exclaimed, hugging and kissing her soundly. "I want to hear everything! You cannot imagine how often I have wondered how Captain Reade took our deception!"

Arm in arm, the two girls went up the steps to the rustic chairs Kate remembered so well. As they sat down, Cecily added, "I must admit George was displeased when he found out I had helped you. He was awake when I returned from rowing you out to the *Camille*, so I had to invent a story about wandering down to the harbor to admire the pleasant night after I visited the necessary, to account for the time I had been gone. I didn't dare tell him until the *Camille* had sailed, you see! He probably would have stormed out there and told your husband! George said it would serve you right if Jack beat you. But he didn't, did he? La, I do so hope not!"

Kate chuckled. "No, but he wanted to, he was so furious with me. So furious he made me stay in the cabin most of the time—all but ignored me for the entire voyage. It wasn't till we reached Statia that he forgave me."

The two spent a happy hour together, Kate relating all her adventures and Cecily telling her about the baby that was due in April. For a moment Kate almost confided her own condition, but finally decided to hold her tongue awhile yet.

"Where is George?" she asked instead. "I must congratulate him on making me an aunt yet again."

"He had to go over to Crow Harbor today. But, Kate, why not come back for supper, so you can see him? He'll walk you home later, and he can take your portmanteau then. It looks heavy. Why lug it out there by yourself or send Tatum back for it?"

Kate agreed, and a time was set. A few minutes later she was walking into her own house, to greet the welcoming slaves. As she washed and changed into one of the gowns she had left at home, Kate realized how good it was to be back. And wouldn't her own bed, those soft goosedown pillows, feel fine after so much time in a hammock!

For a long while she wandered through the rooms of her house, touching the new furniture, admiring the familiar view of the ocean from the windows, and making a list of things she must take care of now she was home.

She was so absorbed in her plans that she forgot the time, and when the clock in the main room struck six, she started. She did not have time to do more than pull a comb through her tangled curls, but as she hurried along the path to Tucker's Town again, she told herself it did not matter. She was only going to see George and Cecily, and they were family.

But when she reached their house, she discovered she was not their only guest. Lounging easily against the veranda railing was a stranger. He was a young man of short stature and wiry build, not much taller than Kate herself.

That he was a stranger to their shores was obvious, for no one in Bermuda dressed so formally, not for a simple supper. His bisque knee breeches, white silk hose, and brocade waistcoat would not have been out of place in a London ballroom, and the way his dark green coat fit his shoulders and narrow waist showed a premier tailor. He had smooth dark-red hair, and his face was smooth too, and curiously bland. Kate thought she had never seen a face so devoid of expression, even now when he was inspecting her from head to toe with such arrogant thoroughness. Her chin went up, and her gray eyes flashed for the liberty he took.

"This is Mr. Bartholomew Findley, Kate," Cecily told her. "He is visiting the islands for a while. My sister-in-law, Mrs. Katherine Reade, sir."

Kate curtsied, her head still high.

"I am sure I must be delighted," Mr. Findley said. He had a deep voice, as devoid of animation as his face.

Kate wondered if he had ever been delighted about anything, he seemed so blasé.

"Where is George?" she asked, looking around and
trying to still her annoyance that a stranger had invaded a
family party.

"He is making us some punch. Mr. Findley so admires
our fresh citrus punches," Cecily told her.

"And your weather, ladies. When I left England it was
still summer, but now, as winter approaches, I am well
aware of how nasty, drear, and gloomy it has become."

He turned to Kate then. "I understand you were in
England a year or so ago, Mrs. Reade. No doubt you
will agree with me."

Kate made herself smile at him. His manner was pleasant now, his conversation unexceptionable. Surely her
first feeling of intense dislike, almost revulsion, had been
most unreasonable. And she had been brought up to the
Bermuda custom of warm hospitality.

"Yes, I do agree with you," she said. "I was miserable
there for my entire stay. But perhaps when you are born
and live all your life in such a paradise as Bermuda is,
you become spoiled."

George came out with a tray of drinks then, and Kate
went to kiss him soundly.

"I see you are still in one piece, sister," he remarked,
his dark gray eyes, so like his twin brother's, twinkling.
"I feared for your safety after you stowed away on the
Camille. Jack does not look like a man who would take
kindly to being tricked by his wife!"

Kate had to tell the whole story again. She noticed that
although her brother laughed heartily, only the faintest
tremor of a smile quirked the stranger's lips.

At supper later, she asked their visitor how long he
intended to remain in Bermuda.

"I am not entirely sure," he said, toying with his mug.
"It may be only another week, or it could be another
year. Who can tell? But my time is my own."

"How fortunate you are," Cecily remarked. "But I am
surprised you chose to stay in Tucker's Town, sir. St.
George Town is so much more populated and lively."

Mr. Findley shrugged his well-clad shoulders. "I find it
pleasant here. Of course, there is no genteel company,

except for yourselves, but it is . . . er, restful. Yes, I shall stay here."

"You will need servants, sir," George pointed out. "Someone more than just your man."

"There are bound to be any number of slaves to buy," Findley murmured.

"Not necessarily," Kate said. "Most of our slaves have been in the same families for years, and few are brought here anymore. There is no need for them, you see, for we have no large plantations to work, like they do in Jamaica or the southern colonies."

"I heard from Father that Tully is to marry the young Kempthorne slave," George remarked. "I imagine that took a bit of negotiating."

Kate chuckled. "Yes, it was a most delicate matter. Mr. Kempthorne wanted to purchase Tully, and Father, of course, held out for Amabella. Father won, although probably only because he and Mr. Kempthorne have been such good friends for so many years. But now, at least, any children from the marriage will not have to be separated, thank heaven!"

"I don't understand," Mr. Findley remarked. "Separated? Why?"

"It's like this, sir," George explained. "When slaves marry, even if the man's master buys the woman, generally their eldest male child is given back to her former master as part of the payment, and half of the rest of the children as well. It is a sad business."

He turned to his sister then. "Do you remember the time one of the Burgess slaves fell in love with a girl from another part of the islands? Ecod, what a to-do!"

Kate's eyes were dancing now, and she said, to include the stranger in their midst, "Colonel Burgess did not want his man to marry anyone but someone he himself chose. But—was it Vernon, George?—yes, Vernon was determined. Colonel Burgess had to resort to chaining him up at night to a stake, to keep him from running off to see her. One morning he discovered Vernon had managed to escape even so, by pulling the stake up and taking it with him. He swam clear across Castle Harbor to reach her, and he almost drowned from the weight of the chain he was wearing. At that show of determination, Colonel Burgess had to accept the inevitable."

"A pleasant little story," Findley murmured. "Still, it is hard to credit slaves with such deep feelings, such devotion. They are no more than animals, after all."

"They are human beings, sir!" Kate said, her voice cold. "And as such, I assure you they feel every emotion man is capable of, and feel them as deeply as we do."

Mr. Findley looked so unconvinced, she longed to hit him. Somehow it made her feel better to see the dark look Cecily's slave Mandy gave him as she set down another plate of fish cakes.

"I hear Vernon and his wife are very happy," Cecily remarked into the little silence that fell.

"But no doubt this Colonel Burgess is not," Findley said. "He should have flogged his brute into submission."

Kate opened her mouth to protest, and quickly closed it. After all, Mr. Findley did not know their ways, nor how they loved their slaves. Why, they were all part of the same family!

As she continued her supper, George said, "We do not flog our slaves ourselves, sir. That is done by a parish official, the few times a year it is necessary. He is called 'the jumper'—for the way he makes people jump, of course."

Mr. Findley remarked he was so glad he had come to Bermuda, for surely it was a most interesting place, with all kinds of unusual customs and behavior.

Later, when Kate announced she must be going, Findley offered to escort her home. To her relief, George was quick to deny him the honor. And on the way there, Kate was able to question her brother about this man— who he was and why he had come here.

"I have no idea," George admitted. "He just showed up one day, looking as dapper as you saw him tonight, and moved into the empty house at the edge of the village. He doesn't seem to do anything, or need anything, and he speaks very little of himself or his past. That valet of his is as reticent as his master. You can barely get a civil word from the man."

"I don't like Mr. Findley, somehow," Kate said slowly. "There is something about him . . ."

"Well, he is different from us, that is true, but he cannot help that," good-natured George admonished her. "But it's just as well you stay away from him anyway,

Kate! You're alone out there on the point, a young married woman, and he's a bachelor."

"For all we know, he may have left a wife in every county of England," Kate said, chuckling a little. "No doubt that's why he's here, having been forced to leave the country to escape their wrath! Why, he might even be a bluebeard!"

"Ecod, will you be serious?" George said, sounding a little exasperated. "Now, listen, Kate, be circumspect, do you hear me? I don't think Jack would like it at all if there was the least bit of gossip about you when he returned."

"There won't be, dear brother," Kate said, glad the darkness hid her little smile. In a few months she would be so heavy with child, no one would think to accuse her of dalliance with another man.

But Kate found it difficult to stay away from Bartholomew Findley, for he seemed determined to seek her out. The very next day, he came to the house on the point and asked to see her. When he suggested she go for a stroll with him, tell him more about the islands, she refused. And when he persisted, coming again the next day, she was forced to tell him outright that as a married woman, she could not be seen in his solitary company. At his air of bland amusement and disbelief, Kate was quick to tell him how happy her marriage was, how much she loved her husband, even how repugnant she found this pursuit of her.

He professed great surprise at her attitude. "Why, ma'am, and here I thought only to do the kind thing, to keep your spirits up while your sailor husband was at sea," he said, his half-closed eyes admiring her narrow waist, the fullness of her breasts in her early pregnancy.

"Besides, he will be gone a long time, I hear. Months and months. I can wait. I'm sure there will come a time when you will miss havng a pair of masculine arms about you, my dear. And another masculine . . . er, *endowment*, now you've grown used to having it so . . . er, *intimately* if I may put it that way? I can wait."

Kate's color was high as she dismissed him without another word. How dare he say such things to her! She resolved to instruct Annie to tell the gentleman Mrs. Reade was not at home to him, if he should call again.

But only the next morning, while she was taking her usual swim in the cove, she was startled to see Bartholomew

Findley taking a seat on a rock at the edge of the little beach. How had he known she would be here at this early hour? she wondered. No one had ever bothered her before.

"This cove is private property, sir," she called from a safe distance away, where she was treading water. "I must ask you to leave at once!"

He strolled over to where she had left her clothes, holding up first one garment and then another in inspection. Kate had to grit her teeth when she saw his hands on her petticoats, her shift.

"But can it be that you are naked, ma'am?" he asked politely. "And you want me to go away? Ecod! It would be impossible for me to do so, now that I know the treat in store. I'll just sit here till you get tired of swimming. You'll have to come out sooner or later, I imagine. And as I mentioned before, I am a very patient man. Besides, I have always admired the Botticelli painting *The Birth of Venus*, you know. And to think I am about to see it in the flesh, so to speak! I am so glad I came!"

Kate was furious. She did not think there was any sense in pleading with the man, trying to appeal to him to behave as a gentleman, even if she would have stooped to such paltry behavior. But what on earth was she to do?

Suddenly she remembered the *Sprite*. It was moored only a short distance away, and she knew there was an old blanket in the cuddy. She and Jack had used it more than once in deserted coves and on lonely beaches.

She swam to the sloop, putting it between her and the man who watched her from shore, before she levered herself up near the bow, making sure only her arms and shoulders were exposed. She was well aware she could not reach inside the cuddy from there, so she groped along the well of the boat for the sounding pole. It was a tedious process, once she finally had it to hand, and she cursed a great deal before she managed to fish the blanket from its hiding place and pull it into the water. All the while, Findley lounged on the beach, looking only mildly curious about what she was doing.

She did not wrap the blanket around herself until she was close to shore, for she could not swim wearing its heavy, sodden weight. But when she finally stood up and left the water, it covered her from head to toe. Striding to her clothes, she bent and snatched them up.

Mr. Findley was watching her closely, a dangerous light of anticipation in his eyes—almost, for the first time, one of animation. Kate shuddered.

"You will leave my husband's property at once, sir, and you will never come here again," Kate ordered quickly, before he could speak or move. Her heart was beating rapidly. She was afraid of this man with his deceptive lassitude, and she admitted it. Somehow he reminded her of a wild beast, one who yawned and stretched in a lazy manner, his tawny eyes half-closed. But a beast nonetheless, who could change in an instant into a clawing, tearing predator intent on making you his next meal.

When Findley only raised an eyebrow and made no move to obey her, Kate went on, "And if you think to force me, because we are alone here, know I shall have you taken up for rape if you do. My father, Roger Hathaway, is one of Governor Bruere's councilmen, and he would be most distressed. *Most* distressed. Indeed, I do not think you would escape the islands with your life."

"But, my dear lady, who said anything about rape?" Findley asked, sounding bewildered. Kate was not fooled.

"No, indeed, that was not my purpose. I only hoped to have a closer look at future delights, I do assure you. And now you have thwarted me. It is too bad."

He shrugged. "Your trick, Mrs. Kate Reade," he murmured. "But one trick does not win the game. I play my cards rather better than that. Reluctantly I give you good-day, madam. *Most* reluctantly."

17

LATER, as Kate ate her breakfast, she noticed for the first time how oppressive a day it was becoming, how hot and still. Another Sarah Bassett day, she thought as she wandered to the window to stare down at the beach that fronted the ocean. Then she frowned. There was another hour to high water, but already the waves had erased the old tide mark. Even taking into account the full moon last night and the subsequent spring tide that could be expected, it was very high.

Her eyes inspected the broad Atlantic that stretched before her to the horizon. Far out, the seas looked glassy calm, but nearer shore, heavy long swells had formed. Kate's eyes widened. She knew full well that the greater the distance between each swell, the more severe the storm that was coming would be. And these were farther apart than any she had ever seen.

She went outside then. There was little wind. Not yet, she reminded herself. It was too soon for that. The sky was filled with thin, wispy bands of clouds, fanning out from low on the horizon.

Wiping the perspiration from her forehead with the back of her hand, Kate went around to the back of the house, where Jack had hung the barometer in a shady place. Bermudians had used this device for years, and trusted it much more than the new, still-rare scientific one. The tightly corked bottle that Kate inspected now held about a cup of shark-liver oil. Normally clear in fair weather, the contents turned cloudy whenever storms were in the offing. Now she frowned again when she saw how murky and dense the shark oil was. And she had never known the barometer to lie.

She needed no other warning. There was a storm coming, and it would be a big one. She only hoped she had enough time to prepare for it before it hit.

As she called the slaves, she suddenly remembered how the sunrise had blazed, all hot orange and crimson, and the old English saw came to mind, "Red sky at dawning, shepherds take warning, red sky at night, shepherds' delight."

She set Annie to cooking food and baking bread for them to eat later, and then to gathering what fruit was ripe on the trees. Manfred was ordered to make as many trips to Tucker's Town as were necessary to fill the water casks, and Kate herself, in company with Tatum, hurried to the cove.

As they reached it, Kate recalled how Bartholomew Findley had surprised her here only a short time ago, and her expression grew severe. She had planned to tell her brother and Cecily about the baby today, but she didn't have time for that now. In a way, she had been sorry she would be forced to disclose her wonderful news in such a way, but she had come to see that to do so would be prudent. For surely Findley would leave her alone now, after he learned of her condition, and that in itself would be worth exposing her secret to the world.

Tatum rowed them out to the *Sprite*. While she busied herself securing all the loose gear on board, he dived overboard to check the mooring chain. Kate set the spare anchor as well, with plenty of line out for the play needed for the height of the tide. She knew the little cove was sheltered, away from the direction of the coming storm, but if a hurricane was on its way, the full force of the blow would be unleashed here later, after the vortex passed. Kate remembered all too well that deceptive period of calm when it was safe to go outdoors, begin assessing the extent of damage to trees and boats and property. And how quickly the winds could begin to howl again, now coming from the opposite direction with renewed fury. Her father had always maintained that the back side of a hurricane packed the stronger punch by far.

For a moment Kate debated hauling the *Sprite* ashore for safety. But she and Tatum and Manfred could not do it alone. And she knew her brother would be too busy at the yard to spare her any of his men. As she remembered George's new venture, she said a small prayer for him. So many boats, so much equipment—even Jack's new brigantine in her cradle hard by the water's edge. Pray God the storm would not take its toll there, that it would not be the disaster the barometer predicted!

At last, having done all she could to safeguard her sloop, she had Tatum row her ashore. But before she left the *Sprite*, she rested her hand for a moment on her varnished coaming, her smooth cedar side. It was almost as if she were trying to give the little sloop comfort, reassure it.

She helped Tatum pull the rowboat well off the beach, tie it securely to two trees. She left him filling it with chunks of limestone so it would not wash away if the tide did manage to reach it.

Back at the house again, Kate busied herself wrapping all the valuables in linens and packing them away in chests. If the roof should go, that might protect them from breakage. And then there were the shutters to check, and limestone to be placed on the plaited palmetto roof of the smaller, more flimsy cedar kitchen house.

It was not until after dinner that afternoon that George arrived on a quick visit. By then the breakers were pounding ashore, and even though the tide had turned now, it was still ominously high.

"The old South Shore is roaring today, isn't it?" George asked. "Ecod, we can even hear it way over in the harbor. Don't like the distance between those swells, either. This will be a real hard storm, Kate!"

His sister nodded. "I've done all I can," she said, standing up from where she had been bent over a chest putting her precious crystal goblets away. She stretched to ease her aching back.

"Come back with me to Tucker's Town, old lady," George begged. "Bring the slaves too. You're exposed to danger here, and Cecily and I are worried about you."

Kate smiled at him. "It's kind of both of you, my dear, but I think I'd feel better staying. The house is on high ground. There's no way the waves can reach it, no matter how high the tide. As for the wind, I'll chance it. I've weathered storms before—more than I like to remember."

George stared at her dubiously for a moment before he nodded curtly. It was Kate's choice, not his, and mayhap she would feel better out here in Jack's house, watching over it for him. Besides, Tatum was a good man, and that Jamaican diver strong and fit. He kissed Kate quickly before he hurried back to the yard. There was so much to do, and so little time!

By late afternoon the wind had risen, but still it was so oppressive that Kate felt it was becoming hard to breathe. And now that she had done all she could, there was nothing to do but wait. She made herself eat a good supper, and insisted the slaves do so as well, and then she began to pace the floor of the big main room. She had had to light the candles, since all the shutters were down and fastened tight. But in that warm, smothering false darkness, there was no sense of security. Kate began to pray then—not for her own safety, but for all the ships at sea. Pray God neither Jack nor Greg was anywhere near this storm! Jack, of course, was well north of it by now, but who could tell what path the hurricane might take after it wreaked its fury on Bermuda? And she had no idea where her brother was. His merry, contented face and lazy grin came to mind then, and she clasped her hands tightly together. Oh, let him be in port somewhere, a thousand miles from danger! she prayed.

She did not seem to be able to keep from going to the door, and so she was there when the sun went down at last in a brassy, lurid finale. Overhead, the darkening sky was veiled in a peculiar mistiness. It was so awesome a sight, so full of malignant portent, that she felt very small. She noted that the wind had begun to howl in earnest now, and the roaring of the breakers as they crashed on the beach was almost a continuous tumult.

It was then she called the slaves into the main house. The kitchen house was not a safe place for them any-more, and soon a torrential downpour would start. She could smell it coming. Tatum and Annie could sleep in the spare bedroom, and Manfred could put his pallet down here on the floor.

The wind was so strong already that even large trees were being whipped and tossed about in it, and Annie had to have help to cross the yard. Her eyes were wild and frightened when they were all safe inside at last.

"Nevah seed nuttin' lak *dis* 'fore, Miz Kate," she mumbled, her voice shaking.

Kate hugged her for a moment. "It's going to be a bad one, all right, but we'll be just fine, you'll see. But I don't trust that palmetto roof on the kitchen house, even though Manfred did weigh it down with stones."

The slaves seemed awkward, sitting there in the big room, but soon they were all talking about hurricanes they had known. Everyone but Manfred. He didn't say much, but then, he never had.

Kate stared at his dark, sullen face where he sat on the floor somewhat apart from the others. She wondered if he had been the one who had told Bartholomew Findley about her early swims. She had never liked Manfred from the moment Jack had bought him. There was some-thing about him that was different from the other slaves, an arrogance to him, almost. Perhaps it was his Jamaican background. That island had seen some terrible slave uprisings! And although he obeyed her orders, there was always that little hesitation before he moved to do her bidding, and he refused to hurry any task. Still, he was an excellent diver. He had helped Jack find so many gold doubloons.

The sudden crash of a large tree falling somewhere nearby made Kate wince. She rubbed her forehead then, trying to ease the headache she had, and wondering, as she did so, why the storm seemed twice as frightening just because it was dark. Was it because they couldn't see the destruction that was taking place? Kate felt bone-tired, but she knew it was no use trying to sleep. Who could sleep in this din?

The eye of the hurricane came with sudden quickness just before midnight. One moment the wind was howling as hard as ever, and the next it was deathly quiet. Kate opened the door almost fearfully. She could not see much in the blackness, but she could hear what the older people called the storm's "barking"—that throbbing beat from the encircling winds. It seemed to be echoing inside her aching head.

As she peered out, she saw that a large sea-grape tree had come down, fortunately nowhere near the house. She sent Manfred and Tatum to the kitchen house then to check for damage, and she was not surprised to learn when they came back that the roof had indeed blown away, and a cedar tree had fallen on the building itself, almost completely demolishing it. Fortunately, their food and water were safe inside the solid limestone walls of the main house.

No one got much sleep that night. After the eye passed, the wind grew in intensity again, now blowing from the northwest. The shrieking it made was wild and tortured, like the sound of a thousand souls in agony. Only toward dawn did the storm begin to abate, and they could all get some rest at last.

At first Kate's slumber was fitful, but eventually sheer exhaustion sent her a more sound sleep. But asleep, she dreamed—wild, unconnected dreams that made no sense to her. She was standing on the *Camille*'s deck, dressed in one of her London ball gowns, and she could see a dark storm approaching. But when she called for help, no one came. It was then she realized she was alone on the big sloop, out of sight of land, and somehow she could not move from where she stood, no matter how she tried. Then another boat passed her, going the other way. It was filled with all her old friends, but no matter how she called out to them and pleaded for help, no one paid any attention to her. It was as if she were invisible as she sailed on alone, to disaster.

That dream faded away, thank the Lord, but another took its place. In this one she was in a dark closet. Frantically she felt along its walls, but there was no way out. And then the closet began to shrink, to close in on her.

Even covered with perspiration as she was, Kate was glad when she woke. She drew a deep, relieved breath, and was not surprised at the scent of the bruised cedar she inhaled. It was often so, after a hurricane. Rising, she washed and hurried to dress. They would all have to eat a cold breakfast, for they had no way to cook until the kitchen house was rebuilt. And then she must see what other damage had been done, and go to Tucker's Town to make sure George and Cecily were all right. As she fastened on her petticoat, she reminded herself to ask her brother to send a message to St. George Town. She knew her mother must be frantic with worry about them all.

When she stepped outside at last, Kate's eyes widened. There didn't appear to be more than a few trees still standing anywhere on the point. Below her, the beach was strewn with debris, and a grinding, heavy surf was pounding the shore relentlessly. The wind was still gusting, so even though there was bright sunlight now, you could not forget the storm that had just passed. But she saw that the moongate was still standing, and for a moment her heart lightened. No matter how bad everything else was, at least Jack's gift to her had survived.

Kate made her way over tree trunks and around uprooted bushes to the remains of the kitchen house. Only the chimney remained of it. Perhaps they could rig a tarpaulin over the grate so Annie could still use it to cook. Kate decided that would be her first priority. And then she smiled—a grim little smile. No, not her first, for she saw the privy had disappeared as well.

She set Tatum and Manfred to work on that before she went down to the cove. Even from the crown of the hill she could see it was empty, and she gasped. And then her eyes searched the littered beach. She did not see the *Sprite* at first, for the beach itself looked so wild, so different. It was covered with debris and with large hunks of coral that had been ripped from the bottom of the harbor. As she walked along it, she saw a great many dead fish, even a dead longtail. The bird was not beautiful now, she thought as she stepped around it. Instead, it was crushed, sadly bedraggled in death. The sand fleas were already busy at work.

And then, ahead of her, she saw her sloop. The *Sprite* had been tossed far above the normal tide line and was lying against a large rock on her side. As Kate hurried toward her, her spirits rose. Perhaps the *Sprite* wasn't damaged too badly, she thought. The side she could see looked intact. But when she reached the boat, her eyes filled with tears. The mast had been snapped, which she had expected, but the side of the sloop down on the sand was completely staved in. And there was a hole in the hull she could have stepped through, even wearing hoops.

Kate knew the *Sprite* would never sail again, and she sat down next to it and put her head down on the smooth cedar that was left. She cried then, cried as hard as she would have for a beloved person who had needlessly, and unexpectedly, died.

How good a boat the *Sprite* had been! she thought, caressing the smooth timbers. How gay and responsive— how yare! And how many wonderful days Kate had spent in her, sailing and swimming and fishing, the *Sprite* ever obedient to her every command. Why, from the age of thirteen she had sailed this boat, cared for her, loved her. She would miss her so much!

Suddenly Kate wanted Jack so badly that she wept even harder. If he had been here, the *Sprite* might have been saved. But she, left here alone, could not even have her hauled out to safety. And it wasn't any good telling herself she had done all she could. She had failed the *Sprite*. Her demise was all Kate's fault, because she was weak. Because she was a woman. And then, for one mad, mindless moment, she hated Jack for leaving her here to deal with all this alone.

It was a long time later before Kate got to her feet, reminding herself there was a great deal to accomplish that had nothing to do with childhood dreams, and she was the only one to see to them. She walked away then, and she didn't look back.

When she checked the rowboat, she saw it had fared better. A tree had crashed nearby and covered it with branches, but from the amount of rainwater it held, she knew it had not been holed.

Kate went over to Tucker's Town after her simple dinner. The walk there took longer than it ever had, for she had to climb over downed trees and sometimes push her way through the bushes when there was no other way to go. She saw that Tatum and Manfred had a lot to do here too.

She was glad to see that the little house by the harbor was intact, but Tucker's Town itself was a shambles. Most of the houses had been built of cedar, and they had all been destroyed. Only the few houses built of limestone were intact. And when her eyes went almost fearfully to the shipyard, she gasped.

As she made her way there, she could see the massive damage that had occurred. An island sloop that had been having its hull cleaned had been smashed against the careening wharf, and a score of smaller boats were lying wrecked on the shore as well. And Jack's new brigantine was gone. Searching the harbor, Kate saw only a few ribs showing, and part of the cradle. It was obvious that the high tide and the winds had torn her loose, to batter her over and over in the shallows.

Kate's shoulders slumped. Then, ahead of her, she saw George. He was standing very still, staring around as if he could not believe his eyes. Her heart went out to him, and she ran to put her arms around him.

"Oh, George, how dreadful all this is!" she mourned, hiding her head on his shoulder.

His arms came around her in turn, to hug her close. When Kate looked up, she was startled by the expression of pain on his face. He appeared to have aged ten years overnight.

"All your work, all your investment gone! I am so very sorry!" she said as she stared around again.

George bent then and picked up a saw and a tangled mass of rope. "Yes, it is very bad," he agreed, his voice steady. "So bad I may have to go to sea again till I get back on my feet. And Jack . . . well, with the brigantine gone, he's lost a great deal as well. But we're young, Kate, all of us. This won't beat us. Eventually we'll come back from it."

Some of the men who had worked in the yard were busy picking up and saving what they could, and stacking what they found by the one remaining wall of the workshop.

"Go and see Cecily, will you, old girl?" George asked. "She is distraught. Comfort her if you can."

Kate nodded, her eyes still suspiciously bright. As she made her way to the house, she thought about what George had said. Yes, they were young. They could fight their way clear of this disaster. And, of course, the only important thing was that they were still alive.

Cecily was upset, but she was trying valiantly to control her tears as she oversaw preparations for the hearty supper she was having cooked for her husband and the men. She and Kate sat in the parlor, for there wasn't a trace of the veranda left. It might never have been there at all.

"Of all the hurricanes I've witnessed in my life, I am sure this one was the worst," Cecily said. "Can you ever remember another like it?"

Kate shook her head. "No, never. I pray Jack and Greg are all right. Oh, that reminds me. I must get word to my parents. My mother will be so worried for our safety."

"George sent a man early this morning. He knows how your mama frets. And we are anxious to find out how those in St. George Town fared. Did you hear about the schooner?"

When Kate shook her head again, Cecily went on, "Last evening, just before sunset, we saw a boat, heavily reefed, trying to reach safe anchorage near Castle Island. After it grew dark, we couldn't see her any longer, although George was sure she would be all right there. But when the storm veered around, she must have dragged her anchor. This morning, there wasn't a trace of her left, nor any survivors. Some of the men have been out there. They say she must have sunk in deep water, and . . . and they found some of the crew's bodies."

Suddenly Cecily put her hands to her face and wept.

Kate was quick to kneel beside her and put her arms around her. "Yes . . . ssh, ssh, my dear. It is a terrible thing, but we must go on. You must be strong for George now. He is so saddened by everything that has happened, the destruction of all his future hopes."

Cecily sniffled and wiped her eyes. "I know. I think I cry because I am so tired. But tell me, Kate, why is it always the women who have to be strong for the men? Why aren't they ever strong for us?"

Kate smiled a little at that ingenuous statement. "I don't know," she admitted. "It doesn't seem fair, does it? Yet that's the way it is. Come, now, I'll help you with supper before I must go home. I have a privy to build, which I'm sure you won't be surprised to learn has been my first order of business out on the point!"

She was glad when Cecily smiled a little then, and offered the use of their own necessary before Kate went home. And Kate thought to tell her about the baby then, thinking such news after so much havoc and destruction would cheer her sister-in-law.

Cecily was so happy for her that Kate was glad she had revealed her secret at last. As the two went arm in arm to help prepare supper, Cecily even giggled about how delightful it would be to have a friend in the same condition, so they could compare notes and help each other waddle around later. Kate laughed at the picture she painted, but she was not looking forward to that stage of her pregnancy at all.

Bartholomew Findley arrived a short time later. Kate left it to Cecily to entertain him, remaining out in the kitchen house with Mandy and her daughter. But she could not avoid the man for long. When George came back to the house, he insisted she stay for supper, and the four of them sat down together again at the table, after George had had a quiet word with his wife.

"Did you sustain much damage in the hurricane, Mrs. Reade?" Findley asked politely as he spread his napkin on his lap.

"Nowhere near as much as you have here, sir," she said. "The kitchen house is gone, and . . . er, another outbuilding, and I lost my sloop."

"No!" George exclaimed, for he had not heard this news. "Not the *Sprite*!"

Kate nodded, saddened by the look of disbelief and regret on his tired face. She wished she had not had to confess that, for George loved the *Sprite* too. He and his twin had learned to sail on her, and she had been part of many of their youthful adventures.

"I did everything I could before the storm arrived, George," Kate hastened to say now. "The cove is sheltered, and I thought it unnecessary to haul her, not with the extra anchor down. But I see I should have insisted on it. With Manfred and Tatum to help me, even Annie, we might have had her high and dry. I . . . I am so sorry."

"What?" George demanded, sounding horrified. "In *your* condition? No, no, Kate! Why, now that Cecily has told me of it, I am most distressed at your exertions yesterday. I think you must be daft to take such chances, you, a woman with child! From now on, you must have a care for yourself! I am sure Jack would agree."

Kate patted his hand and changed the subject. She was glad he had mentioned the baby, even though it was unusual to do so before someone who was not a member of the family. Now Mr. Findley must leave her alone.

But when she rose to leave later, Findley insisted on escorting her home, and George agreed to it, vehement in his insistence that she needed help over the littered path. He said he would have taken her himself, except there was still so much to be done at the yard. Kate could tell he thought her in no danger from Findley now, although she herself was not so sure.

Kate was forced to accept the man's arm, although her eyes flashed as she did so, and her head was slightly averted as they strolled away.

"What very good news I learned at supper about you, ma'am," Findley remarked into the growing silence. "I cannot tell you when I was more encouraged!"

Kate turned and stared at him. Since they were almost of a height, she was very close to that smooth, expressionless face, those curiously blank blue eyes. It was almost as if Mr. Findley had lowered a veil over them, so no one could see into his soul. Yet even so, he was a well-enough-looking man with his regular features and smooth dark-red hair.

"How so?" she asked, curious in spite of herself.

"Why, just see how much easier it is for me now," he said. "Do watch out for that branch, ma'am! Yes, for now, of course, when your husband arrives home, there will be no danger that you might have to confess you are with child, due, let us say, in the autumn. The . . . er, the *damage* has been done already."

Kate drew in a sharp breath, but before she could speak, he went on, "And you are wise not to coddle yourself. My grandmother always maintained it was a mistake for a woman to curtail her usual activities and . . . er, *enjoyments* at this time. Do allow me to hold back this bush for you, my dear Kate."

Kate pulled her arm from his. "Stop this at once!" she said through gritted teeth. "Know I do not like you, sir. And there is no possibility that I will *ever* like you. When you see my husband, you will understand. He is so handsome, so strong! And so *very* tall."

As she spoke, her eyes inspected his five feet, six inches, and she smiled in derision. She was glad when his bland face paled. "My, yes, Jack is quite irreplaceable, I do assure you," she added.

"Oh, I rather doubt he can compare to me in any way that matters," Findley said with some effort. "A colonial menial is not the equal of the brother of a marquess, ma'am. Yes, I am a member of the nobility. I do not fear any serious competition from your lowborn husband."

Kate was smiling more broadly now. "Oh, but didn't you know? Jack is a member of that august band himself. He is Sir John Reade of Hythe, Kent. We do not use his title here, for it seemed inappropriate in Bermuda."

Findley did not speak for a moment, and Kate was delighted she had not only silenced him but also vanquished him.

After a few more steps, however, her companion mused, "But then what is he doing here? Why isn't he at home seeing to his estate? Why is a nobleman engaged in such an ignoble task as captaining a ship?"

Kate made herself shrug, very aware of his intent gaze. "He likes Bermuda," she said as carelessly as she could. "And he adores sailing. No doubt we shall go home eventually, but for now, while we are young, Jack chose to remain here. It is an adventure for him."

She was glad to see the path open up then, and her

house a little distance away. "Thank you for your escort, sir," she said, neglecting her curtsy. "There is no need for you to trouble yourself further."

Findley swept her a deep bow. "It was no trouble at all, dear ma'am. Do feel free to call on me at any time. I am completely at your . . . mmm, service, *Lady* Reade."

The polite words and faint mocking smile angered her, and Kate longed to hit him. Instead, she turned and hurried away. She would never call on him, not for anything!

The next day, Roger Hathaway came to see how they were all doing. He seemed very quiet and sober to his daughter as she showed him around. The privy was up again, and the new kitchen house was already being built, a larger, roomier building of limestone this time. Manfred was clearing the path to Tucker's Town, and things were fast returning to normal.

It was much later that evening, when they were alone, before Mr. Hathaway told Kate what was bothering him. "I have learned of the cargo your husband carries, daughter," he said, his lips compressed and his eyes stern. "I've had my suspicions about him before, and now I have proof."

Kate was startled. "However did you . . . ? But who told you?" she asked. She had never once mentioned that cargo, and she was sure Jack hadn't either, for he knew too well where her father's loyalty lay.

"The night you returned home, Babur told a friend who had rowed out to chat with him. He said he was frightened to be cooking near all that powder and shot. Now news of it is all over St. George Town. You can imagine what people are saying, and Governor Bruere is furious!"

Mr. Hathaway rose then to pace the room, his face turning red as he did so. "What manner of man have you married, Kate? He is a rebel, a traitor to everything any Englishman holds dear—the monarchy, our rightful king! Well, Olivia told me there was something strange about your Jack, and now I perceive she was right! Tell me, why did he come here? Why does he remain? You, of all people, must know!"

Kate was heartsick, but she knew she could not reveal Jack's secret, not even to her dear father.

She studied him now with fresh eyes. He was still trim and upright, even in his fifties—a fine-looking man with great presence. Kate had loved him dearly all her life, even, she realized, more than she had loved her mother. It was hard for her to go against her beliefs and his wishes, to stand with her husband as she knew she must.

"Jack had a good reason for it, Father, but I cannot speak of it, for it is not my secret to tell. And he is not in the least strange! Nor is he a traitor! We are not at war with the colonies, not yet at any rate, and powder and shot are legal cargoes."

"You are quibbling," her father interrupted. "It is only a matter of time before war is declared. And will he stop carrying those cargoes then? He is a disgrace to our name, and I'll not have him in my house again!"

Kate was suddenly angry, and she rose to go to him, confront him. "Is Matt a disgrace too? Will you forbid him your house as well?" she asked quickly. "He was the one who told Jack about the cargoes in the first place, and how needed they are in the colonies. He is on the side of the rebels, for he feels their cause is just. And it is his cause too."

Roger Hathaway looked stunned. "No, I will never believe that," he said slowly. "Not of Matthew! My oldest son—why, I raised him too carefully, and he knows my views."

At the pain in his voice, Kate's anger melted, and she took his arm and rested her head on his shoulder for a moment. My wretched temper! she thought.

She was sorry now she had mentioned Matthew's new loyalty, even though she knew her father would learn of it shortly. Determined to ease his pain, she said, "Yes, that is true, sir, and he respects your views. But he is a man now. He has his own, and you must respect them, in turn. But come! Sit down and let me pour you some wine. And let me tell you my joyous news. I am with child. Isn't that wonderful?"

She was sure her father did not think it wonderful at all, but he made a valiant effort to congratulate her and appear pleased.

Still, Kate was not sorry when he went back to St. George Town early the following morning. She promised to come for a visit as soon as things were back to normal, and she assured him she felt fine. He was to tell her mother that especially, so she would not fret, Kate said, wrinkling her nose at him. Roger Hathaway even chuckled before he kissed her good-bye.

It was getting cooler now that it was mid-November, and Kate stopped going to the cove to swim. She found she did not regret that, for the cove was a different place to her now, the place where Findley had spied on her, and where she could not avoid seeing the sad remains of the *Sprite.* It was no longer possible to go there and remember only the happy times with Jack.

She did not miss her swims, however, for suddenly she seemed more tired than she ever had in her life. She slept for hours past her usual waking time, and still she yawned and had to nap during the day. Annie grinned and told her it was only normal for her to do so, and Cecily said she had felt exactly the same way.

At last, one day in early December, Kate had an answer to her letter to England. George brought it with him when he returned from a trip to St. George Town, joking as he handed it to her about her exalted noble relations. Kate's heart was beating rapidly when she slit the seal after he had left. The letter was bulky; she could hardly wait to read it.

And as she did so, her eyes filled with tears. Weakly she wiped them away. She seemed to cry so often these days. She could not understand that either.

Camille Maxwell, Countess Granbourne, wrote to say she had never been so happy in her life as when she had received Kate's letter. It had been such a long time since she had heard a word of Jack. "And to know he is well and prospering, even married now, has made all the difference in the world to me, and to the earl. I only fear that your great kindness may cause problems for you, my new, already dear daughter-in-law," she wrote. "You never said so in so many words, but I am positive Jack has no idea you have written to me. I would not cause you a moment's trouble, my dear, but I pray—oh, so very hard!—that you will continue to correspond occasionally from now on. Your letters will be my only means of knowing of my beloved son.

"I wish I had a miniature of you, like the one I treasure of Jack, and kiss so often. I would like to be able to picture you. Prithee describe yourself when next you write. But I do not have to see you to know how good you are, nor do I have to wonder if you care for Jack. It is in every line you write. Thank you for loving him so well, and God bless you both, always, and keep you safe.

"You, my dear Katherine, are now always in my prayers."

Kate was so touched that she sat down at Jack's desk at once, and wrote a long letter in reply. And in it she confided that she was carrying Jack's child. As she did so, she smiled. She felt as if it was the first time she had truly smiled in a very long time.

And it would be the last time she would do so for a very long time as well, for the next day the splintered transom of the *Lady Sprite* washed up on Ireland Island.

18

KATE spent very little time at her house on the point in the months that followed that awful discovery. Olivia Hathaway, on learning that her son's sloop had gone down with all hands, almost lost her mind. The only one who seemed able to comfort and soothe her was her daughter. Mrs. Hathaway even refused to see her son George anymore, for he reminded her so of Gregory, she could not bear it. And Roger Hathaway, sunk in depression and sorrowing himself, was of little help.

So Kate found that the burden of caring for her mother became hers alone. It was not easy for her, living in her girlhood home again and dealing with a wailing, disconsolate woman who refused to leave her darkened room. And Kate's rapport with her father had changed somewhat since he had learned of Jack's cargo. He was more formal with her; colder now. The only person Kate felt easy with was Keza. But even Keza's encompassing love could not reach Kate these days.

She felt frozen, as she had ever since the news had been brought. And even when she had seen the transom,

and touched the gold-leafed name painted on it, she had
not been able to cry. She had watched her father and
George grieve, and she had wiped what seemed an ocean
of tears from her mother's cheeks, but Kate herself remained dry-eyed. Keza watched her, a frown on her
broad face, for she was worried about her and the baby.

Kate never told anyone that she could not grieve because of how she had reacted when she first heard the
news. She was ashamed of herself, mortally ashamed.
For for one dark, exultant moment, she had thanked
God that if one of them had had to drown, it had been
Greg and not Jack. The storm gods had had their sacrifice; surely Jack would be safe now. And then, mortified,
she had prayed for forgiveness, although she did not feel
she deserved it. To have thanked God for such a fate for
her beloved brother! Even her great love for Jack could
not excuse her vileness.

The day after the news of the lost ship became general
knowledge, Kate, in her mother's place, received the
many friends who came to offer their condolences. She
allowed the older ladies to weep on her bosom, and
accepted the wordless hugs of their husbands stoically.
Only when Granny Bessie came to call did she feel any
stirring of emotion at all, for she suddenly remembered
that Granny had lost someone dear to her as well—her
slave Samuel.

When she commiserated with the old woman, Granny
only patted her hand. "It is all right, my dear Kate," she
said. "Samuel wouldn't have minded going that way. He
loved the sea, and he knew the dangers just as well as my
own husband, Will, did. And Samuel was old. He didn't
have much time left in any case. I only pray he didn't
worry about me in his last moments, the dear, *dear* man!"

Granny kissed Kate when she left, and told her she
was not to worry about her either. She would be just
fine.

A week later, Bessie Simpson died peacefully in her
sleep. Kate went to the funeral, but still she could not
cry.

That same afternoon, a Mr. Greer came to call on her.
Adolphus Greer was a solicitor in St. George Town, and
he told her that Granny had had him draw up her will
only a short time before. Kate was to receive all the old

lady's valuables—the beautifully fashioned cedar hope chest that her husband had made for her so many years ago, her silver spoons and knives, her precious linen, so delicately sewn and embroidered. And she was to have Granny's small pieces of jewelry and the lace handkerchief she had carried at her wedding as well. Kate had to bow her head at that, and swallow hard, lest she disgrace herself.

"Mrs. Simpson told me that she hoped your daughter would carry it someday, Mrs. Reade," the solicitor told her. "She said she wanted her to do so even if she *didn't* marry a seafaring man. No doubt you will know what she meant by that.

"She has left her cottage to a young couple who are to be married soon. I'm sure you know Ben Swan and Sally Wellman, do you not, ma'am? Since Ben's a sailor, Mrs. Simpson wanted to give them a start."

He sighed then as he packed his papers away in his case. "Such a good lady, Granny Bessie was. How we shall miss her!"

Kate agreed, and after he had bowed and left her, she wandered over to the parlor window to rest her head against the cool pane. When would all this sadness end? she wondered. Would she ever be happy again?

And where was Jack? She needed him so! She needed his warm strength and his love. She knew her world would not come right again until he was with her. Pray he came home soon!

But Jack did not come home. The new year came in without him, and then February and March as well.

Kate was heavier now, and awkward, although physically she felt well. Owing, she was sure, to Keza's bullying. The old woman made her go out every fine day and walk, get away from the house. Whenever Olivia Hathaway protested this regimen and tried to coddle her daughter, Keza stood up to her mistress, arguing Kate's cause.

Mrs. Hathaway had finally left her room, although she still refused to receive callers or even attend church. Instead, she sat in the parlor and stared into space, only sighing heavily now and then. Her needlework, her books and letters, lay neglected, and if it had not been for Keza and Kate, the household would have been neglected as well.

The three Hathaways were seated at the breakfast table one blustery day in early April, eating silently, when Kate finally broke. She had looked up from her plate at her mother's tiny sob, to see her burying her face in her napkin.

"Mama, there will be no . . . more . . . tears!" Kate told her slowly and forcibly as she threw down her own napkin. From the end of the table her father stared at her, amazed into silence.

"No more tears?" Olivia Hathaway's voice quavered. "I shall never cease mourning my dearest Gregory! How can you be so unfeeling, daughter?"

"I am not unfeeling. I have been *feeling* for you for months now," Kate told her. "But it is time to stop, Mama. In the past, you commiserated with many women who had lost their husbands and sons to the sea. You told them they must be brave, go on. Would you now belittle their sacrifice because somehow your *own* loss is so much more important? And why should that be so? What of the other families who lost their men with Greg? They have mourned too, but not like *you*! No, Mama, it is time for you to put your exquisite sensibilities aside now, for I am going home."

"No, no, I cannot bear it!" Olivia Hathaway moaned. "Roger, you must stop her! I will lose my mind if Kate deserts me!"

"No, you will not lose your mind, Mama," Kate said firmly, before her stunned father could speak. "Nor will you hold me here any longer with your excessive demands for all my attention. I have a home of my own to see to, a husband who will be coming there soon—God willing—a child to bear. I have my own life to live, and I intend to get on with it."

"Cruel, so *cruel* and unfeeling," her mother mourned, rocking back and forth in her chair in her distress.

"As you must get on with your life," Kate went on as if she had not spoken. "There is your husband for you to care for. And there are Matt, Alicia, and your granddaughter, as well as George and Cecily. Have you never thought what your banishment of George has done to him—the extra burden you placed on his shoulders by refusing to see him? Dammit, Mama! Wasn't it enough for him to lose his twin brother, and all his hopes for the shipyard, without you making it worse by exiling him from your presence? Are no one's feelings important but yours? You should be ashamed of yourself!"

"Kate, that will be enough!" Roger Hathaway said at last. Kate looked around wildly, for she had forgotten he was even there. She saw that his face was stern but composed. Behind him, in the doorway, Keza stood watching, her arms crossed on her ample stomach. She nodded to Kate, and winked, and Kate felt better.

"I quite agree with everything you say, my dear, but I cannot allow you to continue to speak to your mother that way," her father went on. "But know you have all our thanks and all our love for everything you have done here. You shall go back to Tucker's Town today. Indeed, since there was another case of smallpox announced this morning, it will be safer for you and your baby there. And you are right. You have your own life to live."

"You must take Keza, then!" Olivia Hathaway cried. "You'll not go without Keza to watch over you! Indeed, I'm sure you would prefer her, since you dote so on *her* care, yet refuse your *mother's*!"

Ignoring that provocative statement, for she could see it would just lead to more weeping, more recriminations, Kate thanked her. And she kissed her mother before she went away to begin packing.

At Tucker's Town later, Kate stopped to see Cecily and George, to explain what she had done. Only a few days from term now, Cecily looked huge to her, and she seemed different somehow. Whenever she looked at her husband, there was a new light in her eyes, and her pretty mouth was tightened in her determination to make sure he was all right in spite of the exile imposed by his mother. It was as if she had decided she must be all to him—wife, mother, father, and missing brother.

"I expect you'll be summoned to town soon, George," Kate told him. "I had some plain words with Mama, and with Father too. In fact, I rather surprised myself."

"Din't s'prise me none, Miz Kate, honey," Keza said from where she was sitting in a chair by the door so she could keep her eyes on the crate of bantams she had brought with her.

She had insisted on bringing half her flock, so they could have fresh eggs. The rooster was coming separately. As Keza said, "We-all kin wait for him, an' so kin *dey*!"

" 'Swounds, it doesn't surprise me either," George said now, his eyes twinkling a little. "But then, you always were a firebrand, old lady!"

Kate begged him to tell her all about the yard then, remarking on how prosperous it looked. George told her about several new commissions, and how the repair work he had been swamped with after the hurricane had kept the yard solvent.

As she and Keza were leaving later, Bartholomew Findley arrived to bow and greet her. Kate had almost forgotten him, and now she was delighted that she was so large and ungainly. To her dismay, he did not appear to be at all put off by her obvious pregnancy. His expressionless blue eyes gleamed for a moment, and his mouth curled in a little smile.

"You must allow me the honor of escorting you home, *Lady* Reade," he said, extending his arm. "It has been such a long time since we met, has it not? And we have so much to talk about!"

" 'Tain't no need o' dat, suh," Keza said, coming to take Kate's arm herself. "*I'se* here to see to Miz Kate now."

To Kate's secret amusement, the gentleman was forced to retreat before the old black woman's fierce frown.

As the two walked away from him, Keza snorted. "Who dat mans, honey?" she asked. "Ah feels in mah bones he nuttin' but trouble. Y'all keep out of his way, hear me, girl?"

Kate was only too delighted to agree, and when she stepped into her own sitting room again, to hug Annie, she felt happier than she had for a long time. Even the sudden rain shower that was streaking the windows now could not depress her. It had been dry for a long time, and the rain would be welcome. And perhaps if it continued long enough, the rain might even stem the rising number of smallpox cases in the islands. What with the threat of epidemic and the worry about low food supplies, Bermudians had enough to burden them without adding a lack of good drinking water.

Even though she knew they would hate such plebeian labor, Kate intended to set Manfred and Tatum to build-

ing a coop and hen yard for Keza's bantams, and then to
clearing and tilling a plot for vegetables. It was not that
she did not have enough money for food, for Jack had
left her ample for her needs; it was just that suddenly
there was very little available to buy. Kate had heard
stories that the American colonies were loath to continue
trading with any loyal British colony, and she prayed
they would change their minds. Bermuda could not survive else, for there was little food grown here, and trade
was their lifeline. Who was it who had said that all the
wealth Bermuda had was cedar, salt, and sailors? How
true that was!

But Kate could see she could not just wait for the
Americans to relent. No, she must grow some crops lest
the household have to subsist on fish, a few eggs, and
what native fruits they could gather. And no matter how
Manfred and Tatum felt about tilling the soil, in this
instance they would have to. They, none of them, had
any choice. She had often wondered why the slaves disliked farming so much, yet took to sailing so eagerly. A
sailor's life was just as hard, certainly more uncomfortable, and many times more dangerous.

Kate was a little concerned that Annie would not take
to having Keza in the house, or that Keza herself would
dislike the younger woman. After all, this was Annie's
domain, and Keza a stranger. As it turned out, the two
women became instant allies. When she heard Annie
talking so eagerly to Keza, Kate realized that she must
have been lonely out here by herself all this time, with
only her husband and the sullen Manfred for company.
And as Kate knew very well, there were times only
another woman would do for companionship. In a very
short time, Annie was just like Keza's daughter, and
Tatum another of her sons.

The only occupant of the house on the point that Keza
did not like was Manfred. It was not many days after her
arrival home that Kate saw trouble coming between the
two of them.

Kate had set her two male slaves to clearing and digging a sizable piece of land. Manfred worked so slowly,
his labor was just on the edge of insolent rebellion. One
afternoon, when Kate and Keza went out to see how
much had been accomplished, Keza sniffed in scorn.

"Lazy nigger!" she scoffed. "He tink he too good for dis kind o' work, doan he? Y'all got to git rid o' him, Miz Kate! He trouble, dat one, y'all mark mah words!"

Kate wished she could get rid of him, for she didn't trust Manfred either. Still, when Bartholomew Findley came one morning and asked to buy him, she hesitated. She had heard from George that Findley was intent on searching for treasure at the offshore reefs, and he needed a diver for that.

"Why do you hesitate, ma'am?" Findley asked. He was seated in Jack's favorite chair in the main room, for Kate had not been able to refuse his request for a few moments of her time on a business matter. She had to grit her teeth, however, when she saw the little man he was, lounging where her big, handsome Jack had taken his ease.

"Surely you know how *well* I treat my slaves," Findley went on with a secret little smile. Kate stiffened. Cecily had told her that Bart Findley had bought two pretty twins in their early teens. He had also purchased another, much older, woman to do the cooking and cleaning, for it was common knowledge all over the islands that the twins never did a lick of work. They had been bought for another purpose entirely.

"We don't see nearly as much of him as we used to," Cecily had confided. "Not since we learned what was going on down there. I told George I didn't want such a revolting man in my house."

Kate had not been surprised at the news, knowing Findley as she did. It stood to reason he would have to have someone in his bed, and slaves were all that were available to him.

"Yes, I have heard of your slaves, sir," she remarked as evenly as she could.

He chuckled. "Do you take it personally, ma'am? But you must not, no, indeed! You have been gone for some months now, and I am a virile man. And if white meat is not available, well, then, I make do with dark. I would be happy to change my diet . . . er, even now."

Kate rose from her chair to dismiss him in disgust, but he raised a languid hand and said, "But never mind that now. I want your Manfred for my proposed diving expedition, and I am prepared to pay handsomely for him.

After all, what use is he to you? Your husband may be gone months longer, and Manfred is wasted digging furrows."

"Was he the one who told you about my swimming in the cove?" Kate asked, curious.

Findley nodded, never taking his eyes from her face. "Indeed. There is little that gold can't buy, m'lady."

Kate took her seat again, thinking hard. Only last evening, as Keza had been brushing her hair before bedtime, she had warned Kate again about Manfred. "Ah tell you, honey, dat man bad trouble! He apt to rise up anytime now, and Ah fears for y'all. Git rid o' him as soon as y'all can! We-all do fine wit'out him, you'll see. Dat boy Tatum a good worker, and Ah'll keep at 'im!"

Now Kate nodded. She knew Keza was right, and now that she had proof of Manfred's duplicity, she was more anxious than ever to sell him. "Very well, Mr. Findley," she said. "You may purchase Manfred, if he is willing. I cannot sell any slave without his consent."

"You needn't fear for that, ma'am," Findley told her, rising to bow. "He knows my mind, and he is anxious to work on the reefs for me. I fear he considers the work you have set him to quite beneath his touch. Ridiculous, is it not, to think such animals have standards?"

Kate stood there silently while he counted out the guineas for the slave. She had never liked Manfred, and she would be glad when he was gone, but still she did not envy him such a master.

That same evening, Cecily had her baby—a little girl. Keza was with her for the birth, since her mother, Mrs. Lunne, had been unable to come out from St. George Town. She was too busy nursing Cecily's younger sister, who had the pox.

Cecily and George named the baby Margaret Rose, and in the following days Kate spent a lot of time with them. She was feeling passive and indolent now, not unlike the sleepiness she had suffered in her early months. All the baby clothes were prepared, and the padded basket she intended to use for a cradle. George had brought his own cradle back with him from St. George Town for his daughter to use, after he had gone there to tell his parents the grand news. Secretly, Kate hoped her mother would let her have hers and Gregory's cradle for her own baby, although she hesitated to suggest it, lest her mother begin her weeping again.

Kate was delighted to see that her mother seemed a little more cheerful now. She made the trip to Tucker's Town often, to see her new granddaughter, and her visits brought her close to George again. Since the yard was prospering, and his wife and child doing well, he was content, almost happy.

One evening he walked out to the point to see his sister. Her own time was very near, and he pitied her that she would have to endure it alone, without her husband to support her. Kate was rather glad Jack was not there, for she felt ugly now, awkward and grotesque. And from what Cecily had told her, and Keza as well, men were of no use at such a time, for instead of helping, they placed another burden on their suffering wives.

"I've been thinking of the brigantine, Kate," George told her as he mixed up a citrus punch. "I'd no idea what Jack would want me to do under the circumstances, so I did nothing. But what do you think? Should I begin to build her again? I fear we salvaged little of her that we can use now. We would have to start anew."

Kate thought for a moment, and then she shook her head. "I don't know what to tell you," she said. "We never thought we might have a hurricane and lose her. Perhaps Jack will not want to rebuild her. Perhaps he would rather replace the sloop first."

Both brother's and sister's faces sobered then, and there was silence between them for a long moment.

"I miss Greg still," George admitted finally, his voice full of regret. "Sometimes I can't believe that he won't walk into the yard someday, full of the tales of his adventures. I guess I won't ever be able to really accept the fact that he is gone. We were so close."

"I know, my dear," Kate said, hiding her own pain. "What happened was sad. But I have often wondered why the transom came ashore at Ireland. Do you suppose that Greg was coming home at last, and ran into the storm? How terrible, when he was almost here!"

George nodded, still frowning. "It must have been that. But all his expertise, and old Samuel's as well, were of no use during such a mighty blow. They could not have seen the reefs in time during the gale, and perhaps they were blown off course too. And it was entirely like Greg, you know, being so close, to think he could make harbor, instead of running before the hurricane with only a storms'l up, as any sensible man would have done."

Kate had a sudden vision of Greg's excitement, standing at the wheel with his hair blown wild and his eyes intent; heard his delighted laughter at the challenge; and she knew that was what he had done as surely as if she had been there to see it. She sighed. Her daredevil brother—only this time the gods had not smiled on him.

"Perhaps we should just wait a bit longer," George said, interrupting her musings. "Surely Jack will be home soon. Why, May is half gone, and I know he intended to be back this spring, for he told me he would."

The baby moved then, and Kate clutched her distended abdomen and groaned. "I must say this child is most impolite!" she said tartly. "Not only does he squirm and kick in company, he does so especially when his mama is trying to get to sleep at night."

George grinned at her. "You are so sure the baby will be a boy?" he asked.

Kate grinned back and wrinkled her nose at him. "But of course. No girl would be so horrid!"

The two laughed together then, and when George took his leave, he begged her to call him the moment she felt her pains begin, so he could come to her. Kate changed the subject. This was something she knew she had to do alone, and with Keza beside her, she needed no one else.

Jack Reade was even then setting out for Philadelphia. At his brother-in-law's instigation, he was taking several prominent Bermudians to petition the Second Continental Congress, soon to convene.

Earlier that week he had stopped in Charles Town to visit Matthew Hathaway before going on to Bermuda. He was not at all sure, from the temper of the colonies, when he would have the chance again.

Much earlier, Jack had learned of the loss of the *Lady Sprite* with all hands, from another Bermuda captain in a Caribbean harbor. By now he had overcome his grief for Greg and the crew, and for that graceful sloop he had named for his Kate. Still, the man who sat late over wine with his brother-in-law was vastly different from the man

he had been two years before. He seemed much older
and harder, and a great deal more serious.

"I doubt I will be calling in Charles Town for a long
time, Matt," Jack remarked. "It appears to me we are
already at war, and there is only the formal announce-
ment of revolution left to come."

"Yes, I am aware," his host agreed. "I have been in
touch with Bermuda, even though the crown has forbidden any more intercourse between the islands and the
mainland. My family ties there excuse me from the ban,
at least for now. Things are not going well in Bermuda,
my friend. Some people are on the verge of starving, for
there is no food to buy, and no one in the colonies will
trade with them."

Jack leaned forward, his black hair shining in the candlelight and his handsome face set in hard lines. "Pray
Kate is all right!" he said. "I will go to her as soon as I
can make sail in the morning!"

"I hope I can persuade you to do otherwise, Jack,"
Matthew said as he poured them another glass. "You
must not fear for Kate. My father and my brother, George,
will see she comes to no harm. And only last week I sent
food to them—as a gift, mind you! Governor Bruere is
not aware of this, for I charged my father most strictly
not to tell him. How His Excellency would fume if he
knew! Fool!"

"Why do you say that?" Jack asked.

"Because he is adamant that there will be no clandes-
tine trade with the colonies. Worse, he has demanded
Bermudians provide supplies for British warships and
troops. I heard from Colonel Henry Tucker, who is aboard
a ship in Charles Town harbor now, that the House of
Assembly refused such a request, and most indignantly,
too. For how could they supply others, when they have
so little for their own use? But you see it was an empty
victory they won, for Bruere is a stubborn man, and he is
His Majesty's representative."

"Why did you say you hoped to persuade me not to go
home?" Jack asked. He was anxious to see Kate, hold
her in his arms again. He felt they had been separated for
years, not months, and he hated to delay their reunion
any longer.

"Because Colonel Tucker and several other prominent

Bermudians are bound for Philadelphia to see the Continental Congress that is soon to convene there. They go without official sanction, of course, for the governor would never agree to such a move. Well, but neither will Tucker and others watch their families, friends, and slaves die of hunger. They intend to petition the Congress to permit American vessels to bring food to Bermuda, in return for which they will provide salt for the colonies. I would like you to take them on the next leg of their journey in the *Camille*. It will be safer for them if they travel to Philadelphia in another vessel. That way, no word can leak out about their errand, for no one knows why you are here. And when you bring them back to Charles Town, they can return home in their original ship, and Bruere will be none the wiser. If he did find out what they had been up to, he might have them hanged as traitors."

Jack rose then to pace the room, deep in thought. Matthew Hathaway watched him through half-closed eyes that hid the intensity with which he hoped Jack would accept the plan. And as he waited, he had the irrelevant thought that Jack Reade was one of the handsomest men he had ever seen. But he was more than just handsome, with that strong face, those unusual turquoise eyes, he told himself. He was clever and intelligent as well, and more important, as straight and true as any man he had ever known. Matthew was proud Jack was his friend.

Jack turned suddenly, and Matthew held out his hands, palms up.

"After all, it will not take that long, Jack," he pointed out. "And Kate will still be there in a month or so, will she not? I am delighted you value my sister as you should, even love her so much, but I must say I wish you were not so . . . ardent at this particular time. But what say you?"

"You have not been away from your Alicia for half a year, my friend," Jack remarked. "How very easy it is for you to be so dispassionate!"

As Matthew chuckled, Jack took his seat again. "I suppose I must go," he said, frowning now. "The matter it too important not to. And let us pray the Congress heeds Colonel Tucker and agrees to his plan. But perhaps you might acquire a cargo of foodstuffs for me to carry to Bermuda on my return? To be given away as gifts, of course!"

Matthew agreed, and the two sat late together planning the voyage. It was decided that the Bermudians would come ashore, putting it about that they were going inland to visit Matthew Hathaway's plantation. Then, late at night, they would be rowed secretly to the *Camille* in small boats. And they would remain belowdeck until the sloop was at sea.

"I will not try to deny that this voyage might be dangerous, Jack," Matthew said at last. "The colonies do not look kindly on British vessels. What say you to carrying the South Carolina Colony flag? It would ensure your safe arrival, if you would agree to the subterfuge. Of course, it is a blatant act of rebellion. You could be accused of being a traitor—hanged for it—if taken by a British ship."

Jack stared at him, the frown still between his brows. "Let me think on that, Matt," he said slowly.

He stirred in his chair then, and added, "To do so would precipitate a move I am not ready to make at this time. I am still an Englishman; I cannot in good conscience sail under another's flag. Oh, it is not that I do not sympathize with the colonies, see their dilemma, even wish the crown—Parliament—would moderate its demands and make peace here. But as an Englishman still, your fight cannot be mine."

"Of course you can take your chances," Matthew said easily. "But there are Colonel Tucker and all the others to consider. Bermuda would be ill-served if they were lost in a battle at sea. And I have heard that some of the colonies are even now planning a navy. Indeed, some of the New England colonies are petitioning for one, arming their own vessels. As you must be aware, our few roads are a disgrace. And we have a wilderness at our backs, so the broad ocean before us becomes our highway—the only way we can trade and communicate with each other. I only suggested the flag to keep you safe, my friend. Ecod, Kate would have my heart out if anything happened to you, brother or no brother!"

Jack promised only to think it over, before he said his good-nights and took himself off to bed.

Matthew Hathaway sat on alone at the shining dining-room table, deep in thought. Yes, it was true that Jack was a loyal Englishman. Matthew wondered, however, if he would always be one. Something had forced Jack Reade to immigrate to the New World, but Matthew knew the man had grown to like it here. Jack had mentioned his admiration for too many things—the climate, the people, the breadth of life available to all with the courage to seize it—to leave any doubt of the way he was leaning. Someday, Matthew suspected that Jack would face up to whatever had driven him from England's shores, and return there. But whether he would remain was questionable. For himself, he hoped Jack would choose the colonies. Men of his stamp would be a most valuable asset in the coming years.

Idly he wondered what Jack's dark problem was. It had to be serious indeed, for Jack was no coward. As he rose and yawned, Matthew wondered if Kate knew.

When the *Camille* left the port of Charles Town a few days later, she was flying the British ensign. Captain Jack Reade had decided to take his chances, for there was no way he could bring himself to sail under another's banner without publicly announcing his change of allegiance.

Fortunately, the voyage was uneventful, and although some of the other ships' captains and crews in the port of Philadelphia were unfriendly, the *Camille*'s stay in that port was uneventful as well.

But the voyage was all for nothing. The Continental Congress listened to the Bermudians' plea most courteously, but decided that a trade of food for salt was not to their advantage. The only hope they held out was to say that if the Bermudians could provide them with the gunpowder they were in such dire need of, they might reconsider.

Before they dropped the hook in Charles Town harbor again, Jack and Henry Tucker had many talks together. The colonel was disappointed at the failure of his mission, but he assured Jack he would find a way to overcome the problem, for he could not stand by and watch people starve. And, he said, if it came to it, he would defy the governor, buy the gunpowder at St. Eustatius, and take it to the American colonists himself.

Looking at the older man's set face, that jutting, determined jaw, Jack was sure he would do just that. He told the colonel of Isaac Van Dam then, and as much as he had learned of the trade, and of the inherent dangers Tucker would have to face.

For himself, Jack did not see any way he could continue to transport such cargoes anymore. It had been different when he had first arrived, for the possibility of war had been only a very small cloud on a distant horizon. Now, however, he expected war to be declared any day. And as he had told Matt, he was a loyal Englishman.

As he took his watches on the voyage to Bermuda, Jack pondered this growing problem of his. He missed home even now, and yet the lure of the colonies grew stronger and stronger. Sometimes he even caught himself daydreaming of settling in South Carolina someday, carving out a plantation as Matthew Hathaway had done, with a handsome town house so he could engage in shipping and trade. Bermuda was a lovely place, but its scope was limited both in opportunity and in society. Only the Hathaways and a few others there had inspired him to friendship. But the South Carolinians he had met were men he felt at home with—educated and knowledgeable men who were witty and astute. And there were many of them.

He eased the helm a point and frowned. Perhaps such dreams were a delusion. Perhaps he dreamed them because such a decision would be an easy way out of his dilemma. Because in South Carolina it wouldn't matter that he was not really Sir John Reade.

But he knew that whatever he finally decided, he would go back to England someday, to settle the affair once and for all. And when he did, he could see his mother and Alex again, make his peace with them. And it would be easy to go. He and Kate were childless, all thanks to his precautions. He had only to continue to be careful, and all would be well, for he would be the only impostor to the title. When he died, one of the other Reades would inherit, and the estate would revert to the rightful line.

Ah, Kate, he mused. How good it would be to see her, hold her, love her again. Only a little more time now, and they would be together, and she would be in his arms.

The *Camille* dropped anchor first at Ely Harbor, then at Crow Harbor at the head of the Great Sound before she sailed around to her home port at Tucker's Town. Jack chafed at the delay, for being so close to Kate, yet still apart from her, was agony. But he had to distribute his cargo of foodstuffs at places where they would do the most good. True to his word, he would accept no payment for the food. It was, he assured the astounded islanders, a gift.

He was embarrassed when one old lady threw her arms around his neck, sobbing in gratitude for her bags of flour, sugar, and tea, plus fresh produce, and he tried to make light of his generosity. But when he saw the eager eyes of the children, both black and white, so big in their drawn faces as they stared at him, and observed their skinny little arms and legs, his mouth tightened. Tucker was right. This could not go on.

But he wondered that George Bruere could be so indifferent to the needs of the people he governed in His Majesty's name. Still, no matter how harsh and unrelenting the man was, some way, somehow, a continuous supply of food would have to be assured. And if that meant the men of Bermuda had to deliver gunpowder to the American colonies, so be it.

19

WHEN Jack stepped into the yard of his house on the point one late-June morning, he stopped short, to stare around in amazement.

It was still very early; no one was awake. Indeed, so anxious had he been to see Kate again, he had come ashore before anyone in Tucker's Town was stirring. Time enough to see George later, he told himself as he hurried along the familiar path, his portmanteau on his shoulder.

Now he frowned a little. He had noticed how few trees were left on his way here, due, no doubt, to that ferocious hurricane that had taken the *Lady Sprite*. But the yard looked so different, so much the farm now! His moongate was incongruous in such a setting. Over to one side there was a large vegetable garden, its long furrows just beginning to sport rows of tender green shoots of peas and beans and lettuce. Beyond that, near a new and larger kitchen house, there were a chicken coop and yard. As he watched, a little bantam hen strutted out and squawked at him before she began to scratch in the dirt. And over on the edge of the clearing there was what looked like a pig sty. A pig sty?

Jack shook his head, and then a slow smile curled his lips. Leave it to Kate, he thought as he went toward the house. It was obvious she had foreseen the food shortage and taken care of it as best she could. What a wonder she was, his bright penny!

He opened the door without knocking. He had intended to go to their room and wake her with a kiss, but as he stepped inside, he saw that would not be necessary. Kate was standing in the bedroom doorway, buttoning the neck of her bedgown. She stared at him as if she were seeing a ghost.

"Jack?" he heard her whisper, but she made no move to come to him.

In a moment he was beside her and she was in his arms. He lifted her face to kiss her, and closed his eyes, the better to savor the feel of her slender body, those generous lips opening under his; to smell the healthy clean scent of her skin and the sweet perfume of the lavender sachets she used in her clothes chest.

When he could bear to draw back a little, he stared down into her face and frowned. Kate was so altered! But why should that be? he wondered as one big hand caressed her chestnut curls. Her gray eyes were as steady and honest as they had ever been, her aristocratic features as fine. Even the little golden freckles on the bridge of her nose were the same. Still, there was something different about her he could not put his finger on. He had the sudden thought that he had left a girl behind him all those months ago, and come home to find that a woman had replaced her.

"What is it, Kate?" he asked quietly. "What has happened to you?"

"Oh, Jack, I am so glad you are home," she sighed, snuggling closer to him. "It has been such a long dreary time, and so many bad things have happened!"

He picked her up then and went to his favorite chair to settle down with her on his lap. "Tell me," he said.

Kate began to talk then, at first slowly and hesitantly, and then in a rush. She told him about the hurricane, the loss of the *Sprite* and the brigantine, how the transom of Greg's sloop had been washed ashore.

"It was then we knew that Greg . . . Samuel . . . all of them had been lost in the storm. My mother nearly went out of her mind with grief. I had to spend months with her until she was more stable. It seemed to me I was deluged by one tragedy after another. And now there is a shortage of food, and rampant smallpox. But . . . but I am so sorry about your ships, Jack. What an awful blow for you!"

Jack nodded. He had not seen the brigantine when he sailed into Tucker's Town at dawn, but then, he had not expected to see her, for she should have been launched long ago, and at sea now. His happy anticipation of homecoming died away as he counted up his heavy losses.

"George was in a bad case," Kate went on. "The shipyard was almost destroyed. But he is coming around now. He had a great deal of repair work to do, and now he has some new commissions. We talked about building the brigantine anew, but we did not know if you would want to do that, so we decided to wait until you came home."

"I shall have to see what would be best," Jack said slowly. "This has been a blow to our future, Kate."

Kate's hand caressed his lean face, those high cheek-bones, and he turned his head so he could kiss her palm. Then his arms tightened.

"But time enough to think of such serious matters later, my love," he told her as he rose and set her on her feet. "I have quite another urgent goal in mind at the moment. Come!"

As he turned her toward their room, he wondered why she seemed to hold back, without a smile of agreement on her face.

"Er, Jack, there is one other thing," she said a little breathlessly. "Please, wait! Hear me out!"

Jack was astounded to see how she had paled, how awkward and uncomfortable she looked. "Yes?" he asked, his brows lifted.

Kate stared at him for a moment, and then she moved past him to the bedroom. All the words that came to mind seemed inadequate, for what did you say to a man who did not know he was a father: "Oh, by the way, my dear, the most amusing thing, I have had a baby"? Or: "I have such a surprise for you! You will never guess"? No, better not to say anything.

Perplexed, Jack followed her. And then he had to stop and grasp the doorjamb when he saw the basket by the bed. Kate had stooped and picked up a baby, and he was having trouble breathing as she brought the tiny bundle to him.

"This is your son, Jack," she said softly, smoothing down one side of the blanket so he could see the infant's sleeping face.

"No!" he said harshly. "No, it can't be! I don't believe it, for I was always so careful! And you knew I didn't want children, Kate!"

Kate had been holding the baby out to him, but at those impassioned words she cradled him close to her breast again, as if to protect him from his father's rejection.

"Whether you did or not, you have one now," she said, trying to hide the hurt she felt.

He stared at her, his eyes accusing, and she cried, "Why do you look like that? This isn't all my fault! I hardly managed the thing on my own, you know!"

Jack shook his head. "Knowing you, Kate, I have no doubt you could have, if you put your mind to it."

He seemed to notice her distress then, for he came to her to take the baby from her arms. Kate watched him anxiously as he inspected the little boy. She could not tell from his serious face, those shuttered eyes, what he was feeling.

The only emotion Jack felt was a deep, heart-wrenching disappointment. The child he held—his and Kate's—had no power to move him. For as he stared down at the baby's soft skin, that button nose and tiny rosebud mouth, he realized that this little scrap of humanity he held was as large an obstacle as the most formidable army would have been. For now he could never go home to Hythe. The choice had been taken out of his hands. Without meaning to, he had fathered the next baronet, one, moreover, who, like his father before him, had no claim to the title. A title Jack could never permit him to acknowledge either.

"What did you name him?" he asked quietly.

"John," Kate said.

Jack's head swung up, and his turquoise eyes bored into hers.

"John, for you, of course," she went on, twisting her hands together to keep them from trembling. "He is John Gregory Reade. But I call him Johnny. He is too wee for such formality."

"When was he born?" Jack asked, still staring at her. She wished he would look away.

"June second. He must have been conceived just before we sailed. Remember, Jack? That captivating night of the full moon, the moongate?"

"So you were pregnant even on our voyage?" he asked. "Why didn't you tell me?"

Kate took the baby from him then, and went to put him back in his basket. She was so disappointed! Jack had sounded cold, cold and leaden. And while she had expected him to be surprised, she had never thought he would look at her with such accusation in his eyes, act as if the birth of their child was a tragedy. When she contrasted his reaction to her own joy when she had first held Johnny in her arms, she could have wept.

"Well?" he persisted. "Why didn't you tell me, Kate?"

She straightened up and came to stand before him. "You had so much on your mind," she said, ignoring her aching heart, the tears she could feel clogging her throat. "I didn't want to worry you when you were going on that long journey carrying such a dangerous cargo."

She turned away then, but not soon enough for Jack not to notice the tears in her eyes, hear the little catch in her voice. He was ashamed of himself then, and he reached out to take her in his arms and hold her close. The deed was done. He must make the best of it. Acting as he had was most unfair to Kate.

"To think you went through it alone, love," he murmured against her hair. "Were you all right? Was it hard?"

Kate nodded, but she did not look up at him. "Yes, it was very hard. But Keza was with me. She saw me safely through it."

She stopped then. No need to tell Jack of those long two days of labor, the searing pain that had almost consumed her, how she had barely been able to hang on to her courage. No need for him to know that later she had almost bled to death. She was glad he had not been here to see it, suffer it with her.

"I cannot imagine how you must have looked," Jack said, his voice wondering. "My slender little Kate, big with child."

She leaned back in his arms then. "No, I wasn't big," she said, shaking her head. "I was enormous!"

He was able to smile a little then. "Is he . . . is he all right?" he asked. At her perplexed look, he added, "He is very quiet for a baby."

"He has just been nursed, sir. And he is not at all wet at the moment. But let me warn you. He has a very demanding cry when he wants to get attention. You shall see."

She looked up at him shyly then and said, "He is so beautiful, Jack, so perfect! And although I know you said you never wanted a child, surely you will come to love him as much as I do. He is ours—ours together—conceived in our love for each other."

"I am sure I shall," Jack made himself say. Better this lie than causing her any more distress. But deep inside, he did not think he would ever be able to love this son he had never wanted and tried so hard to avoid having. This son whose existence meant that the deception his father had had to practice would continue for another generation.

"I must tell Annie you are here, so she can make you breakfast," Kate said, going to the door. Jack hurried after her.

"Wait!" he said, his voice a little desperate. "Will he be all right here alone?"

Kate's gray eyes brightened as she said, "But he is not alone. He has his father with him, does he not?"

After she had gone, Jack tiptoed back to stare down into the basket. The baby lay sleeping peacefully, his soft black hair ruffled. As Jack watched, a little hand came out of the blankets, to open and close for a moment. He wondered if he should put it back under the covers, but decided it was better not to disturb Master Johnny in any way. Still, he was not at all at ease until Kate returned. He didn't know anything of babies—indeed, he didn't want to know anything.

At breakfast, Jack heard all the details of the things that had happened in his absence. Kate seemed happier now, more at ease, as if she were relieved that the dreadful moment of discovering he was a father was over. Not that the news she told him was at all happy. Jack was especially sorry to hear about Granny Bessie's death. He had planned to do something for the lady if he could, to ensure she would be comfortable in her old age. And when Kate mentioned the many cases of smallpox, he was glad he had built his house out on the point, isolated from any near neighbors. He gave her the news of Matthew and his family then, told her why he had been delayed coming home.

"Not that it did any good," he said, shaking his head. "I do not see what Bermudians are to do, once war is finally announced. We must have a dependable supply of food, but who will trade with us? Pray the Americans retreat from their current position!"

He told her then of the shipload of foodstuffs the *Camille* carried, and how he had been distributing them. "I intend to sail to St. George Town tomorrow," he said. "What remains, after we take our own supplies, of course, will be given to the hungry there."

"Given?" Kate asked, looking confused. "But where's the profit in that, when we need the money?"

"It has to be done that way. George Bruere continues stubborn, and he refuses to allow any traffic with the colonies anymore. But even he cannot object to an outright gift."

Before Kate could comment, he went on, "I shall of course call on your mother and father. Do they need anything?"

"I don't think so. Matt sent a large shipment only a while ago," Kate said absentmindedly. Then she asked, "But what are we to do? If you cannot trade, how shall we live? And what will you do instead?"

Jack wiped his mouth on his napkin before he threw it down. "I have no idea. Of course, I will not transport arms anymore, and that decision has nothing to do with the governor's restrictions. It is simply because I am still an Englishman. I told Matt that while I do sympathize with the colonists, their battle is not mine. Not yet, at any rate. My only concern is making sure Bermudians do not starve. But perhaps I can find another shipwreck and dive for treasure. Manfred must be bored with nothing to do here but farm."

Kate frowned. "Yes, well, but he is not here. I sold him."

"You *what*?" he demanded, looking fierce. "But he was the best diver on the islands. Why did you do such a harebrained thing?"

"Keza warned me he might try to start a rebellion, and indeed, Jack, he was almost insolent to me. So when Bartholomew Findley came and asked to buy him, I was delighted to let him go. I never thought you would want to dive again."

Jack heard the distress in her voice, and he made himself ask more mildly, "Who is this Findley person?"

He wondered why Kate wrinkled her nose in distaste . . . and noted how stiff her voice became as she explained the stranger who had come to Tucker's Town and who showed no signs of wanting to go home.

"Findley, Findley," Jack mused. "Is he by any chance related to the Marquess of Carden?"

As Kate nodded, he said, "I believe I have heard of the man. But somehow I gather he has not met with your approval, madam wife."

Kate sniffed. "Indeed he has not, sir. Mr. Findley is a disgusting man." She looked up to see Jack's questioning look, and she said hotly, "And don't ask me to tell you why I think so, for I shall not, sir!"

Jack rose from the table. "I'm off for Tucker's Town myself now. I want to see George, and there are the supplies to be unloaded here before I can sail the *Camille* to St. George Town tomorrow."

Kate nodded, but after Jack left, she sat there wishing she was as free as she used to be, able to pick up and go with him wherever he went. But of course, now there was the baby to see to and nurse. She could not restrain a little sigh at her loss of freedom.

Jack saw Keza as he left the house and crossed the yard. She was throwing feed to her chickens, and she beckoned him closer.

"I must thank you with all my heart for what you did for Kate when she was in childbirth, Keza," he said, taking her hand in his and squeezing it. To his surprise, the old black woman's concerned expression did not lighten.

"Cap'n, kin Ah speak plain, suh?" she asked.

At his nod, she went on, "Miz Kate, she almost die den. Ah was some feared for her, de birthin' wuz so hard. Two long days, suh. An' she done bleed so! She some brave lady, Miz Kate! But she weak still. Y'all got to leave her alone now for 'while, Cap'n, hear me?"

Jack nodded again, stunned by what she was saying.

"Miz Kate, she love y'all so much, she prob'ly take you in her bed agin 'fore she should. So y'all got to be de one to say no."

Jack assured her he would, anxious to escape now. But as he walked back to Tucker's Town, he thought about what he had heard. To think Kate had almost died, and he hadn't even known of it! If he had lost her . . . But still, he could not help contrasting this homecoming with the one he had planned, beginning with an exciting romp in bed. He could see this new baby would be responsible for a great many changes in their lives, and thinking about the scope of them did not endear little John Gregory Reade to his father.

When the *Camille* arrived the next morning in St. George Town, Jack found a huge crowd assembled on the Customs House dock. At first he thought they had come down to see a ducking, but it was soon obvious, from their cheers, that they had heard of the food he carried. Jack set the crew to distributing it as soon as the *Camille* was tied up alongside, and he left Chris Abbott to oversee the process. He himself went ashore to talk to the officials, reassure them that he had brought a needed gift and had no cargo to declare. Then he made his way across the square to the State House. He noticed Wilcox Hinson was in the stocks again, and he shook his head. No matter how scarce food might be, the man always seemed to be able to find a supply of rum.

It was apparent that the governor was furious, for his greeting to Jack bordered on rudeness, and his color was very high. Although he could say nothing if the man wanted to give a valuable cargo away, he still could not like it. Reade had been to the colonies and had acquired his cargo there, in direct opposition to his own express orders, and so he told the man in his coldest manner.

"I knew nothing of such orders, Your Excellency," Jack told him, willing himself to speak calmly, although what he really wanted to do was to tell this pompous idiot exactly what he thought of him. "How could I? I have been at sea for seven months. Tell me, sir, how are Bermudians to live if they cannot trade with the colonies? You know we have no farms here, no way to survive without that trade. And I hardly think England will come to our rescue. She has more important things on her mind right now."

Bruere waved a careless hand. "I have no idea," he said. "But my orders will be obeyed, sir! There is to be no more intercourse with rebels, and the man who defies that order will be hanged!"

Jack took his leave shortly thereafter. It was all he could do to be civil, for he considered the governor a damned fool, only concerned lest his own authority be weakened, no matter how many people died. The man was an abomination!

Taking deep breaths to calm himself, he strolled along Water Street, stopping often to greet people he knew. As he climbed the steps of the Hathaway house, he wondered how soon he could decently take his leave. He was anxious to get back to Tucker's Town, and he had never cared that much for either his father or his mother-in-law.

To his surprise, when he entered the parlor, a quivering Olivia Hathaway, dressed all in black, rose to her feet and pointed an accusatory finger at him.

"You *dare*?" she cried. "You dare to come here, you *murderer*?"

"Ma'am, what can you mean?" Jack asked, bewildered. Was she thinking of Kate's narrow escape? But no, that could not be, for Kate was safe, the baby too.

"You know what I mean," she panted, looking more than a little deranged in her fury. "*You* are the cause of my son's death! My beloved Gregory is taken from me forever, all because of *you*. For if he had not been carrying that dangerous cargo, his ship would not have been lost!"

"Mrs. Hathaway, you cannot be well," Jack said. "Please, sit down and let me pour you some wine."

"No, I will take nothing from your hand, *murderer*!" she screamed. Jack retreated a little.

"But I was not the cause of Greg's death, although I regret it most sincerely," he protested. "He was lost in a storm at sea. Everyone knows that. It could have happened to anyone."

"No, he wasn't! His sloop was attacked by an English ship because of the guns and powder it carried," she went on quickly, her eyes shining with demented hatred. "I know this for a fact. The Lord told me about it in a dream."

Jack was relieved when Roger Hathaway entered the room then and hurried to his wife's side.

"Olivia, my dear, you must calm yourself," he said as he led her to a chair. She was weeping now, and tearing her handkerchief in her distress. Jack stood quietly, wondering what he should do.

Then Roger Hathaway turned toward him. There was no smile for his son-in-law on his ravaged face, no hint that he intended to ask Jack's pardon for his wife's outburst, her insane accusations.

"We will never know if Olivia is right or wrong," he said crisply, almost biting off his words. "Greg was probably lost in the storm, but then, there is always the possibility that he was bested in a desperate fight. However, now that I have learned what cargoes you yourself have carried, sir, I cannot in good conscience receive you in my house any longer. You, sir, are a traitor. If there were any justice, you would be hanged for it. And to think I gave my Kate to such a man! I must ask you to leave this house at once, and never return to it."

Shocked, Jack just stood there for a moment, and then he bowed. "Very well, sir, it shall be as you say," he said stiffly. He was so bitter about his reception by Kate's parents that he wanted to rage at them. Only an iron self-control allowed him to restrain himself. "I am sorry you feel this way. It will hurt Kate a great deal."

"Kate knows how I feel," Roger Hathaway said. "When I taxed her with it, she chose to stand beside her husband. But while she will always be welcome here, you, sir, will not."

Abruptly Jack turned on his heel and quit the house. As he strode back along Water Street, he tried to remind himself that he had done nothing wrong, that he had as high standards as Roger Hathaway or any other loyal Englishman.

Can anything else go wrong? he asked himself savagely. First he had come home to discover he was a most unwilling father, and then, besides losing a crew of men who had been his friends, he had lost not one, but two ships. And with those ships, most of his money and the chance to make more. And with the governor's restrictions, his one source of revenue had been taken away from him. He would not be permitted to trade anymore, except with other British possessions in the Caribbean. He certainly had no intention of transporting slaves from Africa, as certain American captains did.

But what else could he do? The coming war might last for years, and even though he had enough money to get through it in comfort, he could not spend the time doing nothing. Not he!

How the mighty have fallen! he scoffed at himself. For Sir John Reade, that privileged and fortunate young man so admired by society, so sought-after and adored, had now become what? A beached sea captain. A man who had even been accused of being a traitor and a murderer. All his hard work for a new life here had come to nothing. And there was nothing he could do to reverse this new destiny of his, no way he could go back and recapture the dream. He couldn't even go home to Hythe, not now, not with that baby son, the next baronet of Hythe, to have to acknowledge. Whether he liked it or not, he was tied to Bermuda now, and war was coming. Not his war, but one that would affect him and his family as surely as it affected those in the colonies. And he had no way to make his fortune now, unless he did it illegally, putting his own principles aside.

He did not think he could do that. Something of pride was left to him. Perhaps it was the only thing, he mused.

He had reached King's Square now, and he pushed his way unseeing through the crowds of people, all thanking him and smiling at him. At least they would not starve for a while yet, he told himself as he swung on board the *Camille*. But as soon as the last bag of flour was unloaded from the hold, he would leave St. George Town and sail the sloop back to Tucker's Town. What else could he do?

From then on, Jack was very preoccupied. Kate watched him nervously. He had not told her in depth of the meeting he had had with her parents, so she did not know her mother had accused him of murder, but from what he did relate, so stern-faced and white-lipped, she was sure he had not had a pleasant visit. It was then she remembered her father's views about Jack's cargoes. Had he taxed him with them? Had they quarreled?

At least Jack seemed easier with Johnny now, she told herself as she watched him with the baby one evening two weeks later. Jack was waving a silver spoon and smiling a little as the baby's blue eyes followed it. And then Kate saw Johnny yawn, and she went to take him from Jack's arms to put him in his basket.

"Well, he's put me in my place, hasn't he?" Jack asked when she returned to the main room. "To yawn in his father's face! He has no manners at all!"

Kate chuckled as she reached for her sewing box. "No, and he is very self-centered beside. I'm sure he will improve as he gets older, though."

Jack nodded as he opened his ledgers, looking preoccupied now. Kate couldn't help sighing a little as she threaded her needle. But as she smoothed the fabric, she remembered a most important conversation she had had with Keza earlier, and she smiled to herself.

Jack was not seeing the columns of numbers on the page before him. Instead he was remembering how protective he had felt this morning when he had helped Kate bathe Johnny. He had been surprised at the warmth, the tenderness, he had experienced when she handed him the dripping baby to wrap in a towel. Johnny was so little still, and yet a perfect specimen of a man, right down to the tiny penis he sported. Jack had learned to keep that covered, after Master Johnny had sprayed him in the eye once.

Poor little man! Deprived even before birth of his rightful place, because his father was a bastard. Silently Jack vowed he would make it up to him somehow—someday. All this was not Johnny's fault. He would see that the boy did not have to pay for it, as his father had had to do.

When Kate put her sewing away and rose, Jack was so lost in his musing, he barely heard her. He had been going to bed later and later these nights. It was not that he was worried he might forget himself, and try to make love to her. No, never that, after what Keza had told him! He still kissed Kate and hugged her on occasion, but after learning how she had almost died, he had made a promise to himself that he would not be intimate with her again. It was just that it was so much easier to keep his promise if she was already sleeping when he sought their bed.

And after all, he rationalized, she had the baby she had wanted so badly, and he kept her very busy. Sometimes Jack was ashamed when he felt pangs of jealousy that he had been usurped by such a tiny mite. But babies, he was discovering, were demanding little things. And he had seen for himself, when he first came home, how tired Kate was every evening, how she often napped during the day as she regained her strength. No, his beloved Kate would never have to suffer the agony of childbirth again, and if that meant he must live like a monk, he would.

It was late when he finally entered their room to undress quietly and slide into bed. A little cynically he wondered how long he would have to sleep uninterrupted before Master Johnny woke up, wailing loudly of his hunger.

Jack settled down on his side away from Kate, and he was startled when she touched him. She had not been asleep after all, he realized as her hands caressed his back in that well-remembered way.

"Jack?" she whispered. "Where have you been this age? I thought I must fall asleep before you finally came to bed."

He forced himself to roll toward her and take her in his arms. His kiss was gentle and brief, and he tried to ignore how eagerly she returned it, how she felt, pressed so close to him. Then he realized she was not wearing her bedgown, and he stiffened. "Go to sleep, Kate," he said. "It is late, and you need your rest."

"No, not tonight," she said, cuddling closer still. "Jack, I spoke to Keza today. She said there wasn't any more need for this celibacy we practice. And indeed, I have been feeling well for a week now. Well, and strong."

Her breath stirred the hair on his chest, and her hands wandered from his arms to his waist, his lean hips. Suddenly he pulled away from her.

"What is it?" she asked. "Please, my darling, hold me . . . love me! It has been so very long, and I . . . I want you so!"

There was silence for a long moment after her whisper died away, and she waited breathlessly for him to crush her in his arms, so she might know again the euphoria she had been without for so long.

But Jack made no move toward her. Instead, he rose, and stopping only to pick up his breeches, left the room, closing the door quietly behind him.

Kate sank back on her pillows, her eyes wide as she stared at the tester so far above her head. But what was the matter? Didn't Jack want her anymore? she wondered. Was it because she had had a baby, changed in some way? She knew her figure was different now, with riper curves, but she had thought Jack might enjoy that. She had always been so slender!

But perhaps this had nothing to do with her figure. Perhaps he was still angry at her for conceiving. He had told her why he did not want a child. But she knew he was beginning to care for Johnny, for she had seen how his face softened whenever he looked at him. And she knew he still cared for her, for he was so kind to her, so good. Didn't he?

Kate rolled over and blinked her tears away as another, most unwelcome thought occurred to her. Perhaps this was God's way of punishing her. Perhaps this was the way he intended her to pay for her sin, by taking away the man she had loved so much she had even been glad her beloved brother had drowned instead of him. She stifled a sob then behind her fist. She could not bear it, she could not!

The next morning at the breakfast table, Kate watched Jack as unobtrusively as she could. He looked tired, as if he had not slept well, and he wore that little frown between his brows that she was afraid was becoming a permanent feature of his handsome face.

But he spoke to her easily, and courteously, asking

about the baby and whether he had allowed his mama her rest last night.

Only Annie's beaming presence as she served them permitted Kate to return an even answer.

After breakfast, Jack announced he intended to borrow George's sloop to try to find another treasure reef to dive on. He told her he was taking Tatum with him, that Keza was making them up a packet of food, so she was not to wait dinner for him. Kate nodded, her eyes troubled. And when he bent to kiss her good-bye, his lips merely brushed hers before he was gone.

In the following days, he was often absent from the house, either sailing or busy at the yard. He had drawn up plans for a small sloop to replace the *Sprite*. Everyone on the islands had some kind of small boat, for it was the only quick way to get from place to place. And few people kept a horse, for there were no roads, only paths between the small settlements. Without the *Sprite*, they had been isolated here.

Jack had returned to their bed again, but Kate had never tried to approach him since the night he had left her so abruptly. She knew he was tired from all his work, from his lonely, vigorous swims, the hours spent pacing the beach. But more important, she knew she could not bear another rejection.

Sometimes she would look out the window at dusk and see him there walking on the sands or just sitting staring out to sea, so immobile she knew he was deep in thought. And when he did come back to the house, he had little to say that was not commonplace. Often he spent the evening holding a book Kate knew he was not reading. She wished she could ask what was troubling him, ask him outright why he didn't want her anymore, but she did not dare.

But still, for all her forbearance, she felt as if she were tiptoeing on fragile glass these days, frightened that the glass would break and plunge her into heaven knew what kind of maelstrom.

One morning, Jack left the house early, for he wanted to be at the shipyard when the workmen began planking the new sloop. When he arrived, he saw that no one was working on her as yet, although the cedar planking lay in neat piles nearby.

He rolled up his sleeves and settled his broad-brimmed palmetto hat more securely in the fresh breeze before he set to work himself. The warm sun beat down on his shoulders, and he could hear the little waves of the cove as they lapped the shore, the familiar noises from the houses clustered around the harbor. The sweet scent of flowers filled his nostrils, and for now at least, he was at peace.

Intent on what he was doing, Jack did not notice the approach of a stranger. Bartholomew Findley watched him idly for a moment, then said, "Sir John Reade? But how very singular, sir, to see you here—and engaged in such a strange occupation, too."

Jack looked up, a frown on his face for the use of his title. Then he rose to his feet to study the man who was so carefully inspecting him. He saw he was a short, wiry man with dark-red hair, dressed much too formally for a hot Bermuda morning. His long-tailed coat sported silver buttons, and he wore a brocade waistcoat over his lace-trimmed linen shirt. His pale breeches fit like a second skin, and his square-toed black shoes had large silver buckles.

Jack forgot the foppish attire as he observed the stranger's smooth, expressionless face, those curiously blank blue eyes.

" 'Tis plain Jack Reade here, sir," he said. "But you seem to have the advantage of me. You are . . . ?"

The gentleman swept him a low, mocking bow. "Mr. Bartholomew Findley, sir. Surely in this isolated place you must have heard of me. Or can it be your sweet wife has never mentioned me?"

"Yes, I have heard of you," Jack told him evenly, determined to ignore the snide reference to Kate.

"I have been longing to speak to you," Findley went on. "I am so intrigued with your mystery. For why, Sir John, does a nobleman live here on these far-distant islands, when he could be at home seeing to his estates, enjoying London and the Season? And why does that same nobleman sail a ship, work in a common boatyard? You must satisfy my curiosity, indeed you must, sir. I shall not rest until I have learned your reasons."

"But there is no mystery about it," Jack said as easily

as he could. "I am here because I like Bermuda, like sailing and boatyards."

"Indeed? Well, of course Bermuda is also our sweet Kate's home, is it not?"

"Why are *you* here, sir?" Jack asked, taking the offensive. There was something about the man he could not like; something that put him on his guard.

"Why, I, myself, am on a repairing lease," Findley admitted. "The dibs, my dear Sir John, have not been in tune for me. By the way, did you know I bought your slave Manfred? A fine diver, although a most sullen, difficult animal. I never turn my back on him, and I have taken to carrying a pistol."

"Have you found any treasure?" Jack asked idly as he knelt to measure another plank.

"Not as yet. We did look at the reef you discovered last year, but Manfred says the wreck is too deep to explore without a diving bell. You wouldn't care to sell . . . ? Ah, no, I understand. But surely there are other reefs in shallower water. I do not despair.

"When are you planning to return to England, Sir John?" he asked next.

Jack looked up to stare at him. "I cannot imagine why that information would interest you," he said coldly.

Findley waved a careless hand. "Merely making conversation, y'know. Or could it be that you left home under a cloud? That you *cannot* return, hmm?"

Jack straightened up and put both hands on his hips. "I find your questions and suppositions impertinent, sir," he said. "We are strangers. And since we are such, I do not choose to discuss my personal affairs."

"Then perhaps you might tell me when you plan to go on another voyage," Findley persisted. "I found it so pleasant spending . . . mm, time with your wife while you were away. That private cove of yours—such a secluded spot, is it not? And she is such a lively, lovely lady too."

Jack strode toward him so fast, Findley had no chance to escape before he was grasped by the neck of his shirt and dangled off the ground in one big hand. " 'Swounds! No one insults my wife, sir!" Jack said through gritted teeth, his turquoise eyes blazing fire. For one mad moment he wanted to kill him, and he tightened his grip.

"But I meant no insult," Findley gasped. "Assure you, have the greatest of admiration for the lady and her charms!"

"You will never speak of her again, do you hear me?" Jack said, shaking him now much as a terrier shakes a rat he has caught. Frantically, Findley clawed at his hand, his face turning purple as he did so.

"Here, Jack, what's to do?" George Hathaway called as he ran toward the pair. He was closely followed by some of the workmen. "Here, I say, put him down! Ecod, man, you're throttling him!"

Jack lowered his captive to the ground. As soon as he was free, Findley said in a voice that sounded more than half-strangled, "Name your seconds, sir! 'Tis to insult me, 'pon my honor!"

To everyone's surprise, Jack only stared at him in disgust. "My seconds?" he asked. "You want satisfaction? But I wouldn't bother to load my pistol for the likes of you."

He turned his back then, and Findley, his face a dark red now, asked, "Are you a coward, Sir John? A coward as well as a most questionable nobleman? One, moreover, who cannot even keep his wife from other men?"

Jack spun around to face him, and with one quick hard fist to the jaw, he knocked him sprawling. As soon as he saw Findley was still conscious, he said, "I am neither a coward nor at all questionable. Your remarks about my wife are a lie. I know Kate. Now, I advise you to make yourself scarce. You were very close to death a moment ago. You still are. But I won't soil my hands on you further unless I am forced to it. Besides, I make it a practice never to exchange fisticuffs with *little* men. It would be so one-sided."

As the workmen chuckled and nudged each other, Findley rose unsteadily to his feet. He was as white now as he had been red a moment ago, and a trickle of blood dripped from his mouth and stained his cravat. He spat out a tooth, and suddenly he reached into his coat pocket for his pistol.

As George called a warning and the workmen fell back, Jack moved quickly to grasp Findley's arm. The pistol fell harmlessly to the sand.

Jack released his captive then, and stooped to pick it

up. He emptied it of powder and shot and handed it back to the furious Mr. Findley. "Here," he said. "You'll probably need this, as frightened as you are of your slaves."

Findley's pale blue eyes never left Jack's face as he took it. Then he said slowly, "I'll not forget this, Reade. Someday you'll pay dearly for the insults you have given me."

Jack walked away from him without another word, to speak to George. The workmen wandered off, disappointed there was to be no bout to enliven their day.

Findley stood quietly for a moment, staring at Jack, and then he straightened his disheveled clothes and started back toward his house. As George watched him go, his gray eyes were somber.

"If I were you, I'd be careful from now on, Jack," he said quietly. "The man's a shark, and like a shark, he's apt to strike when you are least expecting it."

As he saw his brother-in-law shrug, he added, "Mark my words! You've made an enemy today, and a bad one. Be on your guard!"

20

BY the time Jack came home for dinner, Kate had learned all about his fight with Bartholomew Findley. Granted, she had heard such a strange version of it, much embellished by Tatum's imagination, that when Jack walked into the house without a scratch on him, she ran to him in relief.

"I am so glad you were not hurt after all!" she said, reaching up to hug him and kiss his cheek.

"What nonsense is this, Kate?" he asked as he put her away from him. "I gather you have heard about my introduction to your disgusting Mr. Findley. I knocked him down and that was the end of it.

"Ah, Keza, what is that delicious aroma I smell?" he asked the old black woman as she carried a steaming trencher into the room and set it on the table. "Come, Kate, sit down! I'm famished!"

Kate had to wait until Keza and Annie left the room before she could continue to question her husband.

"But why did you knock him down, Jack?" she asked a little warily.

"He insulted you," Jack said.

Kate was relieved that he spoke in a normal tone of voice. "How did he do that?" she persisted.

When Jack raised his brows at her, she lost her temper. "Dammit, Jack! Getting information from you is harder than pulling hen's teeth! Tell me!"

He grinned then. "He implied, madam, that the two of you had several trysts at the cove while I was away."

"He dared to say that?" Kate demanded, her face white now.

"That's when I lifted him off the ground by his fancy neckcloth and shook him. One-handed, too," Jack added, sounding not a little proud of his strength.

Kate refused to compliment him. "What happened then?" she asked.

"When I put him down, he challenged me to a duel. I refused, and he called me a coward, a nobleman with a questionable past, and a man whose wife gave her favors to other men."

As Kate gasped, he went on, "That's when I hit him and sent him sprawling."

He asked Kate to pass him the bread then, and as she did so, she said, "He lied about everything!"

"Oh, I know that. I have to wonder, though, why he did it. Would you have any idea, wife?"

Kate looked down at her clasped hands, a little frown on her face. "He was already living here when I returned from our voyage to Statia, and he . . . he began to bother me. I told him to leave me alone, but he would not. And the day before the hurricane, while I was swimming there early, he came to the cove."

Jack looked up, his dinner forgotten. "What happened?" he asked.

"I had left all my clothes on the beach, as we always did, but I remembered the old blanket we kept on the Sprite. I fished it out of the cuddy with the sounding pole and towed it with me to shore. Then I wrapped it around me before I came out. I told him if he touched me, I would have him before the authorities. He went away, but he did not give up."

She looked up then, her gray eyes steady on his. "Not even when he learned about Johnny. But he left me alone finally, after he bought two young girls for his . . . his amusement. He is an animal! I am glad you hit him. I hope it hurt."

Jack raised his glass of punch to her. "It did, madam, but not, I think, as much as your refusal of him did. Pompous little man! We'll have to have a care to avoid him in future. And perhaps I should teach you how to use my pistol before I sail again."

"You are planning a voyage?" Kate asked as she served him some fruit, all thoughts of Bartholomew Findley gone from her mind.

Jack shrugged. "I don't know. I set George to careening the *Camille* this afternoon, so her keel can be scrubbed. If I can think of a profitable legal cargo, I might be tempted to go."

Kate would have questioned him further, but a knock at the door interrupted them. When she saw Colonel Henry Tucker on the doorstep, she bade him enter. The elderly colonel was a favorite of hers, for he had always had a smile for her, and when she had been a child, he had entertained her many times with his tales of old Bermuda.

The colonel assured them he had eaten dinner, and begged a few minutes of Jack's time. Kate rose and excused herself. She heard the door shut behind the two shortly thereafter, and knew they had quit the house. Idly, as she sorted Johnny's clean gowns and diapers, she wondered what it was all about.

As Jack led the way back to the little cove where the colonel had left his sloop, he said, "You are very stealthy, sir! But no doubt you have good reason for it."

Tucker motioned to some rocks nearby, and the two sat down. "Yes, there is a very good reason," he said. "No one must know I am here. That's why I sailed to the cove instead of going to Tucker's Town. And what I have to tell you must be kept secret, even if you do not agree to help. Is that understood, Captain?"

Jack nodded, somewhat mystified.

"You know the colonists are adamant about not trading food for salt," Tucker went on. "But they are not at all averse to a trade of food for ammunition."

"I remember," Jack said.

"We have a goodly supply of gunpowder in the colony magazine at St. George Town at this moment. One hundred barrels of it. I have recently had a visitor from the colonies, a Mr. Harris. He was sent as an emissary from General Washington. Together we made plans to confiscate that powder, send it to the colonies. In return, they will begin trading with us again and assure us a continuous supply of food."

"Confiscate it?" Jack asked, frowning now.

"Of course we must steal it," Tucker admitted. "But it is not heavily guarded, and if we take it at night, we should be safe from detection. Two American ships will be arriving soon. I expect them within the week. All we have to do is break into the magazine, then roll the barrels of powder to the shore and transport them in whaleboats to the waiting vessels. They can be well offshore by dawn. I have several dependable men already committed to the venture. I would like to have you join us as well. The more men involved, the quicker we can be. It will be safer that way.

"If I can convince you to join us, I want to ask you to take command," he said next, his lined face and faded blue eyes intent in his urgency. "I'm too old to do so."

"Surely not, sir!" Jack protested, but the colonel only waved a dismissive hand.

"As painful as it is for me to admit it, in this case I must," the colonel said. "No, you're the man for the job. You're in the habit of command, and I've noticed how men follow your orders without question. It's a unique talent you have, my boy. A quiet word from you accomplishes as much as another man's harsh blustering."

Jack nodded his thanks, thinking hard now. "We could all be hanged for it," he pointed out.

Tucker nodded grimly. "There is that risk. Governor Bruere will do his utmost to discover the culprits. But none of us will talk, and there will be no proof of our involvement."

"It is an interesting solution, but still it is the act of traitors, no matter how well-intentioned," Jack said.

Tucker put his hand on the younger man's arm. "I know. That pains us all, for none of us are rebels. But if we do not have the colonies' assistance, many people here will starve. I expect this revolution to last a very long time. Bermudians cannot survive even a year without outside help. And since that is the case, we have no choice. In this one instance, we must forget we are loyal Englishmen and put the good of the many before our own standards and beliefs. But what say you, Captain? Are you with us?"

Jack hesitated. The colonel wondered what he was thinking. His expressionless face and hooded eyes gave no hint of which way he would decide to go.

"Do you think the colonies have any chance of success in this revolution, sir?" Jack asked then, considerably surprising Tucker.

Not waiting for an answer, he went on, "It appears to me they face immense difficulties. They are so small, so unorganized, so far-flung. And many people there are loyal still. Besides, they have no navy, no army to speak of, yet they are prepared to take on the might of England with its vast fleets and disciplined military. How can they prevail against such crushing odds? It is like David facing Goliath without his slingshot."

"Of course you are right. But they are still determined to cut all ties with the mother country. It is too bad, but in a way, England herself drove them to it. I would wish Bermuda could remain aloof from all of it, but we cannot."

"As an Englishman, I wish I might remain aloof as well," Jack said.

Tucker rose slowly to pat his shoulder. "I understand, sir. It is a serious step, and no one will think the worse of you for refusing—"

"I do not refuse," Jack interrupted. "You misunderstand me. I was about to go on and say that I would be with you. The circumstances make it impossible for me to remain at arm's length."

The colonel clapped him on the shoulder now and beamed. "Good man!" he said. "Come, let me tell you what I have planned. As commander, you might well want to make some changes. I'm glad you're with us. The other men will be glad as well."

For almost half an hour the two sat, their heads close

together, discussing the procedure to be followed. Jack did indeed have some suggestions, suggestions the colonel was quick to agree to.

Jack did not go back to the house after Tucker sailed away, nor did he return to the shipyard. Instead, he went to the beach and walked down it until he was out of sight of the house. With all his heart, he wished it had not come to this. Roger Hathaway could call him—all of them—traitors now, and speak the truth. But then he recalled Governor Bruere's petulant face, his proud ranting against any trade with the colonies, and his lips tightened. It must be done. There was no other way. In this one isolated instance, patriotism must be put aside in favor of expediency.

Jack stared out to sea, his eyes narrowed. He felt as if he were being drawn ever closer to a final decision, the one that would force him to make a clean choice for either England or the colonies. True, he could stay here in Bermuda and make no choice at all. He sensed, as Colonel Tucker did, that most Bermudians were loyal to the crown and had no wish to join their continental brothers in breaking with it. All of the men who were to be involved in removing the gunpowder from the magazine were loyal, committed to this deed only because they were forced to it for the common good. And when it had been accomplished, they would revert to their former loyalty. None of them intended further acts of treason.

Jack stretched out on the sand then and lay back, his hands behind his head. He closed his eyes and went over the plans he and the colonel had made. They sounded foolproof, but he knew there was always a chance that something could go wrong. He remained on the beach for a long time, probing, testing, making his strategies.

Four days later, on the evening of August 14, Jack dismissed the servants early, saying they would not be needed again till morning. Kate wondered at it, but she did not question him.

It was just dusk when he laid his book aside and rose. He had been very quiet throughout supper, lost in some deep thoughts of his own. From his set expression, Kate could tell they were serious, and she kept her own counsel, even though she knew the day was coming when she would be forced to talk to Jack and bring things out in the open between them. He still had not made love to her, and although she missed the fulfillment his lovemaking brought, she found she missed the closeness that resulted from it even more. Now, instead of standing together, there were only the two of them, standing apart. They were polite and considerate—even affectionate —companions, but they were not lovers anymore. Kate knew it could not go on.

Jack went into the bedroom for a moment. Kate could hear him rummaging through his chest of clothes. When he came back, he was wearing a dark jacket, even though the August night was sultry.

"I must go out," he told her, his turquoise eyes steady on her face. "Do not wait up for me. I do not know how long I will be, and it might be very late. And if by some chance anyone should come looking for me, tell them I have gone to visit a friend at Crow Harbor."

"And are you going there?" Kate asked over the sudden quick beating of her heart.

"I cannot tell you where I am going," he said. "It will be better if you do not know. I must ask you to trust me, Kate."

She nodded as she came to put her arms around him. As she held him close, she felt the weight of the pistol under his jacket, and her eyes widened. "Be very careful," she whispered, lifting her face for his kiss.

"I shall be," he said. "Don't fret."

His kiss was warmer than it had been for a long time, and Kate reveled in it, but it was over much too soon.

She watched him go to the door and hesitate before he turned back to her. "I love you, Kate," he said. "Know I have always loved you."

Her usually brilliant smile was tremulous, and in a moment he was gone.

Jack made his way quietly down the path to the cove. The dory was waiting where he had left it, and after he had climbed in and pushed off, he settled down on the center thwart and fitted the oars in their tholes. It was a long way to the point on St. David's Island, across the harbor.

As he rowed with the steady rhythm he had learned as a boy, he thought about the night ahead. Pray all went well! Late this afternoon, he had seen the signal he had been waiting for across the habor—a driftwood fire on the beach at St. David's. He glanced over his shoulder now to check his direction. He did not want to pass anywhere near the fort on Castle Island.

After he reached the little beach he had chosen earlier, he pulled the dory well up on the sand and pushed through the brush surrounding it. It was full dark now, and he had to stop to light the lantern he had brought with him in the dory. It was shuttered, and gave little light, and he did not think it could be seen. Besides, this part of St. David's was uninhabited. When he reached the opposite shore after many long minutes of walking, he found a whaleboat waiting for him. There were five men in it, and he whistled a soft signal before he joined them.

As he climbed into the boat, he extinguished his lantern. He would need it later. He knew all the men. Both the Abbott brothers were there, as were Aaron Benson and his son Matt; even Rodney Cox was there, one of the governor's circle of friends, bending to his oar with a will.

Much later, Jack saw other whaleboats converging on the same destination, six in all. No one spoke as they came ashore in Tobacco Bay on St. George. Jack motioned the men onward. Following him, they crept up the short, steep hill to where the powder magazine was located on the crest. Colonel Tucker was waiting for them, and as he had promised, there were no guards.

Quietly, Jack set lookouts, and in the dim uncertain light of the one shuttered lantern he held, he could see that young Edward Abbott looked disgusted to be chosen. No doubt he longed to be here where the action was, Jack thought as he turned to survey the magazine.

The stout door proved impossible to breach, not without a battering ram and a great deal of noise they could ill afford. The governor's mansion was nearby. Jack grasped the colonel's arm and pointed to the roof. Tucker nodded. It was made of slate, and much more penetrable than the solid door and limestone walls. Jack and Matt Benson braced themselves against the wall while the thin, wiry Christopher Abbott climbed to their shoulders and scrambled onto the roof. They could hear him breaking

the slates, but it seemed a strident age before he had
made a hole big enough so he could drop inside.

The door was opened quickly then, and the systematic
removal of the barrels stored there began. Everyone
knew his job. Jack had stationed men along the steep
path to the shore to steady the barrels as they were rolled
down.

So far, so good, Jack thought as he positioned another
keg and sent it on its way. Then he heard someone
crashing through the brush beyond them, and he stiffened, reaching inside his coat for his loaded pistol.

"Captain, Captain!" young Edward Abbott whispered
hoarsely. "There's trouble!"

The men stopped what they were doing to gather around
the sentry.

"What is it, Edward?" Jack asked. "Speak up!"

"There was someone coming this way," young Abbott
panted. "I . . . I had to kill him! He would have discovered us, sir!"

Aaron Benson drew in a startled breath, audible to all.

"Who was it, lad?" Jack asked, his voice calm. He
remembered how important it was in a crisis to appear
easy, in control of the situation.

"I don't know," Abbott confessed, sounding distraught.
Jack noticed that Colonel Tucker had put his arm around
the boy's shoulders to steady him.

Abbott took a deep breath before he added, "It was
some French officer—one of those on parole here. God
forgive me! I had to stab him!"

"We'll have to bury him, and quickly, too," Jack said.
"Where did you leave him?"

"He's . . . he's in the governor's garden," Abbott managed to get out. "Lying next to the wall, out of sight. I
. . . I dragged him there."

"All right. Chris, you and Edward live closest. Go
home and get shovels. You had better bury him where he
is. We cannot risk the time moving him. Bury him as
deep as you can, and cover the grave with leaves—try to
disguise the place. Then go home. Your part in this is
over. Hurry, now! The rest of you men, back to work!"

Chris nodded, his face as grim as his brother's, and the
two melted into the blackness.

Jack waved the other men to their tasks as he went

back into the magazine for another barrel. It was a shame a man had had to die merely because he had been in the wrong place at the wrong time. Jack hoped it was not a bad omen for the success of their mission, but he had no time to think of that now.

At last the magazine was empty. It had taken longer than Jack had thought it would, and everyone scrambled back down to the beach to load the barrels on the waiting boats. Jack was covered with perspiration; he was hot and dirty, his mouth completely dry, but still he worked harder than the next three men. There was an underlying sense of urgency in what they did now. Jack suspected the death of that French officer had made the men uneasy, anxious to be gone from the scene, and apprehensive lest they be discovered.

As the boats headed out of the bay at last, the breeze of their passage was welcome. Although still as quiet as they could be, it was possible to discern a lightening in the atmosphere. They had come this far without detection, and the most dangerous part was over. As he bent to his oar, Jack was glad it was a calm night. The boats were so heavy-laden, there was little freeboard.

The *Lady Catherine* of Virginia and the *Charles Town and Savannah Pacquet* of South Carolina were waiting for them just outside the North Rock. With so many sailors to help, the barrels were quickly transferred to the American sloops and stowed in their holds.

Jack's whaleboat was alongside the *Lady Catherine*. As her captain came to the rail and thanked them, he said, "Our thanks will come in the form of food delivered, sir. But make sail now, as fast as you can. The winds are light, and for safety, you must be far offshore by dawn."

The American captain waved and saluted them as the whaleboats pulled away. Jack was tired now, with an ache across his shoulders and down his arms he was sure the others were feeling as well. Old Aaron Benson looked worn and exhausted, but still he wore a satisfied expression now, for a job well done.

By Jack's orders, the men from St. George Town were dropped off first, and then Jack was rowed back to St. David's. As he left the boat and waded ashore, he wondered what time it was. There was no moon tonight; he had no idea how many hours of darkness were left.

By the light of the lantern, he made his way across the island to his own dory. Only a little farther to go, he told himself as he dragged it back to the water.

When he reached the cove below his house at last, the sky was just beginning to show a faint gray line on the horizon. He made the boat secure and climbed the path to the house. He could not remember ever being so tired.

Kate had not been able to sleep. Instead, she had paced the main room until Johnny woke and cried for her. She was absentminded as she changed him and nursed him. She did not know where Jack was, or what he was doing, but she knew he was in danger.

As she put the baby back in his basket to sleep again, she prayed for Jack's safety over and over again. Eventually, worn out, she had dozed for a while, but the slightest sound brought her awake again—the breeze rustling the branches outside the window, a sleepy bird's chirped complaint. And so she was at the door of the bedroom when Jack arrived.

He saw her close her eyes for a moment, the way her lips moved silently, and then she came to put her arms around him.

"Come!" she said. "You will want to wash."

She poured what water there was into the basin. "Take your clothes off," she ordered. "You are filthy! I'll get more water from the barrel. No one will see me. We'll have to hide those clothes until they can be washed later."

As she left the room with the pitcher, Jack began to obey her. He caught a glimpse of his face in the mirror, and was startled at how dirty he really was. He marveled that Kate had not asked him a single question, only hurried to do what had to be done.

She brought not only more water but also the remains of the fruit punch they had had for supper. Jack gulped it thirstily. Nothing had ever tasted so good.

As he climbed into bed and pulled the sheet over him, Jack saw Kate was still standing there, a little frown on her face. "Kate, my love," he murmured. "My bright penny. You are a wonder."

She smiled then. "Go to sleep, my dear," she told him. "Time enough to talk about all this later."

* * *

The news of the gunpowder's disappearance spread quickly all over the islands. Indeed, it was only early afternoon when the news reached Tucker's Town. George came over to the point to tell them about it.

"They say Governor Bruere is livid," he said, his gray eyes twinkling. The three of them were seated at the table, the remains of dinner before them.

"I can well imagine it," Jack remarked, careful not to look at Kate. He had slept until eight, and then insisted on rising as he normally would. He realized that everything he did today must be as usual.

"He's issued a proclamation," George went on. "I brought one for you to see."

He handed Jack the flimsy paper, and Kate rose to see it over his shoulder. "POWDER STEAL," the headline read. "Advt. Save your country from ruin, which may happen hereafter. The Powder stole out of the magazine late last night cannot be carried far as the wind is so light. A GREAT REWARD will be given to any person that can make a proper discovery before the magistrates."

"Has anyone come forward?" Jack asked as he returned the paper.

"Nary a soul!" George said cheerfully. "Furthermore, when Bruere asked some of the Bermudian sloops to go in pursuit of the thieves, try to recover the powder, he could not find a single captain willing to undertake the commission. I heard he intends to send word to General Gage in Boston, tell him what happened, and beg for troops to be quartered here again."

"I doubt he'll have any more luck than he did with his last petition," Jack said. "Gage has a better use for his troops in New England, now that war is coming."

"Still, I wonder who did it," George said next. "They say there were two American sloops tacking about outside the harbor late yesterday afternoon, but they must have had help from someone here. How would they know the location of the magazine else?"

"We'll probably never know," Kate said as she took her seat again.

"I've a mind to go to St. George Town myself, see what people are saying," George said as he rose. "Care to join me, Jack?"

"No, I don't think so," Jack said, rising to walk him to the door. "Kate and I intend to walk the beach this afternoon and swim. But do come and tell us anything you learn."

"Remember me to Mother and Father," Kate told her brother. "Tell them all is well here, and Johnny is thriving."

"You haven't been to see them for a long time, old girl," George remarked. "Why don't you come with me and bring Johnny? You could stay for a visit. I know how Mama must miss you. And come to think of it, she hasn't seen the baby for a long time, has she? Her first grandson, too!"

Kate's color was high now, and Jack was about to intervene when she said with a great deal of dignity, "I'm afraid that won't be possible, George. There is . . . there is a little trouble between us right now."

Her brother frowned for a moment, and then he hugged her. "Never mind, old lady," he told her. "Mama will come around, and it will all come right in the end."

After the sound of his footsteps died away, Kate turned to her husband. "Will it come right, Jack?" she asked.

He came to her then and put his hands on her shoulders. "I don't know," he said. "Your mother has it in her head that I was responsible for Greg's death, and your father . . . well, he has forbidden me the house. He called me a traitor. I cannot foresee any change in their feelings for me, although you know how they love you. Why don't you go with George, Kate? It might do you good, the change."

"No," she said. "That would not be right. You are my husband, and by insulting you, they insult me as well."

He dropped a kiss on the bridge of her nose. "Can we walk now? Or is Johnny about to wake and howl?"

Kate smiled over the ache in her heart for what he had told her. "He was fed only a while ago. I'll just tell Keza, so she can watch him," she said.

The two of them strolled down the beach, and as they did so, Jack told her about last night's raid and why it had been carried out. Kate's eyes were wide, and, he thought, more than a little troubled.

"You think what I did was wrong, don't you?" he asked her at last.

Kate nodded as she sank down on the sand. Jack hesitated, and then he joined her there. "Yes, I do," she said reluctantly. "That gunpowder has gone to England's enemies. It will be used to kill English soldiers."

"I know. You will never know what a hard decision it was for me to make," Jack said, his voice grim. "I kept seeing men from Kent, and wondering if any of them had joined up—men like my farmers' sons, the innkeeper's and the blacksmith's boys. Even some of my own friends—the younger sons of the nobility. But I had to do it. It was the lesser of two evils. We must have food here to survive. Could I stand by and watch children and old people starve? Have that on my conscience? 'Swounds, I could not! I would make the same decision again!"

Kate sensed his anguish and she reached out to take his hand, even though she sighed a little. "Of course you must do what you think is right," she told him. "I . . . I just wish it had never had to happen."

Jack yawned then, and covered his mouth. "Forgive me, Kate. I predict an early bedtime. I only hope I do not fall asleep over supper. It is important to act normally."

"But surely there is no danger, especially for you!" Kate said. "Why, who would ever suspect that anyone from Tucker's Town would make that long trip there and back at night? No, no! I'm sure they'll concentrate their search in St. George Town. There are enough men there who have voiced their disapproval of the governor's tactics, and they will be under suspicion. Oh, I pray none will be hanged for this!"

"No one will talk. We are all pledged to secrecy," Jack said. Then he remembered the French soldier. He wondered if his disappearance had been noted as yet, if anyone had connected it with the theft of the gunpowder. He had not told Kate about the man's death. He hoped he would not have to.

He turned to Kate then, and was startled to see how she was shivering. "What is it?" he asked, his voice urgent. "Are you ill?"

"Suddenly I feel so frightened!" she whispered, wringing her hands together.

Jack put his arms around her and pulled her close. "Sssh," he said. "There is nothing to be frightened about, indeed, there is not."

It was a moment before he felt Kate relax and sigh a little as she rested her head on his chest. His hands caressed her back, and he kissed the top of her head. How dear this slip of a girl is, he thought. How precious to me.

"Jack?" she asked, her hands stealing up around his neck. "Jack?"

He looked down into the face she had raised, and he saw the question in her gray eyes. At once his hands were still.

"What is wrong, my dear?" she asked then. "Why did you leave me that night? And why don't we ever make love anymore?"

He would have put her away from him then, but she held on tight. "No," she said. "*Dammit*, Jack, I have a right to know!"

Now it was his turn to sigh. "Yes, I suppose you do. It is because of what Keza told me about Johnny's birth, how hard it was, how you almost died. I made myself a promise that I would not touch you that way again. I could not bear it if you were taken from me."

Kate's face had cleared as he spoke, and her eyes began to shine with brilliant light. "Oh, Jack, if you knew what I have been thinking!" she said, shaking her head. "But although the birth was very bad, I didn't die, did I? And I have no intention of dying in the future, no matter how many babies we have."

"There will be no more babies," he commanded, his voice and eyes cold. "I cannot take that risk."

"But if I am ready to take it, why can't you?" she argued. "Besides, we can be as careful as we were before."

She reached up then and pulled his head down to hers. Her warm kiss turned passionate, and he found he had to return it. He had meant to say that being careful had not worked, and might not work again, but Kate, ah, Kate was too persuasive, too erotic and tempting now that she was in his arms again.

When he raised his head at last, her eyes were closed and a tentative smile played over her lips. He stared down at her, frowning now at the ache in his loins, as she whispered, "Why is it, sir, that I am always the one seducing you? It hardly seems fair, and I thought it was supposed to be the other way around!"

Jack had to smile a little at that as he buried his face in her chestnut curls. The sweet scent of her stirred his senses, and he closed his eyes for a moment before he said, his voice husky, "Shall I seduce you, Kate? Shall I?"

She chuckled then, her hands busy on the buttons of his shirt. "I do not think it will be necessary, my love," she whispered. "Jack, oh, Jack!"

Their lovemaking was a wild celebration of reunion at long last, fevered, impatient, demanding—on both sides. And after they had gone for a swim, Jack fell asleep. Kate sat beside him quietly for a long time, content to watch his handsome face, relaxed, at peace. And she smiled to herself as she did so. He loved her still. She felt nothing could hurt them now that they were one again.

It was much later before they hurried home, suddenly concerned for Johnny. He was wailing when they reached the house, but Keza just gave her rich chuckle when Jack expressed his concern. "Doan you fret 'bout dat baby, suh," she said as she went to the door. "Do him good to learn he ain't goan git what he wants when he wants it, not ev'ry time. 'Sides, crying makes strong lungs, and Massa Johnny, he got a fine pair o' lungs!"

Jack agreed, but he was glad when the baby's wails stopped abruptly. He went into the bedroom then to watch, something he had not done before. He had not been able to bear seeing Johnny at Kate's breast. Now, somehow, it was all different.

That night, Jack did go to bed early, but he did not sleep, not right away. When he joined Kate under the netting, he saw that she had discarded her bedgown, and he caught his breath at her beauty. Her breasts were so much fuller since she was nursing, and she looked riper as well—her hips, all her curves. The girl she had been had disappeared. Now it was a woman who opened her arms to him, to draw him close to kiss and caress.

"Are you sure it will be all right, so soon again?" he asked, his hands gently cupping her breasts. "I would cause you no discomfort, love."

"Sssh, I am fine, and as eager as you are," she admitted.

Jack bent to kiss her breasts, and she closed her eyes. For some reason she was still afire tonight, as if their passion on the beach had never happened at all. That had been wonderful, of course, but it had been frenzied, hurried, with both of them aware that someone might come along and see them. Yet in their desire, they had not taken the time to leave the beach, seek the shelter of the trees. But tonight, alone in their own room, they could make love as she had been longing to do. Slowly, savoring every kiss and caress—mingling, exploring, tasting. Experiencing that wonderful flood of passion that built from a warm glow to brilliant fulfillment.

Now Kate reveled in the touch of Jack's hands on her body, the feel of *him*, so long and powerful and smooth-muscled; his skin against hers, his breath in her mouth; the way his turquoise eyes blazed down at her. And then, just when she was throbbing with the need for them to be closer still, he drew back.

Kate's eyes flew open, to see him frowning. "What is it, Jack? Why did you stop?" she asked breathlessly. "Oh, prithee, not *now*!"

"I can't," he admitted.

Kate stared down the long length of him. To her amazement, she saw he could not, indeed.

"But what is the matter?" she asked, confused. "Is it . . . is it my fault? Something I did?"

"No, it's the baby," he said.

Kate could only gape at him.

"I feel as if he's watching me," Jack explained.

There was a stunned silence for a moment, and then Kate burst out laughing. "Oh, Jack," she gasped at last. "Johnny's fast asleep! And even if he were not, he couldn't see all the way up here from his basket. And he's only two and a half months old, my love! Oh, Jack, I . . . I . . ."

Her laughter began to echo off the thick white walls again, and Jack put his hand over her mouth. "It's not funny!" he told her sternly.

Her laughter still gurgled behind his hand, and her eyes were dancing so, he chuckled weakly himself as he removed that hand.

"We could always put out the candle," Kate said when she could speak again. "And we could whisper, or . . . or not say a word. Oh, my . . ."

As she started to laugh again, Jack realized he was not going to get a sensible word out of her for some time to come, and to forestall any more laughter, he bent and kissed her open mouth slowly and thoroughly. She was quiet when he raised his head at last. Quiet, but not quiescent, for she was moving against him now, all provocative smooth tempting flesh, and she was driving him mad. Forgetting the baby completely, he moved with her, wrapping his arms and legs around her in passionate possession. Her caressing hands seemed to burn him everywhere they touched. He could wait no longer.

Later, as they lay close together in each other's arms, Jack wondered at Kate's tears. She had begun to cry at the crest of their lovemaking, and she was still sobbing a little. He stroked her back, reveling in the familiar scent of her, the satin of her skin as he tried to soothe her. But tonight Kate could not be soothed.

"What is it, love?" he asked at last. "Why do you cry so?"

"I think I am crying for Greg," she murmured. His arms tightened, and she went on, "I never did cry for him, or grieve, you know. I . . . I couldn't, because . . . No, I cannot tell that even to you."

"You can tell me anything," he said. "Try. It might make it easier for you."

She turned away from him a little until all he could see was her profile. "When I heard the news, my first thought—my very first thought, mind you!—was that if one of you had to be drowned, I was glad it was Greg and not you," she whispered. "I am so ashamed! How could I have been so *vile*? My own dear brother, and I was *glad* he had died!"

Jack took hold of her chin and made her turn and face him. "No, you were not glad he died, nor were you vile, love," he told her. "But I can tell you have been torturing yourself with guilt over it for months. That was not right. What you thought was only what anyone would think, faced with a situation like that. For, Kate, if there was ever a situation when I had to choose between saving you and saving my mother, I would choose you."

She stared up at him, hope dawning in her eyes. "Do you mean that?" she asked fiercely. "*Really* mean it? You're not just saying it to make me feel better?"

He nodded. "I mean it. We cannot love everyone

equally. I love my mother very much, I always will. But you are dearer to me by far even than she is."

He saw the tears in her eyes starting to fall again, and he wiped her eyes with a corner of the sheet. "No more tears, madam!" he ordered. "You'll have us awash if you keep it up!"

The baby whimpered then, and he said, "See what you've done? Now you have Johnny crying for you."

Kate laughed as she swung her feet over the bed, to pad over to the basket. "If you think he's crying in sympathy, you're wrong. He's too self-centered for that," she said as she bent to pick him up. "Besides, he's only wet and hungry—again!"

21

WHEN George returned to Tucker's Town the next day, he saw that Jack was at the yard working on his new sloop, and he went to tell him what he had learned. To Jack's satisfaction, everything was as Colonel Tucker had claimed it would be. The American sloops had gotten clean away, and no one in St. George Town knew anything about the theft, not how it had been done, nor who had been involved. Even the governor's offer of a large reward had brought him no information.

As he sanded the sloop's coaming, Jack began to relax. He could almost feel his muscles ease, the tension in his neck and shoulders begin to dissipate, and he realized how eagerly he had been awaiting such good news. For if the governor knew nothing now, there was small chance he would discover anything pertinent as the days went on. And eventually it would all be forgotten.

But only two days later, Jack received a message from Governor Bruere, summoning him to the State House on what the governor claimed was a matter of serious import to the crown.

Kate was there when a boy brought it to the house, and Jack could not avoid showing it to her. Her face paled as she read it, and her voice was a mere whisper as she said, "But what can it be about? Did he find out, do you think?"

"I am sure he has not," Jack told her, trying for a nonchalant tone. "He is casting about for suspects, and naturally, because of those cargoes of mine, I came to mind. I suppose I must go to St. George Town tomorrow and deal with this."

"You'll not go alone!" Kate said swiftly. "Johnny and I will come with you! I can visit one of my friends there while you are . . . are engaged."

Jack wanted to refuse her, but he did not know how. "I mean to leave very early," he said, hoping to discourage her. "I do not plan to remain overnight."

"I can be ready. So can Johnny," Kate told him.

Defeated, Jack turned away. Unless the morning poured rain or was stormy, Kate would be there, baby in tow. Somehow he knew it would be a fine clear day, with just enough wind to speed them to St. George Town and back. Kate's luck.

They arrived at the Custom House dock at nine in the morning. Jack escorted Kate to the Abbotts' house just off the square, carrying the baby's basket for her. Mrs. Abbott and her daughter Belinda were delighted to welcome them and have a chance to admire the baby, and Mrs. Abbott insisted they remain for dinner after the captain's business was completed. She said both Chris and Edward would be glad of a chance to visit with Jack then. Belinda told him pertly that she hoped such a visit would cheer her brothers up, so solemn and gloomy as they had been lately.

Jack put the Abbotts from his mind as he passed through King's Square. He sensed he would need all his wits about him in the coming confrontation.

The square was crowded this morning, even as early as it was, with women carrying shopping baskets on their arms, children playing tag, and the usual bustle near the Customs House dock. There were also several men outside the tavern. Jack's face darkened when he saw Bartholomew Findley among their number, and he was not surprised when Findley turned his back on him and waved another man away.

The State House Jack made his way toward had been

one of the first buildings in Bermuda to be constructed
entirely of Aeolian limestone, back in 1620. It had small
windows and a flat roof in the Italianate fashion, and it
was one of St. George's most admired buildings, although to Jack's eyes it seemed very unpretentious.

He was conducted to Governor Bruere's private room.
So, he thought as he followed the governor's servant, the
councilmen were not all in session. There could have
been no formal accusation made as yet, in that case.

As he entered the room the servant indicated, Jack
saw the governor seated behind his desk, and Kate's
father, council president Henry Tucker, and another man
he did not know well. They were all of them looking very
solemn, with nary a smile of greeting among them, and
he steeled himself even as he bowed.

"You wished to see me, Your Excellency?" he asked,
his voice easy. "How may I serve you?"

Bruere fussed with some papers on his desk, his florid
face, under his gray periwig, set in a mighty frown.

"We have received a serious accusation against you,
sir," the governor began. "Most serious, indeed."

He fell silent then, to cough a little behind his hand.

"Indeed?" Jack prompted. "What kind of accusation?"

As he spoke, he pulled a chair forward. "If I may?" he
asked even as he took his seat and made himself lean
back and cross his arms. He had no intention of standing
before his accusers like some prisoner in the dock.

Bruere glared at the liberty, but decided to ignore it.
The young Sir John Reade had an air he knew well. An
air of privilege, family, and an impressive lineage. He
might call himself plain Jack Reade here, but the governor was well aware of his connections in England. He
must go carefully.

"A witness has come forward, placing you in St. George
Town on August 14, m'lord, the night the gunpowder
was stolen," he said, looking very stern and accusing.

Before he could go on, Jack said firmly, "That cannot
be. I was not in St. George Town that night." He paused
for a moment, as if to think, and then he asked, "That
would have been four nights ago, sir? Impossible! I was
not here—indeed, I have not been here since we last
met, when I returned from my voyaging, if you recall."

"I am afraid the witness was most positive, sir," Henry

Tucker volunteered. Jack saw he was looking mournful, almost distraught, and he remembered that Tucker was married to the governor's sister, Frances. And if the man suspected that his own father, the colonel, had been involved in the theft, as Jack was sure he did, knowing the old man's outspoken views, all this must have been a nightmare for him.

"The witness said he saw you clearly. You were near the governor's mansion at the time, in company with a group of men he could not identify," Roger Hathaway said coldly. "He said when you saw you had been observed, you hurried away. In the direction of the magazine."

"Strange, that," Jack mused, as if only mildly interested in his father-in-law's statement, his accusing face. "I mean, how strange he could see *me* clearly, and no one else. Did he tell you I was carrying a lantern?"

"He did not!" the governor broke in, as if displeased that others had taken over his interrogation. "He said he knew you instantly, from your height, the length of your stride, your distinctive profile."

"He saw all that in a brief moment in the dark?" Jack asked, his voice wondering. "What keen—albeit *selective*—eyesight he has!"

He rose then and went to lean his hands on the governor's desk. "I deny this charge, Your Excellency," he said firmly. "And I repeat, I was not in St. George Town on the night in question."

The governor coughed again and moved his papers in an aimless fashion. "It is to be expected that you would," he said at last. "However, unless you can bring corroborative witnesses to your whereabouts that night, it is your word against his."

"There is only my wife," Jack said, setting his jaw hard. "We were alone in our house near Tucker's Town."

"No!" Roger Hathaway exclaimed. "You'll not bring Kate into this, force her to lie for you, you blackguard!"

As Jack whirled to face him, the other gentleman in the room said in a high, nervous tenor, "Hear, I say, Roger! Easily over the ground there, man! M'lord is only here to answer our questions. He has not been formally charged."

"Indeed, indeed," Governor Bruere agreed.

Jack forced himself to take his seat again, his mind

working furiously. Someone had accused him, although
he knew very well no one had seen him—or, indeed, any
of the others—that night. Who could it be? Who could
hate him so badly that, even without knowing of his
presence, he thought to malign him this way? And then
the answer was plain. Findley! He had threatened ven-
geance, had he not? This had to be his doing.

The governor's voice forced him to put his thoughts
aside and concentrate. "Then there is the matter of those
cargoes you carry, sir. Guns, powder, shot—and all taken
to the northern colonies."

"Not in all cases, Your Excellency," Jack told him. "I
have also delivered them to Charles Town and Philadelphia
on occasion. A most profitable cargo they are, too."

"And a dastardly one!" Roger Hathaway interrupted,
his eyes cold with his dislike.

"If you please, Roger?" the governor requested, looking annoyed.

Mr. Hathaway subsided.

"Do you deny that those cargoes will be used in the
coming confrontation between the colonies and the crown,
sirrah?" Bruere demanded, his face growing red again.

Jack shrugged. "I have no idea to what use they will be
put," he said. "When I contracted to transport them,
they were legal cargoes. No one in the government de-
nies that. One might as well ask what becomes of the
Africans who are brought here. Their slavery is legal too.
Yet many think it an abomination. I do myself."

The governor rapped his desk. "We are not concerned
with the problem of slavery here, m'lord. The cases are
somewhat different."

Jack nodded, as if in perfect agreement, which did not
appear to placate His Excellency at all. His face was
turning purple in his rage now.

"Can you deny you have a great deal of sympathy for
the colonies, sir?" Bruere asked. "Deny that you find
their cause just?"

"My opinion of the colonies has no bearing on the
issue. I may sympathize with their plight, but as I am a
loyal subject of King George, their quarrel with the crown
is not mine," Jack said.

Suddenly, as if wearying of being on the defensive, he

asked, "Who is this brave witness of yours, Your Excellency? Might I know his name?"

Bruere looked at his councilmen before he sniffed and said, "I cannot reveal his identity, sir. If anything were to happen to him, there would be no case against you. He must be kept safe, and a secret."

He noted Sir John did not look unduly disturbed; indeed, he nodded, as if in agreement. What a strange young man! Bruere thought. Doesn't he realize the magnitude of the accusation? Contemplate the distinct possibility that he might be hanged for treason?

"I see," Jack said, leaning back in his chair again. "No matter. I have a very good idea who he is. May I tell you something, Your Excellency? Gentlemen?"

He waited for the governor's nod before he went on. "Several days ago I was in a fight with a Mr. Bartholomew Findley, that stranger to our shores I am sure you all know. Mr. Findley insulted my wife, and taking exception to this, I knocked him to the ground. He swore revenge. I do assure you I have several witnesses to his threat—God-fearing men, industrious and *sober*."

He paused for a moment then, looking around. Henry Tucker was shifting in his seat and would not meet his eye, and, encouraged, Jack continued, "As I crossed the square this morning, I saw that same Mr. Findley deep in conversation with Wilcox Hinson. A most unlikely pair, wouldn't you say? With very little in common? It occurs to me now that Findley might have used the man's weakness for rum as a vehicle for his revenge against me.

"And if your witness is indeed Wilcox Hinson, gentlemen, I must question your acceptance of his word. The man is a sot, more often in the stocks for it than not. Doesn't it seem entirely possible, nay, almost a certainty, that for a supply of the endless rum he craves, Hinson could have been persuaded to fabricate a tale? For that is all it is, nothing but a tale. Hinson never saw me that night. Even if he had been capable of seeing straight in the dark, castaway as he usually is that late at night, he could not have seen me. I was not here."

Governor Bruere cleared his throat then, shuffling his papers as if to regain control of the proceedings. "What you say has merit, m'lord, certainly. The matter will be sifted. Most carefully sifted, indeed."

He rose ponderously then and bowed a little. Jack rose in turn.

"You are excused, sirrah. For now. We will continue our investigation, and of course may require you to appear before us again."

Jack swept a bow. "But of course, Your Excellency," he said. "I am, naturally, completely at your service. Gentlemen? A good day to you."

As Jack walked back to the Abbott house moments later, he forced himself to appear normal, no small task when he was so furious. There was no sign of Findley or Hinson in the square, which was fortunate for them if they valued their continued presence on the earth.

He was so furious, it was all he could do to eat his dinner calmly and chat with the Abbott family as if nothing had happened. But as he cut his chicken, and complimented Mrs. Abbott on her fruit cobbler, he could think of nothing but the lies Findley had paid Hinson to tell. Mr. Findley had a day of reckoning coming, he promised himself.

Kate was delighted when Jack announced they must be off to Tucker's Town right after dinner, for she could not wait to hear what had happened to him in the governor's chambers. Chris and Edward Abbott seemed disappointed, and she wondered briefly, through her own anxiety, why they looked so grim. It was only when Jack mentioned another voyage for the *Camille* that they brightened.

Jack had easily explained his summons by the governor as a request that the *Camille* be sent after the American sloops to try to discover where the gunpowder had been taken, and by whom.

It was then that Mrs. Abbott mentioned the French soldier who had disappeared so inexplicably that very same night. She said people were wondering if he had had a hand in the theft, in return for a passage on one of the American sloops, in order to make his escape. Chris Abbott changed the subject almost at once, and Belinda began to chatter about how dear a baby Johnny was. Nothing more was said about the theft of the gunpowder, although Kate saw Jack having a private word with Edward Abbott just before they left. He grasped the man's arm as he did so, and patted his shoulder, and she wondered what it was all about.

Fortunately, Johnny slept as well at sea as his father did. They had no more than cleared the harbor than the baby settled down for a long nap, and Kate and Jack were free to talk.

He reached out for his wife then with his free hand, to pull her close to him on the windward bench, and shelter her in his arm.

"It's all right, Kate. It's all right," he said.

Kate sighed in relief, and closed her eyes as she nestled against his side, her face raised to the golden sun. The morning, spent gossiping with Belinda and Mrs. Abbott, had seemed endless to her. Even Belinda's demure confession that Aaron Evans was courting her now had not brought more than a moment's respite from her worries about Jack and how he was faring.

Now she begged him to tell her everything that had happened. Jack gave her a brief version of his mock trial and the questions he had had to answer. Then he told her how Wilcox Hinson had claimed to have seen him that night, and how he was sure Bartholomew Findley was behind the old drunkard's lies.

Kate sat up straight then, her gray eyes flashing. "Why, to think of such a dastardly thing! The man's a lizard. And dammit, if I ever get my hands on either one of them, they'll be sorry!"

Jack laughed and pulled her down beside him again. "My avenging angel!" he said. Then, in an effort to diffuse her anger and calm her, he added, "There is no need for you to take up arms for me, love. I . . . er, I am noted for being able to take care of myself, you know."

Kate was frowning now, and she only nodded absentmindedly. "But, Jack," she said slowly, "if Hinson is believed, it is only your word against his! But you must not be concerned! If necessary, I'll go to the governor myself, swear you were with me all that night!"

He hugged her close and kissed her for that before he said, "I doubt it will come to that, but I thank you, ma'am. To think you are prepared to lie for me!"

Later, when they were on a broad reach for Stoke's Bay and home, Kate suddenly thought of something. "Jack, you won't do anything foolish, will you?" she pleaded.

He looked a question, and she went on, "I mean about

Bart Findley. After all, there is no real proof that he was involved, and much as I wish him dead, I'd not lose you to the hangman's noose for murder."

Jack answered her easily, but somehow Kate hoped Mr. Findley would remain in St. George Town for some time to come.

She did not know it, but Jack certainly planned to confront the man as soon as possible and get him to admit his part in all this. And if that meant he had to pummel him till he was unconscious, he would do it without a qualm. And when he had his written confession, duly witnessed, he told himself he would see that Findley had that duel he wanted so badly, so he could kill him. For Jack had no doubt whatsoever that Findley had plotted his downfall. He knew Findley had gone to St. George Town right after their confrontation in the yard. And of course it was there he had met Hinson and formulated his plans after hearing of the gunpowder theft. It had been common knowledge that the royal governor, General George Henry Bruere, so proud and pompous, had been determined to find a scapegoat if he could not get his hands on the real culprits. Findley must have thought just Hinson's placing him at the scene would sway the balance.

Jack quite understood, even excused the governor's zeal. It would not look well on his record to have been duped so neatly and held responsible for the loss of those precious barrels of powder. Not with war coming, it wouldn't. Any scapegoat the governor could hang would weigh in his favor when he returned to England.

A few days after their trip to town, a wide-eyed George appeared at their door to announce that Findley had just come back, and he had no sooner arrived than he had killed his slave Manfred.

Darting a glance at Jack, Kate saw he looked disgusted at the news.

"But what on earth?" she asked as George sank panting in a chair, having run all the way. "Why would he do that?"

"He claims Manfred threatened him with a knife," George told them. "I was in the shipyard, and I heard the shot clearly. Then those twin slaves of his began to scream, and everyone ran to the house."

Jack leaned forward, looking more interested now. "Why did Manfred threaten him?" he asked. "Was Findley beating him?"

"I have no idea," George admitted. "But there is one curious thing. Manfred was found lying in Findley's own bed. Indeed, there was blood all over the sheets and hangings."

"Ugh!" Kate exclaimed.

Jack was rubbing his jaw now, deep in thought. "Has anyone questioned those other slaves of his?" he asked.

"It wouldn't be any use to try," George told him. "They're having what appears will be endless hysterics. And no one can get a word out of that man of his, Withers. We never could.

"But Findley has assured us he will return to St. George Town tomorrow, to report the incident."

His good-natured face twisted in a grimace then. "What an odious creature he is!" he said, looking as if he had just tasted something rotten. "Do you know what he said at the end? He said he didn't know what all the fuss was about! After all, Manfred was only an animal, and his property, bought like any dog or horse with good coin of the realm. If he wanted to shoot him, surely that was his prerogative."

"Ugh!" Kate retorted, looking truly disgusted now. Neither her husband nor her brother reprimanded her for such an unladylike expression. It was obvious they more than shared her opinion of the man.

True to his word, Findley left Tucker's Town early the next day, attended by the faithful Withers with all their baggage. By nightfall, rumors began to spread, first among the men in the shipyard, and then to their horrified women.

Kate heard the story late that afternoon when she took Johnny on a visit to her sister-in-law's. Cecily's pure green eyes were huge as she told her the news.

"Those slaves say the reason Manfred was shot was that when Mr. Findley came home, he discovered Manfred with the two twins." Cecily lowered her voice then, as if she did not want the babies to hear. "They were all of them naked, Kate! Imagine!"

Kate's eyes sparkled. "Was that why Manfred's body

was found in Findley's bedroom?" she asked. "Never tell me they were all in bed together!"

Cecily nodded. "They say Findley was more furious about that than he was about the three of them cavorting together. He screamed at them because they were defiling *his* sheets! That was when he shot Manfred in the heart, while the twins were still on either side of him. Oh, Kate, isn't it just awful?"

Kate agreed with her, for she could see how shocked and horrified Cecily was. But later, when she was telling Jack the same story, she looked pensive.

"Now, what are you thinking, scamp?" he asked, ruffling her curls. They were lying in bed side by side, talking privately, as they often did before they went to sleep.

"I was wondering what it must have been like," she admitted.

"What? The shooting?" he asked. "But what a bloodthirsty little thing you are, ma'am!"

"No, no, not that!" she protested. "I just wondered what it must have been like to be making love to two people at once. Surely it must be difficult. I mean, how would you manage it? After all . . ."

Jack choked a little as he turned toward her to take hold of her shoulders. "That, madam wife, is something you will never know. I suggest you go to sleep now. What a thing to think about!"

Kate grinned up at him. "Oh, I do assure you I don't want to try it. You are quite adequate for me, sir. I was only . . . just wondering."

"Go to sleep now," he said firmly before he kissed the bridge of her nose. "Think pure thoughts. Say your prayers. Good night."

He sounded stern, but as she composed herself for sleep, Kate heard his little chuckle, and she knew he was not really provoked with her at all.

In spite of Findley's assertion that Manfred had threatened him, and he had only acted in self-defense, he was not believed in St. George Town. Perhaps the rumors arrived there sooner than he had thought they would.

In any case, Governor Bruere announced that Mr. Bartholomew Findley would no longer be welcome in Bermuda, and suggested he make immediate plans to leave. When Findley would have demurred, the governor made his departure a direct order. Brother of a marquess or not, this was too much. Besides, unlike the theft of the gunpowder, Findley's expulsion was something he could control, something that would provide him with a sense of power once again.

Mr. Findley and his man left two days later on a sloop bound for Barbados.

22

KATE was both delighted and relieved when she learned that Bartholomew Findley had left the islands. She had been so worried that Jack planned to challenge him to a duel. And if Jack had been killed, or even injured, she could not have borne it.

But if her mood lightened from then on, Jack's did not. Oh, he still smiled at her, and played with the baby, and their lovemaking was as satisfying as it had always been, but he resumed his solitary walks on the beach. Sometimes he would sit brooding over his papers and books for an entire evening, and his good appetite seemed to have deserted him. Kate began to hope he would plan another voyage. Surely that would revive his spirits, and if it did, it was worth it, no matter how badly she would miss him when he was gone.

But Jack did not speak of traveling or trading. Instead, he finished the small new sloop and named her the *Grace*. When Kate questioned him, he told her that was the name of his little sister back in England, and his eyes were bleak as he did so.

At last Kate knew she had to seek Keza's counsel. Jack had gone to the shipyard right after breakfast one morning, and she went out to the chicken yard, where Keza was throwing feed to her flock. The old slave frowned and put her pan down when she saw Kate's worried face.

"Wot's de matter, honey?" she asked as she wrapped a

comforting arm about Kate's shoulders. "Ah knows dat look! Y'all in trouble?"

"No, I'm not, but I'm afraid Jack is," Kate admitted as she led the way to a rustic seat near the moongate. "And I don't know what to do about it. He is so depressed, even though he tries to hide it from me. And he broods so! I never thought the governor's suspicions would affect him this way."

As Keza settled her ample girth on the seat, she leaned over to pat her mistress's hand. " 'Tain't lakly it dat 'tall, chile," she said. Kate stared at her wide-eyed as she went on, "Massuh Jack, he got a look on him I seed on mens afore. Doan bode no good, neither, when dat look comes over dem."

"Whatever do you mean?" Kate asked, bewildered. "What look?"

"Ah s'pects dat man's yearnin' for his homeland. It muss be dat! Ah seed mens die o' dat, long time ago. When we wuz taken by de slavers, herded into dat ship, some of de mens, dey jess turn dere faces to de wall an' die. An' even when we all gits here and gits sold, why, some of dem die den. Dey jess fade away wit hankerin', chile!"

Kate frowned. "But why would he feel that way now?" she asked. "He's been in Bermuda for three long years."

Keza shrugged. "Cain't say, Miz Kate. Mebbe it jess come on him sudden. 'Cause he ain't had good luck here, losin' his ships an' all, mebbe? An' yestiday, when Ah wuz in Tucker's Town takin' a little toy Ah made for Miz Cecily's baby, Ah seed someone treat Massuh Jack rude."

Kate ruffled up, just as Keza's bantam hens were wont to do. "What do you mean, rude?" she asked fiercely. "How? Why?"

"Doan know, chile. Diz mans from St. George Town, he done turn hiz back on Massuh Jack. Ah heered him say he doan talk to traitors!"

Kate's frown was ferocious now. "I wish I'd been there!" she muttered, clenching her hands into two tight fists. "I'd have given him a piece of my mind!"

Keza's chuckle was rich and deep. "Ah'm sure you would o', honey! But Massuh Jack doan want y'all standin' up fer him. He all a mans, dat one."

Kate nodded, deep in thought now. At last she turned

to the old slave and asked, "But what can I do, Keza?
How can I make things better for him?"

She sounded so bewildered, hurt even, that she and
the baby were not enough to make Jack happy, that Keza
hugged her close. "Seems to me dere's only one way.
Y'all got to git Massuh Jack back to hiz home, iffen y'all
kin. Den he be better, be happy 'gin."

"Back to England?" Kate asked, her gray eyes apprehensive. "Why, I couldn't let him go, Keza! I would miss
him every minute for the rest of my life!"

"Y'all not thinkin'!" Keza said tartly. " 'Course y'all
got to go wit him, and de baby too. Y'all got to live dere
den."

Kate shook her head, looking stubborn. "No, I hate
England!" she said. "It's so cold and damp, and the
people are so strange, and cold too. And it's so formal! I
wouldn't be free there, be at all comfortable. In fact, I'd
be miserable!"

Annie called Keza then from the cookhouse door, and
the old slave rose. As she smoothed her apron over her
ample hips, she said, "Den y'all got to be prepared for
bad tings, chile."

"Oh, not more bad things!" Kate exclaimed. "Surely I
have had enough of *them* to last me a lifetime!"

Keza shook her head, her wise old eyes full of sadness.
"Oh, Miz Kate, honey! Ain't y'all figgered it out yet?
Life full o' bad tings, an' dey jess keeps comin' all de time!"

She went away then, shaking her head as she did so,
but Kate remained on the rustic seat, thinking hard. As
she did so, she stared out at the ocean beyond, all turquoise and green and blue, except where it was scalloped
with white filigree near the inshore reefs. A small island
sloop was tacking toward a favorite fishing ground, and
on the beach below her, some little boys from Tucker's
Town were playing in the gentle surf. She could hear
their happy laughter as a wave surprised them and spilled
them on the sand, a tangle of gleaming wet arms and
legs, both black and white. A gentle breeze lifted the
curls on her brow and brought a land scent of flowers
with it, and the warm sun smiled down on her and kissed
her cheeks. To leave Bermuda, this beautiful place she
loved so much! She couldn't do it! There *had* to be some
other way.

Maybe Keza was only seeing the dark side. Wasn't it entirely possible that after a while, when all the furor over the gunpowder was forgotten, Jack might be more cheerful again?

Perhaps if she tried harder to amuse him and interest him, he might forget England in time. She resolved to ask him to teach her to play piquet this very evening, and at dinner she would tell him all she knew of the Canary Islands. There was many a fine exotic cargo to be had there, from trading ships coming from India and China.

She heard Johnny crying then, and rose to go to him. As she made her way back to the house, she told herself that Jack was not a weakling. There was no danger he would waste away with his longing, no matter what Keza said. Not Jack! The very idea was ludicrous.

But still, even when Johnny was happy suckling, she could not help but think that accepting a situation—trying to be content—was not the same as being happy. And she knew that if Jack were not happy, she would not be able to be either. It was a terrible problem.

Colonel Tucker came out that afternoon to see Jack. He left his sloop in the cove, as he had before, and suggested the two of them take a walk up the beach. Once they were alone, strolling the sand, Jack asked him for the news of St. George Town. The colonel frowned.

" 'Tis not good, Jack," he said slowly. "The governor seems determined not to let the matter of the gunpowder rest. I thought that surely by now he would have given up his search for the culprits, but the man is as stubborn as he is pompous. But I do have some good news! I have received a letter from Mr. Harris, and he tells me that food supplies for the islands are being arranged even now. New York and Pennsylvania are to provide meat and flour, and the southern colonies peas, corn, beans, and other vegetables. We're to have rice from South Carolina as well. Harris tells me we should receive the first of many such shipments by late November. We did it, Jack! We did it, and now the people of Bermuda are safe from starvation."

Jack smiled down at the happy old man, so content that his plan had succeeded. "This is grand news indeed, sir. You can be proud you were instrumental in bringing it to pass."

"I'm proud for another reason as well," the colonel said, a little gruffly now. He stopped walking then and reached into his coat pocket to withdraw a letter he unfolded almost reverently. "This was enclosed in Harris' letter. 'Tis from General George Washington himself. Here, you read it."

Jack took the letter he was holding out, to study it. The general wrote most elegantly about this situation the colonies found themselves in. He elaborated on all the reasons they had been forced to civil war, and he reminded the colonel that as Englishmen, they were freemen, as committed to the cause of virtue and liberty as Bermudians themselves were. And in closing, he assured the colonel that he would use his influence with the Continental Congress to ensure that Bermuda would not only be supplied with provisions but also "experience every other mark of affection and friendship which the grateful citizens of a free country can bestow on its brethren and benefactors."

"Most impressive, sir!" Jack said admiringly. "You'll have to keep this in a safe place. Someday it will be an important piece of Bermuda's history."

Colonel Tucker's old eyes crinkled shut as he chuckled. "Aye, I'll do that, never fear! But just for now, with George Bruere on the rampage, I think I'll keep it only between the two of us."

The two began to walk again, and his face sobered. "Jack, I admit I'm worried," he said at last.

As Jack turned to stare at him, he went on, "I've heard rumors that Bruere has been interviewing Wilcox Hinson again. It seems the man continues stubborn, insists he did see you in St. George Town that night. He's lying, of course, for no one saw any of us, but nothing will shake his story."

He glanced sideways to see Jack's frowning look of concern, and added, "No doubt, having lost Mr. Findley's ready supply of money, Hinson has decided to try for that handsome reward. That would keep him in rum till he died drinking it. 'Sblood! That happy day cannot come soon enough for me!"

"But there is no proof, other than his story," Jack said, as if to reassure himself as much as remind the colonel of that fact. "No matter what he says, they cannot bring charges. Or can they?"

The colonel shook his head. "I've no idea. You know that no one will talk, but even so, it is a danger. And even if you are just accused, and later acquitted by the council, it will go hard for you. There are many loyal Tories in Bermuda, and you would be reviled. Indeed, you are being reviled here now by some of our most fervent citizens." He snorted in derision before he added, "I am so sorry, Jack. I never thought to see you into danger when I suggested you join us."

Jack waved a dismissive hand. "It appears there is nothing I can do but wait and see," he said slowly.

The colonel nodded, but his brow was still furrowed. After a few moments he said a little diffidently, "You don't think it might be better to leave Bermuda for a time? Perhaps you should go on a long trading voyage. Out of sight, you know . . ."

"Running away is the coward's choice," Jack told him. "And it is an admission of guilt, is it not?"

"Surely not!" Tucker protested. "You have been on several voyages before. And you have been here for some time now. I'm sure no one would think a thing of it."

He saw Jack was looking stubborn, and he put his hand on his arm. "Think about it seriously, Jack," he said. "It is not weak to retreat at prudent times, you know, but the sign of a wise man. And he who fights and runs away, lives to fight another day, remember."

Jack promised only to consider it seriously, and with this the colonel had to be content. But as he sailed home again, he shook his head more than once. The temper in St. George Town was growing ugly. People were demanding a victim so they could put the gunpowder theft behind them once and for all. And Jack Reade was the only suspect they had. The colonel wished suddenly that he had thought to have a word with little Kate. She was the man's wife. Perhaps she would have been able to convince him to leave, whereas he himself had not been successful.

As it happened, it was her brother George who finally told Kate what was happening. Jack was offshore sailing when he came over to the house a few days later. He had been to St. George Town the day before, searching for a particular brass fitting, and he had heard the talk there. People were calling quite openly for Jack's arrest and hanging, and no matter what George said to defend him, they only stared at him before they turned their backs, to mutter among themselves once again. How quickly they forget! George thought bitterly. Only a short time ago Jack had been a hero to them, bringing much-needed supplies, all of which were given away without thought of payment. And now those same eager recipients of his gift wanted to see him hang.

He told Kate all about it, soberly and slowly, and he watched her face pale as he did so, until the golden freckles on the bridge of her nose stood out in bold relief.

"But how terrible! I did not know," she whispered as he finished.

George looked away from her then, to run a hand through his dark brown hair. "There's worse, Kate," he said, his voice sounding strangled.

"Yes?" she prompted as she saw him hesitate.

"One of those who were the most vocal against Jack was our father," George said finally. At Kate's muffled exclamation, he hurried on, as if anxious now to be done. "He says that even if Jack is his son-in-law, he cannot stand by and see him escape punishment. He says he knows him for a traitor: those cargoes of guns and shot he carried, the time he spent in New England ports—all pointing to his guilt."

George stopped then, worried his sister might faint. Kate stared at him stoically, and he went on, "Be that as it may, Father has been believed. His views are the most damning, because he speaks out against family. You may be sure I taxed him with it, but he is adamant. He will not change his mind. Sometimes, old lady, I don't feel I know Father at all anymore. And Mama! She is even worse. This has become a personal mission for her, a way she thinks to avenge Greg's death. She urges Father on. It is . . . it is too bad."

Kate rose then to pace the big main room, her hands clenched together so George would not see how they were trembling. "It is more than too bad, George," she said finally. "But . . . but what can we do?"

Her brother looked grim. "I cannot see anything that
will change the mood of the people now. There is nothing we can do."

"But if we don't do something, Jack may be arrested
. . . hanged!" Kate cried. "We must prevent that at all
costs!"

She turned to her brother then and said, "How much
time do you think we have before they come for him?"

George spread his hands. "I have no idea. Perhaps a
few days—no more. I have heard there is to be a special
council meeting on Thursday morning. I imagine a vote
will be taken then."

"That's only three days!" Kate exclaimed. "So short a
time!"

"I think we must get Jack away from here before
then," George told her. "There's no sense in his thinking
he can stay and fight this. Not when the minds of the
authorities—all the people—are made up. No, better for
him to gather his crew and take the *Camille* on a long
voyage. He can return when the war is over. Perhaps he
can even come back sooner."

Kate nodded, her brow knit in thought. Yes, she quite
saw that Jack's only hope lay in flight, no matter how
that would look to his accusers. But how to convince him
of it?

She was preoccupied throughout the rest of her brother's visit, so preoccupied she even forgot to send her love
to Cecily and the baby. When she kissed him good-bye,
she promised to let him know the minute they had
decided what to do.

Kate thought Jack would never return home. As she
ate her solitary dinner, attended by a silent Keza, she
thought hard. Jack could of course go to another British
island in the Caribbean—Jamaica, Barbados, even to
Grenada or St. Kitts, if it came to that. But wouldn't he
be safer somewhere else?

Keza shook her head at the little Kate had eaten when
she pushed her plate away and rose at last. Kate ignored
the old slave's sniffs as she went to the window that
faced the ocean, to rest her forehead against the cool pane.

Jack would be safest in England, a little imp in her
mind whispered. Safe, and something more. He would be
happy, for he would be home then. No! Kate cried si-

lently. I cannot bear for him to leave me, go so far away! But, the imp reminded her, as Keza pointed out, you and Johnny could go with him. And isn't this the perfect opportunity to get him to return where he never intended to go again, but where he wants to be so badly?

No, there must be some other way! Kate cried to herself as she searched her mind for possibilities. Not England! Never England!

Jack had taken the little sloop *Grace* almost out of sight of the islands of Bermuda that day. As always, sailing eased his mind, and he was able to relax. But still, he spent the time pondering his problem. Colonel Tucker had told him he was in danger if he remained here, and he respected the colonel's judgment. The old man was not one to see a threat where none existed, and if he said it was time to go, it behooved a wise man to take heed and make immediate plans to do so. It still bothered him to play a coward's role, however, but in all his thinking about it, he had been able to come to no better solution.

Very well, I must leave Bermuda, Jack told himself. But where can I go? The other British islands in the Caribbean were a safe refuge, of course, but that was all they were. No more than Bermudians could their sea captains trade with the colonies.

Then there was South Carolina. He knew Matthew Hathaway would be delighted to help him get established there, but if he went, and war was declared, he would have to pledge his allegiance to that colony. And he was not at all sure even now that that was what he really wanted to do.

And then there was England herself, and Hythe. He had always promised himself he would go back one day, to see his mother and the earl. Perhaps it would be expedient to do so now.

In his mind's eye, then, he saw the old gray-stone mansion set in the gardens his mother had cared for so well. Now, at the end of August, they would be in full, riotous bloom. And beyond them, the fields of Hythe would be rich with the coming harvest of fruit and grain and hops. The cattle in the fields would be fat and prospering, and over it all, the sun and rain would be blessing the land in turn.

He frowned then, and brought the sloop about, to sail back to the place he had called home for the past three years.

If he went to Hythe—anywhere—it might be quite a while before he would be able to return, he thought as he tightened the mainsheet. Could he bear to be apart from Kate that long? And how would she fare, left here, the wife of a man who had chosen to run rather than face trial? Even her brother and her father could do little to shield her from the scorn and sneers of the loyalists.

Perhaps he could convince her to go to Charles Town with the baby. But what would become of them if war broke out? Charles Town was an important port. There might very well be a battle for control of it, and the thought of Kate and Johnny caught in the middle of it made his blood run cold. No, they could not go there. They would be better off in Bermuda. He smiled a little then, remembering his Kate. She would know exactly how to handle any snide remarks about his absence, and she would do it with aplomb.

It was late when he arrived home, and Kate barely gave him time to kiss her before she began to tell him of her brother's visit and the things he had said. Jack poured himself a fruit punch laced with rum as she talked.

"You do see you must go away, and at once, don't you, Jack?" she finished as he took his seat.

"It is truly amazing," he remarked, beckoning her to come and sit on his lap. As he put his arms around her, he added, "I have spent all afternoon making plans to do just that, madam."

"You have?" Kate asked in wonder, her mouth falling open a little.

Jack could not resist kissing it before he went on, "The very same! Colonel Tucker warned me of the temper in St. George Town on his last visit, and I've no mind to hang.

"Today I decided to sail to England. There's little I can do now in the West Indies, with war coming, and I have had it in mind to visit my mother and Hythe for some time now."

"You are going to England," Kate repeated. "I don't believe it!"

"Why ever not?" he asked. "You yourself have pointed

out any number of times that I will be Sir John Reade
until I die. There is no way I can change that. So why
shouldn't I pay a visit to Hythe, if only as its faithful
steward?"

"There is no reason you can't, of course," Kate said
slowly. Then she sat up straight and took a deep breath.
"It is really too bad of you, Jack! Here I have spent
hours fussing and fuming, and marshaling all my most
potent arguments to make you go home, and you march
in here and blithely announce that very destination. I was
never so provoked!"

As she shook her head, he laughed at her. "Perhaps
matrimony does that to people. Having the same thoughts
at the exact same time, I mean."

He saw Kate was not really attending, and he asked,
"What is it? There is a problem still?"

"I was planning something else as well this afternoon,
Jack," she told him. Her gray eyes were steady on his
face as she added, "I want you to take Johnny and me to
England too."

"What?" he asked, completely astonished. "But, Kate,
you hate England!"

"I see it was not fair for me to make such a sweeping
statement on so little acquaintance," she told him. "And
you may be gone for a long time. A very long time.
Dammit, Jack! Don't you see? Wherever you are is my
home now, be it Bermuda, England, or . . . or Timbuctu!"

Jack smiled a little then at her vehemence before he
bent his head to kiss the freckles on the bridge of her
nose. Determined, Kate pulled his head down so she
could kiss him, long and hard. In spite of her intensity,
that kiss ended in tenderness—a tenderness born of deep
love and a renewed commitment. When he took his lips
from hers at last, Kate realized she had never felt so
close to him before, no, not even when lovemaking made
them one. In spite of her revulsion for the course they
must take, she knew a fierce stab of exultation.

Jack stood up then, putting her aside to pace the room.
"But there's Johnny," he said, a frown creasing his brow.
"If I take him to Hythe, I acknowledge him as the next
baronet."

"He is that whether you do so or not," Kate told him.
"And he is only three months old. I hardly think he will

be overwhelmed by the distinction. He will not even know of it. And no doubt we will be gone again before he learns how exalted he is. I do so hope so!"

Jack smiled a little at her biting tone, but Kate saw he was retreating into his own thoughts again, and she asked quickly, "Whom will you get for crew?"

"The Abbotts, of course. I've sent them a message already, for I know they are with me. None of the slaves, though. I might not be able to find ship's passage for them right away, and the blacks would not be happy in an English winter. But Chris will know whom we should have."

"Did you tell him all this must be kept as silent as the grave? No one must suspect what you are about, lest they try to stop you."

"I know. We must slip away secretly. Like criminals," Jack said, looking grim at the thought.

"Keza will go back to my parents' house, but what of Tatum and Annie?" Kate asked. "What will become of them when we are gone?"

"I'll put them in George's charge, I think," Jack told her. "But, Kate, will you be able to care for Johnny without another woman to help you? It is a hard voyage to England, and without favorable winds, it might take as long as three months. Perhaps, no matter how much I would miss you both, it would be wiser for you to stay here. You love Bermuda, and you would be safe here—"

"No!" Kate cried. "If you go, we all go, and that's the end of it! Please, Jack! You'll see. It will be all right." Hiding her distaste for the voyage to come—the sleet, the snow, the damp cold fogs—she added, "As far as Johnny is concerned, I doubt he'll even know he is not here at home. But I will need warm clothes for him, and blankets. And warm clothes for me as well. I'll see to that at once."

"I must go and talk to George now," Jack said. "You had best start making lists of what you want to take with you. None of the furniture, of course. We'll leave that here, against our return. For I promise you, my bright penny, we *will* return someday. You have my word on it."

As he blew her a kiss and hurried away, Kate shook her head. She had her doubts about that. It might be she would not see Bermuda again for years. Indeed, she might never see it again.

She had fought a battle with herself all afternoon, before she finally came to understand that if Jack were ever to be safe and happy, she must put her own desires aside. Still, she prayed his happiness would be enough for both of them; that basking in its reflective glow, she could find acceptance, even peace. She did not expect to find joy in England. That was too much to ask.

Pushing such depressing thoughts from her mind, she went to the desk for writing material. There was so much to do, and so little time to do it in the short time before they must be gone. Besides, she would have plenty of time to consider this step they were taking on the ocean crossing.

She spent the rest of the afternoon making lists and searching out her warmest clothes. She had only a few, for three years ago when she had traveled to England, spring had been coming on, and she had left there in early summer. Even her boat cloak was not particularly cozy. She wondered if Cecily had any flannel. She knew she could not take the time to go to St. George Town to shop for some, even if such a trip would have been wise.

As she folded her warmest gowns and set them aside, she realized she must take some wool and knitting needles, as well as her sewing basket. She would have to make Johnny warm mittens and booties on the voyage, and some heavy stockings for herself as well. Johnny had almost outgrown the pale blue sweater she had made for him before he was born. Perhaps she should take it anyway, so she could unravel it and use the wool again.

As she set it aside, she remembered she must write to her parents to inform them of her departure. Obviously she would have to leave the letter with George, to be delivered after they were safely away. Her mouth twisted in a grimace then, and she shook her head. It had been hard enough to accept her mother's crazed assessment of Jack, but to know now that her beloved father was in some way responsible for this new development to bring him to trial and hang him hurt her deeply. How could he do this to me, he who has always claimed to love me so much? she cried inwardly. How could he destroy my happiness, my very life?

When Jack came back, she was still hard at work, for she wanted to pack her most precious possessions away herself, to be sure they would be safe in her absence. Those silver spoons and the tea set, the fragile, crystal goblets. She had not called Annie or Keza to help her, for this was something she had to do herself. As she wrapped them securely and laid them in Granny Bessie's cedar chest, she inhaled the aromatic wood deeply. She wished she could at least bring Granny's chest, to remind her of home, but she knew removing their furniture would look suspicious and cry out that they were leaving for good; running away.

Jack set himself to the task of listing supplies they would need on the journey. He told her he expected the crew to arrive sometime tomorrow.

"We'll put our baggage and the food aboard then," he told her. "The men can do the loading, and George has promised to help as well. I'm glad now I had the *Camille* careened. A clean hull will speed us on our way."

After supper, Jack called the slaves into the big main room of the house to tell them his plans. He did not mention why they were leaving; the less the slaves knew, the better.

Annie looked distressed, and she began to cry a little as he explained. Keza moved closer to put her arm around the girl, and she whispered in her ear when Jack took Tatum aside for a few private words. Kate sat on at the table, staring at them all. She had wanted to go and comfort Annie herself, but she had not dared, lest she begin to weep as well.

Late, when they had gone back to the kitchen house, Kate made herself write that letter to her parents. It took her several attempts before she had it right. Somehow, all her resentment and her anger at them kept creeping into her sentences. Her final copy was short and to the point. In it she did not admit that they were going in order to save Jack's life. Instead, she said only that Jack wanted to return to his estate in England for a while, and she had begged to go with him. She promised she would write again on their arrival, and she would look forward to that day when they would all be reunited again. She signed the letter with her love and obedience, but she felt it was a poor, stiff effort for all that.

Jack was busy writing as well. A letter to Colonel Tucker, and a long one to Matthew Hathaway, as well as a note to George about how he wanted the house, the sloop, and the dory kept in his absence.

Both of them were tired when they finally went to bed. Yet Kate lay on her back and stared up at the tester above her head long after Jack had kissed her good night and rolled over on his other side to sleep. England, her mind kept repeating. England, where you vowed you would never go again. It was very late when she finally fell asleep.

Johnny woke her early the next morning, and she was glad he had, even though she was still tired. She had dreamed deeply through the night—strange, disconnected dreams of her childhood, of Greg and George, and Matt and her parents. In one dream she had been standing in a large bright room with them, and people she had known growing up had appeared to her and then faded away. She had not wanted to leave the comfort of that warm room, the gentle murmur of their voices, the encompassing love that emanated from them and was almost a living presence. But the room had a door that she could not avoid. When she forced herself to open the door at last and step outside, there had been nothing there but a cold, icy darkness. Yet when she had tried to return to the warm room, she found the door to it had disappeared.

Cecily came over to see her very early, bringing her baby with her. She set Margaret Rose down on a blanket in the main room and took some knitting from the calico bag she carried.

"It is a little cap for Johnny, my dear, and I intend to work on it all day until it is finished," she said, her needles flashing in the sunlight. "Where you are going, he will need a warm cap. I'm going to line it with flannel for extra warmth, and see, Kate? I've put a flap on the bottom that you can tuck inside his gown to keep his neck warm."

Kate's eyes filled with tears as she bent to kiss her sister-in-law, her friend.

"You'll write, won't you, dear?" Cecily begged, her own green eyes brimming with tears that she dashed angrily away. "I'll write often to you too, and tell you everything that's happening here. It is too bad you must run away like this. As if Jack had anything to do with the theft! It makes me angry even to think of how unjustly he has been accused."

Kate changed the subject then by asking Cecily if she had any flannel or wool that she might take with her. Successfully diverted, Cecily promised to have her entire supply packed and ready when the Reades went on board that night.

"I hope you'll plan to share a last supper with us before you go," she said. "That way the slaves will be free to help with the packing. And you're not to worry about Tatum and Annie. I'll see they're just fine. Tatum can work in the shipyard, and Annie can help Mandy and her daughter. We've plenty of room for them. And I'll come over here often and make sure all is well. Did you know, Keza has offered me the bantam flock she had here? She is so kind!"

All the time they talked, Cecily's fingers flew over the cap she was making for her little nephew. At her feet, her daughter smiled and gurgled and tried to catch a sunbeam in her tiny fist. Kate smiled down at her, so fair and so pretty, before she went back to her own task of hemming more diapers.

By late afternoon everything was ready. The Abbots had sailed over from St. George Town earlier with their portmanteaus. Later, by another sloop and by ferry and on foot, came several other seamen. The Benson boy and his cousin Albert; Ben Swan and Jeremiah Tucker. They were excellent seamen, every one of them; a fine crew. Kate's heart swelled with pride that these good men, at least, believed in Jack and would throw in their lot with him, no matter how he was maligned by others.

The baggage and food supplies were quickly loaded on the *Camille*. George had told the men at the yard that Jack and his crew were planning a voyage to Jamaica and would be gone only a few weeks, lest someone grow suspicious and hurry to report the sailing to the governor.

Kate and Johnny were to be rowed out to the sloop well after dark. Just before supper, Kate left Cecily finishing the knit cap and went out to seek Keza for a private farewell.

The old black woman was sitting on a bench near the kitchen house, but when she caught a glimpse of Kate's

woebegone face, she rose and held her arms open wide.
Kate was sobbing in earnest as she ran into them.

"Heah, now, chile! Doan y'all take on so!" Keza chided
her as she patted her back with her big hands. "Y'all be
doin' de right ting, and in yo' heart, y'all knows it."

"I know, I know," Kate whispered, wiping her eyes as
she did so. "It's just that it's so hard to leave here, leave
you. Why, I may never see . . ."

Her voice died away, as if even voicing such a terrible
possibility might make it come true somehow.

"Yas, we goan be 'part, chile, but we never goan be
separated. No, 'cause yo' still mah baby. Y'all always
wuz. Listen to me, now. Even now Ah has mah father
wit' me, an' Ah ain't seed him fo' fifty years. Ah knows
he dead now, 'cause Ah old myself. But still, he wit' me.
Dem y'all loves be wit' y'all even when dey dead and
buried."

As Kate sobbed again, she went on, "Hush, now! Dis
jess one o' dose bad tings Ah told y'all happens all de
time. But y'all strong. Y'all kin go on. An Massa Jack,
he doan need no weeping wimmens! He be happy 'gin
soon, an' den y'all kin be happy too. Ah knows."

Kate nodded, but still she sat close to her old friend—no,
her dear second *mother*—holding her hand until Cecily
called her to supper. But when she went aboard the dory
to be rowed out to the *Camille* much later, she only
hugged and kissed Keza just as she did Tatum and Annie, lest she start crying again. Keza was right. Jack
needed a wife now, not a weeping, helpless woman. She
did not even cry when George hugged his "old lady" so
tight her ribs were in danger, nor when Cecily wept in
her arms, distraught at their coming separation.

The *Camille*'s anchor was pulled inboard and stowed
just at dawn. There was a little smoke coming from some
of the chimneys in Tucker's Town, but the hamlet itself
was quiet. As the sloop's sails filled and she began a
slow, ghostly voyage to the mouth of the harbor in the
light breeze, Kate stood by the rail in the waist of the
sloop, Johnny in her arms.

Jack was at the helm, and very much in command.
And in the gray light of dawn, Kate saw that his face was
calm and content, and his turquoise eyes were full of a
light that made her want to weep in envy.

Johnny stirred in her arms then, and she tucked his
blanket around him more securely as she whispered,
"Breathe deep, Johnny! This is the land of your birth,
your own homeland. We'll come back someday, and until
we do, I'll tell you stories of Bermuda to keep it fresh
and green for you."

She stared astern then. Tucker's Town was already
only a smudge in the background, the sloops at anchor
there indistinguishable from the shoreline. And suddenly
she was reminded of the Williamses, how Maryanne had
stared rapt in the direction of England, while her husband, Farley, bent his brooding gaze ashore. And that
gaze had been one of regret and longing for all that he
was giving up. Kate remembered that she had wondered,
as she watched them sail away, if all marriages were like
theirs, in which one partner had to give more to secure
the other's happiness. It appeared that it was true after
all.

As the sun rose, turning the gray dawn into rosy wonder, and the waves the *Camille* was cleaving so neatly
became their customary aquamarine, Kate saw Jack hand
the helm over to Chris Abbott and come toward her. She
saw his look of concern, and she made herself smile. She
promised herself he would never know what this voyage—
their destination—cost her. She saw that as he took the
baby from her arms, he did not stop searching her face.

Her smile broadened then at his obvious love and
regard for her, and she was glad when his own expression
brightened. She was even able to laugh when Johnny
yawned widely again in his father's face, completely un-
impressed by Jack's tale of the great adventure they were
all going to share, and how exciting it would be.

But over Jack's shoulder, Kate could see a pair of
longtails heading for the offshore reefs, and the familiar
sight of their graceful beauty, in controlled, effortless
flight, caused her to tighten her hands for a moment on
the *Camille*'s polished cedar railing.

23

THE butler entered the drawing room at Hythe with his usual slow, measured steps. Earlier he had sent the new footman here to build up the fire, and he wanted to look over his handiwork. As he had suspected, the fire was only smoldering rather sullenly, and he made a sound of disapproval as he bent to push and prod the sea coals into a heartier conflagration. He was very much afraid that Wilfred was not going to do at all. No, not at all.

When he rose, he noticed that the curtain at one of the front windows was slightly disarranged, and he went to adjust it. As he stood there, he saw an old mud-stained carriage coming up the drive, and he peered at it. Few people came to Hythe, now that m'lord was never in residence. He wondered who could be calling on this raw, rainy December day.

His breath caught in his throat when a tall, somber gentleman descended the steps to stare up at the stone walls of Hythe. The butler bent closer to the panes, his brow furrowed. But surely that was Sir John, home at last! For a moment he had not been sure, for the new arrival was so unlike the young man who had left here with a twinkle in his turquoise eyes and a gay smile on his handsome face. This man was very different indeed. He had a definite air of severity that he had never had before. The butler realized that Sir John had become a man in truth, but he wondered what could have happened to him to bring that sober cast to his face.

Faintly, he heard the knocker sound on the front door then, and he started. One of the grooms must have come ahead to alert the house, and now, for the first time in many years, the butler actually ran back to the hall. If he should not be there to welcome his master home after all this time! It did not bear thinking about!

He gave a number of quick orders which sent the footmen scurrying. Harry was sent out with the umbrella to shelter m'lord, while Wilfred was to see to the unloading of m'lord's baggage. The boot boy, attracted by the commotion, was dispatched to the back of the house to alert the housekeeper and the rest of the staff. The butler himself stood by the open front door, a welcoming smile on his face.

That smile faltered for a moment when he saw the young woman held close in Sir John's right arm. She was carrying a blanket-wrapped bundle that looked very much like a baby. But could it be? the butler wondered. Had Sir John married and fathered a child? He could hardly wait to apprise the housekeeper of such a joyous event!

"Welcome home, m'lord! Welcome home!" he said fervently as Jack Reade stepped inside, the lady beside him still sheltered in his arm. "How very good it is to see you here again, sir!"

The smile that lit that lean face brought the old Jack Reade vividly to life again, and the butler smiled even more broadly.

" 'Tis very good to be here, Greyson," Jack said before he turned to the lady at his side and said, "Here we are at last, Kate, and now you can be comfortable. Let me take your cloak, love."

"Please, sir, allow me," Greyson said, hurrying to assist the lady. "If you would permit, madam?"

Kate nodded as she put back the hood that had half-concealed her face. Greyson was hard put to keep his expression neutral. The lady looked worn to a thread, and under the fading tan she sported, her face was pale and strained. As he took her cloak, the butler could see how very thin she was, and he suspected that even when she was blooming with health, she would not be an outstanding beauty. She was hardly the mate he had thought Sir John would choose.

"Kate, my love, this is Greyson. He has been my butler for several years now."

He turned to his butler then and said, "My wife, Lady Reade. And this little mite is my son. He is named John too, but we call him Johnny."

The butler beamed at them all as he bowed. Much would be forgiven the lady who had produced the next baronet. "I have summoned the housekeeper, m'lord," he said. "She will assign a maid to take charge of the baby until permanent staff can be found. And she will see to it that your rooms are prepared for you at once."

"Oh, no, she must not do that!" the new Lady Reade exclaimed, and then she covered her mouth with one thin hand.

As the butler stared at her perplexed, she whispered, "It is just that I have always taken care of Johnny myself. I . . . I would prefer to continue to do so."

A little discomposed by this most unusual arrangement, Greyson only bowed. He saw Lady Reade's hand tremble as she adjusted her son's blanket, and he wondered if she were ill. In that case, surely another attendant for the baby would be more prudent?

A door at the back of the hall opened then, and Camille Maxwell, Countess Granbourne, entered. Behind her, the housekeeper peered over her shoulder, the blue eyes under her neat mobcap round with excitement.

"Jack! Oh, my dear, is it really you?" the countess cried. As she hurried forward, arms outstretched, her eyes never ceased inspecting her son's face.

It was not until she was closer that she noticed the girl beside him, and she stopped short and frowned. Greyson had been waiting for her to rush into Sir John's arms, weeping and exclaiming, and he was startled when she said, "Oh, how could you, Jack? How *could* you?"

"Mrs. Nearing, please take the baby," she ordered as she herself hurried to put her arms around the new Lady Reade. "My dear Katherine! But you are ill, child!"

Greyson saw the young lady close her eyes for a moment, almost collapse in the countess's arms, and he edged closer just in case she fainted. Beside her, Sir John stared at his mother in complete confusion. She knew Kate's name? But how?

"Had you no care for your wife, Jack?" the countess demanded, sounding as fierce as the butler had ever heard her. "How could you allow this dear girl to get in such a state? I have never been so angry!"

"No, no, indeed, ma'am, 'tis but a momentary weakness," Lady Reade murmured. "And it is not Jack's fault."

The countess shook her head as she brushed the girl's limp chestnut curls from her brow. "You are feverish, Katherine," she said, her voice concerned. "We must get

you to bed. Mrs. Nearing, see to Lady Reade's rooms
first, and send up some hot tea as well. And please
summon a maid to take charge of the baby."

"Certainly, m'lady," the housekeeper said, looking a
little confused as to what she was supposed to do with the
baby she had been so delighted to receive only a moment
ago.

"I'll take him, Mrs. Nearing. We appear to be engaged
in a game of hunt the slipper, with Johnny as the slipper," Jack said, sounding a little amused in spite of his
mother's less-than-effusive greeting. "Indeed, Mama, I
did not realize that Kate was feeling poorly. She hides
such things from me, you see," he added as the housekeeper hurried away.

His mother only nodded absently. "I will put her to
bed at once. Greyson, please send someone for Dr.
Lincoln!"

As she spoke, she had been urging Lady Reade to the
stairs. "Come along now, Katherine," she said. "You
will soon feel better. Oh, how glad I am to see you at
last, dear girl! And you are not to worry about your
baby. He will be well cared for here. Ah, there you are,
Betsy! Kindly take the baby to Mrs. Nearing's room until
we can have the nursery fire made up."

The maid curtsied before she took the baby from him,
and Jack watched his mother and his wife begin a slow
ascent of the stairs. He was frowning now, wondering if
he should go after them and help. But no, he decided.
He would only be in the way. Better to wait until his
mother had put Kate to bed.

He had known Kate was feeling pulled from the journey here, but he had not realized how ill she really was.
Surely his mother was right. He ought to have noticed
that, even as concerned as he had been about the continuous gales they had encountered on the ocean crossing;
the fogs that had impeded their safe landfall here. He
shook his head at his imperception before he removed his
cloak and handed it to his butler.

"Some wine, if you would be so good, Greyson. 'Tis a
raw day," he said. "I'll wait in the drawing room for my
mother to come down."

The butler bowed as the footman brought in another
load of baggage. Then he scowled as Wilfred dropped a

large portmanteau and it landed on the carpet with a heavy thud.

Jack walked quickly into the drawing room, looking eagerly around as he did so. And then he stopped short, for over the mantel, in the place of honor, was a life-size full-length portrait of him. He knew he had never posed for it, but he recognized Sir Joshua Reynolds' expert hand at once. The lean face and crow-black hair were the same as the miniature he had had done just before he left England, but the figure could have been anyone's. Still, it was remarkable how much it did resemble him.

"Was I ever that young and careless?" he murmured as he moved closer to study it. From the canvas, the handsome young man he had been smiled down at him. He looked as if he had never had a single problem or sorrow in his life; as if he were, in truth, one of those golden youths much smiled on and indulged by the gods.

Jack's mouth twisted in a wry grimace. The real Jack Reade knew one thing that careless golden young man would never know. He knew how to survive, and by his own efforts, too.

Greyson brought in a bottle of canary and some glasses on a silver tray then, and as he poured his master a glass, Jack questioned him about the portrait.

"The countess commissioned it, m'lord," the butler told him. "She said Hythe must have a portrait of the current baronet, hanging in its proper place. And it did serve to remind us of you, help us remember that someday you would be coming back to Hythe."

He paused for a moment before he added, "May I say again, sir, how happy we are to welcome you home. And your lady as well."

"You are forgetting our son," Jack reminded him with a rueful smile. "I do assure you, Greyson, he will soon make his presence known. Master Johnny has an excellent pair of lungs."

The butler nodded, not at all perturbed at the prospect. "If I may venture an opinion, sir?" he asked, and he waited for Jack's nod before he went on, "We do not have a full staff at the moment, but I'll set about remedying that at once. And we shall need a nanny, now that m'lady is ill, and maids for the nursery. Perhaps your own nanny, Mrs. Bell, could be persuaded out of retirement. Do you remember her? Mrs. Nearing mentioned she lives in Folkestone."

"Nanny Bell! Of course I do," Jack said, smiling as he took a seat by the fire. "But she would be how old now?"

"I believe in her fifties, m'lord. Shall I send for her?"

Jack nodded. "Yes, we must have a nanny for Johnny, no matter what Kate says. Beside, she will soon be busy here with other matters when she recovers from her indisposition."

He frowned then before he said, "Have you sent for the doctor? I am most concerned for my wife."

"A groom is already on his way to the village, m'lord."

Jack waved his dismissal. "Apprise me at once of the doctor's arrival, and send the countess to me when she can leave my wife."

Jack sat on, close to the comfortable fire, thoroughly enjoying its warmth. For some weeks he had only been cold, or wet, or both. Faintly he could hear the sounds of the staff as they hurried about making the house more comfortable. He closed his eyes for a moment then, trying to picture them doing so. The footmen, of course, were taking the baggage to his rooms and Kate's, or setting the dining-room table, while the maids were busy making beds and stoking fires. Three stories above him, maids would be busy as well, warming the nursery and putting fresh bedding in the old oaken cradle he had slept in himself. He wondered how Master Johnny was faring in the housekeeper's room. Kate had nursed him in the carriage only a short time ago. No doubt Johnny was fast asleep and as good as gold, giving the staff a most erroneous impression of his saintliness.

And down in the kitchen, the cook and her minions were scurrying about preparing a welcoming feast. Jack smiled a little. How long had it been since he had cut into a thick, juicy slab of the roast beef of old England, he wondered, or spread some ripe blue-veined Stilton on a cracker? How very good it was to be home!

He thought of his crew then, hoping they were enjoying some good English food as well. He had left the *Camille* off Folkestone, and hired the local livery carriage to transport his family to Hythe. The crew had been happy to be ensconced in Folkestone's best inn to await his return. Until that time, they would trade watches on the sloop and oversee her needed repairs. It had been a very rough crossing, for they had encountered gale after gale after a few deceptive days of perfect weather when first they had left Bermuda. Even Ben Swan, the hardiest man in the crew, had been troubled with seasickness, and Jack himself, who had never felt nauseated at sea, had known moments of discomfort. He knew Kate had been afflicted too. The only member of the company who had appeared completely happy had been the baby. Secure in the tiny hammock his father had made for him and strung on gimbals, Johnny had slept away the crossing, waking only to nurse and have his diapers changed and to play with his toes, which he had recently discovered and which seemed to fascinate him. Jack frowned, wondering how Kate had managed to keep him in diapers. It had taken so long for anything to dry once they had reached the cold, damp northern waters.

Upstairs, Jack's mother was discovering how. As she helped Kate undress, she saw the remains of the girl's ragged petticoats, and Kate confessed she had taken to ripping them to pieces so her son would be comfortable toward the end of the journey.

Reminded of Johnny again, she grasped the countess's hand before she climbed into the bed that looked so welcoming with its clean sheets newly warmed by a covered pan of coals. But she had to know how Johnny was before she could rest. "Please, ma'am, where is my baby?" she asked. "I have never left him before. I'm . . . I'm worried."

Camille Maxwell patted her hand. "You must not fret about your little son, dear Katherine. He is fine, and no doubt has captured the heart of every female in the house by now. I am most anxious to see my first grandchild and hold him myself! Come, now, climb into bed. The doctor will be here soon. Tell me, how do you feel?"

As Kate sank down on the soft goosedown pillows and sighed, she said, "So very strange! I can't stop shivering, but my head feels as if it were on fire. And I am so dizzy! But no doubt I am only tired. It was a fearsome journey. Sometimes I was afraid none of us would survive it, and I have never been frightened at sea before. Indeed, if it had not been for Jack, we might never have reached

England. He is a superb seaman, and a much-respected captain. He held us all together and gave us hope."

As the countess tucked the covers closer around Kate's shoulders, she said, "I want to hear all about it, and why you and Jack have come home at last, although I do thank the Lord most fervently for that! But now you must sleep until Dr. Lincoln arrives to see you."

Kate smiled at her and closed her eyes, and the countess waited until she knew she had fallen asleep. Then she rang for a maid to sit with her, before she hurried back downstairs to finally greet her beloved son properly. How very glad she was that she had chosen this particular afternoon to come and inspect Hythe and have one of her occasional conferences with the staff!

This time, when she entered the drawing room, she wore a welcoming smile, and she put her arms around her tall son to hug him close to her. Tears sparkled in her eyelashes as she kissed him soundly.

"Dare I hope this means you have forgiven me my treatment of Kate, Mother?" Jack asked, to tease her a little.

She rapped his hand. "It was very bad of you, and you know it! That dear, dear girl! I shall never forget how she wrote to give me news of you. And how brave she is! I'm sure any other woman would have told you the minute she began to feel unwell."

"How is she?" he asked as he went to pour his mother some wine.

"Still feverish, and worried about the baby. I left her sleeping. We must pray the doctor says it is only a minor illness, although I do suspect influenza. But, Jack, we must do something quickly about a wet nurse. No doubt the baby will be crying shortly—you always did!—and Katherine is in no condition to nurse him. Besides, it would not be good for little John, now she is ill."

Jack frowned. "You're right, of course. I wonder if there is anyone available close by."

"I have already asked Mrs. Nearing about that," the countess confessed. "She assured me one of your farmers' wives recently gave birth, and she is a good clean woman. A message has been sent to her. There is no reason she cannot nurse both John and her own baby.

And she will be delighted to do so. It is quite a cachet, you know, to be chosen to nurse the future baronet."

Jack's face darkened even more, and she stared at him, perplexed. "Never tell me you are still troubled by that, Jack?" she asked quietly. "And if you are, why, then, did you come home? I . . . I thought it was because you had accepted it and forgiven me and Alex at last."

Jack stared at her as he considered his answer. His mother looked so much older to him than she had three years ago. Her face was lined now, and thinner, and there were many more strands of white than black in her hair. He felt a guilty pang then as he realized his self-imposed exile had probably had a great deal to do with the acquisition of that white hair, those lines on her fair skin.

"I forgave you a long time ago, Mother, and I always intended to return someday, if only for a visit," he said, rising to pace the room. "However, I was given no choice in the matter."

The countess settled back in her chair and folded her hands as she prepared to listen.

"I did not make an unqualified success of my new life in Bermuda," Jack confessed. "I lost valuable ships to a hurricane, and the revolution that is coming in the colonies took away any chance I might have had of trading and recouping my losses. It was a bitter pill for your son to swallow, madam, to learn he is not infallible."

He shook his head then, a rueful smile on his handsome face.

"Life's reverses do not denote failure, Jack," his mother reminded him. "But it had to be more than that, did it not?"

"However did you know?" he wondered. "Ah, but I never was able to keep anything from you, was I? Yes, I was forced to flee Bermuda. The governor there was about to hang me as a traitor."

"And were you one?" she asked, her voice steady.

"In his eyes, perhaps, but not in my own. What I and a great many other loyal men did was only so the people of Bermuda would not starve in the coming years of war."

Camille Maxwell nodded, her lovely face serene. "I am sorry, son, but I must admit I am glad circumstances were such you did have to return home. I have missed you every day since you left. Alexander has too. It was only after Katherine's first letter arrived that I was able to feel easier. She is a wonderful young woman, so caring and kind! You were very fortunate in your choice of wife."

Jack's expression had brightened as she talked of Kate. "Yes, my bright penny is unique. I pray she will be happy here."

Before the countess could ask him what he meant, the butler knocked and came in to tell them the doctor had just arrived. Both Jack and the countess went up to Kate's room with him, Jack forced to endure a profusion of congratulations on his homecoming, his marriage, and the birth of his heir.

Jack insisted on remaining in the room when Dr. Lincoln examined Kate. He could see for himself now how the fever had taken hold of her, the sheen of perspiration on her face, the slightly vacant look in her eyes. And he knew how ill she must be when she did not even ask him about Johnny. He was very worried then. Perhaps he should summon another physician. Perhaps one from London. He had always thought Dr. Lincoln a competent man, but still . . .

The doctor finished at last. He measured out some powders for the fever, concocted a saline draft, and gave instructions that Lady Reade was to be encouraged to drink as much liquid as possible. She was also to be kept warm, and her rest must not be disturbed. He assured Jack he would return in the morning.

As his mother hurried away to make arrangements for maids to sit with Kate throughout the night, Jack escorted the doctor to the drawing room and poured him a glass of wine. "How bad is she?" he asked gruffly. "Be open with me, if you please!"

"I am not sure as yet, m'lord," the doctor admitted. "She may wake tomorrow morning feeling much better, or she may be a lot worse. You must prepare yourself for the possibility of a long, serious illness. And on no account is she to be allowed to nurse her child! If she has influenza, as I suspect she does, she could infect him as well."

"Influenza!" Jack exclaimed, frowning mightily now.

The doctor nodded, looking grave. "I am afraid we must consider the prospect of it. And m'lady is very thin.

She probably had little defense against the infection. But she is also young and strong. I have every hope of her recovery. And now, m'lord, you must excuse me. I'm expecting a childbirth in the village this evening. And that reminds me, have you arranged for a wet nurse?"

Jack assured him it was being taken care of, and the doctor bowed and took his leave, once again promising to come back to Hythe the first thing in the morning.

Jack went upstairs then, to Kate's room. He knew his mother had sent a message to Willows, telling Alex of his return and begging him to join them for supper as well as bring enough clothes for her so she might stay here and nurse Kate. Until Alex arrived, Jack intended to remain by his wife's side.

The maid who was watching over her curtsied and went to the dressing room. Jack could hear her unpacking Kate's things, but he forgot her as he went up to the bed. Kate was twisting and turning now in her fever, and muttering to herself. Jack bent closer, but he could not make any sense out of her disjointed words. He saw a basin of water and a cloth on the stand near the bed then, and he wet the cloth and wrung it out before be began to bathe her flushed face. The cool cloth seemed to soothe her, and he applied it again and again. At last he took her icy hand in his and caressed it, and as he did so, he prayed harder than he had ever prayed before. Kate must recover, she must! He could not even contemplate a life spent without her. His love, his bright penny, his darling Lady Sprite!

"Beg pardon, your lordship, but may I ask you what I'm to do with these?" the maid's voice from behind him asked timidly. "I found them in her ladyship's things."

Jack turned to see her holding something in her hands, and he beckoned her closer. She held out several shells for his inspection, and a small wooden box. He took it from her and opened it to discover it was packed with cedar shavings. Even without raising it to his face, he could smell its distinctive aroma.

"Put them down on the bedside stand so she can see them when she awakes," he said, his voice constricted.

As the maid obeyed and left him, Jack shook his head. A few small shells and a box of wood shavings were very little to have to remind you of your home, he thought.

For he knew that was why Kate had brought them, to take them out occasionally so she could recall the islands that she loved so well, set like jewels in their aquamarine waters. God's Own Garden—far, far away.

It was a week before Kate was out of danger, and over another before she was strong enough to think of rising. Christmas passed, and the new year came in, and she was not even aware of it. Still, the first time her fever went down slightly, she tried to get up. It had been in the darkest hours just before dawn. Jack had been sitting with her, for he was used to rising to take the early watch at sea, and this way he could spell his mother and the maids. He had dozed off a little in the warm room, and when a small sound woke him, he was startled to see Kate trying to struggle into her gown. As he rose to go to her, she collapsed in an untidy heap on the floor.

He undressed her again and carried her back to bed. She recovered consciousness then, and when she saw his worried face bent over hers, she cried, "Let me up! Jack, I must go to Johnny! He needs me!"

"Hush, Kate," Jack told her, holding her struggling body down with both hands. "Johnny is fine. We've found a wet nurse for him, and he is doing spendidly. And you cannot see him. You are very ill."

"A wet nurse?" she whispered, her gray eyes huge in her thin, drawn face. "Oh, no, not a wet nurse!"

"But of course," Jack told her. "You have influenza, love. And if you went near Johnny, even held him, he might get it too. You do see how dangerous that would be for a little baby, don't you?"

Tensely he waited until he heard her sigh and felt her body relax under his hands.

"I suppose you are right," she said, easy tears sliding down her pale cheeks. "I wouldn't put him in any danger for the world, but . . . but . . ."

Jack bent to kiss the bridge of her nose. "There's a good girl," he said. "Now, let me give you some of this lemonade. You must drink a lot of liquid if you want to get well again soon."

As he propped her up in one arm so she might drink, she said wonderingly, "Lemonade? In England? In the winter?"

"Alex, my . . . stepfather, sent them over from his greenhouse at Willows."

Kate nodded, but her eyes closed again after only a few sips. Jack laid her back down on her pillows and adjusted her covers.

After that, her recovery was slow but steady. Sometimes she would slip back into delirium, thrashing about in the big bed with a strength that surprised her attendants, as she called for Jack and her son. Only Jack was able to soothe her, make her rest. But those spells grew further and further apart, and at last she felt well enough to sit up in bed for short periods, and then to rise and totter to a soft chair near the fire. She was impatient with her weakness, for she had the generally healthy person's disdain for illness of any sort.

At last Dr. Lincoln proclaimed her quite recovered and in no danger of infecting others. Kate had smiled at him then, one of the old smiles that lit her face and turned it radiant. The doctor realized suddenly that the new Lady Reade was a much-better-looking young woman than he had first supposed.

The first place Kate decided to go when she left her room at last was to the nursery. She had risen early that morning, and she had not summoned a maid. As she dressed, her hands still weak and clumsy, she cursed a little, even though she was glad that the maids' constant surveillance was a thing of the past.

Jack had told her the nursery was located on the floor above, and she climbed the stairs eagerly. She could hear a soft murmur of voices behind a closed door, and she hurried to it to knock.

Not waiting for permission, she entered on her knock. She saw the old oaken cradle at once, and another, smaller, less elaborate one nearby, and ignoring the maids who had entered the room, she hurried to her son.

Johnny was sleeping in his favorite position, on his stomach, and he had his thumb in his mouth. Tears came to her eyes and dimmed her vision as she stared down at him, so plump and healthy, and with such good color in his cheeks. She knelt to lift him into her arms.

"Oh, no, m'lady, you must not!" an authoritative voice behind her said. Kate turned, perplexed.

"Is it wise, so soon, ma'am?" an older woman asked.

She was wearing a dressing gown, her gray hair braided in one long twist, but still her superior status was obvious. "You have only recently recovered, ma'am, and we must take no chances with Master John's health."

"I call him Johnny," Kate told her, lifting her chin defiantly. "And who are you?"

As she rose to her feet, Kate looked around. She could see two other women whispering together in a doorway, both still dressed in their bedgowns with shawls over them. She did not wonder at the shawls. The room seemed very cold to her for a nursery, and there was a definite draft swirling around her ankles. She shivered.

"I am Mrs. Bell, the nanny," the older woman said. "I used to be your husband's nanny years ago. You may be sure that your son will be well-cared-for in my charge, m'lady. You must not worry about him."

Kate just stared at her. Her arms ached to hold her baby and suckle him, even though she knew she could never do that again. Her milk had gone during her illness.

"He is sleeping, too," the nanny went on in her quiet voice. "It is not good practice to be waking babies and encouraging them to deviate from their normal routine. I do assure you, m'lady, I shall be happy to bring Master John to you every afternoon at three, as soon as there is no danger of any lingering infection."

"His name is Johnny," Kate repeated, frowning now. Every afternoon at three? But what of all those other hours he was awake? She turned back to her son then, to watch him sucking his thumb in his sleep. He had never done that before. Was he getting enough milk?

Nanny Bell came to lead her away. "You should go back to bed now, m'lady," she said. "You do not look well, and it is obvious you are still weak. Susan, escort m'lady back to her rooms, lest she fall."

Kate let herself be taken away, but even after the maid had curtsied and left her, she was thinking hard. This situation was intolerable! Johnny was *her* baby, and she knew what was best for him. She resolved to speak to Jack about it as soon as she could. She had to be able to see Johnny whenever she liked; she wanted to have his cradle next to her bed, where it had always been; she longed to pick him up and cuddle him, and his new "normal" routine be damned!

Countess Granbourne had gone back to her own home, now that Kate was out of danger, so Kate could not talk to her about this. Besides, she was hesitant to do so. Jack's mother was such a lovely yet grand lady, as formal as she was kind, and Kate did not feel easy with her as yet. But the countess had promised to come and visit often, and bring her daughters Constance and Grace with her when she did so. She had told Kate how eager they were to meet their new half-sister-in-law, and how they could not wait to see the baby and play with him. Kate reminded herself she must be sure they came only at three in the afternoon—the royal visiting hour!

Kate mentioned her dilemma to Jack later at her first breakfast belowstairs, but she thought he seemed almost indifferent to her plight. He was much involved in other matters now—problems to do with the estate, as well as the finding of a ship for the Bermudian crew to return home on. And he planned a trip to London in the near future, now that she was well again. His agent had written, pleading for his attendance there.

"But I don't see the problem, love," he said from his end of the breakfast table. In his mother's old place opposite, Kate felt a mile away from him.

"Of course you can go to the nursery anytime you like. But Nanny Bell is in charge of Johnny now. And after all, she didn't do so badly with me, now, did she?" he teased, his unusual eyes twinkling. Kate was not to be diverted.

"But why can't Johnny sleep in my room, as he has always done?" she persisted. "I . . . I miss him so! And it should be his mother who goes to him when he calls, not a . . . a nanny or a maid!"

Jack looked confused. "But that's how it's always done here," he said vaguely. "And do consider, love, how busy you will be, managing the house now. You will not have time to be at Johnny's beck and call. And soon we will be having visitors, no doubt, and you will be meeting all kinds of new people. I know how anxious everyone is to make your acquaintance. Only your illness has kept the local gentry away."

Kate would still have protested, but he wiped his mouth on his napkin then and rose.

"I must be off. One of my farmers is involved in a

boundary dispute with his neighbor. Ecod, Kate! Sometimes I wonder how they all muddled through without me these past three years."

He came to draw her to her feet then and kiss her. "Don't fret, love," he whispered. "Just get well and strong again for me, please!"

As he walked to the door, he said over his shoulder, "I think it would be a good idea for you to see Mrs. Nearing today. As housekeeper, she has been waiting for you to give her direction—tell her how you wish things done now. And then there are the menus to approve, the housework to oversee. And do ask either Mrs. Nearing or Greyson to give you a tour of the house if you feel up to it."

He was gone then, closing the breakfast-room door behind him.

Kate sat back down at the table. Her coffee grew cold, and her breakfast was forgotten. This is too much! she thought, crumbling a muffin absentmindedly. I cannot bear it!

Then she grimaced. She was reminded how often she had cried those same words before. She couldn't *bear* to be separated from Jack, she couldn't *bear* to leave Keza, she couldn't *bear* her father's coldness and distrust of her husband. But she had borne all those things, and now she knew she must learn how to bear this strange new life as well.

But in the days that followed, she was more often miserable than not. She had gone to the nursery unbidden only once, for when she had arrived, the wet nurse had been suckling Johnny, and it had been all she could do not to tear him from her arms. The wet nurse was a plump girl, and she had smiled shyly at Kate, but still, Kate had had to turn away.

It was then that she noticed the old rocking horse in one corner, and to avoid the sight of her baby at another woman's breast, she had gone to inspect it. The once bright paint was faded and chipped, and it was missing one eye, as well as most of its mane and tail.

"That was Sir John's old rocking horse," Nanny Bell told her with a reminiscent little smile. "How he loved his Peter Pony! He had it brought down from the attics for his son."

"Johnny will not be able to ride it for a long time," Kate remarked.

Nanny Bell nodded. "No, indeed, but Sir John insisted we have it painted and refurbished as soon as possible. As you can see, m'lady, he pulled out most of the horse-hair when he was a little boy. One of the estate carpenters is going to fix it just like new."

Before she went away, Kate reached down to caress the painted saddle, trying to picture Jack rocking away, clutching the mane in both hands, a pleased grin on his little boy's face. She nodded slightly to Mrs. Bell and the others as she took her leave. She was an interloper here, and it made her very uncomfortable when they all curtsied to her. She had not been able to get used to that, nor to the way they called her "m'lady." She was Kate, Mrs. Jack Reade; she was not "m'lady" anybody!

The servants here were so different from the slaves at home, with their beaming smiles and slow, smooth, informal speech. Oh, what she wouldn't give to hear Keza call her "Miz Kate, honey" right now! Keza, dressed in her old calico gown with a calico kerchief knotted on her head! But here Kate was surrounded by men in livery, or, in the case of the butler, somber black, and the maids wore dark dresses with aprons and caps so stiff with starch they crackled. And they were so cold and unfriendly! Hardly a smile from any of them! They didn't even hum or sing as they went about their chores.

As for the housekeeper, Kate had tried to avoid her. She felt she could hardly admit she didn't know the first thing about running a grand house this size. Instead, she had asked Mrs. Nearing to continue as she had always done, and to approve the menus as well, for she had no intention of interfering. She thought the housekeeper had looked startled even as she agreed, and Kate was sure she was despising her for her ineptitude.

She couldn't even ask Lady Granbourne for help. For what did they have in common, besides Jack? Why, she would be willing to wager anything you liked that Camille Maxwell had never cursed in her life! And when she had seen Jack with his little sisters, seen how easy he was with that forbidding-looking earl, Alexander Maxwell, she had felt very much the outsider.

But then, she did not feel close to Jack anymore. He

was so busy with his own concerns, and he seldom seemed
to have time for her. And they had separate bedrooms
too. Of course, there was a connecting door, but even
now that she was well again, Jack never stayed beside
her. How she missed him! How she missed waking up
and cuddling next to his warm bare back, or rolling
sleepily into his arms to doze for a few more minutes,
breathing deeply of the distinctive scent of his skin, their
baby sleeping peacefully in his cradle nearby.

Kate shivered then. The morning-room fire seemed
very meager. Perhaps it would be warmer in the library.

As she crossed the hall, the footmen bowed in unison,
and the butler hastened to open the door for her. Even
as she nodded her thanks to him, she wanted to scream
that she wasn't helpless.

She went to stand beside the fire, as close as she could
get without singeing her skirts. It was another bitter day.
The frost still glistened in icy patches on the shaded
sections of the lawn, and in the cold wind, the branches
of a tree just outside one of the leaded windows tapped
brittle fingers on the panes. Kate rubbed her arms and
pulled her shawl closer to her breast. If she had not been
so concerned about what the servants would think, she
would have gone back to bed, pulled the covers over her
head, and closed her eyes so she could pretend she was
home again. Bermuda was so very far away now.

24

JACK Reade went up to town the following week. He
had not planned to be away for long, but his business
with his agent, the people he wanted to see, and some
things he intended to do took more time than he had
thought they would. Now, as he rode back to Hythe in
his comfortable carriage, he was at peace with himself at
long last. And he had used the time for more than just
business. In assorted boxes and bundles on the seat opposite him, he had many surprises for Kate, and toys for

the baby as well. In a way, he wanted to make up for the quiet Christmas they had all spent, with the house so unnaturally somber because of Kate's illness.

He had brought one of her old gowns to London with him, so he could purchase new ones. And he had had some petticoats and shifts made up for her in soft, fine wool. He had noted how she hugged the fireside, how she shivered sometimes passing through the halls.

There were cozy wool shawls as well, and warm stockings, even a new cloak. He had purchased several new sets of clothes for himself as well. He had not intended to spend so much money, but he had justified it by telling himself that since they were Sir John and Lady Reade here, they must dress the part. And Kate's few gowns were old and outdated. He hoped she would approve his choices.

There was one he especially admired. A formal gown, it was made of copper-colored taffeta, the exact shade of her hair, in a new style the dressmaker had called a robe *à la française*. It had a low square neckline and a tight bodice, and elbow sleeves that ended in flounces of creamy lace. Meant to be worn over large hoops, it opened in front over a matching lacy petticoat. He could hardly wait to see Kate in it, some evening soon.

Since Willows was on his way, he had decided he would stop there first. He had bought new dolls for Constance and Grace, and he was anxious to see his mother and Alex.

The hall he entered was full of baggage. The butler explained that the earl and his family were shortly to leave for Styne. Jack's brows rose at that, and when he learned the earl was alone in the library, he asked the butler to wait half an hour before informing his mother of his arrival. There were things he wanted to discuss with Alex first.

He found his father sitting in a chair by the fire, reading.

"Now, what is this, sir?" he asked as he came forward to bow. "Off to Styne, are you, when I have just returned?"

Alexander grasped his son's shoulders before he indicated the chair opposite. "We always intended to spend Christmas there, Jack," he said. "We only delayed because of your wife's illness, and, of course, so we might enjoy your company after your long absence."

"Can't I persuade you to enjoy it longer, sir?" Jack asked. "I shall miss you all when you are gone."

The earl shook his head. "It would not be wise," he said in a somber voice. At Jack's questioning look, he explained, "I know you will be entertaining soon, to introduce your bride to the local gentry. And you and I do appear very similar, especially since your experiences in the colonies have hardened you, aged you slightly. No, better I be far, far away. No one can remark a resemblance if there is no resemblance to remark. I would do nothing to harm you, Jack, or your Kate, or my . . . grandson.

"You had a successful trip to town?" he asked next in the little silence that fell between them then.

"Very successful. There were the usual problems to do with the estates, the monies that had accrued from them. Ecod, I thought Mr. Botts would never have done," Jack told him. "But I'd several other purposes there as well, the most frivolous being to surprise Kate with some new gowns."

"Tell me, is she content here?" the earl asked. "I have often wondered."

Jack frowned a little. "No, I do not think she is. But the decision I made in London will soon have her feeling much better. You see, I have decided to leave England permanently. I intend to sail to the colony of South Carolina in the spring, make our home there."

"So, it is true what Camille told me. You haven't fully accepted your position as Sir John Reade, have you?"

Jack stared at his father. "I do not choose the colonies for that reason, sir," he said quietly. "However, I admit I am ever mindful I live a lie here."

Alexander made an impatient gesture. "I hope I can change your mind. Hear me out, if you please.

"I gather you have not seen any of your Reade cousins since your return to England," he went on after Jack had nodded his agreement. "If you had, you would understand immediately why Sir John was so anxious for *you* to be his heir. Robert Reade's sons are very like him, just as greedy and sly. I shudder to think that any of them might get his hands on Hythe, plundering it of its wealth, and with no concern for the faithful people who serve it. Sir John knew this. Besides loving your mother as he did, he took the only step he knew that would keep the other family members from ruining his heritage. And now you would shame his name, and him as well, by denying him what he wanted and planned for all along? It is most perverse of you, Jack! And what of your own son? The next baronet? Think you to deny him that heritage as well?"

"Johnny must decide about that when he is a man," Jack said calmly. "I intend to tell him everything when he is older, so he will understand the choices he has."

"No, you must never do that!" the earl exclaimed in a harsh voice. "You must *never* tell him the truth! Why burden him with everything you have suffered? He is Sir John's grandson in the eyes of the law—his legal heir. Let him accept that, embrace it, without any dark shadows from the past to color his future. Isn't it bad enough that you and I have had to live with the pain those shadows bring? At least let your Johnny escape our fate! And no one knows what the future may bring. It may be that someday Johnny will decide to return to Hythe, make his own life here.

"No, do not speak! Let me tell you something, and I beg you heed me well. You are not the first imposter foisted on an unsuspecting nobility, nor will you be the last. There will always be wives who present their husbands with love children, indeed, some who do so with their impotent husbands' blessings, lest the titles they hold dear should die out. And the king can create new nobles, or banish others by whim. Our titles are not graven in stone, ordained from the Almighty himself, although some peers act as if they were.

"Sometimes I think that is why the nobility has remained so strong and vital—that it is the infusion of new blood that keeps us all from producing drooling idiots. For just consider the inbreeding that goes on even now. There are only so many of the peerage in England, and most of them meet somewhere on their family trees. Even my first wife and I were distantly related."

He saw that Jack looked only mildly interested, and he continued, "Ecod, 'tis not only perverse of you, this determination of yours to give up Hythe, it is disobedient as well. For in doing so, you go against all of Sir John's express wishes. Fine thanks for a man who loved you and cared for you, gave you his own name."

The earl's voice had grown harsher and colder as he spoke, and his face wore a look of deep disgust. Jack was sorry for it and he made himself say calmly, "Yes, I understand, sir. But I am a man grown now, and I shall make my own choices. And I do not choose to be Sir John Reade. I've quite another goal in mind."

Alexander shrugged. "Your scruples do you honor, no doubt, as misguided as they are in this particular case. But if I can live with what happened, the evil my father did that kept me from marrying Camille and acknowledging you as my son, why can't you? For in a fairer world, you would have been the next Earl of Granbourne, and your son—my *grandson*, I remind you, dear boy—its ninth earl. If *I* have been able to accept that that can never be, why do you demur at taking a much lesser title? You would have been a viscount now, living at Styne and waiting to come into your richer inheritance. You are noble, Jack, as is John Gregory after you. And since you have been cheated of being an earl, why should you not embrace a baronetcy, as that good man, the former lord, wanted?"

He saw Jack's intent look, and knew he had not considered the situation in that light before. He wondered if it would be enough to keep him here.

"Let me tell you something I have never told another soul, my son," the earl said quietly, frowning again. "When your mother and I were finally married, I prayed we would never have another child. I wanted no one to replace you, even if I could not acknowledge you. I wanted that even more than I wanted to deny my dead father the most important thing in the world to him— Granbourne's next earl. When Camille found herself with child, I tried to hide my disappointment from her. But then Constance was born, and Grace, and I knew God was good. By giving us only daughters, he himself saw to my father's punishment. And so now you can remain, in my heart and mind, my son and rightful heir, even though the earldom will cease to exist at my death. A fitting ending to our story, don't you think?"

When Jack made no reply, the earl said in a rallying

voice, "Come, Jack! Put this fantasy of emigrating away, and accept your rightful place as baronet at last! For when you do, the wickedness of my father will be over. Never again can that evil pride that drove him touch you, or me, or anyone we love. I beg you to reconsider."

As Jack sat deep in thought, Alexander Maxwell rose to go to the decanter on a table near the wall. "Join me in a glass of wine, Jack," he said as he poured them out. "And perhaps soon you will be able to lift a glass to your son, toast him as the next baronet of Hythe. I shall pray you will do so."

Jack took the glass and sipped before he said, "And now, sir, as I listened to you, I must ask you to give me a hearing as well. Perhaps when I tell you what is in my heart and mind, you will understand why I have chosen the course I have, and why I will not, *cannot*, deviate from it."

The earl looked disappointed, but he only settled back in his chair and nodded.

"If you remember, when I first learned I was a bastard, I was distraught," Jack began. "And I was angry—very angry at you and at my mother. But even after I learned from your letters that what had happened was not your fault, I could not make myself live a lie. And so I went to Bermuda to find my own way there as plain Jack Reade."

His little laugh was rueful, and he shook his head. "You can have no conception of how hard it was for *me* to play the commoner. I think I learned a dozen humbling lessons every day. For, being brought up to privilege as I had been had not prepared me for taking a lesser role; becoming no more, no less, than any other man. Because, you see, in my mind's eye I was still Sir John Reade, the baronet."

He spread his hands and shrugged before he went on, "But I learned those lessons, Father, and I learned them well. And I learned something else too. And that was that I could depend on myself to see to my future without help from others, or an exalted background. Of course, I did not have an easy time of it. I have told you of my reverses. Sometimes it seemed to me as if fate, not content with dealing me one bitter blow, was determined to pummel me with more and more disaster, as if to test my breaking point.

"That kind of thinking was weak, of course. I do no believe in fate. A man makes his own way, for better o worse, and the strong ones manage, no matter how ad verse the prevailing winds."

He took another sip of his wine then. The earl waite patiently for him to continue, impressed in spite of him self by his calm maturity, his reasoned speech. This wa not a quick decision Jack had come to, he knew. No instead it was the result of hours of deliberation, and h could only respect it, much as he regretted it.

"Some good came out of it all; it was not all bad,' Jack said. "I found Kate and married her, and she brough love into my life again. And I found happiness in othe ways too, building my ships, sailing and trading. Hardly gentleman's occupations, were they? But they brough me contentment.

"And in my travels I saw a great deal of the colonie and all the New World. And what I saw appealed to me It was so different from England, so fresh and unfet tered, so challenging.

"Still, I could not take the final step of embracing it. told myself I was loyal still, no matter how empathetic felt toward others' struggles to live free. And when I wa forced to leave Bermuda, I decided I had to come hom before I made my final choice. For I knew I had to make that choice, for England or the colonies, sooner or later."

One of Jack's hands caressed his jaw then as he stare into the fire, brooding deep. Alexander waited.

"At first it was good to be home, I'll not deny that. I spite of my worries for Kate's health, I reveled in it, and in being reunited with my mother, and you, sir, and my little sisters. And I saw how dear Hythe was to me Indeed, for the first time I was able to value it as should, and not just take it for granted.

"I went up to London for a number of reasons. One of course, was to see my agent, as I have told you. But also sought out my old friends, talked to them, and listened. And I was shocked to discover we had little in common anymore. Even Sir Dudley seemed superficia to me, with his endless gossip of the *ton,* his preoccupa tion with his wagers and horses, and the set of his coats.

"I also approached many other members of Parlia ment, to question them about the government's plans fo the colonies. And from one and all, I heard the same old story. The colonies must conform. They must pay any taxes levied on them without question. They must be brought into line. They would not have a voice."

Jack sighed in exasperation then, and ran an impatient hand over his hair. "I tried to tell them their errors, tried to explain the colonists' viewpoints, and why they felt so strongly. And desperately I tried to convince all those who would give me ear that revolution was coming. They did not heed me. Instead, they scoffed at me. Even those few who agreed that war was probably inevitable, were convinced that England would prevail.

"Perhaps she will. She has the might, and a sizable advantage in soldiers and ships. But it came to me then, that if war did come, I did not care to be here to see it from afar. That although I loved England, and my boyhood home here, I had somehow outgrown them. Does that sound arrogant to you, sir? I pray not, for it is the truth!

"You see, I don't want to be a baronet. I don't want to spend my days overseeing my farmers and counting up my profits. I don't want to take my seat in Parliament or travel to town for the Season."

"But if you were to do so, you might be able to bring about a change in policy," the earl remarked, speaking for the first time.

Jack shook his head. "One voice? And a young one at that, among so many graybeards who cannot, or will not, see beyond the end of their noses? I think not, sir. Besides, I would rather have a hand in making history, not just preserving the past."

"Ah, I perceive you are still an adventurer," the earl remarked as he set his empty glass down on the table beside him.

"Do you think that is all I am, sir?" Jack asked quietly.

The earl shook his head. "No, I know there is much more to you, my son. I can tell you did not come to this decision without a great deal of reasoned thought. And much as I regret it, I must accept it. But what of your own son? It seems to me you are taking his heritage—his future—away from him for your own selfish desires."

Jack rose then to lean against the mantel. "I am not so careless. As soon as I change my allegiance, I shall name

Johnny baronet. I rely on you to keep that title safe for him, sir. And I shall see that Johnny is educated for the role, sent to Eton when it's time. Then, when he is a man grown, he shall have the option of deciding which life he wants to live—as an English lord or as a plain American.

"But for now, as the current baronet, I intend to use the monies that have accumulated over these past three years at Hythe to give me a new beginning."

Alexander strove to keep his voice even over the ache in his heart as he asked, "When do you plan to leave?"

"Not until spring. There is much to do here, much to arrange. And I would not put Kate and the baby to the rigors of another winter crossing. No, we'll stay here til May at least. I've written to Kate's brother Matthew Hathaway and told him my plans. He will see we have a home waiting in Charles Town when we arrive, and he'll help me get started. You'd like him, sir. He is a true gentleman, and my friend."

"But what of the war you say is coming?" Alexander asked. "Won't it be dangerous to travel?"

"I do not believe war is imminent, not yet. From my estimates, I would wager it might even be another year before independence is declared. You see, many of the colonists strive even now to resolve the matter without bloodshed. But war will come, and when it does, I will take my part in it without question. I not only plan to live in America, I plan to give that new country my loyalty."

Alexander stared at his dear son, so tall and strong and handsome—so invincible. The crucible of fire he had gone through to bring him to this point had tempered him well. With all his heart, Alexander wished he would remain in England, but he was forced to accept Jack's choice. His son was a man now.

He heard his daughters' excited voices coming closer, and he rose and said, "Plan to spend a month with us at Styne before you go, won't you? You can sail for America just as easily from Plymouth as you can from Folkestone. Why, you might even say we are on your way! And it would ease your mother's mind, before losing you again."

Jack went to him then and hugged him close. "I shall, sir," he said, his voice constricted. "Why is it, whenever you make a choice, there is some pain attached? This decision of mine does give me pain, as well as satisfaction, for I will miss you all, more than I can say."

The little girls danced into the library then, closely followed by the countess, and it was not very long before they had all learned of the Reade family's coming visit to Styne.

Jack talked quietly with Alex and his mother as Constance and Grace sat at their feet playing with their new dolls. When he rose to leave at last, Jack kissed his mother tenderly, exchanged wordless hugs with Alexander, and picked the little girls up, one by one, for a final embrace.

Last, Grace took his face between her two little hands to stare deep into his eyes. Once again Jack was reminded what a solemn mite she was, so different from her more mercurial sister.

"You *won't* go away, ever again!" she ordered in her gruff little voice. "I *wanted* you, Jack, but you weren't here! Promise me you won't leave me again."

"I cannot promise you that, m'lady," Jack told her as he kissed the tip of her nose. "But know I shall expect you and Constance to come and visit me someday, far, far across the sea. You will like South Carolina, it is so warm and beautiful. And I shall teach you how to swim, and sail the *Grace*, the little sloop I named for you."

"That sounds nice, but still, I'd rather you didn't go back there at all," Grace told him, looking fierce.

The earl shook his head. "It is rude to be so persistent, lovey," he said as he took her into his own arms.

"Don't care! Want Jack *here*!" his unrepentant daughter insisted.

"Shall you name a boat for me someday, Jack?" Constance asked eagerly. "Shall you? I should like that, if she is a pretty one!"

He assured her he would do so, before he wished them all a safe journey.

"My dearest love to Katherine, Jack," his mother reminded him. "Take good care of her now, you hear? And I will be counting the days till spring, and your visit."

Jack kissed her again, and he blew them all a kiss as he hurried out to his coach.

The little girls hurried away to show their nanny their

new dolls, but the earl and countess remained at the
door, watching Jack's coach disappear down the drive.

Alexander glanced at his wife. She wore a pensive air
but she did not look as sad as he had expected, after
hearing of Jack's coming defection to the colonies.

She looked up at him then and smiled a little, and he
caught up her hand and kissed it. "You are all right
Camille?" he asked.

She nodded. "Yes, my dear. You were afraid I would
be distraught at losing Jack again, were you not? Oh
Alexander! I lost him the minute he married dear Katherine! It was ever thus."

When Jack entered the hall at Hythe, he gave the
butler instructions to have all the packages he had brought
taken up to his rooms.

"And where is my wife?" he asked, handing his cloak
and tricorne to a footman as he looked around.

"Lady Reade is receiving company this afternoon
m'lord," Greyson told him. "Lady Whitaker and Miss
Penelope Whitaker have called, and Miss Clorinda Reade
as well."

Jack's brows rose. "Indeed? Then I shall join them
They are in the drawing room?"

As he strode toward that door, he was thinking hard
Alexander had told him earlier that it was not only possible but also highly probable that his cousin Clorinda had
been the one who had written the poisonous letter that
had sent him fleeing from England; how the Reades had
come to Willows with a solicitor to confront him. And
yet Clorinda was here today? How very arrogant she
was!

As he entered the room, the ladies gathered around a
tea tray all turned.

"Here I am at last, Kate!" Jack said with a wide grin as
he strode to her side. He noted how pale she was, even
how distressed she seemed, and he wondered what had
been going on.

Kate tried to return his smile, but when he drew her to
her feet to kiss her lightly, he could feel her trembling.
'Fore gad, if Clorinda had upset her in any way, he
would see she paid for it!

Reminded of the guests then, he turned to them, still

holding Kate in his arm. "Lady Whitaker, how very nice to see you," he said, bowing a little. "And is this really little Penelope? My word, child, how changed you are!"

The young lady dimpled up at him, using her long lashes as expertly as the most hardened flirt. Jack was amused. Penelope Whitaker had been only thirteen when he had sailed away—a shy, gangling girl afflicted with a stammer and a spotty complexion. How could a short three years have turned her into such a raving beauty, all peaches and cream and big brown eyes and shining gold ringlets? he wondered. It was truly a miracle.

He glanced next to his cousin, and his eyes widened. Clorinda Reade had become enormously fat in that same time, so obese that he worried about the gilt chair she was currently overflowing. Her eyes had nearly disappeared in folds of fat, but he could see how she glared at him, note the petulant set of her little mouth. She was dressed in deepest black mourning, although he had learned that her mother, Martha Reade, had passed away shortly after he had left England.

"Sincere condolences on the loss of your mother, Clorinda," he said. "Kindly extend them to your father as well."

Lady Whitaker tittered. "Prithee, but didn't you know, m'lord?" she asked in her plummy voice. "Mr. Reade remarried two years ago. La, 'twas on the very anniversary of the day his first wife died, was it not, Miss Reade?"

Jack looked at Clorinda again. She was sniffing, almost as if someone had slipped a rotten fish onto the mounded plate of cream puffs she held. "Yes," she said in her shrill voice. "But at least *he* waited for a year to pass, unlike some others I could name!"

"Is it really true his new wife is even younger than you are, Miss Reade?" Penelope Whitaker asked, her brown eyes alight at the very thought of such a ridiculous thing.

Clorinda did not deign to answer. Instead, she only sniffed again as she picked up another cream puff.

As Jack took the seat on the sofa next to his wife, Clorinda Reade brooded over the horrid turn of fate she had had to endure. For not only had she lost her sainted mother so suddenly, she had been forced to watch her father make a complete fool of himself over a younger woman. One, moreover, whom Clorinda did not consider outstanding in any way. Miss Eleanor Egglesford had had no great degree of either beauty or wit, and she was of spare build. The only attribute she could claim was that she was an heiress, although one who had been well past her last prayers. And it was rumored that her father had made his fortune in *trade*. A twenty-six-year-old spinster! How *could* Papa? she thought as she devoured her cream puff. And the new Mrs. Reade had made it very clear that she did not care for her new stepdaughter, and would be delighted to see the back of her. It was too much!

Seeing that his cousin was totally involved in eating, and not caring in the slightest to watch her at it, Jack turned his attentions to the other guests. "How very good it was for you to call on Kate in my absence, m'lady," he said.

"We were most anxious to meet the paragon who could tempt *you* to matrimony, m'lord," Lady Whitaker told him.

Her eyes wandered over Kate's slender body and drawn face then, as if in shocked disbelief. Lady Whitaker had been enjoying herself very much this afternoon. She had no sooner entered the drawing room than she had taken this provincial little nobody's measure, and she had spent the last twenty minutes putting her firmly in her place. M'lady had long had plans for nuptials between her daughter and the baronet, and her disappointment that he had married while in the colonies made her cruel. I hope he regrets what he has missed! she thought viciously as she compared her daughter's full, high bosom and tiny waist, her lovely face and smart London gown, to the unprepossessing Lady Reade's appearance in her dowdy clothes.

Jack did not appear to be doing so. As he accepted a cup of tea from his wife, he smiled tenderly at her. "Ah, yes, my Kate is a paragon indeed, and I the luckiest of men," he said, his voice caressing. "But, my love, you do not appear to be feeling well this afternoon. I miss your usual vivacity. Have you been overdoing things in my absence?"

Not waiting for her reply, he remarked, "Kate was very ill when we first arrived home, with a severe case of influenza. She has not as yet fully regained her strength."

"Yes, you're right. I am not feeling well," Kate told him. It was the first time she had spoken since he had come in, and he noticed how constrained she sounded.

He also saw the little pleading in her gray eyes, and he rose at once to help her to her feet. "Then off you go, love! I am sure our guests will excuse you. Do go and rest. I shall entertain the ladies."

The guests all murmured most insincere wishes for the return of Lady Reade's good health as Kate curtsied to them. Jack insisted on taking her to the door himself, squeezing her arm in reassurance as he did so.

As he rejoined his guests, he said, "I do so hope Kate will be more herself in a few days' time. I've a mind to give an evening reception to introduce her to the neighborhood."

"But what fun!" Penelope Whitaker exclaimed. "The country can be so *boring* this time of year."

"Of course I will send you invitations. Shall we say for sometime early next week, if Kate is feeling up to it?" Jack asked. Then he turned to his cousin and said, "Do try the cake, Clorinda. It appears to have escaped your notice. Tell me, do you still reside with your father?"

Clorinda bristled. "Of course I do!" she said. "Where else would I live? It is my home!"

"I only asked because I thought you might have removed to one of your brothers' establishments," Jack said mildly. "Newlyweds, of *any* age, being what they are . . ."

Clorinda's face reddened, and she sputtered into her tea. Jack knew as surely as if she had admitted it aloud that her new stepmother had been busy trying to accomplish just that removal. But he was also very sure none of dear Clorinda's brothers or their wives had been at all anxious to house her.

"We must ask your father and his bride to join us, and the other members of the family as well," Jack said. "We shall be quite the party!"

Penelope Whitaker's eyes were dancing. "I am sure we will all enjoy it tremendously, m'lord," she said. "And now I have someplace to wear the beautiful new gown I received for Christmas. I vow you will stare when you see it! My very first grown-up gown!"

Lady Whitaker patted her daughter's hand. "No doubt

Lady Reade will also be dressed most becomingly, my dear. That is, unless she has only provincial garments with her, m'lord? Somehow I received the impression that your wife was not interested in fashions."

"Kate?" Jack asked, sounding amazed. "Ah, but I tell no secrets! No, I shall leave that for you to discover the evening of the party, ma'am. But I think I can promise you will not be . . . er . . . disappointed. Or is that the word I should use?"

Lady Whitaker smiled thinly at him, her brown eyes hard. Tiring of the game they were all playing, Jack said, "And now you must excuse me. I am anxious to make sure Kate is all right. Besides, it looks remarkably like snow, and I would not like you to have any difficulty getting home. I noticed several flakes falling on my way here from Willows."

"You have been to Willows?" Clorinda asked, shocked. "Prithee do not tell me the Earl and Countess of Granbourne are to attend your party! I very much fear none of the Reades will care to be present in *that* case."

"But of course they would be, if they were going to be here," Jack said, smiling to hide his anger. "However, they are even now preparing to return to their estate in Devon, and so must miss the occasion. I am sorry they are going, for it has been so good to see my beloved mother and my dear stepfather again after my long absence."

He rose then and bowed. "Ladies? May I see you to the door?"

The guests gathered their gloves and reticules, and rose. As Jack watched his cousin struggle to her feet, he had to hide a shudder. Now that she was standing, Clorinda Reade looked even more obese, and in her mourning she reminded him of a fat black spider. He rather thought the coming party would be the last *any* of the Reades would be invited to attend at Hythe, at least while he was here.

As soon as his guests were safely on their way, Jack ran up the stairs two at a time.

He went first to his own rooms to gather up all the boxes and parcels that contained his gifts for his wife. Then, with a smile on his face, he opened the connecting door between their bedrooms.

His mouth fell open in surprise when he saw Kate lying facedown on her big four poster, sobbing. He dropped everything he carried then, and hurried to her side.

"Kate! What is it? Why do you weep so?" he asked as he sat down and gathered her in his arms.

She only shook her head, her eyes streaming. Jack reached into his pocket for his handkerchief. "Damn those women!" he muttered. "How dare they upset you?"

All his efforts to wipe her eyes could not stem the flood of tears, and he dropped the handkerchief. Instead, he drew her close to his chest and cradled her head, rocking her gently in his arms. "Ssh, love, ssh," he whispered. "Tell me what is troubling you."

Kate made a valiant effort to control herself, and at last her sobs died away to little hiccups. Jack wiped her eyes and face again, and ordered her to blow her nose.

After she had done so, he said quietly, "Tell me."

Kate drew away from him a little, but she did not turn aside. Instead, her gray eyes regarded him steadily. "Yes, the guests did upset me, but then, I suppose I should not have been surprised at that. Lady Whitaker treated me like some sort of crude colonist because I was born in Bermuda. Well, it is no more than what I am, and I am not ashamed of it! And even your mother, as kind and loving as she is, doesn't understand me. And she insists on calling me 'Katherine,' just as my Aunt Mary did. I *hate* my Aunt Mary!"

When Jack would have spoken, she raised a trembling hand. "No, please let me finish. Ever since we arrived here, I have seen how ill-suited I am to be your wife. I don't fit at Hythe, Jack! And I . . . I dislike it here so! I do thank you for pretending that you are content with me, even that you love me, but I can see it is only an act, since there is nothing else you can do.

"I never should have married you. And admit it, you married me only because you *had* to, forced as a gentleman to rescue me from folly of my own making, and your bad luck. And since then, I have done nothing but make your life a misery. Keeping you tied to Bermuda, stowing away on your ship and shaming you before your crew, having a child you never wanted, embroiling you in my family problems—dammit, it is too much! And now I am here at Hythe, and I continue to do nothing but shame

you. Your friends scoff at me, and the servants despise
me, as well they should. I know nothing about running a
house this size in this climate. And I don't know how to
deal with them, so stiff and cold and forbidding and
disapproving as they are!

"And you don't need me anymore. You won't even
sleep in my bed! As for Johnny, well, he doesn't need me
either."

Tears welled up in her gray eyes then, and she dashed
them away angrily. "Johnny is perfectly happy with his
proper English nanny and her rigid routine for him here,
a substitute mother to nurse him, and maids to change
his diapers and wash him. I am . . . I am nothing more to
him than I am to you, not anymore."

Her voice died away and she took a deep breath. "I
would like to go home," she said with quiet dignity.
"You will not miss me."

"Have you quite finished?" Jack asked politely.

Not fooled, Kate paled. Now she saw that his taut
mouth was bracketed by white lines, and those turquoise
eyes of his were blazing. Startled, she drew back.

"Not miss you?" he asked. "Why, madam, I cannot
live without you! And as for your going home, I must
insist you wait till spring. You see, we are all leaving England then. For good."

Kate's eyes were shining. "We are? But why, Jack?
Hythe is your home!"

"It *was* my home," he corrected her. "But since I have
returned, I have seen it can never be that again. It has
nothing to do with the title. I want to live in the colonies,
Kate."

"Not Bermuda?" she whispered. "But when the theft
of the gunpowder is forgotten, we can go back again."

Jack shook his head. "No. I am sorry, for I know how
much you love it there, but I've a mind to settle in South
Carolina, near your brother. Bermuda is lovely, but it
holds no prospects for me. In the colonies, I will have the
chance to get ahead, create a future for Johnny, if that is
where he decides to stay someday. I told Alex what I was
planning just a little while ago, and I promised him I
would let Johnny himself choose between being an English lord and an American when he is old enough.

"I could see Alex did not understand me. To him, the

peerage, heirs, inheritance, are all. Well, he is older. And he has never known any other way of life. Certainly he has never seen the opportunities the colonies offer.

"But it's different for me. I find everything here so staid and predictable. And nothing changes. My farmers will still be arguing about a boundary line, or rights of way, years from now. And those years will pass exactly the same way. Spring planting, autumn harvest. The all-important London Season. But London does not please me anymore. The dirt of it, the noise, even the *smell*! It reminds me of a decaying carcass that no one has had the decency to bury.

"Can you understand my disillusionment, Kate? I've lived so long, dreaming of home, and now that I'm here, I find it's not 'home' at all. It's where I used to live when I was a child."

He smiled a little then. "Not that the colonies are Eden, you understand. Bermuda comes closest to that, but even there, there is not one, but many snakes in the garden."

"Bermuda doesn't have any snakes!" Kate protested.

"I was speaking metaphorically, my dear," he told her.

Kate was not interested in debating the issue. "Oh, do we have to wait till spring?" she asked eagerly. "Prithee, say we can go tomorrow. I can be ready! And after all, you can't want me to stay here all that time, mortifying you before your friends and your servants."

"Mortifying me?" he asked in a wondering voice. "You could never do that! I do not know where you got this impression that the servants were sneering at you. It is completely erroneous. Perhaps what you took for disdain, madam, was in fact awe. Yes, you stare, but their admiration for your courage is unbounded. I heard two of the maids talking a while ago about how noble you were to endure a life alone while I was off on my trading voyages, how fearless you had been giving birth to the baby without a proper midwife to care for you, and how brave to sail across an ocean without even another woman to help you with Johnny—how they never would have dared! And Greyson himself told me that everyone was stunned that even as ill as you were, you were still able to care for the baby and not collapse with the fever until you had him safely home. You see, they do look up to you."

Kate's eyes were huge now as he went on, "And if you didn't know how to treat them or order things in the house, why didn't you tell me so? Or ask Mrs. Nearing to help you?"

"I . . . I was ashamed of my lack of housewifely skills in such a great establishment," Kate muttered, wishing Jack would take her in his arms and hold her close again.

"But forget the servants for a moment," he said instead. "As far as Lady Whitaker and her beauteous, hen-witted daughter are concerned, or that grotesque cousin of mine, you are worth a dozen of 'em. Or any other society woman. They would be having hysterics when you would rise calmly and competently to the occasion. Can you imagine *them* coping with a hurricane alone? But you did! They are only little dolls, while *you* are a *real* woman. I do assure you, there is not a man in England who would not envy me such a wife!

"And as far as our separate rooms are concerned, that is a matter of custom here, as are separate nurseries for the children. We can change all that in a twinkling. Indeed, I don't know why I didn't suggest it earlier.

"Listen to me, Kate!" he said, grasping her shoulders then and shaking her a little. His eyes, so intense with his feelings, bored down into hers. "I love you. I have always loved you, yes, even before our marriage! I may have been forced into that, and you know why I never intended to marry anyone, but you also know how eagerly I embraced marriage—and you. I can see that I grew careless once I was home again at Hythe, put the estate and its concerns before your needs, and I most humbly apologize for that, my dear. For I do love you. How could any man not love a Lady Sprite, with her generous, giving ardor, her heartfelt smiles? I meant what I said in the drawing room. I am the luckiest of men."

Kate's eyes were shining now. "Do you mean it, Jack? Truly?" she whispered.

"Idiot!" he muttered just before he bent his head and kissed her. His arms crushed her to him, and she closed her eyes, feeling for a moment as if she might faint with joy.

"Will you *talk* to me from now on? Tell me what is bothering you?" he asked moments later, his lips only an inch from hers. "How can I see to your happiness if I do not know what is troubling you?"

"Very well," she whispered back. "But only if you will do the same, not brood alone as you have been so wont to do. After all, if I am not some little doll, I deserve to share all your life, and not be closed out of the sad parts of it. For we are partners, sir, are we not?"

He nodded, his eyes intent on her soft lips. "Partners indeed," he said as he caressed her. "And you'll see, Kate. You'll like living in South Carolina. You'll be near Matt and Alicia, and you'll be able to visit Bermuda often. Why, we might even spend our summers there, to enjoy the offshore breezes. The lowlands of the South can be oppressive then."

As he spoke, he had been unlacing her gown, and now he bent to kiss her breasts. "And there will be so many people for you to make friends with, so many things to do! We'll have a fine home on the Battery, and a plantation out of town, all done up in grand style—whatever you like," he promised, his warm breath on her skin making her shiver.

Kate closed her eyes. "Why, Jack," she said, chuckling a little, "I do believe you are seducing *me* for the first time! What a nice change!"

He slipped her gown from her shoulders and pushed it to the floor. The hoops she wore followed. As his fingers caught the bottom of her shift to lift it over her head, he said, "Come to bed, Kate. I've a mind to show you how much I love you, and I cannot wait."

25

IT was quite a long while later, and Jack had just risen to add more coals to the dying fire, when he spotted the packages he had brought, lying forgotten on the carpet.

"Here, sit up and wrap this comforter around you," he ordered as he handed it to her. "I have some surprises for you."

Forgetting the delicious languor she felt, Kate did as she was told. "Presents, Jack?" she asked, as excited as any child.

He dropped the packages around her on the bed. "Open them," he said with a smile.

The first large box Kate untied contained the copper-colored gown, and she sighed as she held it up to her in wonder. "How beautiful it is!" she said.

"Yes, it is my favorite. I plan to have you wear it at the evening reception we are giving next week to introduce you to the local gentry."

Kate dropped the gown from suddenly nerveless fingers. "A reception here? Oh, no!" she cried.

"Oh, yes!" he said firmly. "And you shall outshine every lady there, my Lady Sprite. See here," he said as he rummaged through the other packages. "Here's a stole embroidered in gold thread to match, and there's a pair of shoes somewhere. Why, there's even a fan!"

Kate wrinkled her nose and grinned at him as she opened the fan and regarded him over its pleated edge. "A fan? In January?" she asked demurely.

"Maybe I did get a little carried away," Jack admitted. "But perhaps you could carry it for effect.

"Look," he said, opening another box. "Here's a warmer cloak with a hood and muff to match, so you won't feel the chill when you go out. And some fine wool shawls . . . gowns for morning, noon, and night . . . even a warmer robe."

"They are lovely," Kate said, her voice trembling now as he thrust them all into her hands. He did not notice, for he was opening the last bulky package.

"Do look at this, Kate!" he said. "New petticoats and shifts of white wool. You need never shiver again in Hythe's chilly halls."

Kate's face crumpled as she took them from him, to hold them against her cheek. "Oh, Jack," she said brokenly, just before she burst into tears again.

Jack swept the presents to one side, to gather her into his arms again. "No more tears, madam," he ordered gruffly. "Do you want the servants to think I've been beating you?"

"It's no more than I deserve," Kate told him, sniffling. "To think I even imagined for one moment that you didn't love me! I am so ashamed!"

The clock chimed then, and Jack rose. "Time for us to dress for dinner. Then we will send for Johnny, have him brought down to the drawing room. I do assure you you could have sent for him at any time. A nanny's routines take a distant second place to a parent's wishes, you know. And if Nanny Bell can't adjust to ours, she'll have to go. Besides, I have some presents for our son too. I can't wait for him to see them."

Kate slid off the bed, her hand caressing the beautiful things he had brought for her. "What did you get for Johnny?" she asked as she put on her new robe.

"Now, let me see. A top and a ball, and a wonderful toy sailing ship. And there's a fishing rod, and his first gun, and—"

"But, Jack, he is only a baby!" Kate exclaimed, trying to hide her laughter.

She saw her husband's face fall, and she ran to him to put her arms around him and hug him tight. "But no doubt he will grow up very fast," she reassured him. "Oh, my dearest!"

The very next morning, Jack moved into her room, and Johnny's cradle was brought downstairs so he could sleep in the room across the hall. Jack told Kate she must make a choice between her husband or her son. He said he had no mind to have nursery maids bustling in and out when he wanted to kiss her, or Johnny interrupting them when they were involved in . . . other matters. Kate quickly agreed that across the hall was quite close enough.

Still, in the days that followed, she found she loved being able to go to her son whenever she liked, or to ring and have him brought to her. And if he was sleepy, she put him down on her own bed, protected by a nest of pillows, so she could watch him. She could tell that Nanny Bell did not approve of the new arrangement, although she was trying hard to adjust to these strange colonial ways. But the young wet nurse, Molly Dawson, confided shyly to Kate that she understood completely. Why, if her Nan had been taken away from her, she said, she would have cried her eyes out, that she would, milady!

Kate had admitted her ignorance about grand establishments to both Mrs. Nearing and the butler, and begged their pardon for her earlier attitude. Completely disarmed, the two old retainers had assured her they would

be delighted to help her. As she trailed after them,
learning how to go on, Kate found she was happy in a
way she had not been for a very long time.

For just to be able to wake up with Jack beside her, to
observe his contented face and hear his laughter—see the
return of all his old spirits—was heavenly. And to know
they would be sailing westward in only a few months
made her feel warmer, no matter how chilly the day.
They were going to make a fresh start, and they would be
doing it together.

Of course, it would be in South Carolina, not Bermuda, but even that seemed unimportant. For she would
have some of her family close by, and Bermuda would be
just over the horizon.

It was not that she thought she would not miss Bermuda, for she knew she always would. She had cried
over Cecily's first letter, although she had hidden all
signs of it from Jack. Cecily wrote to say the gunpowder
theft had been all but forgotten, for Governor Bruere
had never been able to discover the names of the men
involved. And after Wilcox Hinson's untimely death,
brought about when he fell off the Custom House dock
and drowned late one night after he staggered from the
tavern, Jack's possible part in it was never mentioned at
all.

Cecily also wrote that both Kate's parents were well,
as was all the family, and that little Margaret Rose was
thriving. Food from the colonies came regularly, and
Bermudians were very busy with the salt trade in exchange.

Keza had sent her love. Cecily wrote that the old slave
was failing now, but she was well-cared-for by her sons
and new daughter-in-law.

Kate and Jack's house on the point overlooking the
ocean had come through the latest hurricane with no
damage at all, as had the new sloop and the dory. Cecily
had been over there only shortly before she wrote, to see
to its cleaning and air it out lest it get musty.

Someday, Kate told herself as she folded the letter,
someday I will see it again, be it only for visits. And I can
wait. *Now* I can wait.

The afternoon of the reception, Kate had a bath in the
tin tub pulled close to the fire. She had put her hair up in

rag curlers earlier, for she wanted to look her best for Jack's guests.

She was feeling more than a little apprehensive about the evening to come, even though she was sure it was not apparent to any of the servants, or, more important, to Jack. For some reason, this evening meant a great deal to him, she could tell. He had mentioned that he intended to name Johnny his heir to the baronetcy when the time came that he himself had to relinquish it. And he had told her that he had promised the earl that Johnny would be the one to decide whether to keep it or not.

Kate was not concerned about that. She could not imagine her son opting for life in England, not after he had grown up in the freedom of the New World.

Now, as she stepped from the tub and reached for the towel warming on the fire screen, she reviewed the preparations for the party again.

Mrs. Nearing had seen to it that the main rooms had been cleaned to a fare-thee-well, and Jack had engaged a string trio to play for the guests, and raided the greenhouse at Willows for fresh flowers. Cook had outdone herself planning a most lavish supper, and a profusion of sweets to end it. And Mr. Greyson had overseen the wines to be served, and given many lectures to the footmen and the maids chosen to attend the ladies, as they polished the silver and washed every crystal drop on the chandeliers.

Kate herself had walked through the rooms with the housekeeper only a short time ago, and she had been impressed at how lovely Hythe looked, dressed as it was *en fête*. She planned to thank all the servants tomorrow for their extra work.

Now, as the maids removed the tub, Kate made herself go and lie down on the bed to rest until it was time to dress.

A moment later, the door opened and Jack entered and came up to the bed to sit down beside her.

Kate immediately pulled a pillow over her head. "*Dammit*, Jack, go away!" her muffled voice exclaimed. "I won't have you seeing me like this!"

"Like what?" he asked. "I can't see you at all."

"Good! Go away!" the pillow told him, and he grinned.

"But aren't you afraid you'll smother under there?" he asked as he reached out to whisk it away.

Kate tried to hide her rag curlers with her hands, but when Jack burst out laughing at her, she was quick to join in.

"It is too bad of you," she said when she could speak again. "Now, why couldn't you wait until tonight, when I shall be a vision in my smart gown and perfect curly coiffure?"

Jack reached down and slipped his hands under her robe, to softly stroke her soft skin. As his fingers moved from her breasts, to trail down her belly to her thighs, Kate's eyes widened.

"But I couldn't wait for tonight," he confessed. "I had to see you now. And at the moment, I am not the least bit interested in your smart gown or your curls, or even, mm, the lack of them."

His hands parted her thighs then, and Kate sighed and put her arms around his neck. He bent to drop a score of feathery kisses on her face and neck. "How delicious you smell," he whispered. "All jasmine and honey. Kate?"

His wife opened her eyes, and when she saw the naked desire for her on his face, she smiled at him.

"My love," he murmured, his touch beginning to send little waves of warmth coursing through her body. As she held him closer, he added, "My Lady Sprite! So warm, so giving, so dear!"

Miss Adelaide Cross and her younger sister, Miss Violet, were always the first to arrive at any party in that part of Kent. They told themselves it was the result of old-fashioned attention to punctuality, but everyone, including themselves, knew it was because they couldn't bear to miss a thing. This way, they were assured the most comfortable seats in any room, seats with an excellent view of the proceedings.

Of course they were the first guests at Hythe that evening, and after greeting Sir John with the affection they felt for one they had known since babyhood, they were delighted to be introduced to his bride. As they went and took their places on a sofa in the drawing room, Miss Violet whispered, "My, what a stunning young woman! And that beautiful gown, exactly matching her curls. London, I'm sure. The topaz-and-gold jewelry was the perfect choice to set it—and her—off."

"Yes, she is not one in the common way, either," her sister agreed. "Excellent bones! I do believe dear Jack will be very happy in his marriage. Did you note her lovely smile, how warm it was?"

Miss Violet sighed, for she was an incurable romantic. "Yes, and Jack's smile for her as well. How proud of her he is, how fond, the dear boy! You can see it in his eyes. And he is as handsome as ever in that gold brocade coat, those buff unmentionables. Such strong calves! I do so like a well-set-up man, don't you?"

"Look, here comes the Reades," Miss Cross murmured. "Clorinda does not look well, does she? I do wish she would put off that dreary mourning! It is so out of place when her father has remarried now. But I'm not at all sure the new Mrs. Reade should have chosen that pale pink with all those cherry bows. How . . . how *deedy*!"

"Obvious. Very obvious. She has no taste at all. Well, *trade*, you know," Miss Violet agreed, smoothing her own elegant gray alemade skirts. "But do look, sister! Lady Reade is so slim and elegant, she makes Clorinda seem twice as large as she is."

"She is *more* than twice as large," Miss Cross said tartly. "Oh, and there are all her brothers and their wives as well. Tch, tch. It is true indeed that while we may choose our friends, we cannot choose our families. La, I pray none of them will come over *here*."

Miss Violet tittered. "They appear to be content to cluster together. Kindly notice how young Reginald Reade is looking around. I am sure he is assessing the worth of the furnishings, and picturing himself here, and not for the first time, either. Thank heaven there is no danger of *that*, not now, with that dear little heir sleeping upstairs. I do so long to see him!"

"I must say that Penelope Whitaker has turned into a pretty girl. I used to worry about her so," Miss Cross confided. "She was so very gawky, and spotty to boot."

"Her mother had better marry her off quickly," her sister said. "Beauty such as hers fades quickly. Oh, I wonder if her mother is unwell? La, Lady Whitaker turned quite pale when she greeted Lady Reade."

"There is Lord Whitaker, and behind him, dear Gareth and Caroline Ward. Caroline is about Lady Reade's age,

is she not? And such a kind, pleasant girl! Perhaps they
will be friends."

"And here come the Pearsons," Miss Violet murmured.
"Oh, dear. I see that Mrs. Pearson is increasing again. Tch,
tch, some men! That will be ten children now, won't it?"

"Eleven. You forgot the twins," her sister, Adelaide,
reminded her. "Ecod, Violet, I am very glad we never
married, aren't you?"

Miss Violet sighed. She supposed she was, but Sir
John—dear Jack!—was so outstanding a specimen of mas-
culinity, so tall and handsome, she was not at all sure. If
only he had been born earlier, or she later!

The string trio began to play then, and soon the drawing room was full of people, all chatting and laughing and
sipping the wine presented by Hythe's well-trained
footmen.

The two elderly spinsters continued to hold court on
their sofa, greeting all the guests in turn. They were
especially delighted when Lady Reade herself came up to
make sure they were comfortable; to ask if she could get
anything for them.

And when she left them, they were not the only guests to
notice how proudly the baronet's eyes followed her, or his
warm smile when their eyes met, and her answering blush.

Only once was the general merriment of the evening
disturbed. Robert Reade and his daughter, Clorinda,
could be seen speaking most seriously with Sir John, and
ending with a direct question. Looking very cold and
haughty now, he returned only a short reply before he
left them abruptly, quite forgetting his bow.

Miss Cross nudged her sister and nodded her head in
their direction, just as Robert Reade turned a dark red.
Both ladies could see how the second Mrs. Reade tugged
his sleeve, a frown on her face. And then she whirled to
say several things to her stepdaughter. Things, Miss Violet observed, that dear Clorinda did not appear to relish
hearing at all.

Much later, after there was nothing left but crumbs of
the sumptuous supper, and every one of Cook's candied
violets and comfits had disappeared, Sir John had a word
with his butler. Greyson nodded and left the room. Several minutes later, the footmen circulated among the
guests with trays of champagne glasses.

Sir John clapped his hands then, and the large room grew quiet. With everyone watching, he went to his wife's side and slipped his arm around her waist. He smiled down at her before he raised his glass and said, "M'lords, m'ladies, all our honored guests. I would like to propose a toast to my bride. She has completed my life and brought me happiness I never thought to know. To my beloved wife, Kate!"

"Hear, hear," some of the gentlemen called as they raised their own glasses. "To Lady Reade! Your health, ma'am!"

There was a stir by the door then, and the two Cross sisters inched forward on their sofa expectantly as an older woman came in carrying a baby. As all those assembled exclaimed and murmured to each other, Lady Reade looked at her husband in some confusion. He bent his head to whisper to her before she took her son from the nanny's arms.

"I give you another toast now, and a very special one it is, too," he said, raising his glass again and looking around. Miss Cross saw his glance linger on the rest of the Reade family for a long moment, and as she watched, his face grew cold. But had she only imagined that? she wondered. He was certainly smiling now!

"Ladies and gentlemen, I give you my son, John Gregory Reade," he said. He sounded so proud that several of the ladies had to wipe their eyes as he continued, "Please join me in drinking to the *next* baronet of Hythe—to his continued good health and his future prosperity. To my son!"

As the guests cheered and raised their glasses again, the baby awoke to favor them with a wide grin.

Over their son's dark head, Jack Reade and his Kate exchanged a smile so loving and intimate that both the Misses Cross sighed in unison.

About the Author

Barbara Hazard is the award-winning author of twenty-five regency novels. There are two million of her books in print, both here and abroad.

The book you have just read is the sequel to her previous historical romance, CALL BACK THE DREAM, also available in an NAL Onyx edition.